TABLE OF CONTENTS

- 02 BLACK & WHITE & RED ALL OVER
- 04 TERRINLE TOP 10 CANNIBALS
- 06 MANSON / SNYDER INTERVIEW
- 13 JACK THE RIPPER LETTER
- 14 MUSIC TO MURDER TO
- 17 JURY OF FEARS / MATCH MADE IN HELL
- 18 ED GEIN'S HOUSE OF HORRORS
- 21 CHAINSAWS & SATANISTS
- 22 KEMPER : THE CO-ED KILLER
- 23 IN DEFENSE OF MURDERABELIA
- 24 LAST SUPPER - DEATH ROW MEALS
- 25 SERIAL KILLER TRIVIA
- 26 WARNING SIGNS
- 27 IS MY SON A SERIAL KILLER
- 28 LETTERS FROM HELL - SON OF SAM
- 30 COLD CASE - BLACK DAHLIA
- 31 SON OF SAM & THE SATANIC CULT
- 32 THE ART OF MURDER
- 34 HOME SWEET CELL
- 35 THE HANDS OF DEATH
- 39 BITS AND PIECES
- 42 BUNDYS LAST INTERVIEW
- 44 COOKING WITH CANNIBALS
- 45 WHATS YOUR SERIAL KILLER IQ
- 46 ANY LAST WORRDS
- 47 SERIAL KILLER CROSSWORD
- 48 IF LOOKS COULD KILL
- 50 THE ART OF MURDER - KIMBERLY BAILEY
- 51 THE BEAST OF THE ARDENNES
- 54 MANSON POEMS AND SONGS
- 58 VAIN WOMAN OR URBAN MYTH
- 60 SERIAL KILLERS - WOULD YOU KNOW
- 61 JOSEPH EDWARD DUNCAN III
- 62 PATRICK MACKAY
- 63 HIGHWAY OF TEARS
- 64 ALBERT FISH COMIC
- 70 NIGHTSTALKER LETTER
- 72 THE ICEMAN COMETH
- 78 WHY DO WOMEN KILL
- 79 BUNDY WANTED POSTER
- 80 THE MOTIVES OF SERIAL KILLERS
- 82 LETTER FROM LEE BELCHER
- 83 TED BUNDY QUOTES
- 84 CHARLES STARKWEATHER
- 86 VICTIM OF CHOICE
- 90 MAKING A LIVING
- 92 REEL TO REAL
- 94 ANGEL RESENDIZ COMIC

THE HUMAN MACHINE WORKS IS CAP MOST UNFATHOMABLE HATRED. DESPITE ALL THE ADVANCES SOCIETY HAS MADE IN THE EXPLORATION OF THE MIND, WE STILL KNOW VERY LITTLE ABOUT WHAT DRIVES A SMALL PORTION OF US TO KILL. IT IS THIS MYSTERY THAT MAKES SERIAL KILLERS SUCH A COMPELLING SUBJECT. THEIR VERY EXISTENCE ON THIS PLANET PRESENTS US WITH A COMPLICATED AND UNPLEASANT TRUTH ABOUT THE HUMAN CONDITION AND REFLECTS A SIDE OF MANKIND THAT MOST OF US WOULD RATHER PRETEND DOES NOT EXIST AT ALL. THE REASON THAT MANY PEOPLE FIND THESE MONSTERS APPALLING IS THE VERY SAME REASON THAT MILLIONS OF OTHERS FIND THEM FASCINATING. THEY REPRESENT A DARK SIDE OF OUR SOCIETY THAT LIES JUST BENEATH OUR COLLECTIVE SKIN, THE HYDE TO OUR COLLECTIVE DR. JECKLES." IT IS IMPORTANT TO UNDERSTAND THAT THE STAFF OF SERIAL KILLER MAGAZINE DOES NOT IN ANY WAY CONDONE OR ADMIRE THE ACTIONS OF THESE MONSTERS. IN FACT, MANY OF US HAVE LOST LOVED ONES AT THE HANDS OF SUCH KILLERS. WE DO HOWEVER, FIND THEM THE MOST INTERESTING OF SUBJECTS AND WE HOPE THAT OUR EFFORTS IN RECORDING THEIR DEEDS WILL HELP TO SOLVE THE AGE OLD MYSTERY OF WHY THEY KILL.

- JAMES GILKS (EDITOR AND CHEIF)

"WE SERIAL KILLERS ARE YOUR SONS, WE ARE YOUR HUSBANDS, WE ARE EVERYWHERE. AND THERE WILL BE MORE OF YOUR CHILDREN DEAD TOMORROW."

- TED BUNY

artwork by johnny machine

BLACK AND WHITE AND READ ALL OVER

1. MARCH 14, 2008

Condemned killer William Bradford, a double murderer who implied to his jury he had other victims, has died of natural causes while awaiting execution in a California prison. He was 61. Bradford died Monday of natural causes at a prison medical facility in Vacaville, the California Department of Corrections and Rehabilitation said in a statement Wednesday. It did not elaborate on the cause of death. Bradford was sentenced to death in 1988 for the murders four years earlier of Shari Miller, 21, who he met in a bar, and Tracey Campbell, 15, a neighbor.

2. MARCH 24, 2008

A suitcase possibly containing the body of a New Jersey woman missing since June was fished out of a pond on Staten Island yesterday, authorities said. New Jersey authorities went to the site off Route 440 near the foot of the Outerbridge Crossing – linking Perth Amboy and Staten Island – to search for the remains of Hightstown resident Amy Gior dano, whose married boyfriend has been charged with her murder, authorities said.

3. MARCH 25, 2008

ANCHORAGE, Alaska - A young man wielding a 5-inch knife stabbed four people to death in a small Alaska fishing and tourist town on Tuesday before officers subdued him with a stun gun, police said. The 18-year-old man was taken to the jail in Sitka and is awaiting charges, Police Chief Sheldon Schmitt said. Officers found the bodies of three people just before noon at a two-story home just two blocks from the police station, police said. A fourth person found in the house later died at a hospital. The suspect's relatives owned the home, police said, though they did not release their identities.

4. APRIL 01, 2008

The second survivor of the 50-shot police shooting that killed Sean Bell picked out Det. Gescard Isnora today as the gunman who fired on them "like he was crazy." Mopping his face with a blue handkerchief, Joseph Guzman recounted on the stand how Isnora suddenly began shooting at him as he sat in Bell's car with their buddy, Trent Benefield. "He's still shooting like he's crazy, like he was out of his mind," he said. "Like he's trying to kill us, like he's shooting at a tank." Guzman said he had no idea that Isnora was a cop and denied he was reaching for a gun when the shooting started. "The dude was crazed," he said. Guzman testified a day after Benefield was battered on the stand by defense attorneys trying to cast doubts on his claim that police fired without warning - and without identifying themselves.

5. APRIL 02, 2008

WAYCROSS, GA -- A group of third-graders plotted to attack their teacher, bringing a broken steak knife, handcuffs, duct tape and other items for the job and assigning children tasks including covering the windows and cleaning up afterward, police said Tuesday. The plot by as many as nine boys and girls at Center Elementary School in south Georgia was a serious threat, Waycross Police Chief Tony Tanner said. "We did not hear anybody say they intended to kill her, but could they have accidentally killed her? Absolutely," Tanner said. "We feel like if they weren't interrupted, there would have been an attempt. Would they have been successful? We don't know." The children, ages 8 and 9, were apparently mad at the teacher because she had scolded one of them for standing on a chair, Tanner said. A prosecutor said they are too young to be charged with a crime under Georgia law.

6 | APRIL 02, 2008

Public officials rallied for tougher gun laws Tuesday in the wake of yet another teen shooting, but of the nearly 1,000 Chicago public school students who joined them at the Thompson Center, many said the solutions are more complicated. In the chanting, sign-waving crowd, Corine Minniefield, a junior at Banner Linc Academy, said school officials need to get truants and drop-outs back in class and that police need to tighten up their protection. "I'm just tired of turning on the news and seeing my people get killed. I can't go to no more funerals. I'm tired of going to funerals," said Minniefield, 18, whose cousin Ruben Ivy was killed at Crane High School last month.

7 | APRIL 02, 2008

SPRINGFIELD, BUCKS COUNTY - April 2, 2008 (WPVI) -- A 65-year-old woman has been charged with last January's church murder in rural Bucks County.

8 | COMPANY NEWS

Well folks, if you are reading this, then you already know the big news at SerialKillerCalendar.com this month. It is the first release of our new Serial Killer Magazine. We have also added over 100 new serial killer t-shirts, pillows, wall posters, stickers, postcards, coffee mugs, DVDs and... well, I would need a whole magazine just to list them all. As most of our loyal fans already know, we started this company in 2006 with little idea how big it would get. Thanks to customers like you, we have been able to make Serial Killer calendar a household name. Thanks again to those who have stuck with us and be sure to check out the site as often as you can!

ARTWORK BY MATT VERGES

TERRIBLE TOP TEN
HISTORY'S MOST NOTORIOUS CANNIBALS

10 IDI AMIN: Idi Amin Dada was an army officer, Field Marshal and President of Uganda. It has been estimated that the death toll during Amin's regime was somewhere between 80,000 and 500,000 people. Amin would boast of being a "reluctant" cannibal - human flesh, he said, was too salty.

09 SASCHA SPESIWTSEW: Sascha Spesiwtsew is a Russian killer who practised cannibalism on his victims. When authorities entered the flat they saw blood covering the walls. In the kitchen there were bowls with pieces of human bodies. In the bathtub they found a mutilated, headless body. Olga Galtseva was found, also mutilated but still alive.

08 ARMIN MEIWES: Armin Meiwes is a German cannibal who achieved international notoriety for eating the penis of a voluntary victim he had found via the Internet. After eating the penis, Meiwes killed his victim, and continued to eat a large amount of his flesh.

07 FRITZ HAARMANN: Haarmann was a notorious serial killer born in Hannover, Germany. From 1919 to 1924, Haarmann committed at least 24 murders. Rumours had it that Haarmann would then peddle meat from the bodies of his victims as black market pork.

06 ANDREI CHIKATILO: Andrei Chikatilo was a Russian serial killer and cannibal, nicknamed the Rostov Ripper. He was convicted of the murder of 53 women and children between 1978 and 1990. During his trial he was kept in a cage in the center of the courtroom.

05 ALFERD PACKER: In winter of 1873, Packer was with a party of 21 who left Provo, Utah, bound for the Colorado gold country. At an unknown date, the party got hopelessly lost, ran out of provisions, and became snowbound in the Rocky Mountains. It was later discovered that Packer ate many members of his party. Packer was eventually sentenced to 40 years in prison after being convicted of manslaughter.

04 DONNER PARTY: The Donner Party was a group of California-bound American settlers in the 1940s. After becoming snowbound in the Sierra Nevada in the winter of 1846, some of the emigrants resorted to cannibalism.

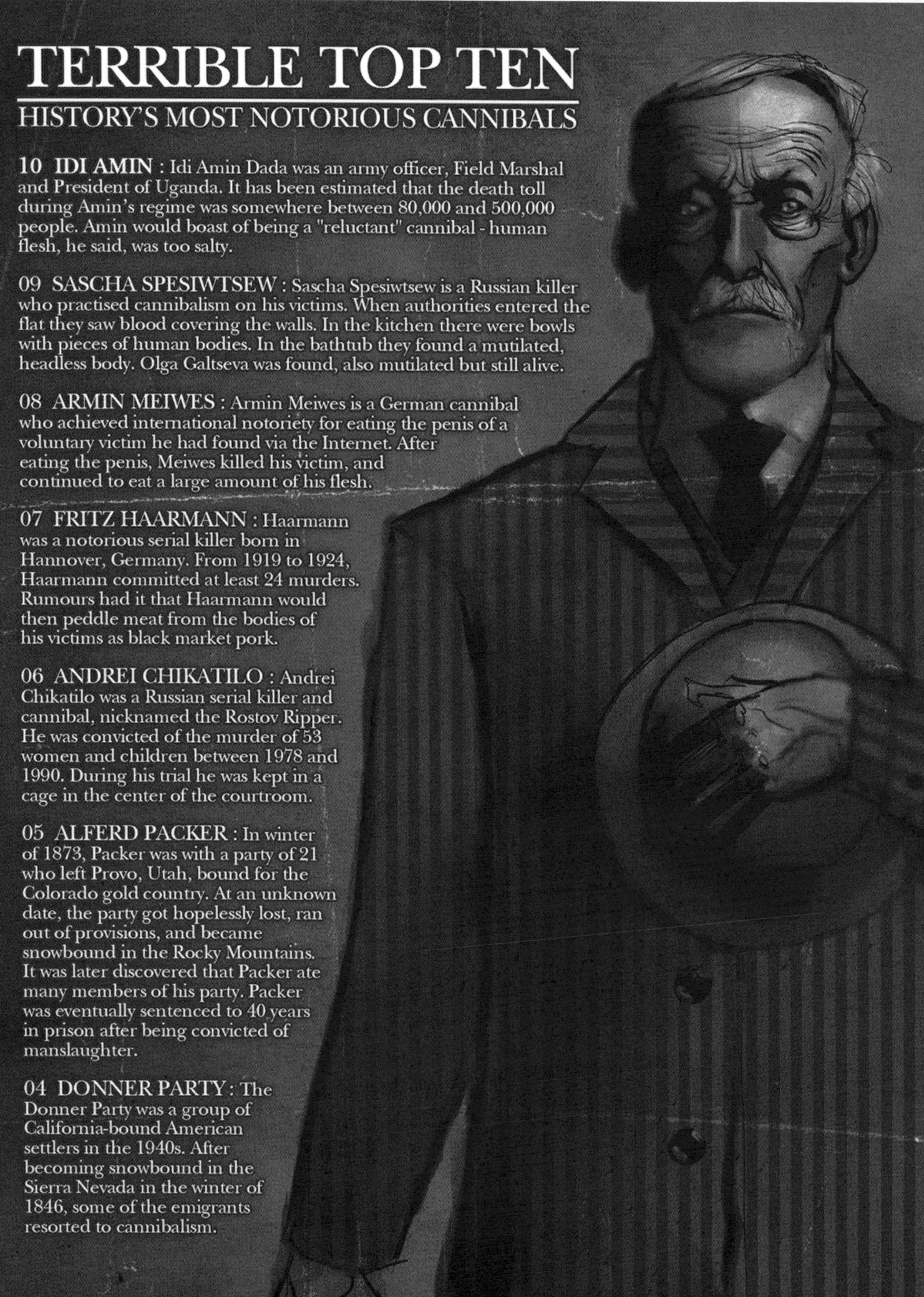

03 ALBERT FISH: Albert Hamilton Fish was an American serial killer and cannibal. He was known as the Gray Man, the Werewolf of Wysteria and the Brooklyn Vampire. He boasted he molested over 100 children, and was a suspect in at least five killings. Fish also sent a letter home to the family of one young victim. In this letter he wrote "First I stripped her naked. How she did kick — bite and scratch. I choked her to death, then cut her in small pieces so I could take my meat to my rooms. Cook and eat it. How sweet and tender her little ass was roasted in the oven. It took me 9 days to eat her entire body."

02 ED GEIN: Edward Gein, was an American serial killer, cannibal and grave robber. He is perhaps most infamous for wearing the skin of dead women and using human bones as household items. His actions where the inspiration of such classic horror movies as The Texas Chainsaw Masacre and Psycho.

01 JEFFREY DAHMER: Jeffrey Lionel Dahmer was an American serial killer. He murdered at least 17 men between 1978 and 1991. His murders involved acts of necrophilia and cannibalism. Dahmer chose to plead not guilty by reason of insanity, arguing that his urges were so strong that he could not control them. The court found Dahmer sane and guilty on 15 counts of murder and sentenced him to 937 years in prison.

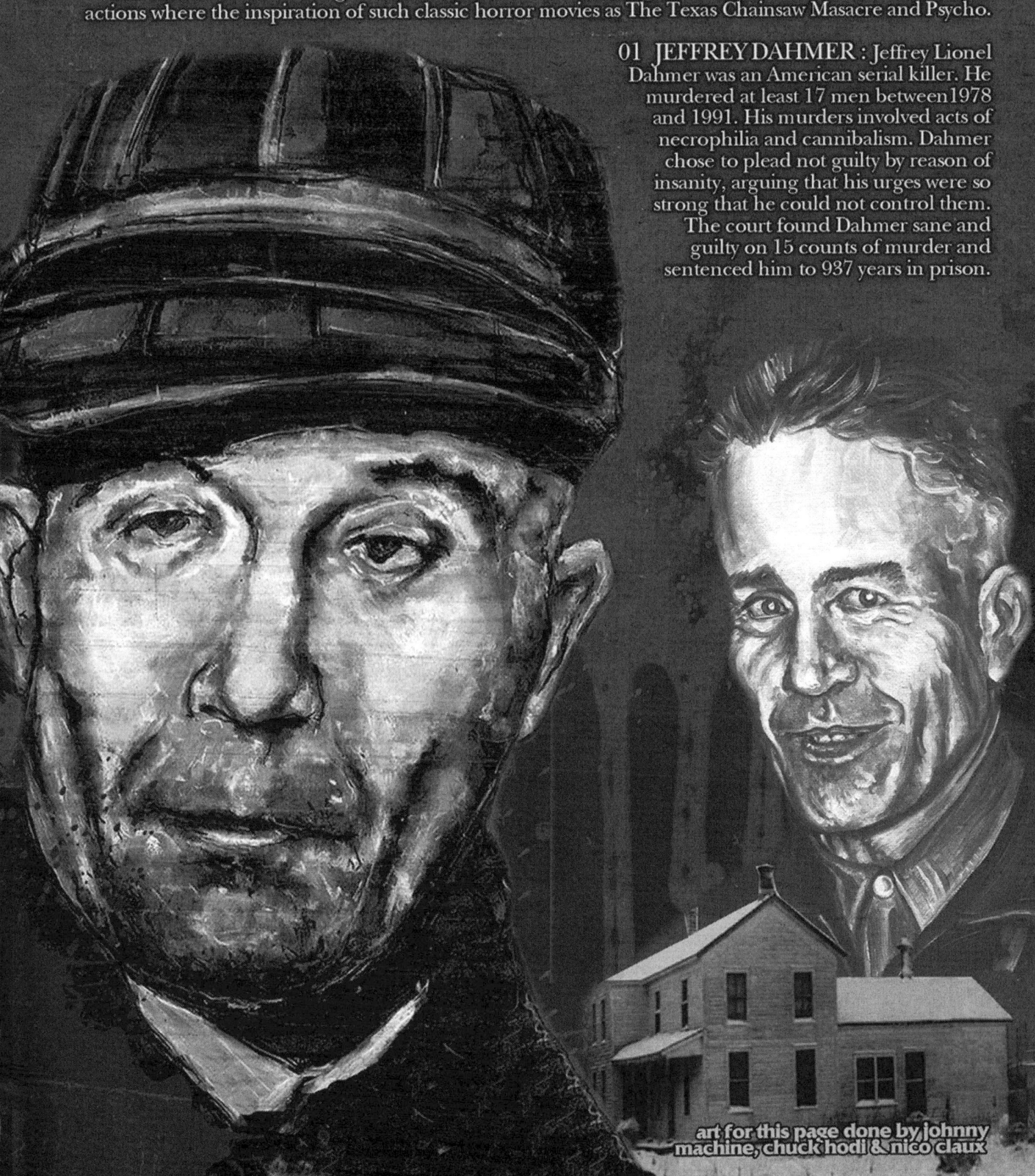

art for this page done by johnny machine, chuck hodi & nico claux

P4RT ON3 OF THE 1981 INTERVIEW WITH TOM SNYDER AND CHARLES MANSON

Tom: Tell me about life here in prison, do you read newspapers? Do you listen to the radio? Do you watch television? Do you communicate with people on the outside? What goes on for Charles Manson in this prison?

Manson: Well, I can feel the grass growin' out there on the lawn and there's a few trees that's got some leaves on that I can feel. And I've been in jail all my life so I'm actually right here at home, uh how long have I been in jail? 34 years? 34 years so um..

Tom: Out of 47 you've been here 34.

Manson: I've been in jail, uh prison, uh a long time. All my life. I was raised up in here, so I understand jail so I understand myself so I can deal with that. I sit in my cell and do my number like a convict does his number.

Tom : You like jail don't you?

Manson: I uh, don't dislike or like.

Tom: Let's go back to 1967, the time you were winding up serving a term of a number of years, ten years, and written accounts indicate that you told the authorities "Don't let me out, I can't cope with the outside world." Do you have a recollection of that? And do you...

Manson: You're making a desperate plea out of something, man. There's no desperate plea out of it. I said I can't handle the maniacs outside, let me back in.

Tom: I didn't use the word desperate, that's your word Charles.

Manson: Yeah, well, your inflection and your voice tones were, uh, implications there.

Tom: Well, uh, You use the word maniacs on the outside. How are you different from the maniacs on the outside, and why do you call them maniacs? Because you know something? They think you're one.

Manson: Yeah, it would reflect. If you hold a negative up to the light, you don't see the light you just see the negative. So I'm a reflection of your negative, there's no doubt about that and I can handle that also. I been handling ain't I?.

Tom: I don't know have you?

Manson: Well, I've been up and down in these damn hallways, in and out of these nut wards for the last ten years. You think you can follow that act?

Tom: Don't want to follow that act, I don't want to get in, why do you want to get into that?

Manson: What crowd you playing for?

Tom: Huh?

Manson: I'm playing for my life. (chuckles) You're working for money.

Tom: What does that mean, you're playing for your life?

Manson: I'm working for my life mister. I'm not playing for money, I'm playing for keeps.

Tom: What do you mean you're working for your life?

Manson: I'm playing for real.

Tom: What does that mean, you're playing for real. How are you playing for your life?

Manson: Well That's something you can't buy.

Tom: When you say you're playing for your life am I to assume to you think that someday you're going to get out of here?

Manson: (chuckles) Get out of here? Hmmm…get out of here? Where would I go now see.

Tom: What would you do if you got out of here?

Manson: If I got out of here…

Tom: What if they said, they said to you tomorrow morning "Charles, hey listen, you're free" You could go where ever you wanna go, do whatever you wanna do. What would you do?

Manson: I'd probably go out front in the grass and sit down.

Tom: For how long?

Manson: For, uh, right now. How long? I wouldn't, I could put a track record on it or I could, um, put a computer on it.

Tom: Come on down, no no come on down. Get off computers and get off tracks. If you got out of here, there are a lot of people who think you'd go start killing people again.

Manson: Again? (chuckles) Well you guys are misinformed. I haven't killed anyone.

Tom: What about, uh, what about Shea?

Manson: What about him?

Tom: Well, what about him?

Manson: He got killed.

Tom: Well, the word is you killed him.

Manson: Who?

Tom: Word is you stabbed him.

Manson: Oh, Word.

Tom: What does it feel to kill someone Charles?

Manson: Word…word is that you're an old woman. Word is you have turkey in sky. Word is…I don't know what word is. Someone else tell you that, I didn't tell you that.

Tom: Did you kill Shea?

Manson: Hell no.

Tom: Did you cut, uh, Hinman's ear off?

Manson: Hell ….yes. Yeah.

Tom : Why'd you, How'd that feel when you cut his ear off?

Manson: Uh, I felt bad about it.

Tom: The truth's fun now, isn't the truth fun now when you... ok ok ok, you cut his ear off what did it feel like..

Manson: Yeah Yeah sure, sure. Is the truth fun? (chuckles) My Goodness.

Tom: What did it feel like when you cut his ear off?

Manson: Huh?

Tom: Tell me about it, come on.

Manson: What did it feel like?

Tom: Yeah

Manson: Well I had done what he said for about 20 years. I done everything he told me to do. And I got to thinking now, why don't this guy do something I tell him to do? And he said uh, "no". And I said "well how comes I'm always doing what you tell me to do but then you never do what I say to?" And he said 'Well blah blah blah" So I said "now you do what I say". And he said "no." I said "you do exactly what I say!" And he said "no." "I'm telling you! I'm not asking you! I'm telling you! You do exactly what I say!" He said 'Wow, where'd you get that ?" I said "I got it from my father in prison. He gave it to me. I had a little charm bracelet I used to carry it on when I was about that big."

artwork by nico claux

PART TWO OF THE 1981 INTERVIEW WITH TOM SNYDER AND CHARLES MANSON

Tom: Why was it so important for him to do what you say? Why do you like having people to do what you want them to do?

Manson: Because....

Tom: Why do you like to control them Charles?

Manson: Because. Wait a minute, no, no I was asked. The dude asked he says "are you my brother" I said "yeah I'm your brother", he said "how much are you my brother?" I said "completely". See if I'm gonna explain it to you, it's not gonna be that easy. So you're gonna have to bare with me. So Bobby said, he was a young dude, he said."I'm your brother" so I said "ok"

Tom: Bobby?

Manson: I'm your brother. Beausoleil, Beausoleil. I just got out of prison.

Tom: Wait wait, wait, wait, wait

Manson: Yeah

Tom: Let me interrupt you for a second.

Manson: Yeah, well then we're gone with that thought.

Tom: No, no, no, no no because you're getting on to something...

Manson: Then we'll go onto another one and you'll make me look crazy.

Tom: No, no, no. You can make yourself look crazy, Charles, I can't make you look crazy and please believe me.

Manson: Alright, I'll believe you.

Tom: Let me...

Manson: and I'll put it in my left hand pocket for later.

Tom: Let me, let me take you back to you wanting this man Hinman...

Manson: I cut the dude's ear off because he was fucking over Bobby. And Bobby was a youngster and really didn't know what the hell he was doing, and he was a kid and he never had no man show him nothing, see, so I was telling the boy, I said, uh, the guy says "You got my money?", I said "go over there and get your money or leave him alone."

Tom: You're taking me to another story.
Tom: Why was it so important for him to do what you say? Why do you like having people to do what you want them to do?

Manson: Because...

Tom: Why do you like to control them Charles?

Manson: Because. Wait a minute, no, no I was asked. The dude asked he says "are you my brother" I said "yeah I'm your brother", he said "how much are you my brother?" I said "completely". See if I'm gonna explain it to you, it's not gonna be that easy. So you're gonna have to bare with me. So Bobby said, he was a young dude, he said "I'm your brother" so I said "ok"

Tom: Bobby?

Manson: I'm your brother. Beausoleil, Beausoleil. I just got out of prison.

Tom: Wait wait, wait, wait, wait

Manson: Yeah

Tom: Let me interrupt you for a second.

Manson: Yeah, well then we're gone with that thought.

Tom: No, no, no, no no because you're getting on to something...

Manson: Then we'll go onto another one and you'll make me look crazy.

Tom: No, no, no. You can make yourself look crazy, Charles, I can't make you look crazy and please believe me.

Manson: Alright, I'll believe you.

Tom: Let me...

Manson: and I'll put it in my left hand pocket for later.

Tom: Let me, let me take you back to you wanting this man Hinman...

Manson: I cut the dude's ear off because he was fucking over Bobby. And Bobby was a youngster and really didn't know what the hell he was doing, and he was a kid and he never had no man show him nothing, see, so I was telling the boy, I said, uh, the guy says "You got my money?", I said "go over there and get your money or leave him alone."

Tom: You're taking me to another story.

Manson: No I'm trying to tell you the same thing. And we'll be here for a thousand years unless you let me finish.

Tom: No, no, no, no we won't be here that long at all if you just speak to this one point.

Manson: Ok, I made the point. Why I cut the dude's ear off, man, that's the point.

Tom: I, I didn't ask you that, I said why was it important to you to make Hinman do what you wanted him to do. If one follows your story...

Manson: Because the dude had a gun.

Tom: Ok, and if one follows your story

Manson: Yeah

Tom: through the times at the ranch

Manson: Yeah

Tom: in southern California, it was important to Charles Manson to be a leader,

Manson: No

Tom: to have people follow him.

Manson: Come on district attorney! See you're full of brainwarsh. That's the district attorney. I'm nobody's fucking leader and I'm nobody's follower. I got a parole officer. I got a sleeping bag and a guitar and I'm standing at old blind man's ranch and that's about the extent of it. All this occult and that hocus pocus stuff that you guys are playing, I don't nothing about all that.

Tom: You know nothing about something called Helter Skelter? You know nothing about it?

Manson: Yeah I know about Helter Skelter! It was a song that some people sang!

Tom: And that's all it was?

Manson: and some other kids picked it up in their minds. And they said "What do you think Helter Skelter is" and I say "Well I get out of the penitentiary in the 50's and everybody's going (claps) "dun....dun....dun" (claps) and they're walking like that. I get locked back up, and I get out of the penitentiary in 65 and it's going (claps faster) "dun..dun..dun..dun" And locked up again I come out in 69 and it's going (claps very fast) "dundundundundundundun" and I was thinking "Wow man, wow far out"

Tom: Wow what? Wow what? Come on keep going, Charles, keep going.

Manson: I was a beatnik, I was a beatnik in the 50's before the hippies came along. You know, and I cut a rut down through Acapulco, and I smoked Acapulco before you knew what it was, and I lived in the tombs and I was in the Cook County jail in Chicago when you were playing cricket in, uh, high school. See, like you live in another world. I live in street peoples world.

Tom: Manson had a plot, "Helter Skelter."

Manson: Yeah..

Tom: Manson had uh a little scheme called creepy crawlers. He'd send people in to move furniture around. Is that all a figment of someone's imagination so far or is there any truth to that? Tell me Charles, I don't know.

Manson: It's a fairy tale. It's worse than a fairy tale.

Tom: It's a fairy tale?

Manson: It's, uh, it's, it's a comedy. It's a comedy tragedy, uh, opera that (chuckles) was played in the, uh, early morning.

Tom: Come on Charles off.

Manson: It was sickening. You know?

Tom: Get off the space shuttle.

Manson: Well that's what the D.A. gave you as reality.

Tom: Ok

Manson: He stood in the courtroom and said "this man did this and this man did that", and you all believed him. He said "this man did that" and I said "Your honor may I speak?" and he said "No you can't speak" and I said "your honor I got a voice, let me talk" then he said "No sit down and shut up" and then he handcuffed me and took me to the back and whipped my (inaudible) what are you gonna do? I come out and sit down, I ain't gonna get whipped again.

Tom: Didn't you, uh, stand up in that courtroom?

Manson: Sure

Tom: and by the way, by the way, let me just go back...

Manson: and I felt the reproductions of it in the back of it.

Tom: Ok ok, but you say the whole thing is a fairy tail. You say the whole thing is make-believe.

Manson: Yeah, that's his Helter Skelter, it wasn't mine.

Tom: Uh huh, uh huh. The body of Sharon Tate is make believe isn't it?

Manson: Uh that's make believe..

Tom: Make believe,....

Manson: That's make believe to the people that went in there and did what they did.

Tom: And who were those people? You know...

Manson: Yeah

Tom: You know, but you know who those people were.

Manson: Sure I know who they were.

Tom: They were with you at the Spahn's Ranch. They were part of this thing

Manson: Yeah

Tom: if not the Manson Family or the Manson Cult, the Manson Ranch, call it what you will.

Manson: So then? What?

Tom: And Tex Watson testified in a court of law that you told him "go to the house that Terry Melcher used to live in and kill those people in the most gruesome way." A man that was once your associate said that of you and now you sit here and say that's not true, that's all make believe?

Manson: You've got a stone wall there, won't you take it down a little bit. Look here, I'll explain something to you.. Um, Tex took the witness stand, and this is record, and he said "I don't know whether I'm Charlie Manson or my mother" Tex didn't have his own mind one way or the other . He was balanced back and forth because I had already took his mind in another game down the road that I was playing with some Hell's Angels that you don't know nothing about and you probably never will know nothing about it. Because you would have to know those people to get in that thought, see. But there's different colors on different peoples backs doing different things. It's a different world. I love the world I live in too just like Reagan loves the world he lives in.

HIGHEST BODY COUNT

Pedro Alonso Lopez
Pedro Alonso López (born 8 October 1948 in Santa Isabel, Colombia) is a confessed serial killer from South America, accused of killing more than 300 girls.

Henty Lee Lucas and Ottis Toole
This duo of deadly killers are suspected of killing somewhere between 6 and 200 people.

H.H. Holmes
Holmes trapped and murdered possibly hundreds of guests at his Chicago hotel, which he opened for the 1893 World's Fair. He confessed to 27 murders but others suspect the number is close to 200.

Gilles de Rais
A French noble that was later accused and ultimately convicted of torturing, raping and murdering dozens, if not hundreds, of young children, mainly boys.

Dr. Harold Shipman
He was convicted on 15 sample charges in 2000 and sentenced to 15 concurrent life sentences. After his trial, an inquest decided that there was enough evidence to suggest that Shipman had killed a total of 215 people.

Pee Wee Gaskins
Donald Henry Gaskins, Jr. (March 31, 1933 - September 6, 1991) was an American serial killer, possibly connected to over 200 murders.

P4RT THR33 OF THE 1981 INTERVIEW WITH TOM SNYDER AND CHARLES MANSON

Tom: You love the world you live in?

Manson: (chuckles) Most a surely. It's me.

Tom: You love all the pain that you've caused people?

Manson: OH!

Tom: All the anguish that you've .....

Manson: Oh! I don't know pain! I don't know pain! I have no depth of pain! I have no depth of suffering! I don't know ridicule! I don't know all the bad things! I haven't been punished by you all my life since I was 10 years old! I've been in every reform school you've got across the country. I used to have to lay down and get my ass whipped till I couldn't walk. Tell me about some pain. Yeah.

Tom: And that's our fault, it's all these peoples fault?

Manson: No, no one fault, make strong, good pain, understand pain. Not bad. Pain's not bad, it's good. It teaches you things. It teaches you things. Like when you put your hand in the fire, OW! You know not to do that again. Yeah I understand that.

Tom: But how come you didn't learn

Manson: That's the reason come I never stick my hand in fire.

Tom: But, excuse me! You've been putting your hand in the fire sense you were a little boy.

Manson: I have?

Tom: By, you just told me a couple minutes ago.

Manson : I did?

Tom: that out of 47 years you've spent 34 of them behind bars, now if isn't keep putting your hand in the fire, I don't know what is.

Manson: Yeah, yeah, what year was that?

Tom: It's uh, uh, the year's not important.

Manson : Oh.

Tom: What's important is you just say you learn by pain not to experience it again to put your hand in the fire. Why have you been in and out of prisons for the last 34 out your 47 years. Do you call that normal behavior Charles? Is that something you're proud of?

Manson: No, no, no. I never thought I was normal, never tried to be normal. Normal runs in that little rut down there. I don't know nothing about being normal. I've been in jail all my life, man. I lived on the handball court. This guy raised me up. All the men in the joint raised me up, told me what to do, what was right and wrong, told me where to sit down , where to stand up, I just did whatever I was told. You know, and I got to the end of it and I just turned around and said "Wow, far out."

Tom: Alright, now that's....

Manson: Then I went outside and all these little kids got a hold of me and said "We want to stop the Vietnam War and we want to do this." What? there was a war,? I don't know what's happening. I just got out of prison. I never had any vocational, did you ever see me go to any vocational training, rehabilitation?

I never played no rehabilitation. I sweep the floor in the kitchen then go play handball. I'm still 10 years old in your world. Your world I'm still a kid, I'm not gonna grow up, I'm not gonna go to college.

Tom: How old are you in your world?

Manson: Um, Forever. Since breakfast... I can't remember.

Tom: I don't know what that means, come on off the space shuttle Charles.

Manson: Yes ...off the space shuttle.

Tom: How old are you in your world?

Manson: How old am I? I'm as old as my mother told me (chuckles). How's that?

Tom: Your mother? Tell me about your mother, what did your mother tell you?

Manson: My mother told me that when she worked on death row and they took that dude into hanging and his head popped off and went down them 13 stairs and rolled over by her, it scared the shit out of her. (chuckles) you know, and I said "Wow, that sure is a far out trip Moms". So then when I got up on Death Row in cell 13 for 9 counts of murder 1969, and I looked at, at her fears of that guy's head popping off of that hanging noose, and I said to myself "My goodness, what the hell am I doing here, I didn't want to come here." I didn't break the law. The judge knew that. But the people didn't want to hear it. The Judge knew it. He washed his hands. He said "I know it but what can I do? The people want this."

Tom: The judge never said that.

Manson: Yeah

Tom: The judge never said that.

Manson: that's what Older said.

Tom: No, the judge never said that.

Manson: He got off and shook their hands, didn't he?

Tom: The judge did not say he washed his hands

Manson: He's a Flying Tiger man, from Madam Shanghai's Shack. I just wrote him a letter today.

Tom: The judge did not say you were innocent Charles.

Manson: Innocent?

Tom: Let's go back to your mother, what..

Manson: Innocent?

Tom: What is...

Manson: Wait a minute, wait a minute, let's get back to that word innocent. Are you so white and pure?

Tom: The judge didn't say you were innocent.

Manson: Are you innocent?

Tom: Innocent of what?

Manson: Oh. That's what I'm saying.

Tom: None of us are innocent.

Manson: Yeah, just because you're convicted in a court room doesn't mean you're guilty of something.

Tom: What does mean you're guilty.

Manson: When you know you're guilty.

Tom: And how do you feel about yourself, tell me about...

Manson: I feel, I feel pretty good.

Tom: (sighs) Let me take you back to your mom.

Manson: Take me back to old river..

Tom: What else did see talk to you about besides the fellow who's head popped off?

Manson: The head popped off, yeah. She was living in the Blue Moon Café and she hit a dude in the head with one of them bottles of uh, Jim Beam Whiskey. She tried to hustle a few dollars on the corner but there wasn't no money, so when she jammed this whiskey bottle upside that clown's head, he went down and she took his bread and come up and got me and we left and went to Indiana.

Tom: When you were a boy, did you love your mother?

Manson: Uh, I didn't know what that was.

Tom: Did you respect your mother? How did you feel about, how do you feel about your mom right now? If your mother, I don't know if she is alive Charles or not.

Manson: Yeah you don't huh?

Tom: Do you?

Manson: Hmmm. Let's see. Alive now...yeah, yeah, maybe..

Tom: I mean, if she could be watching this right now..

Manson: She could watching this right now..

Tom: What would you say to her Charles?

Manson: Oh well, what would I say to her...

Tom: What would you say?

Manson: I'd say, "you sure did go through a lot of changes to get me as far as you did. And you did a damn good job with the help of my grandma." My grandma was a mountain girl (chuckles) from Kentucky up in the mountains. And uh she never did drink or smoke or cuss or lie. She used to cook for the Salvation Army and she was a human being, a good one. I'd go to Church down there and sweep the floor for her.

Tom: Well how were you in school? I've heard that you weren't too good, but maybe I've heard wrong.

Manson: Depends on which school. I did very well in reform school.

Tom: (chuckles) yeah...

Manson: I did good in uh, in uh, every place that I was ever told to go good in. As much as I was allowed to do, you know. Lot of times good for some may not be the same for others. Sometimes it kind a bumps heads but when it does um, I just chew on my pipe and think about it and do the best I can.

Tom: Mmmmhmmm ... but..

Manson: You dealt, you dealt the hand down there in LA. You and that press, you and that uh, LA Times. You dealt the hand. You put me on "Life Magazine" and had me convicted before I walked into the courtroom. You had what people wanted to buy. When they wanted to buy it they didn't give a damn if they had to convict the District Attorney. They'd convicted the whole building to get that dollar bill going there.. They had big bucks going there. They made twenty seven million, thousand, hundred, billion and I'm bumming fifteen dollars from a friend here..

Tom: Here's another newspaper account that you can now speak to since you haven't done it before. That on the night following the, uh, killings of the house on Cielo Drive in Los Angeles, you accompanied four people to a home occupied by Mr. & Mrs. Leo LaBianca.

Manson : Yeah

Tom: That you went inside that house

Manson : mmmhmmm

Tom: And you tied them up

Manson : mmmmhmm

Tom: And assured them that they were not going to be hurt

Manson : mmmmhmmm

Tom: That you went back outside

Manson : mmmmhmmm

Tom : And sent Kasabian and Krenwinkel and Watson and Atkins inside the house to kill them.

Manson : mmmmhmmm

Tom : True or False?

Manson : mmmmhmmm (long pause)

Tom : Cause you know something Charles, that's what you were convicted of among other things.

Manson : Alright.

Tom: Is it true or false?

Manson: Do you deserve and in theory do you..

Tom: No no no. It's, it's a yes or no.

Manson: No, no, no, no, nothing's played...

Tom: But it's so simple. Try it, try it, try it.

Manson :No, nothing's yes or no. No. You, you go, go, go through your little boxes and things. You know, look, look here, uh, first you have to see where I'm coming from.

Tom: Not on that question, there's no coming from anywhere on that question Charles. (long pause) Did you do that?

Manson : (very long silence)

Tom : Chair's getting hot huh? (long silence)

Get mad, get angry, come over here and hit me if you like, but why don't you answer the question?

Manson : Hit you?

Tom: If you'd like

Manson : Nah.

Tom : But answer the question

Manson : I don't want to hit you. I, uh, got out of prison and I went up in the streams and I saw a big fat dead rat laying in the water.

Tom : I'm gonna ask the question again Charles

Manson : Uh-huh

Tom : I'm gonna ask the same question again

Manson : (long pause) Same question again. (pause) Did I break the law? Is that your question?

Tom : No, the question was that on the night following the murders or the killings or whatever else you want to call it at the Melcher home

Manson : Mmmmhmmm

Tom: On Cielo Drive in Los Angeles, newspaper accounts claim that you, Krenwinkel, Atkins, Kasabian and Watson went to the home of Mr. & Mrs. LaBianca in Los Angeles, that you went inside the house, tied them up, assured them that they would not be hurt, then went back outside and sent the other four in.

Manson : Who told you that?

Tom : Newspaper accounts...I do.. newspaper accounts and this is one of the things that for which you were convicted of in a courtroom in Los Angeles. Now here's your chance before the whole world to tell it straight once and for all. Did you do that?

art by pete berg

PART FOUR OF THE 1981 INTERVIEW WITH TOM SNYDER AND CHARLES MANSON

Tom: No, did you go in and tie up the LaBiancas that night? Very simple question.

Manson: That night..

Tom: August 10th 1969

Manson: That night, August the 10th, 1969

Tom: Did you? Why duck it, why dodge it? why not answer yes or no once and for all put it behind you?

Manson: (very long pause) mhmm (long pause) Did I kill anyone?

Tom: Did you tie up the LaBiancas? (long pause) Atkins testified you did.

Manson: (long pause) That's what Susie said?

Tom: That's what she said

Manson: Yeah?

Tom: And you remember it. You were in the courtroom when she said it.

Manson: (chuckles) She's written three books, and each time she's said something different.

Tom: Mmmhmmm

Manson: Each time.

Tom: Did you time them up?

Manson: Did I?

Tom: Mmmhmm

Manson: (long silence) Well, we came down from Aberdeen, and uh

Tom: Let's stay in Los Angeles August 10th, 1969

Manson: And there was a hole-in-the-wall gang there.

Tom: (long pause) Why don't you want to talk about it Charles? Why don't you want...

Manson: Because I'm an outlaw and I go so far and then that's all you know.

Tom: And if you did.

Manson: That's like asking Jessie James "are you going to shoot somebody?"

Tom: And if, and if, and if, and if as others have written and others have testified and as the media has reported you did that ,and you sent your friends back in to do the deed, aren't you a coward?

Manson: Oh my friends back in to do the terrible deed .

Tom: Doesn't that make you..

Manson: The wicked deed. Um, did we have the castle there with the vampires and the Frankenstein, and the bugs and lizards dying in the desert? Did we have the water that is dying and the whales that are being killed and the seals…

Tom: Here we go again, lay it off on someone else.

Manson: Well

Tom: Let's point to all the other injustices

Manson: Oh I'm in the world all by myself?

Tom: Yeah, on this one you are. Yeah.

Manson: Yeah, hmmm, it's ok, if that's the way you see it for you.

Tom: Well, whether you like it or not Charles, all those things that happened that August in Los Angeles are identified as the Manson Killings.

Manson: Yeah, that's what your history book will tell you.

Tom: So you can sit here and talk about the whales and Hiroshima and you can sit and talk about the environment and the Great Lakes and that's all fine, but what it really comes down to in this particular instance is that this one is your ballgame.

Manson: Well if I could get some help from the doctor then I could get my mind straightened out a little bit and I come back and play like a human.

Tom: Well, you've never talked about this before, but I'm gonna try it one more time.

Manson: Yeah. Now, now, now

Tom: You can see

Manson: You got a pistol on you?

Tom: No sir. They wouldn't let me in here if I had a pistol, you know that as well as I do, so why even ask the question? Okay?

Manson: Well, I just thought you might not like what I have done and want to do something about it.

Tom: I don't much care for what you've done.

Manson: Yeah.

Tom: A lot of people don't. How do you feel about that?

Manson: Well

Tom: They think you are a monster Charles.

Manson: Yeah, they think you are a monster because you reflect this news media on me. Cult leader. I never had long hair before I got busted. I never had a beard before I got busted. I went to shave and the guy's "No, you can't shave", I said "I need a razor to shave", he said "No you can't shave" I said "Let me get a hair cut" he said "no we don't want you to change your appearance." So when you , first put that camera on me you got long hair and a beard. First time in my life I've got long hair and a beard.

Tom: You want, you want a shave and get a hair cut? I'll shut them off and you'll get a shave and a hair cut.

Manson: Am I telling him right? I'm not of this generation.

Tom: You want a shave and a hair cut right now? I'll shut them down right now if you want a shave and a hair cut.

Manson: Yeah, yeah I was trying to explain to you man, that a lot of what they pushed of on me is not me. They said I had a great family and I was the followers and leader. There was no followers and leaders, bunch of kids out at the ranch playing, to me.

Tom: Playing at what?

Manson: Playing at living.

Tom: The accounts say that you, that you gave them dope. I'm just saying what the accounts say.

Manson: Oh yeah.

Tom: I'm not saying I know it to be so. So here's your chance to say that it wasn't true.

Manson: Yeah, yeah

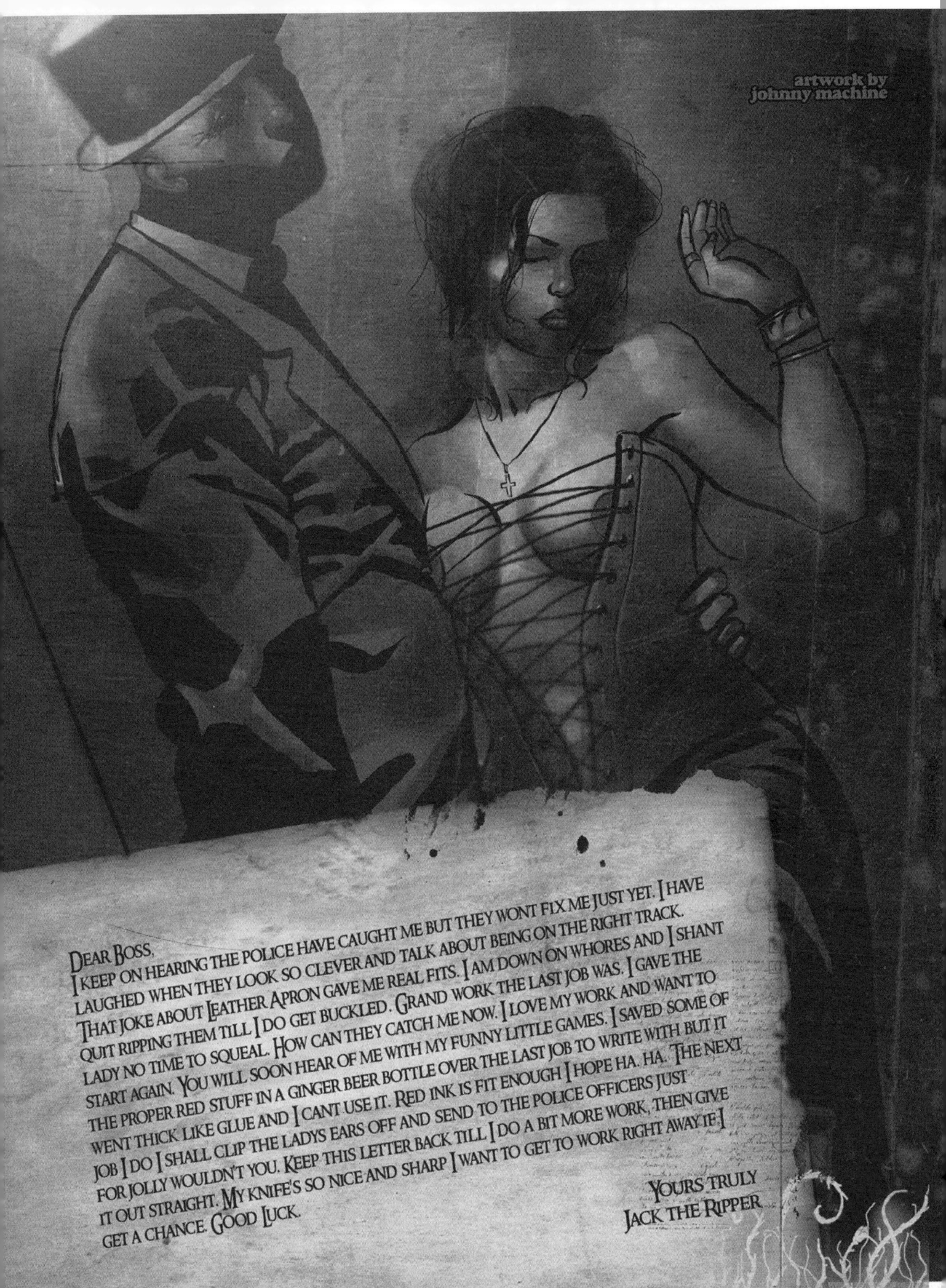

MUSIC TO MURDER TO
LYRICS TO SONGS WRITTEN BY CHARLES MANSON

art by jack malebranche

SICK CITY
Sick city, yeah, restless people
From the sick city burnt their houses down
To make the sky look pretty
What can I do, I'm just a person
This is the line we always seem to hear
You just sit, things get worse
And watch TV and drink your beer
Walking all alone
Not going anywhere
Nobody seemed to care
Restless as the wind
This town is killing me
Got to put an end to this restless misery
I'm just one of those restless people
Can never seem to be satisfied
With living in this sick old sick old
Sick city
It may be too late for me to say goodbye
And I might be too late
To watch this sick old city die
Going on the road
Yeah I'm gonna try
To say sick city so long farewell
And die

LOOK AT YOUR GAME GIRL
There's a time for living
Time keeps on flying
Think you're loving baby
But all your doing is crying

[chorus]
Can you feel
Are those feelings real
Look at your game, girl
Look at your game, girl

What a mad delusion
Living in that confusion
Frustration and doubt
Can you ever live without the game

The sad, sad game
Mad game
Just to say loves' not enough
?? it can't be true
Oh, you can tell those lies
Baby but you're only fooling you

[chorus]

You feel
I those feelings ain't real
Then you better stop trying
Or you're gonna play crying
Stop trying

That's the game
Sad sad game
Mad game
Sad game

P4RT F1V3 OF THE 1981 INTERVIEW WITH TOM SNYDER AND CHARLES MANSON

Manson: That's what they said.

Tom: Alright that's what they said, well are they wrong?

Manson: Oh! Well! I went down to Haight-Ashbury and a little kid 10 years old came up and said "You want an acid pill?" I said "what's that?" he said "This is good. Make colors go" I said "No, I've heard of them things. I don't want none of that." And then, then another little kid was rolling a joint, and they were sitting there smoking a joint and asked me if I wanted one.

Tom: What'd you say?

Manson: I said "I used to smoke this stuff in the 60's but it never, or the 50's but it really, really wasn't, you know, it was funny but it's not..."

Tom: How much dope did you do in your lifetime? Were you a heavy user of dope?

Manson: No. I smoked a little grass and I've taken some acid, mescaline, uh, psilocybin, peyote, mushroom. But actually take uh dope, no. Nothing. I'd never take anything that I feel would actually hurt me.

Tom: Do you feel that those things that you just mentioned hurt you at all Charles?

Manson: Uh, physically or spiritually?

Tom: Mentally.

Manson: And then on what level? On the level of society the way you view the norm?

Tom: No, no, no, no, no, no. Stop the hogwash. Do you feel that the drugs that you did use in your earlier life time confused you, altered your mind, uh juggled, scrambled, made you see things differently, uh stay on that level if you can.

Manson: Maybe I find a uh, spirit of uh, cave man-think-through-brain.

Tom: Let me try it again

Manson: (laughs)

Tom: Do you think the drugs you used hurt you?

Manson: Nah. Drugs hurt me? No I don't think the drugs have hurt me. If I overdone it I think it would.

Tom: You don't want to be anybody's leader do you?

Manson: No.

Tom: Never did want to be anybody's leader?

Manson: No. Don't like attention.

Tom: Mmmmhmm. Then why do you

Manson: Most insecure people need attention. I don't

Tom: I was just going to say then, if you don't want attention, why do you keep, why all your life have you kept waving your arms saying "Hey look at me"?

Manson: That's what I've been doing all my life?

Tom: Well I have to say a young man.

Manson: Let me see if I've got that documented.

Tom: who by the time he's 20 years old has been in and out of jails and reform schools for a variety of offenses that include wife beating... homo...

Manson: (chuckles) Wife beating?! Now that bullshit, I've never whipped my old lady.

Tom: Didn't you?

Manson: No, I punched my mother out once.

Tom: Oh you did, alright, we'll call it mother beating. Uh, forging checks

Manson: But she was wrong. She lied to me and beat me for my money, and she, she didn't do right. You know what I mean?

Tom: Forging checks, uh car theft, I mean these are ways of waving your arms and saying "Look at me, give me some attention"

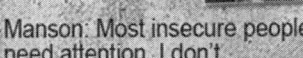

Manson: Yeah.

Tom: And you say you don't want attention. Now Charles, that's a contradiction.

Manson: Yeah.

Tom: That doesn't make any sense.

Manson: Well over a period of about 20 years, I would imagine you'd would want to change something. I'm not very wise to many things. But I am wise to one thing, you know.

Tom: What's that?

Manson: Well I'm not gonna to tell you.

Tom: Ok. You punch your mother, did you hate your mother?

Manson: Nah, I loved my mother, she's a good girl.

Tom: What about your wife, you were married once weren't you?

Manson: Yeah.

Tom: How'd that go? Why'd you wanna get married? That's kinda conventional, that's kind of normal. that's kinda of in the rut as you say to get married isn't it?

Manson: (laughs)I got married, cause I wanted to get in that (inaudible) That's why I got married.

Tom: oh yeah? Married for sex was the reason you got married?

Manson: Yeah, I did know what was happening. I knew something was happening but no one would tell me so I had to find out, you know, I didn't have books like you guys, you know, "Playboys" and stuff in them days. I had to find out for myself.

Tom: Mmmmhmmm. Why do you think that all us guys are playboys? That we can't

Manson: AH MAN! I didn't say you were playboys, I was talking about "Playboy" magazine-type thought man!

Tom: Ok, ok, ok, ok, ok, ok. You had a son by that marriage didn't you?

Manson: Uh Yeah, I got a kid somewhere.

Tom: Do you think about him?

Manson: Uh, not, about as much as my father did me.

Tom: So two wrongs make a right, Charles?

Manson: No I didn't say there's anything wrong with the way my dad's been taking care of me. He lets me live, (laughs) I'm alive, you know.

Tom: I remember you saying, or being quoted...

Manson: Thank you.

Tom: In a courtroom in Los Angeles as saying "The children who came at you with knives are your children."

Manson: Yeah, I didn't raise 'em. You raised 'em.

Tom: "You are the ones that kicked them out. You are responsible for what they've done."

Manson: That's right, just as much as I am.

Tom: Mmmhmmm, so you, in my mind, were criticizing society for kicking their children out.

Manson: Sure.

Tom: And yet I've just seen you sit here and say "Yeah, I've got a kid somewhere."

Manson: Yeah

Tom: How can you criticize other people for kicking their kids out and you did the same thing?

Manson: Difference, difference, difference on many levels. Difference See my old lady left me and run off with a truck driver. She said "let's steal a car and go to California." and I said "Man, I ain't gonna steal no car and go off to California and go back to jail." She said "We won't get caught". Well we didn't get caught, just I got caught. She didn't get caught. So then she had a kid and then some truck driver came along, and I was a green kid and didn't know what I was doin', you know. So she says "You know, I got a ride, you know, see you later." So she took off and got married to someone else, you know. She's a good girl.

PART SIX OF THE 1981 INTERVIEW WITH TOM SNYDER AND CHARLES MANSON

Tom: And besides the son from your marriage, you've got, what, four other children somewhere?

Manson: Oh I don't, uh, uh, think I've been uh, uh, uh, responsible for as much as you people want to lay on me.

Tom: Well how many children do you have Charles?

Manson: How many children do I have? Uh, I don't know, I've got lots of children, man. Uh, in fact sometimes I even think that you're a child.

Tom: But you just said you don't have any children, you don't have any family in the context of the Ranch. I'm talking about children that (sighs) are your, uh, natural children.

Manson: How many are my natural ego?

Tom: No, children.

Manson: Oh children? I would divide one child from the other?

Tom: Alright, somewhere out there, somewhere there's at least one son that we know of that is your child, who's probably about 25 or 26 years old right now.

Manson: Is that right?

Tom: Yeah. Look into that camera. What do you say to that kid? What do you say to your son out there, who's watching his old man on television. Maybe the first time he's ever seen his old man with his face all carved up and his eyes glowering. You talk to that kid, what are you going say to him?

Manson: You gotta catch it on your own boy. The train's hard. The road's ruff.

Tom: And that's it?

Manson: That's all I knew. That's all anyone ever told me.

Tom: Alright. (sighs)

Manson: And you wanna hear something?

Tom: Yeah.

Manson: He'll do it better than me. (chuckles)

Tom: Do what?

Manson: Whatever he does, (chuckles) he'll do it a little better. Kids do, don't they?

Tom: Sometimes.

Manson: Yeah, (chuckles) that's what makes them such a gas. They always seem to get through.

Tom: (sighs) There was a story of a celebrity hit list.

Manson: Was you ever a kid once?

Tom: Absolutely.

Manson: Yeah?

Tom: Still am in many ways.

Manson: Hmmmmm.

Tom: But not, not, not your way.

Manson: Oh my way? I don't know what my way is, everybody keeps telling me I got all these things. I read the other day where I had magical powers, and I told everybody in the chapel, I said "ZAP-ZAP-ZAP-ZAP". I said "where's my magical powers?" Well you can't, you can't believe what you read in the press. I ain't got no magical powers and mystical trips and all that kind of crap.

(pause) Yeah, it's kind of silly. Yeah, you got witches and devils and uh. One guy came up and said "I heard you said your Jesus" I said "Nah man, I ain't said nothing." He said "I'm glad" He said "I'm damn glad." I said "Why?" He said "I know you ain't him." I said "How do you know?" He said "Because I am." (laughs) I said "Ok". But I mean, you know I've been in the nut ward for the last 10 years, so you can't expect me to, uh, to rationally take thing stuff serious.

Tom: Don't you think that you belong in the nut ward?

Manson: It's alright. I can deal with that.

Tom: I'm mean don't you belong there?

Manson: Belong, where, I belong where I am allowed to go, man like, uh, you know, I belong there...

Tom: Let me nail down one of the real simple ones, listen how simple this is Charles. There was a story in the media, back when the trial was going on that Charles Manson had a celebrity hit list. I don't know who was on it, maybe there never was such a list. But was there a list of people, famous people that you thought about harassing, bothering?

Manson: If I wanted to harass them I just wouldn't watch their TV show.

Tom: Talk to me about your life in prison in terms of you being in isolation. You are not on what is called the main line. You don't, you're not in with the prison population here, how do you feel about that?

Manson: How do I feel about it? I don't feel about it.

Tom: Would you rather not be in isolation?

Manson: Oh I've been trying to get on the main line, I've been trying to get to the prison for the last 13 years.

Tom: Why?

Manson: Why? Walk around, play some handball, play a little guitar. Uh, do my number, do my time like any convict does. Like I've always done. Like my mind been set to do. Like my uh, past lives have been in jail, doing time in jail. In fact when I got out I just got outside and sat down. I wasn't

Tom: If you were on the mainline, wouldn't you be exposed to some dangers?

Manson: Come on man,

Tom: What?

Manson: if you're thinking exposure to danger, then that danger you're thinking is coming around you.

Tom: Well look what happened to James Earl Ray? Heard about didn't you?

Manson: Uh, James Early Ray's got his problems, I've got mine.

Tom: Have you heard? He got stuck.

Manson: Yeah.

Tom: 22 Times.

Manson: Some people died in India too.

Tom: Got stuck.

Manson: And some other people died in Hawaii.

Tom: You wouldn't be scared.

Manson: People are dieing all over.

Tom: You wouldn't be frightened or afraid then of the uh, of the uh, prison population trying to make a hit on you.

Manson: Man, I've been staying alive in prison this long without no help.

Tom: What is "S Ward?"

Manson: It's a nut ward.

Tom: What goes on there?

Manson: Uh, what ever goes on in there. You'd have to ask the people responsible for that.

Tom: Well, do you they do things to you in there?

Manson: Do they do things to me?

Tom: Mmmhmmm

Manson: Uh, That depends.

Tom: Do they give you medication here?

Manson: Yeah, they give you medication here.

Tom: (long pause) You on medication now?

Manson: No. No. It took me about a few years to get off the medication. The medication has toned me down quite a bit. (pause) A whole lot. (chuckles) That's the reason I like the desert, was I get out in the desert then I can let it out and say if I see you within 50 miles then we'll know something. Yeah I used to love that desert, out in the woods and things. I didn't know you could get out in the woods for 30 years.

Tom: How do you feel about spending the rest of your life in prison?

Manson: Well, we're our own prisons. We each our own wardens and we do our own times. We get stuck in our own little trips and we kind a judge ourselves the way we do. You know, I can't judge uh, nobody else, best thing I can do is try to judge myself and live with that."

A JURY OF FEARS

On August 3, 1988, the Los Angeles Times reported that some jail employees overheard Ramírez planning to shoot the prosecutor with a gun, which Ramírez intended to have smuggled into the courtroom. Consequently, a metal detector was installed outside of the courtroom and intensive searches were conducted on people entering. On August 14, the trial was interrupted because one of the jurors, Phyllis Singletary, did not arrive to the courtroom. Later that day she was found shot dead in her apartment. The jury was terrified; they could not help but wonder if Ramírez had somehow directed this event from inside his prison cell, and if he could reach other jury members. However, Ramírez was not responsible for Singletary's death; she had been shot and killed by her boyfriend, who later killed himself with the same weapon in a hotel. The alternative juror who replaced Singletary was too frightened to return to her home.

MATCH MADE IN HELL

By the time of the trial, Ramírez had fans who were writing him letters and paying him visits. Since 1985, freelance magazine editor Doreen Lioy wrote him nearly 75 letters during his incarceration. In 1988 he proposed to her, and on October 3, 1996, they were married in California's San Quentin State Prison. Lioy has stated that she will commit suicide when Ramírez is executed.

artwork by johnny machine

HOUSE OF HORRORS

Police suspected Gein to be involved in the disappearance of a store clerk, Bernice Worden, in Plainfield on November 16, 1957. Upon entering a shed on his property, they made their first horrific discovery of the night: Worden's corpse. She had been decapitated, her headless body hung upside down by means of ropes at her wrists and a crossbar at her ankles. Most horribly, the body's torso was empty, the ribcage split and the body "dressed out" like that of a deer. These mutilations had been performed postmortem; she had been shot at close-range with a .22-caliber rifle.

Searching the house, authorities found:

* Human skulls mounted upon the corner posts of his bed;

* Skin fashioned into a lampshade and used to upholster chair seats;

* Breasts used as cup holders

* Human skullcaps, apparently in use as soup bowls;

* A human heart (it is disputed where the heart was found; the deputies' reports all claim that the heart was in a saucepan on the stove, with some crime scene photographers claiming it was in a paper bag);

* Skin from the face of Mary Hogan, a local tavern owner, found in a paper bag;

* A window shade pull consisting of human lips;

* A "mammary vest" crafted from the skin of a woman's torso;

* A belt made from several human nipples, among many other such grisly objects;

* Socks made from human flesh.

* A sheath made from human skin.

* A box of preserved vulvas that Ed admitted to wearing.

Gein's most notorious creations were an array of "shrunken heads." Various neighborhood children — whom Gein occasionally babysat — had seen or heard of these objects, which Gein offhandedly described as relics from the South Seas, purportedly sent by a cousin who had served in World War II. Upon investigation, these turned out to be human facial skins, carefully peeled from cadavers and used by Gein as masks.

Gein eventually admitted under questioning that he would dig up the graves of recently buried middle-aged women he thought resembled his mother and take the bodies home, where he tanned their skin to make his macabre possessions. One writer describes Gein's practice of putting on the tanned skins of women as an "insane transvestite ritual". Gein denied having sex with the bodies he exhumed, explaining, "They smelled too bad." During interrogation, Gein also admitted to the shooting death of Mary Hogan, who had been missing since 1954.

PART SEVEN OF THE 1981 INTERVIEW WITH TOM SNYDER AND CHARLES MANSON

Manson: See, what other people do is not really my affair, unless they approach me with it, and want me to do something about it, uh, then I'll uh take into consideration what has to be done. But other than that I just uh, try to do my number, and do my time. Get out on the main line, play some tennis, walk around, make the chow a little better, you know. And then there's the possibility the preacher can teach me something, because the preacher, the reverend is, is quite a guy. And I'm finding they got two or three doctors here that got a lot of sense. I mean as far as I'm concerned they got a lot of sense in my world, you know. And I've tried to shake two or three of them, but they, they're pretty smart. And uh. then they got some uh, pretty good inmates here, trying to get out and work their lives into a decent sort of way. Trying to promote harmony. Pull ourselves together and be right and do right and have the understanding of what it is in a congenial form for world peace. There's a lot of people working for world peace.

Tom: Let's assume that one day you were paroled. Let's just…

Manson: Parole?

Tom: Let's just make believe. Do you ever think you will be?

Manson: Yeah, do I ever think I will be? Well I've never been paroled before. I went up to the board and they never would, they said I was incorrigible. And uh, not only was I incorrigible, I'd never grow up. And I kind a agreed with them. I had a..

Tom: I mean let's just make believe here for a second.

Manson: Make believe?

Tom: Let's make believe, let's make believe that you're getting out tomorrow.

Manson: Tomorrow.

Tom: Okay?

Manson: Tomorrow creeps it's petty pace. Yeah.

Tom: Would you go after anybody Charles??

Manson: After anybody? Hell no.

Tom: Do you feel, do, let me try another way,

Manson: I'll come after you, man.

Tom: Do you, do you feel, do you feel that you have any scores to settle with anyone on the outside?

Manson: Hmm, let me think. Do I have any scores out there? Now we're making believe right?

Tom: Mmmhmmm

Manson: Well, I'll tell you buddy.. (laughs) (long pause) Well, I don't rightly know. I'm stupid (chuckles) to the point to where I'm not really sure, and if you'll ask the question again, maybe the answer will come to you. What was it again?

Tom: If you got out tomorrow do you have any scores to settle on the outside?

Manson: Scores? You mean people that have done me wrong?

Tom: Or that you feel that have done you wrong?

Manson: That feel that I've done them wrong?

Tom: No, feel that they've done you wrong.

Manson: Oh

Tom: That you feel that done you wrong?

Manson: Oh well most people do themselves wrong.

Tom: But would you want, would you want to go get anybody if you got out.

Manson: No.

Tom: No.

Manson: They push, see what they do, see they take all that bad and then they push it off on each other. I told the dude, "You're doing this to yourself man". You know, I've been sitting in there, in other words I'm the cell, right, and they let me out, and I walk around and the guy says "If you don't do this we're gonna lock you back up." I said "ok, I don't care anyway." Already gave up that thought. Prison's in your mind, man, like you know.

Tom: Okay. Okay.

Manson: You sit in the cell, and they guy asks "You in prison?" I say "no, I'm just here." He says "what you doin'?" I say "I'm just sitting waiting for these uh, people to get done doin' what they're doing so I can get out."

Tom: Do you have a television set? Do you watch television?

Manson: Yeah, I used to watch it a little bit, but kinda it looks, I don't really like it that much.

Tom: Ok, What about newspapers. Do you get newspapers?

Manson: No I don't bother with those. I know that they're jiving there.

Tom: Ok, Radio? Listen to the radio?

Manson: I listen to the Hearts and Space Program. I like that. And the rest of it is just like a bunch of (gibberish) There's no uh..

Tom: What about your music?

Manson: I get some classical music on the 98 station that saying something'..

Tom: Okay, but what about your own music? I remember reading

Manson: Well..

Tom: that you at one time you had a recording stint at a studio in Hollywood, that you liked guitar, that you wrote music, or that you sang music. Do you still do that?

Manson: Yeah, yeah I do that. Yeah I do that. But uh, the way I do it, ain't the same way you guys do it. And the way I do it scares you guys. So I didn't want to scare you guys out of the neighborhood right away. (chuckles) So I just took a can and started banging on it, you know.

But we used to have some cosmic gatherings back in the mountains that would probably shake a Mormon Tabernacle Quire's eardrums.

Tom: You said, the kind of music you play scares people. Why shouldn't people be scared by you?

Manson: There's only one person you should be a-scared of and that's yourself. Afraid of what, loosing your bank account? Afraid of your wife going uh, away? You have all those things. I'm not afraid of loosing my watch or someone taking my money or robbing me. I went down to Mexico in the 50's down where the Yakees was, and they said "Man you don't go down to where the Yakees are. They're terrible" I said "Why?" he said "Well, they don't like people like you." I says "Well they didn't say anything."

Tom: Yeah. I asked that question in the context of, would you believe it or not, there's a lot of people on the outside, that think about the possibility of you coming out of here, and they're genially scared of you.

Manson: Oh boy I might just, just make dust, everything terrible. One little guy, terrible. Oooo. Boy, how insecure are we as human beings put all our fear on one little guy? And afraid to let him out, he might break all the toys. (laughs)

Tom: Why do you say little guy?

Manson: Because I'm not the guy you trying to make out of me. That's not me. That's some guy in somebody's imagination that want to make a couple hundred million dollars for himself. He got rich. He had a good game going. He had a better game going than I did. But he had a good mother to help him. She helped him in a nice game. I was kind a over on the sidelines. See, I had to get around that game and look over the tracks.

Tom: Ok, Now, here we go again on mother for a second. You said he had a nice mother to help him, does that mean you did not have a nice mother to help you?

Manson: Oh, well, I imagine I have got a whole lot of nice mothers that would help me. If I I would help them you know. How much would you help yourself?

Tom: When I asked you why you got married you said for sex. Uh..

Manson: That's when I was 20 years old.

Tom: Yeah, what kind (chuckles) This is funny, what kind of sex life is there for Charles in this prison?

Manson: Well I (inaudible) get a little bit now and then.

PART EIGHT OF THE 1981 INTERVIEW WITH TOM SNYDER AND CHARLES MANSON

Manson: I try to hide it not to embarrass other people. But I've been doing it ever since I was 10. (laughs) I get to thinking, here I am an old man sitting in this cell, (laughs) that's the damnest thing I ever seen, you know. It looks like I grow up, but I really don't know how yet. I'm learning. Preacher's teaching me how to grow up.

Tom: Do you miss women?

Manson: Certainly. My goodness, yeah, damn right, yeah. (laughs)

Tom: What do you think of women?

Manson: Oh I like them. They're nice. If they're put together well, and everything and they're soft and spongy, yeah, they're nice. As long as they keep they're mouth shut and do what they're do what they're supposed to do.

Tom: Why do you say that?

Manson: 'cause that's what a woman's supposed to do.

Tom: Keep her mouth shut and do what she's supposed to do?

Manson: Sure.

Tom: Who taught you that?

Manson: Well, I don't want her snitchin' on me.

Tom: How do you feel about dieing?

Manson: Dieing is.

Tom: You know you were sentenced to the gas chamber and then they modified the death penalty, were you happy when that was done?

Manson: Was I happy when what was done?

Tom: When you found out that you weren't going to the gas chamber.

Manson: You talking about dieing now it gets me nervous.

Tom: Why?

Manson: Did you have any thoughts about something? Was you wanting to go anywhere?

Tom: Were you happy when you found out you weren't gonna go to the gas chamber, Charles?

Manson: Uh, I knew I wasn't gonna go to the gas chamber, cause I hadn't done anything wrong.

Tom: You scared to die?

Manson: (pause) Sometimes I feel I'm a-scared to live. Living is what scares me. Dieing is easy. Getting up everyday and going through this again and again is hard. See I'm carrying a heavier thought, see, the thought I'm carrying is very heavy. Like I'm on a football team, and everybody's, and, and I'm a little guy, I don't have no supp, I don't have no home team. You got all the home, I got one, one uh cheerleader (chuckles) or one uh, uh coach. See you got me in a disadvantage because I'm on your ground see. So, and this is your street I recon, you got the cameras and the money and the things. But you can believe me that um, Bugliosi has you on a rib, and all them guys that sold you most of that stuff, sold you a bunch of things that weren't uh, weren't real. Not to me. We used to have games we would play on the movie set. We would take on different people. I'd be Riff Raff Rackus, Steve would be John Jones, just a-come in from Minneapolis and driving a truck. And we'd just take other people, and play act other people. And then we lost track of who we were. (chuckles) And it went off into other dimensions and levels of thought and understandings and comprehensions that were beyond most people minds, functions, computers, data.

So, um, all I did was watch and learn everything I could from everybody I ever met. Then when I got out of prison I just walked around. I didn't tell nobody to do nothing. I said do what you want to do. (inaudible) Don't tell me what to do. I don't like people telling me what to do. I just come from place where they told me what to do all my life, you know. I want to find out what to do for myself, you know. Never did. Not yet. But I was gonna take a trade, one of these days. Maybe learn to be a welder or something. (long pause) Til I can get to the front gate anyway.

Tom: They got you involved in this whole drama where people got killed. How did you get involved in that drama?

Manson: Well I was borned illegitimately that put me on the other side of the law. I've been an outlaw ever since I was borned. I went to reform school when I was about 10. And I learned to box and cry, and I learned to do all the things that you do in reform school.

And then I went to , uh, I escaped there a bunch of times and I went to prison. And I learned everything that you do in prison. And I talked to all the guys and asked them everything they knew, and they told me all the things they knew. And then I went to the end of it and then old man would be ready to die and he'd say "Well son, un, sincerity is the best gimmick remember that." and I say "Alright, be sincere, that'll win it?" He says "That's it." Sincerity and honesty he said will do it, it'll trick 'em every time. (laughs) I said "Well, sincere and honesty, I've never tried that. I've tried everything else but maybe I'll try sincere and honesty." So then I looked in a book and it said "The wages of sin is death." Now I figured well, I don't want to die, so maybe I have been sinful here. Maybe I am wrong. Maybe I'll take a look at my life and say "well, I'm gonna change it and start all over." You know, and I know I go to God and say "Hey man, are you gonna forgive me?" And he's gonna say "What do you do? You gonna forgive you? What you come to me for? Forgive yourself man, don't be botherin' me." You know, and I think well he must be a big mighty god, man. He just, you know, he ain't got time, you gotta make an appointment or something, you know. So I see the whole aspect of the whole trip for children to play, you know, then I get stuck in the game of playing the goat here, or the lamb, or the, the some other trip. I was a teddy bear, then I was the goof ball, whatever, and uh, what is the real one, where is the real one. I don't know where the real one is. He's in a nut ward somewhere.

Interview over

CHAINSAWS & SATANISTS
A FEW WORDS WITH BILL MOSELEY

William Moseley is an American actor and musician who has starred in a number of cult classic horror films. His first big role was in The Texas Chainsaw Massacre Part 2 as Chop Top. He also played Ottis Driftwood in the Devil's Rejects and evil Ash in Army of Darkness.

James Gilks:
In your film career, you have played many fictional killers. Where any of these characters modeled after real life murderers?

Bill Moseley:
Some might say Otis Driftwood, especially in "The Devil's Rejects," was similar to Charles Manson, but you'd have to ask Rob Zombie about that. Otis was much different in "House of 1000 Corpses," so it's hard to tell. In prepping that role, I didn't base it on anyone in particular, I just read the script a bunch of times, used my imagination and tried to find the truth in each scene!

James:
What kind of preparation or research do you have to undertake to play such a convincing killer?

Bill:
About the only rule of thumb for me in playing psychos is knowing that I'm the only sane one in the world! If you try to play "crazy," it looks dopey. For preparation, I use my imagination- a supremely powerful tool for most people!

James:
Are there any real life killers that you are interested in or would be interested in playing on film?

Bill:
I don't know any real life killers i'd like to play. I'm not all that interested in exploring the psyches of serial killers vs. any other kinds of folks. i say, bring em all on! serial killers are not exactly a happy bunch, and I like to play characters with a sense of humor. Now, maybe I'm wrong, maybe serial killers whistle while they work. if so, I'm more than happy to get into their skin.

THE CO-ED KILLER
THE STRANGE TALE OF EDMUND KEMPER

Between May 1972 and February 1973, Kemper embarked on a spree of murders, picking up female students hitchhiking, taking them to isolated rural areas and killing them. He would stab, shoot or smother the victims and afterwards take the bodies back to his apartment where he would have sex with them and then dissect them. He would often dump the bodies in ravines or bury them in fields, although on one occasion he buried the severed head of a 15-year-old girl in his mother's garden as a kind of sick joke, later remarking that his mother "always wanted people to look up to her." He killed six college girls (including two students from UC Santa Cruz, where his mother worked, and one from Cabrillo College). He would often go hunting for victims after arguing with his mother.

In April 1973, Kemper battered his mother to death with a pick hammer while she slept. He performed a sexual indignity to her decapitated head before using it as a dartboard. He also cut out her vocal cords and put them in the garbage disposal, but the machine could not break the tough tissue down and regurgitated it back into the sink. "That seemed appropriate," Ed said after his arrest, "as much as she'd bitched and screamed and yelled at me over so many years." His murderous urges not yet satiated, he then invited his mother's best friend over and killed her too, by strangulation. He then drove eastward, but when no word of his crimes hit the radio airwaves he became discouraged, stopped the car, called the police and confessed to being the Co-ed Killer. He told them what he had done and waited for them to pick him up, seemingly unashamed as he confessed to necrophilia and cannibalism. At his trial he pleaded insanity, but he was found guilty of eight counts of murder. He asked for the death penalty, but with capital punishment suspended at that time, he instead received life imprisonment.

At the time of Kemper's murder spree in Santa Cruz, another serial killer named Herbert Mullin was also active, earning the small California town the title of "Murder Capital Of The World." And, adding to the college town's infamy was the fact that these multiple murders were preceded three years earlier by multiple murders committed by John Linley Frazier. In a manner similar to the Charles Manson murders, Frazier murdered a Santa Cruz family of five, eye surgeon Victor Ohta and family. Kemper and Mullin were briefly held in adjoining cells, with the former angrily accusing the latter of stealing his body-dumping sites. Edmund Kemper remains among the general prison population and is incarcerated at Vacaville State Prison.

artwork by johnny machine

IN DEFENSE OF MURDERABELIA

BY TOD BOHANNON OF MURDERAUCTION.COM

Opponents of collectors of killer-related items claim that by allowing the sale of these items we are "rewarding" the inmate for the crimes that they have committed. I would like to share some truths about the money that some of these inmates receive. Many inmates are required to pay restitution as part of their sentence. California's restitution requires 55% of any funds deposited into an inmates account to be kept as restitution. Other California institutions supply indigent inmates (those inmates who have no money), with 5 postage-paid envelopes per month. If that inmate later receives any money, the prison promptly deducts 55% for restitution and then they deduct the cost of the envelopes and postage. However, if the inmate doesn't receive any money in the account within 30 days, the cost for the envelopes and postage is erased. If that inmate has any money remaining after the restitution and postage is paid - then the inmate is required to buy their next set of toiletries. Shampoo, tooth paste, tooth brush, deodorant and soap, just to name a few. Then, if the inmate has any funds remaining, they are allowed to purchase items from the commissary. So, do the math, on $10 or $20 and see exactly how much these inmates will have left to spend. Not much. Not all facilities allow just anyone to send money to the inmates. Some require that the sender be listed on the inmates' visitation list. And the list, in some cases, can only be changed by the inmate 2 times each year. Some prisons allow only a specific amount to be spent per month on commissary items. The Telford Unit in Texas allows inmates to spend $40 per month from January through November. In December, they are allowed to spend $80.

It's not only the internet dealers who sell items related to the inmates. San Quentin has an actual store, where artwork and crafts, made by the inmates, are sold to the public. Louisiana has their own rodeo twice a year, where inmates sell their arts and crafts - and the inmates are allowed to actually participate in the rodeo! Most facilities do offer a hobby craft program for the inmates. Prisoners have nothing but time, some use this time to express themselves through art and crafts. Others just paint or make crafts just to pass time. And, in most cases, the prisoners have to buy - with money from their account, the supplies that they use. Some inmates are allowed to work and earn wages from the prison while serving their time. They are paid anywhere from 8 cents to 30 cents per hour. Do we consider this to be a profit or rewarding them for what they've done? Most inmates aren't looking for notoriety. They want no mention of themselves or their crimes mentioned on the Internet. They are still human. Most of the inmates are looking for companionship - interaction with anybody else from outside of the prison. They realize that most people write them in hopes of attaining their autograph, but would they otherwise have a chance to interact with other people on the outside? How many inmates convicted of murder actually do artwork? And out of those few, how many create artwork related to their crime? How many create artwork that's considered violent? How many letters can you locate that were written by a convicted murderer, which actually depicts the violent details of their crime? And of these convicted murderers and serial killers, how many actually have names that are notorious or infamous? I've had names turn up on my website that I had to research just to know who they were, such as Alfred Gaynor and Mark Hacking. I sent an email and asked that you pick a few random items from MurderAuction and watch them over the course of a week. I would have no way of knowing the items that you had selected, and therefore I had no way of altering any of the results. So, you tell me, how many of the items that you selected actually sold?

With Murder Auction up and running the public is able to see what is being sold or traded on the internet. They can monitor who is buying, who is selling, and what items are selling and at what price. Without Murder Auction, the public is no longer privy to this information. And collectors and crime-enthusiasts would simply find other avenues from which to procure the items. Where is Andy Kahan's proof that I, or any other dealers or collectors are making money? Where is his proof that the inmates are making a profit? Media sensationalizes these murder cases and the convicted murderers. This causes a keen interest in the merchandise and collectors and dealers then put a price on the items. Without this notoriety, the artwork and other items would probably receive little notice.

If the argument is that prisoners are profiting from the sale of these items, then let's go and see how much profit Ted Bundy, John Gacy, Jeffrey Dahmer, Gary Hedinik, and Ed Gein profited recently. You can find T-shirts, board games, coffee mugs, key rings, dolls, and trading cards for sale, all related to these men and their crimes. Where would we send their profit to?

Did you know that Lizzie Borden's house is a Bed & Breakfast? Certainly, they are profiting off of crime. The price per day ranges depending on what room in the house you choose. And they stay booked 6 months in advance! Lizzie is really making lots of profit. Why is the gun that Lynette Fromme used in an assassination attempt on Gerald Ford kept on display in the Gerald Ford Museum? Why did people run up to John Dillenger after he was shot dead and use handkerchiefs and other related items to get samples of Dillenger's blood? Authorities buried him underneath 6 foot of concrete to ensure that no one would dig him up.

Why were outlaws such as "Billy the Kid", displayed inside their caskets for the public to see before burial? And why was there always such a good turn-out for public hangings? Rappers involved in what is called "Gangsta Rap" take on either a bastardization of old gangster names or the actual name. How much violence is reported annually that involves the individuals involved in the "Gangsta Rap" industry? Do these artists profit from songs that glorify violence or drug use? Do they make any money off of these songs that make it to the Top 20 list? Then there's the television program Law & Order. Do you suppose that they are making a profit? How many times has the name Charles Manson been mentioned on their show? Several. Then there's A&E Specials, Discovery Time, Discovery, Most Evil, 20/20, 48 Hours Mystery, just to name a few. Are they giving away that air time for commercials? Court TV covered the trials of O.J. Simpson, Robert Blake, and Phil Specter, all celebrities and all charged with murder. I feel safe to say that I bet a profit was made from airing those trials. And there seems to be an increase in the number of this type of public broadcasting.

The BTK trial and segments of the trial were aired repeatedly on the news. As part of the "BTK"'s plea agreement, he had to describe his crimes in detail - on national television! Do you think that the networks that aired these segments had any financial gain in mind, or did they air this just to cause additional pain to the victim's families? And, if any profit was made, did they gift it to the families? Don't you think that the families of Radar's victims were disturbed and hurt by hearing this? Were these networks accused of making money off of the victim's pain? There is now, as there has always been, a cultural fascination with murder, mayhem, and with the people beyond the pale - those who exhibit the extremes of human behavior and violence. And with that fascination comes the collectors of the art and artifacts of those who are "notorious".

Last Supper
THE TOP TEN MOST INTERESTING DEATH ROW MEALS

10. GARY GILMORE, UTAH, 1977-- The alpha. The first person executed when the death penalty was reinstated. Hamburger, eggs, potatoes and contraband bourbon. Happy about winning his legal battle for immediate execution, Gilmore spent his last evening dancing with relatives and tossing back a few mini-bottles of smuggled bourbon.

9. THOMAS GRASSO, OKLAHOMA, 1995-- The signature meal in "Last Suppers". Mr. Grasso devoured a dozen steamed mussels, a Burger King double cheeseburger with mustard, mayonnaise, lettuce and tomato, a can of Franco-American spaghetti with meatballs, a mango, half of a pumpkin pie with whipped cream, and a strawberry milkshake. But, there was a problem. Mr. Grasso had been served spaghetti and meatballs, but had actually requested Spaghetti-O's. He did not take this slight lightly, his last words included this complaint, "I did not get my Spaghetti-O's. I got spaghetti. I want the press to know this!"

8. TED BUNDY, FLORIDA, 1989-- The scourge of Chi-O's across America, Bundy didn't eat a special last meal. His dinner the night before was a burrito and Mexican rice.

7. GERALD MITCHELL, TEXAS, 2001 -- one bag of assorted Jolly Ranchers & LEWIS GILBERT, OKLAHOMA, 2003-- a half-gallon of vanilla ice cream, a box of assorted cones and a box of Whoppers.

6. TIMOTHY MCVEIGH, THE FEDS, 2001 -- 2 pints of mint chocolate chip ice cream. Federal criminals are limited to a frugal $20 tab for their last meal requests. During the time leading up to his execution, the radical, self-serving, asinine, propagandizing, deluded animal rights group, PETA, spent time corresponding with McVeigh, imploring him to order a meatless last meal.

5. THE IDEALISTS--ROBERT MADDEN, TEXAS, 1997-- He asked that his final meal be provided to a homeless person. His request was denied. & ODELL BARNES, JR., TEXAS, 2000--Justice, Equality, World Peace. His request was denied.

4. AILEEN WUORNOS, FLORIDA, 2002-- One from the softer side of death row. Wuornos didn't order a last meal and skipped the regular fare of barbecued chicken, mashed potatoes, apple crisp and tea but had a cup of coffee about 12:30 a.m. Instead, ate a hamburger and other snack food from the prison's canteen. Later, she drank a cup of coffee. Her story has been portrayed in two movies, three books and an opera.

3. WALTER LAGRAND, ARIZONA, 1999-- LaGrand asked for six fried eggs, 16 strips of bacon, one large serving of hash browns, a pint of pineapple sherbet, a breakfast steak, a cup of ice, 7-Up, Dr Pepper, Coke, hot sauce, coffee, two sugar packs. And, as a final item: four Rolaids.

2. JOHN WAYNE GACY, ILLINOIS, 1994-- Kentucky Fried Chicken, fried shrimp, french fries, strawberries and Diet Coke. Once you get the Colonel's recipe of secret herbs and spices in your blood, it's pretty tough to shake. Gacy, the killer of at least 33 young men, was a former manager of a KFC.

1. ROBERT BUELL, OHIO, 2002--A single black, unpitted olive. Actually, Buell was paying homage to Victor Ferguer, the last prisoner executed by the federal government until Timothy McVeigh. Ferguer was hanged in 1963. His last meal--an olive with the pit still in it. He told prison officials that he hoped it would sprout from his body an olive tree -- a sign of peace. Ferguer's body was unclaimed by family and was quickly taken away by a funeral home after the execution and buried. His unmarked grave in a barren corner of a public cemetery bears no olive tree.

The last meal is a symbol of our empathy. Even though we may be putting to death the most despicable person on the planet, those of us who are not despicable still feel some consternation and sometimes even sympathy. It's our attempt to ease the individual's suffering and somehow make their final journey, (this time pardon the pun), more palatable.

SERIAL KILLER TRIVIA

Most people know that Marilyn Manson took his name from a combination of Marilyn Monroe and Charles Manson but did you know that his drummer Ginger Fish's stage name was derived in part from Albert Fish. Former member Zsa Zsa Speck formed the name from Zsa Zsa Gabor's first name and Richard Speck's last name.

Buffalo Bill, the main antagonist in The Silence of the Lambs, was modeled (in part) after Ed Gein. Both Bill and Old Eddie made vests from women's skin. Thomas Harris was in court the day of the infamous bite mark testimony in Bundy's 1979 trial (he had a press pass). Harris was then inspired to create the character Francis Dolarhyde for his novel Red Dragon. Also, many references to Bundy abound in Red Dragon: the teeth the killer uses are identical to Bundy's; and t-shirt slogans that appeared after Bundy's second escape (e.g. "Ted Bundy Is A One Night Stand") are attributed to the fictional killer in the novel.

David Byrne, lead singer of Talking Heads, said the song "Psycho Killer" (from the album Talking Heads:77 (1977)) is about the Son of Sam.

By 1974, the original Manson "family" had dwindled to only Fromme and Sandra Good. Motivated by Manson's new ideology, they sent a series of threatening letters to heads of corporations, making threats unless they stopped polluting the environment.

David Berkowitz (the son of sam) is mentioned as one of the disembodied brains in the book Krokodil Tears (1990) by Jack Yeovil as part of the Dark Future series.

Writer of X Files (Glen Morgan) once read an article about Richard Ramirez. Before his capture it was rumored that he entered the homes of his victims by the small window in the bathroom. This rumor would later be debunked after his arrest, but the story intrigued Morgan so much that it was the basis for the creation of the character Eugene Victor Tooms. To flesh out the story, the writers drew their inspiration from Jack the Ripper and a large ventilation shaft outside their office.

Jeffrey Dahmer's younger brother David changed his last name and lives in anonymity. Many relatives of famous serial killers have been forced to do this in order to lead normal lives.

System of a Down's song "Forever" (aka "Fortress" or "Outer Space") from the leaked album "Toxicity II" contains lyrics referencing Kemper including "Edmund Kemper solved it all, He fooled the shrinks." The song was later dropped from the released "Steal This Album!"

In the popular Japanese manga Rurouni Kenshin, there is a character named simply "Gein", who makes life-sized dolls out of flesh salvaged from corpses. In a creator's notes section in Volume 24, creator Nobuhiro Watsuki notes that the character was indeed inspired by Edward Gein.

Charlize Theron won the academy award for playing Aileen Wuornos on 29 February 2004, Aileen Wuornos's birthday. The biker bar scenes were filmed at "the Last Resort" - a bar frequented by the real life Aileen Wuornos, and the site where she was actually arrested. The bar owner (who capitalized on Wuornos' infamy by hanging a sign out in front of the bar advertising "cool beer and Killer Women") makes a cameo as the bartender who threatens to cut off Wuornos for being over her tab limit.

Henry lee Lucas claimed to have been part of a cannibalistic, satanic cult called "The Hand of Death" to have taken part in snuff films, to have killed Jimmy Hoffa, and to have delivered poison to cult leader Jim Jones in Jonestown prior to the notorious mass murder/suicide of Jones's group.

John Wayne Gacy was voted "Man of the Year" in his home town by the community group the Jaycees.

artwork by johnny machine

Warning Signs
COMMON CHARACTERISTICS OF A SERIAL KILLER

art by chuck hodi

14 Characteristics of Serial Killers

Over 90% of serial killers are male.

They tend to be intelligent, with IQ's in the "bright normal" range.

They do poorly in school, have trouble holding down jobs, and often work as unskilled laborers.

They tend to come from very unstable families.

As children, they are abandoned by their fathers and raised by domineering mothers.

Their families often have criminal, psychiatric and alcoholic histories.

They often hate their fathers and mothers.

They are commonly abused as children — psychologically, physically and sexually. Often the abuse is by a family member.

Many serial killers spend time in institutions as children and have records of psychiatric problems.

They have high rates of suicide attempts.

From an early age, many are intensely interested in voyeurism, fetishism, and sado-masochistic pornography.

More than 60 percent of serial killers wet their beds beyond the age of 12.

Many serial killers are fascinated with fire starting.

They are involved with sadistic activity or tormenting small creatures.

Victim Characteristics

*Serial killers enjoy extending the suffering of their victims. Many feel a lot of power by determining whether their victim will live or die. They may torture their victim for several days to obtain as much pleasure as possible.

*Victims of serial killers have no profile. Most victims are chosen at random, just being in the wrong place at the wrong time. Some serial killers have a preference for their victims, choosing to eliminate a certain group of people (prostitutes, young women, children, etc.).

*Unlike mass murderers, serial killers select the victim. The killer will fantasize about the murder until the fantasy is no longer enough to bring about pleasure, and he must commit the crime. The serial killer will survey the location, and take every precaution to not get caught. Then they seek out the victim and murder them.

*Serial killers are seeking an object or prop to victimize, not a partner. Jeffrey Dahmer was searching for a living, breathing zombie who would do whatever he wanted and would never refuse or leave. The victims share personality traits such as vulnerability and confusion.

Is My Son A Serial Killer?

We get many interesting emails at SerialKillerCalendar.com and although we try to answer all questions to best of our ability, every now and then we get asked something that is outside of our own expertise. That's when we try to draw on the knowledge and experience of others. The woman who sent us this email has asked a very difficult and important question, "is my son in danger of becoming a serial killer?" With her permission, we have decided to reprint the email in it's entirety. If any of our readers can provide help in better answering this question, please email James Gilks directly at MadHatterDesign@gmail.com

Hello,
Found your site today when I was looking for info about Jeffrey Gorton. I am interested in him because he has the same type of fetish my (17) son has and has had since about the age of 8 or 9. My son also has some other personality and mental problems and I think it's only responsible for me to be as educated as possible in all areas that may become a problem for him in life and try to be as aware as possible. Of course no mother ever wants to entertain the idea that their child might be developing the traits of a serial killer, but I don't think it would be helpful to turn a blind eye to the similarities either. Anyway, it's a long story and I have been trying to help my son for years now and nobody wants to take the time to figure out why this is going on. I think it could be genetic or physiological or cognitive because he doesn't come from an abusive or tragic childhood. I wish I could find somone to test him or study him or something helpful. Let me know if you can think of anybody that may be helpful. I have tried everything. In fact, I would like to correspond with this Jeff Gorton guy to see if he would help me understand how he became a criminal and what he thinks may have helped him avoid it if anything could have. My main question is when is your magazine going to be available? I would be interested in reading the articles. I must say I am not sure how I feel about the way you have chosen to approach and display information about crime, it seems to be somewhat offensive to me on many levels but I think the information is valid, and if it causes society to question and explore then that's a good thing. Not to mention that if I don't like it, I don't have to read, buy, support, etc. it. It's really that simple. Simply portraying unsettling material hasn't been shown to cause the bad behavior it represents. Because I have tried to become as educated as possible in what my son may be experiencing and how I may be able to help, I have an interest in the information you are making available. It helps me to understand the reality of these types of behaviors which is the only way I know of to be helpful. A limited or inaccurate understanding is not helpful. I've gone on long enough now. Let me know when/if your magazine will be available or if you would be interested in a story about a mom that discovers that she may be raising someone that could become a criminal. That is my greatest fear, for him and any potential victims as well.

Thank You,
Respectfully,
Mindy

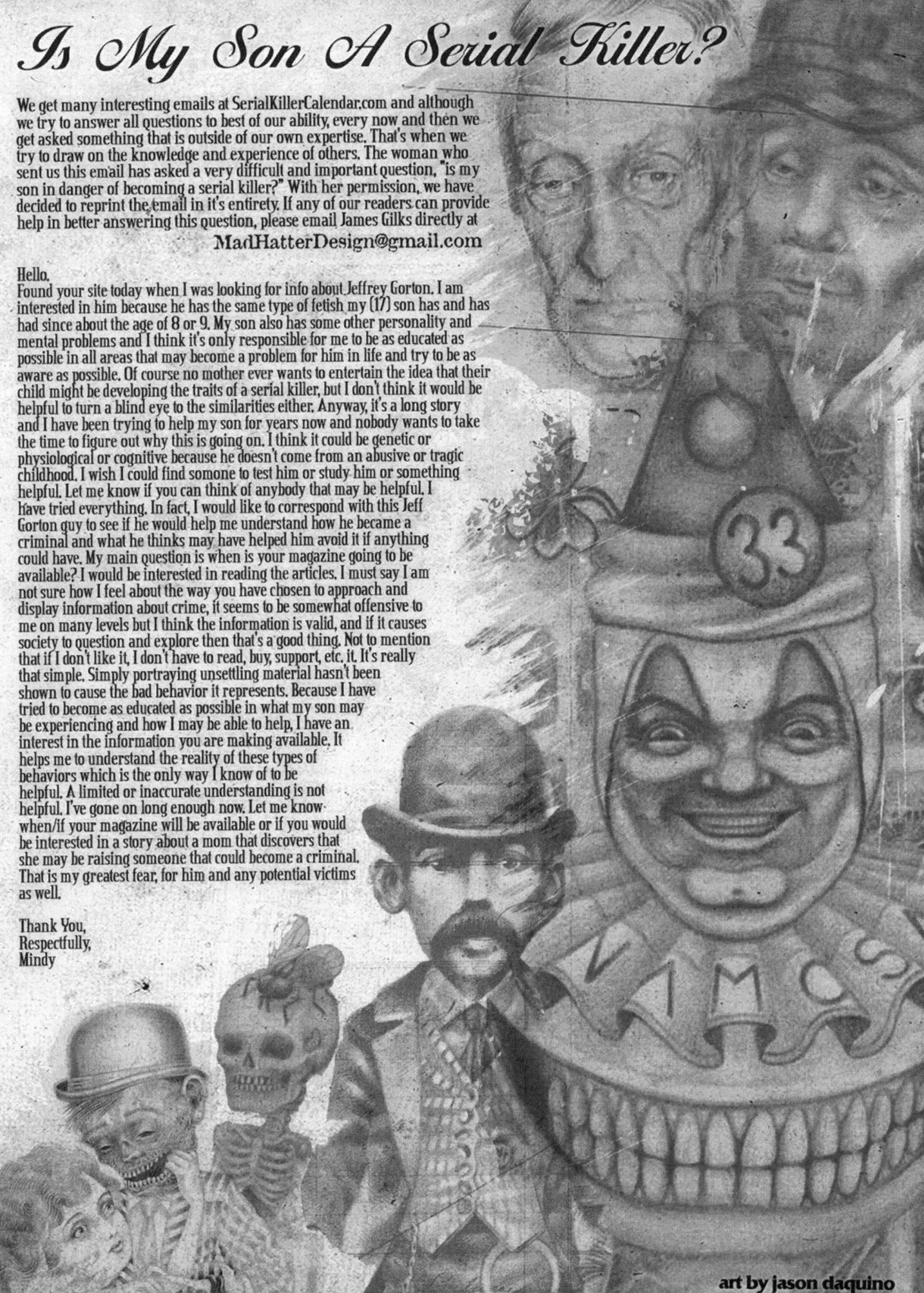

art by jason daquino

LETTERS FROM HELL
THE SON OF SAM TAUNTS POLICE IN NEW YORK

DEAR CAPTAIN JOSEPH BORRELLI

I AM DEEPLY HURT BY YOUR CALLING ME A WEMON HATER. I AM NOT. BUT I AM A MONSTER. I AM THE SON OF SAM. I AM A LITTLE BRAT. WHEN FATHER SAM GETS DRUNK HE GETS MEAN. HE BEATS HIS FAMILY. SOMETIMES HE TIES ME UP TO THE BACK OF THE HOUSE. OTHER TIMES HE LOCKS ME IN THE GARAGE. SAM LOVES TO DRINK BLOOD. GO OUT AND KILL, COMMANDS FATHER SAM. BEHIND OUR HOUSE SOME REST. MOSTLY YOUNG -- RAPED AND SLAUGHTERED -- THEIR BLOOD DRAINED -- JUST BONES NOW. PAPA SAM KEEPS ME LOCKED IN THE ATTIC TOO. I CAN'T GET OUT BUT I LOOK OUT THE ATTIC WINDOW AND WATCH THE WORLD GO BY. I FEEL LIKE AN OUTSIDER. I AM ON A DIFFERENT WAVELENGTH THEN EVERYBODY ELSE -- PROGRAMMED TOO KILL. HOWEVER, TO STOP ME YOU MUST KILL ME. ATTENTION ALL POLICE: SHOOT ME FIRST -- SHOOT TO KILL OR ELSE KEEP OUT OF MY WAY OR YOU WILL DIE! PAPA SAM IS OLD NOW. HE NEEDS SOME BLOOD TO PRESERVE HIS YOUTH. HE HAS HAD TOO MANY HEART ATTACKS. UGH, ME HOOT, IT HURTS, SONNY BOY. I MISS MY PRETTY PRINCESS MOST OF ALL. SHE'S RESTING IN OUR LADIES HOUSE. BUT I'LL SEE HER SOON. I AM THE MONSTER -- BEELZEBUB -- THE CHUBBY BEHEMOUTH. I LOVE TO HUNT. PROWLING THE STREETS LOOKING FOR FAIR GAME -- TASTY MEAT. THE WEMON OF QUEENS ARE PRETTYIST OF ALL. IT MUST BE THE WATER THEY DRINK. I LIVE FOR THE HUNT -- MY LIFE. BLOOD FOR PAPA. MR. BORRELLI, SIR, I DON'T WANT TO KILL ANYMORE. NO SUR, NO MORE BUT I
MUST, HONOUR THY FATHER. I WANT TO MAKE LOVE TO THE WORLD. I LOVE PEOPLE. I DON'T BELONG ON EARTH. RETURN ME TO YAHOOS. TO THE PEOPLE OF QUEENS, I LOVE YOU. AND I WANT TO WISH ALL OF YOU A HAPPY EASTER. MAY GOD BLESS YOU IN THIS LIFE AND IN THE NEXT.

THE LETTER DID NOT HAVE ANY USEFUL FINGERPRINTS AND THE ENVELOPE HAD BEEN HANDLED BY SO MANY PEOPLE THAT IF THERE WERE ANY OF THE MURDERER'S PRINTS THEY WERE LOST. THIS LETTER WAS LEAKED TO THE PRESS IN EARLY JUNE AND THE WORLD FINALLY HEARD THE NAME: SON OF SAM

ONE WEEK BEFORE THE LATEST SON OF SAM MURDER, A RETIRED CITY WORKER NAMED SAM CARR WHO LIVED IN YONKERS, N.Y. WITH HIS WIFE AND CHILDREN RECEIVED AN ANONYMOUS LETTER ABOUT HIS BLACK LABRADOR HARVEY. THE WRITER WAS COMPLAINING ABOUT HARVEY'S BARKING. ON APRIL 19, TWO DAYS AFTER THE LATEST MURDER, ANOTHER LETTER IN THE SAME HANDWRITING CAME IN THE MAIL

"I HAVE ASKED YOU KINDLY TO STOP THAT DOG FROM HOWLING ALL DAY LONG, YET HE CONTINUES TO DO SO. I PLEADED WITH YOU. I TOLD YOU HOW THIS IS DESTROYING MY FAMILY. WE HAVE NO PEACE, NO REST. NOW I KNOW WHAT KIND OF A PERSON YOU ARE AND WHAT KIND OF A FAMILY YOU ARE. YOU ARE CRUEL AND INCONSIDERATE. YOU HAVE NO LOVE FOR ANY OTHER HUMAN BEINGS. YOUR SELFISH, MR. CARR. MY LIFE IS DESTROYED NOW. I HAVE NOTHING TO LOSE ANYMORE. I CAN SEE THAT THERE SHALL BE NO PEACE IN MY LIFE, OR MY FAMILIES LIFE UNTIL I END YOURS."

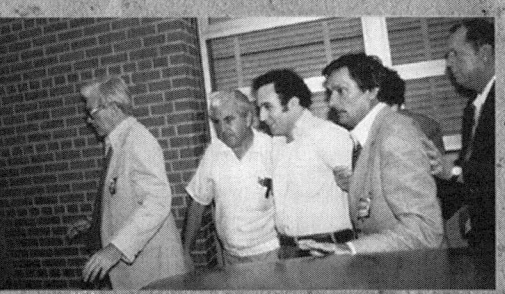

WHILE THE POLICE WERE CHASING DOWN EVERY SUSPECT, CHECKING REGISTRATIONS FOR .44 WEAPONS, TRACING ACTIVITIES OF FORMER MENTAL PATIENTS AND GENERALLY RUNNING THEMSELVES RAGGED, THE SON OF SAM HAD BECOME EMBOLDENED BY THE PUBLICITY. HE DECIDED TO WRITE TO JIMMY BRESLIN, A REPORTER FOR THE DAILY NEWS.

"HELLO FROM THE CRACKS IN THE SIDEWALKS OF NYC AND FROM THE ANTS THAT DWELL IN THESE CRACKS AND FEED IN THE DRIED BLOOD OF THE DEAD THAT HAS SETTLED INTO THE CRACKS. HELLO FROM THE GUTTERS OF NYC, WHICH IS FILLED WITH DOG MANURE, VOMIT, STALE WINE, URINE, AND BLOOD. HELLO FROM THE SEWERS OF NYC WHICH SWALLOW UP THESE DELICACIES WHEN THEY ARE WASHED AWAY BY THE SWEEPER TRUCKS. DON'T THINK BECAUSE YOU HAVEN'T HEARD [FROM ME] FOR A WHILE THAT I WENT TO SLEEP. NO, RATHER, I AM STILL HERE. LIKE A SPIRIT ROAMING THE NIGHT THIRSTY, HUNGRY, SELDOM STOPPING TO REST; ANXIOUS TO PLEASE SAM.

SAM'S A THIRSTY LAD. HE WON'T LET ME STOP KILLING UNTIL HE GETS HIS FILL OF BLOOD. TELL ME, JIM, WHAT WILL YOU HAVE FOR JULY 29? YOU CAN FORGET ABOUT ME IF YOU LIKE BECAUSE I DON'T CARE FOR PUBLICITY. HOWEVER, YOU MUST NOT FORGET DONNA LAURIA AND YOU CANNOT LET THE PEOPLE FORGET HER EITHER. SHE WAS A VERY SWEET GIRL.

NOT KNOWING WHAT THE FUTURE HOLDS, I SHALL SAY FAREWELL AND I WILL SEE YOU AT THE NEXT JOB? OR SHOULD I SAY YOU WILL SEE MY HANDIWORK AT THE NEXT JOB? REMEMBER MS. LAURIA. THANK YOU.

IN THEIR BLOOD AND FROM THE GUTTER-- SAM'S CREATION .44

DUKE OF DEATH. WICKED KING WICKER. THE TWENTY-TWO DISCIPLES OF HELL. AND LASTLY, JOHN WHEATIES, RAPIST AND SUFFOCATOR OF YOUNG GIRLS. P.S., DRIVE ON, THINK POSITIVE, GET OFF YOUR BUTTS, KNOCK ON COFFINS, ETC."

PARTIAL FINGERPRINTS WERE SALVAGED FROM THE LETTER WHICH WERE VALUABLE TO MATCH AGAINST A SUSPECT ONCE CAPTURED.

COLD CASE

THE BLACK DAHLIA

Elizabeth Short (July 29, 1924 – ca. January 15, 1947) was an American woman who was the victim of a gruesome and much-publicized murder. Nicknamed the Black Dahlia, Short was found severely mutilated, with her body severed, on January 15, 1947 in Leimert Park, Los Angeles, California. The murder, which remains unsolved, has been the source of widespread speculation as well as several books and film adaptations.

Elizabeth Short was born in Hyde Park, Massachusetts. She was raised in Medford, by her mother, Phoebe Mae, after her father, Cleo Short, abandoned her and her four sisters in October 1930.

Troubled by asthma, Short spent summers in Medford and winters in Florida. At the age of 19, she went to Vallejo, California, to live with her father. The two moved to Los Angeles in early 1943, but after an argument, she departed, getting a job at one of the post exchanges at Camp Cooke (now Vandenberg Air Force Base), near Lompoc. She moved to Santa Barbara, where she was arrested on September 23, 1943 for underage drinking and was sent back to Medford by juvenile authorities. In the few years following, she resided in various cities in Florida, with occasional trips back to Massachusetts, earning money mostly as a waitress.

In Florida, Short met Major Matthew M. Gordon Jr., who was part of the 2nd Air Commandos and training for deployment in the China Burma India theater of operations. Short told friends that Gordon wrote a letter from India proposing marriage while recovering from an airplane crash he suffered while trying to rescue a downed flier. (He was, according to his obituary in the Pueblo, Colorado newspaper, awarded a Silver Star, Distinguished Flying Cross, Bronze Star, the Air Medal with 15 oak leaf clusters, and Purple Heart). She accepted his proposal, but he died in a crash on August 10, 1945, before he could return to the U.S. She later embellished this story, saying that they were married and had a child who died. Although Gordon's friends in the air commandos confirm that Gordon and Short were engaged, his family subsequently denied any connection after Short's murder.

Short returned to Southern California in July 1946 to see an old boyfriend she met in Florida during the war, Lt. Gordon Fickling, who was stationed in Long Beach. For the six months prior to her death, she remained in Southern California, mainly in the Los Angeles area. During this time, she lived in several hotels, apartment buildings, rooming houses, and private homes, never staying anywhere for more than a few weeks.

The body of Elizabeth Short was found on January 15th, 1947, in Leimert Park, Los Angeles, severely mutilated, cut in half, and drained of blood. Her face was slashed from the corners of her mouth toward her ears.

According to newspaper reports shortly after the murder, Short received the nickname "Black Dahlia" at a Long Beach drugstore in the summer of 1946, as a play on the then-current movie The Blue Dahlia. However, Los Angeles County district attorney investigators' reports state the nickname was invented by newspaper reporters covering the murder. In either case, Short was not generally known as the "Black Dahlia" during her lifetime.

A number of people, none of whom knew Short in life, contacted police and the newspapers, claiming to have seen her during her so-called "missing week" between the time of her disappearance January 9 and the time her body was found on January 15. Police and district attorney investigators ruled out each of these alleged sightings, sometimes identifying other women that witnesses had mistaken for Short.

art by matthew aaron

NEW ALBUM OUT NOW!!!
CD + T-SHIRT PACKAGE DEAL
GET OUR NEW CD "BLOOD OFFERINGS" AND CHOOSE 1 OF 4 DIFFERENT T-SHIRT DESIGNS!
ONLY $16.00 - FREE SHIPPING TO US RESIDENTS ONLY.
OUTSIDE US PLEASE ADD $4.00 FOR SHIPPING.
VISIT WWW.KROTALUS.COM FOR MORE DETAILS.
CD ALSO AVAILABLE AT WWW.CDBABY.COM AND WWW.OPENGRAVESHOP.COM

"Fans of all that is intense about Death Metal will bang their heads to bloody stumps to this one" - David Horn, SOD Magazine

"When you compare Krotalus to the lot of 80's worshipping novelty acts like Merciless Death, Evile, Warbringer, etc., it's amazing to hear how much more sophisticatedly mature they approach their art." - Rob Aloi, Diabolical Conquest Webzine

"All the tracks on 'Blood Offerings' are tremendous! Breakdowns in that ol' 80's Possessed meets Slayer style treats listeners to more chords and crushed notes than bodies left on a WW1 battlefield." Mike Lidia, Unholy Cult Webzine

WWW.KROTALUS.COM • WWW.MYSPACE.COM/KROTALUS

KROTALUS — BLOOD OFFERINGS

SPEED METAL AND THRASH WITH BLACK METAL INFLUENCES

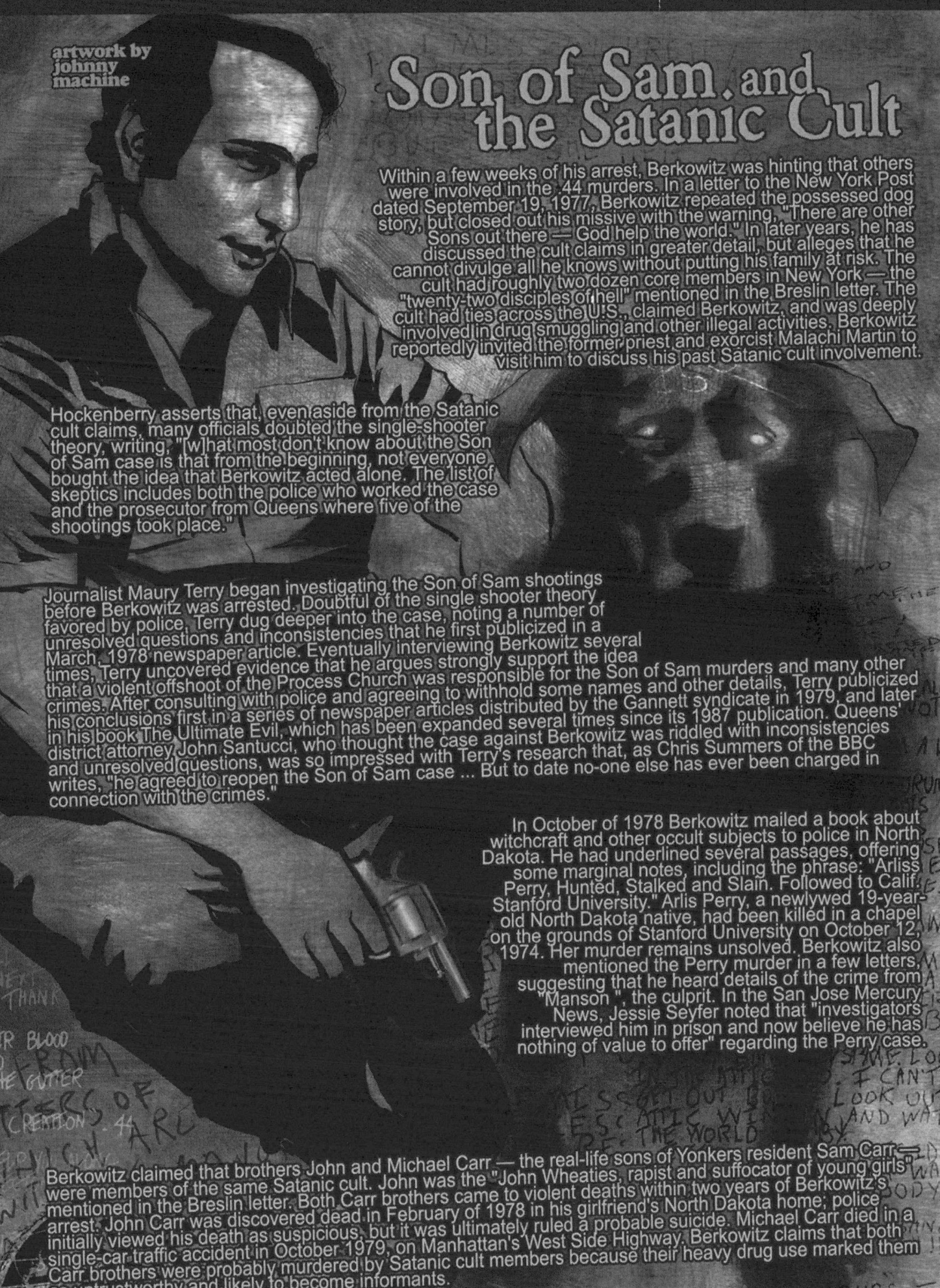

artwork by johnny machine

Son of Sam and the Satanic Cult

Within a few weeks of his arrest, Berkowitz was hinting that others were involved in the .44 murders. In a letter to the New York Post dated September 19, 1977, Berkowitz repeated the possessed dog story, but closed out his missive with the warning, "There are other Sons out there — God help the world." In later years, he has discussed the cult claims in greater detail, but alleges that he cannot divulge all he knows without putting his family at risk. The cult had roughly two dozen core members in New York — the "twenty-two disciples of hell" mentioned in the Breslin letter. The cult had ties across the U.S., claimed Berkowitz, and was deeply involved in drug smuggling and other illegal activities. Berkowitz reportedly invited the former priest and exorcist Malachi Martin to visit him to discuss his past Satanic cult involvement.

Hockenberry asserts that, even aside from the Satanic cult claims, many officials doubted the single-shooter theory, writing, "[w]hat most don't know about the Son of Sam case is that from the beginning, not everyone bought the idea that Berkowitz acted alone. The list of skeptics includes both the police who worked the case and the prosecutor from Queens where five of the shootings took place."

Journalist Maury Terry began investigating the Son of Sam shootings before Berkowitz was arrested. Doubtful of the single shooter theory favored by police, Terry dug deeper into the case, noting a number of unresolved questions and inconsistencies that he first publicized in a March, 1978 newspaper article. Eventually interviewing Berkowitz several times, Terry uncovered evidence that he argues strongly support the idea that a violent offshoot of the Process Church was responsible for the Son of Sam murders and many other crimes. After consulting with police and agreeing to withhold some names and other details, Terry publicized his conclusions first in a series of newspaper articles distributed by the Gannett syndicate in 1979, and later in his book The Ultimate Evil, which has been expanded several times since its 1987 publication. Queens' district attorney John Santucci, who thought the case against Berkowitz was riddled with inconsistencies and unresolved questions, was so impressed with Terry's research that, as Chris Summers of the BBC writes, "he agreed to reopen the Son of Sam case ... But to date no-one else has ever been charged in connection with the crimes."

In October of 1978 Berkowitz mailed a book about witchcraft and other occult subjects to police in North Dakota. He had underlined several passages, offering some marginal notes, including the phrase: "Arliss Perry, Hunted, Stalked and Slain. Followed to Calif. Stanford University." Arlis Perry, a newlywed 19-year-old North Dakota native, had been killed in a chapel on the grounds of Stanford University on October 12, 1974. Her murder remains unsolved. Berkowitz also mentioned the Perry murder in a few letters, suggesting that he heard details of the crime from "Manson ", the culprit. In the San Jose Mercury News, Jessie Seyfer noted that "investigators interviewed him in prison and now believe he has nothing of value to offer" regarding the Perry case.

Berkowitz claimed that brothers John and Michael Carr — the real-life sons of Yonkers resident Sam Carr — were members of the same Satanic cult. John was the "John Wheaties, rapist and suffocator of young girls" mentioned in the Breslin letter. Both Carr brothers came to violent deaths within two years of Berkowitz's arrest. John Carr was discovered dead in February of 1978 in his girlfriend's North Dakota home; police initially viewed his death as suspicious, but it was ultimately ruled a probable suicide. Michael Carr died in a single-car traffic accident in October 1979, on Manhattan's West Side Highway. Berkowitz claims that both Carr brothers were probably murdered by Satanic cult members because their heavy drug use marked them as untrustworthy and likely to become informants.

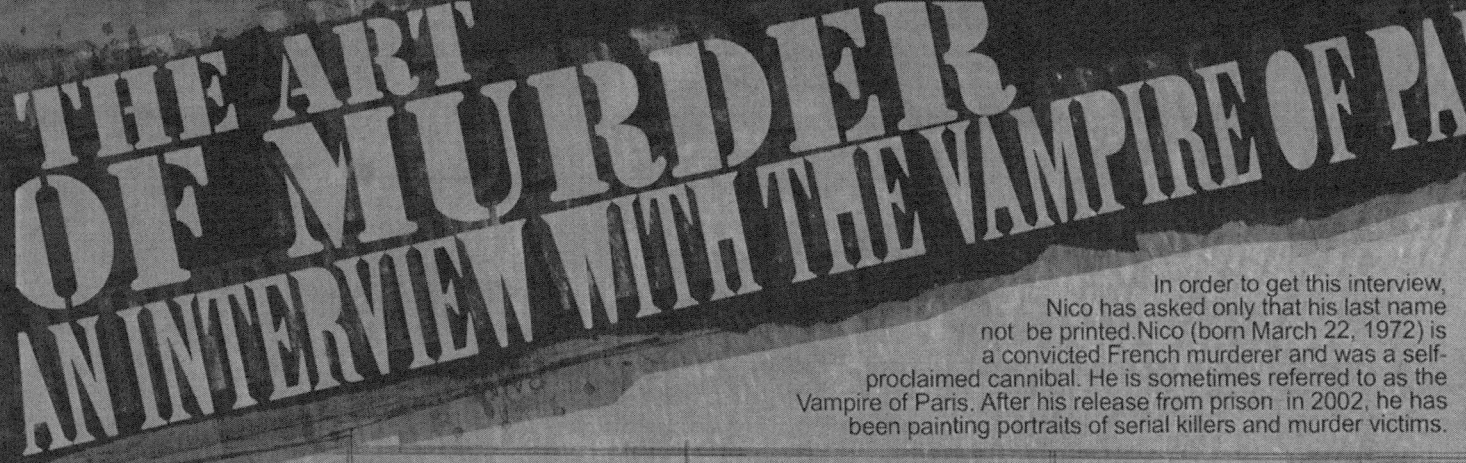

THE ART OF MURDER
AN INTERVIEW WITH THE VAMPIRE OF PARIS

In order to get this interview, Nico has asked only that his last name not be printed. Nico (born March 22, 1972) is a convicted French murderer and was a self-proclaimed cannibal. He is sometimes referred to as the Vampire of Paris. After his release from prison in 2002, he has been painting portraits of serial killers and murder victims.

JAMES GILKS: What were you charged with?

NICO C. - Murder among other things.

JAMES - Could you tell us about your time in prison? How long where you in and what events transpired while you served your time?

NICO - I served 8 years out of twelve. This is where i learned to paint. I also learned how to steal cars, but i dont use this in my everyday life.

JAMES - What did you do after being released from prison? Was it difficult to adjust to life on the outside?

NICO - I travelled a bit, visited a few places, travelled around the world some. I found a job in a morgue, so i decided to settle, but i still travell once in a while.

JAMES - In your opinion, why are so many people fascinated with serial killers, murder or crime in general?

NICO - it's a power trip. People are fascinated by power. Killers and specially serial killers have much more power than the most famous of rock stars or politicians. People remember who was Jack the ripper, but they dont know who was the most famous actress or politician in London at the time. Fear is the only real thing that everybody respects on this planet. Fear is true power..

JAMES - What are your religious views?

NICO - I am a traditional satanist. I am a student of several Left Hand Path traditions, like Ahrimanic sorcery, Setian Magick, Palo Mayombe, Aghori wisdom, all things you wont read in Anton Lavey's Satanic Bible ;)

JAMES - What, in your opinion, drives certain individuals to murder?

NICO - Most act out on basic human emotions, anger, jealousy, love, hate, and under certain circomstances, they cross the line, and think about it later. Thats how most murders happen. Even series.

JAMES - As far as serial killers go, who do you believe was the worst and which killer do you find most interesting?

NICO - Torture killers are the worst. Its not numbers. Bob Berdella is much more interesting than gary ridgeway, there is no doubt. Torture killers are the most interesting to me because i am a huge fan of torture. The word torture itself sparks something special in my mind. Thats how i can tell if somebody is just an average true crime fan, or if there is potential for something else. If he prefers Gary Heidnick over Ed Gein, than there is potential. Its a proof of good taste.

JAMES - When and how did you begin painting?

NICO - in prison around 1997. I have read books and studied other inmates paint. than i developed my techniques.

JAMES - What compels you to paint the subject matter you do? (i.e. serial killers).

NICO - I like to paint human monsters, psychopaths, freaks of nature, people with facial amputations. The thing in common is, faces who inspire terror. I like that.

JAMES - you have created some very impressive paintings throughout the years. Are there any pieces in particular that you are most proud of?

NICO - I like the Ted Bundy portrait that i have done. The eyes are perfect. Insane. It s the same eyes his victims saw before they died. I had an idea of doing just a painting of his eyes, with shades of his victims in the iris.

JAMES - You sometimes take on commission work. What do you normally charge for this service?

NICO - Between $500 and $1000, it depends on the time it will take.

JAMES - Many people find the idea of a reformed killer being on myspace to be unusual. Others are thrilled to have such an easy contact with someone as interesting and talented as you. Could you tell us a little about your myspace account and the myspace community?

NICO - I have two accounts, one public for the painting, and one private where i keep contact with friends. Myspace is good for taking commissions and meeting fellow artists. Other than that i dont do social things. I am not a social person. I am not online to talk with people.

JAMES - Your work has gained a considerable fan base and perhaps even more controversy. Do you have any stories regarding people or groups who are opposed to what you do?

NICO - A few stories. a guy who liked my art carved out his grandmother's heart in UK, and the cops found an interview i did on his coffeetable. They talked about it in the british parliament and it was in Bizarre magazine a while back. I am not welcomed in the UK. The french police are after me since 2002 but they are losers. I had an investigation going on in sweden cause i lived there. Interpol is after me too but their files are based on hearsay. I must sound paranoid, but its probably less than i know regarding who is monitoring what i do. But anyways i am like a snake, its hard to track me down. Few people actually know what i do these days.

JAMES - You have engaged in several debates on murderabelia and also been the subject of numerous attacks from anti murderabelia groups. What are your views on this subject?

NICO - I dont have any convictions in the usa, so i am above any anti murderabilia laws. Those laws dont apply here where i live. If they dont like the art, fuck them. If they dont like the fact that I am free, fuck them harder.

JAMES - What are your views on the world today?

NICO - I hope that the usa will nuke iran to the stone age. but then the economy is so bad in the us, that they better keep ammo for china, cause the chinese might kick the usa's ass in the near future, and even invade them.

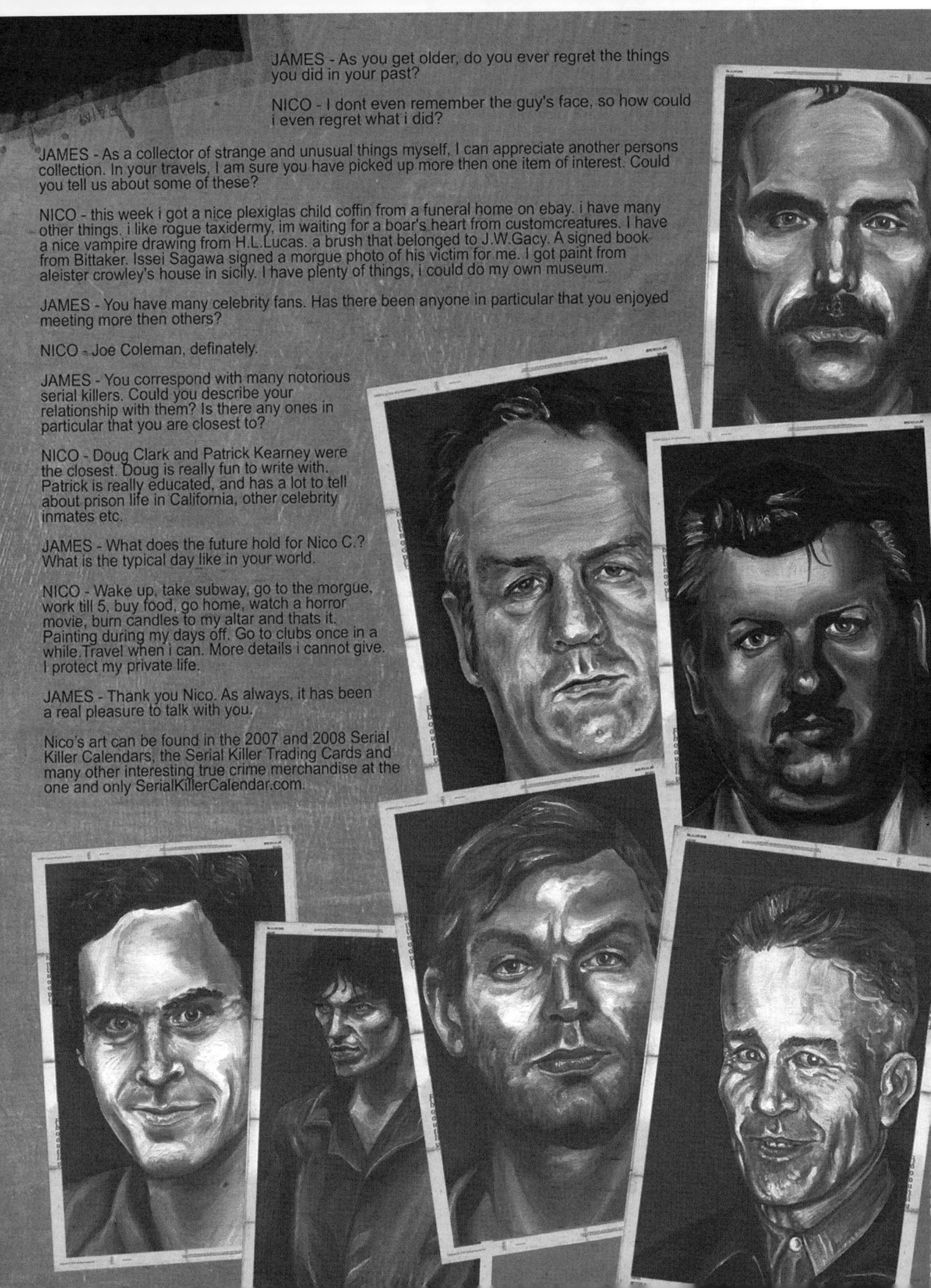

JAMES - As you get older, do you ever regret the things you did in your past?

NICO - I dont even remember the guy's face, so how could i even regret what i did?

JAMES - As a collector of strange and unusual things myself, I can appreciate another persons collection. In your travels, I am sure you have picked up more then one item of interest. Could you tell us about some of these?

NICO - this week i got a nice plexiglas child coffin from a funeral home on ebay. i have many other things. i like rogue taxidermy, im waiting for a boar's heart from customcreatures. I have a nice vampire drawing from H.L.Lucas. a brush that belonged to J.W.Gacy. A signed book from Bittaker. Issei Sagawa signed a morgue photo of his victim for me. I got paint from aleister crowley's house in sicily. I have plenty of things, i could do my own museum.

JAMES - You have many celebrity fans. Has there been anyone in particular that you enjoyed meeting more then others?

NICO - Joe Coleman, definately.

JAMES - You correspond with many notorious serial killers. Could you describe your relationship with them? Is there any ones in particular that you are closest to?

NICO - Doug Clark and Patrick Kearney were the closest. Doug is really fun to write with. Patrick is really educated, and has a lot to tell about prison life in California, other celebrity inmates etc.

JAMES - What does the future hold for Nico C.? What is the typical day like in your world.

NICO - Wake up, take subway, go to the morgue, work till 5, buy food, go home, watch a horror movie, burn candles to my altar and thats it. Painting during my days off. Go to clubs once in a while.Travel when i can. More details i cannot give. I protect my private life.

JAMES - Thank you Nico. As always, it has been a real pleasure to talk with you.

Nico's art can be found in the 2007 and 2008 Serial Killer Calendars, the Serial Killer Trading Cards and many other interesting true crime merchandise at the one and only SerialKillerCalendar.com.

HOME SWEET CELL
SERIAL KILLER MAILING ADDRESSES

John Eric Armstrong 362407-2084912M
Earnest C. Brooks Correctional Facility
2500 S. Sheridan Drive
Muskegon Heights, MI 49444

David Berkowitz #78A1976
Sullivan Correctional Facility
Box 116 Riverside Drive
Fallsburg, NY 12733

Kenneth Bianchi #SD14266961
Washington State Penitentiary
P.O. Box 520
Walla Walla, WA 99362-0520

DOUGLAS CLARK #C6300
SAN QUENTIN STATE PRISON
SAN QUENTIN, CA 94964

Edmund Kemper #B52453
California Medical Facility
1600 California Drive
P.O. Box 2000
Vacaville, CA 95696-2000

Bobby Joe Long #494041
Union Correctional Institution
P.O. Box 221 State Rd. 16
Raiford, FL 32083-0221

Ivan Milat
Goulburn Correctional Centre
PO BOX 264
Goulborn NSW 2580
Australia

Patrick Kearny B-88913
California State Prison
PO BOX 5002 D-4-160-L
Calipatria CA 92233

David Carpenter C 96500
San Quentin State Prison
San Quentin CA 94694

OBA CHANDLER 056979
UNION CORRECTIONAL
FACILTY
PO BOX 221
STATE ROAD 16
RAIFORD FL 32083-0221

WILLIAM HEIRENS #C06103
DIXON CORRECTIONAL FACILITY
2600 N. BRINTON AVE.
DIXON, IL 61021

CHARLES MANSON
#B33920/4A 4R-23
P.O. BOX 3476
CORCORAN, CA 93212

Damien Echols SK931
2501 State Farm Rd.
Tucker, AR 72618

Jessie Misskelley Jr.
#103072
C/O Jene O'Keefe
P.O. Box 13727
New Orleans, LA 70185-3727

HERIBERTO SEDA #98A4814
ATTICA CORRECTIONAL FACILITY
BOX 149
ATTICA, NY 14011

Peter Sutcliffe
Broadmore Hospital
Crawthorn, Berkshire
R6II-7E6
United Kingdom

Charles Ng P-46001
San Quentin State Prison
San Quentin CA 94964

HENRY WALLACE 0422350
CENTRAL PRISON
1300 WESTERN BOULEVARD
RALEIGH NC 27606

Dennis Nilsen
#B62006
HMP Whitemour
Long Hill Road
March, Cambridgeshire
United Kingdom

ANGELO BUONO C19329
CALIFORNIA STATE PRISON
BOX 5002 D-2-111L
CALIPATRIA CA
92233-5002

Arthur Shawcross
#91B-0193 A-S-132
Sullivan
Correctional Facility
P.O. Box 116
325 Riverside Drive
Fallsburg, NY 12733-0116

RICHARD RAMIREZ
#E37101
SAN QUENTIN
PRISON
SAN QUENTIN,
CA 94964

ANGEL
RESENDIZ
999356
3872 FM
SOUTH
LIVINGSTON
TEXAS 77351

JOEL RIFKIN
#95A6514
CLINTO
CORRECTIONAL
FACILITY
P.O. BOX 2000
DANNEMORA,
NY 12929

art by nico claux

THE HANDS OF DEATH

OTTIS TOOLE, HENRY LEE LUCAS AND THE CULT OF SATANIC CANNIBALS

{ BY ANNA M. GRIFFY }

Henry Lee Lucas and Ottis Toole were by many accounts the most prolific serial killers in history. They were notorious for the many women they raped and killed and allegedly engaged in a homosexual relationship themselves. But from their humble beginnings, a merging of two minds became a cross-country killing spree that may have been touched by the hand of Satan, and a cult called The Hand Of Death. While there have been many rumors and some killers have suggested to be part of the cult, Lucas and Toole were the most vocal about their participation in the training, crimes and activities.

Lucas was born in Blacksburg, Virginia on August 23, 1936. From all accounts his early years were spent in a miserable, filth-strewn two-room cabin. His parents brewed liquor and his mother, Viola was the local prostitute. Henry later claimed that while she turned the tricks of her trade, she would force him to watch. This, coupled with her grim amusement in dressing Henry in girls dresses, styling his hair in curly ringlets and laughingly parading him about, left a psychological imprint that would result in her bloodshed years later.

Henry's father, Anderson, had suffered a railroad accident, which had taken both his legs. His days were limited to dragging himself around the house, drinking himself into a stupor and avoiding the wrath of Viola as much as possible. Although Henry had 9 siblings, most of them were sent into foster care. Being one of the two children considered lucky enough to remain at home, he suffered abuse, mostly at the hands of Viola.

Anderson died from a case of pneumonia after refusing to watch Viola's sex show, he crawled out into the frigid Virginia night and the hypothermic snow proved to be too much for his drunken state. Henry was with Viola and her lovers. It was up to him to survive, and in a fashion, he did. He was bashed in the head with a plank of wood and was unconscious for several days. He had to be given a glass eye, courtesy of another of Viola's fits of temper.

But the thing that made the biggest imprint on Henry's young mind at this time was that he learned about sex. First from Viola, who occasionally beat him if he wouldn't watch her service the local men who came by to purchase her homemade liquor, then from her live in lover who moved in after Anderson died. "Uncle Bernie" showed him that animals could be used for sex, torturing and killing them after using them sexually.

artwork by johnny machine

THE HANDS OF DEATH

OTTIS TOOLE, HENRY LEE LUCAS & THE CULT OF SATANIC CANNIBALS

{ BY ANNA M. GRIFFY }

Having watched his mother for so long, at age 15 Henry finally decided to try and have sex with a girl for the first time. Being inexperienced and far from attractive, Henry picked up a local girl and made advances. When she rebuffed him, Henry strangled her and buried her corpse-after he had made use of her sexually, beginning a practice that would last for many years. A dead woman can't say no, and Henry realized that becoming a killer was probably the easiest thing he'd ever done. If all he had to do was kill to get his way, then life was going to be easier and a lot more fun than he thought.

Henry knew that a life of crime would be the easiest way to earn a living and he became involved with a number of small time crooks and petty thieves. He was arrested and spent time in prison for robbing a bank with several others and while he managed to escape twice, he spent about 6 years in prison. When he was released in September of 1959, he went to stay with his half sister in Tecumseh, Michigan. This would wind up being the scene of his final confrontation with his mother. Viola showed up there, looking for Henry and at age 74, she was hardly in the position to fight him. Still, while drinking and bickering with Henry about returning to the family home in Blacksburg, they became violent. She swore at him that he had a duty to care for her in her old age, and struck at him with a broom. He responded by grabbing a knife and stabbing her to death, then raping her corpse. When he was later confessing to many of his crimes while incarcerated, he said he never raped her that he'd made the whole thing up. But he'd already shown a predilection for necrophilia that makes it hard to know what the truth was. He was convicted in 1960 and given a sentence of 20 to 40 years. He was to spend part of his sentence in a hospital for the criminally insane, and was released in 1970. Heading back to Michigan to stay with family seemed like the best idea to him, and he took a job, briefly marrying the widow of a cousin of his. But traditional home and family was something Henry had never known, and this wasn't going to work out. He had been accused of molesting not only two teenage girls, but also the two daughters from his wife's former marriage and she divorced him in the summer of 1977.

Murderous Minds Meet

About this time, in late 1976 Henry met Ottis Toole, a drifter and criminal not unlike himself. Being that he was divorcing his cousin's widow named Betty, he needed a friend and Ottis turned out to be just that, and much more. Women of course would always be their preference but there has long been speculation that the two were occasional homosexual lovers. Henry boasted to his new friend that he'd slashed a killing field as far as Maryland and beyond. Ottis had many a tale of his own: blazing an arson and murder trail across the country. They smiled at each other, I'm sure and at that moment the blood of hundreds of innocents were destined to be spilled. Some strangers, some prostitutes, some kind souls wanting to help the two drifters, and some relatives, such as Ottis's own sister, Becky.

When they found themselves without a home, Ottis told Henry he'd done more killing than he told him about. He'd been made a member of the Satanic cult the Hand of Death and wanted Henry to join, too. This wasn't the first time that Henry would have killed, raped or even possibly cannibalized another human. But this was very detailed and had repercussions that would lead to your death without exception. Lucas later confessed that he wanted to join and told Ottis. He understood he would be killed if he did anything to betray the cult and that the only way out was death. His parents hadn't taught him about religion, so there was nothing in Henry's way of becoming a Satanist. Worshipping the Devil really meant nothing to him. When confessing all this to police years later, many people didn't believe Henry's claims. But in other cases, there was evidence and the police were convinced enough to organize a task force.

Ottis told Henry that the Satanic rituals would keep them safe and from being caught. There was a power there they would be protected by, as long as they obeyed the cult. Henry and Ottis went to Florida to have Henry see the training camp that was set up in the Everglades. There, in an isolated spot, they met a man named Don that Ottis seemed to know well. It was becoming clear to Henry that Ottis had already proved himself to the cult many times over and now he must do the same if he wanted to join. They went to a tent where a young man was drinking and smoking. Don looked at Henry and told him, "Kill him. And make it clean. Only then will you be one of us."

The man was a student, had betrayed his oath to the cult and must be killed, Don explained. Ottis had a bottle of whisky and was ready to go. They walked down to the water with the young man, who was still drinking and talking. Henry waited until he stood at the edge of the water and was tipping his head back for a drink, when he grabbed him from behind and slit his throat so deeply that the whisky poured out, mingled with blood, flowing down his hands.

Don smiled at such a clean kill. The body, according to Henry, was used in a cult ritual where the body was mutilitated, the heart cut out and some of the flesh eaten.

After that, Henry was a member and in training, according to him, all new members had a sponsor. The camp had both men and women and had both day and night activities: days were for training in all forms of crime: Murder, kidnapping, rape, drug selling and the making of pornographic movies and photos. At night, there were liquor and drugs for everyone and Henry claimed sex was plentiful. There were evening sacrifices, transient people or sometimes people who had in some way or another betrayed the cult and was considered a liability. It was as if there were no shortage of bodies to kill, and Henry was quite willing to kill as many as he possibly could. Engaging in the training activities with his partner assigned by the cult, Henry was trained for 7 weeks in almost every form of criminal activity imaginable. Shortly after his training was completed, he was assigned to the kidnapping division of the organization. Ottis was there to work with him and they were told they could make a lot of money by kidnapping. There would be no killing and it would be much easier. In 1978 the chances of being caught were much slimmer, the Amber Alert not having been instituted yet. Henry and Ottis took their first job by kidnapping 3 babies and running them across the border of Mexico to a ranch in Chihuahua. Henry claimed he and Ottis also kidnapped several teenage girls that were used in pornographic snuff films. Knowing they would die at the end wasn't troubling for him. By that time, he'd killed so many people; he said it just didn't matter anymore. But the stakes were higher in the killing game than in the kidnapping operations and after nearly a year, Henry asked to be transferred there.

artwork by nico claux

THE HANDS OF DEATH

OTTIS TOOLE, HENRY LEE LUCAS & THE CULT OF SATANIC CANNIBALS

{ BY ANNA M. GRIFFY }

In a year, he claimed to have carried out 6 high profile executions. Most of these were in Texas and Mexico, with one in Canada. He told the police at the time of his incarceration that he was offered the job of delivering the cyanide to Jim Jones in Guyana and assassinating then President Jimmy Carter. How much all of this is fact and not a figment of Henry's imagination, one is left to speculate. But what happened next is fact, and not open to interpretation.

Henry and Ottis had traveled extensively, killing and raping at their discretion. But Ottis had a young niece named Becky that Henry had his eye on for a long time. He'd met her when she was 10, when he and Ottis had first started crashing around. But now she was in a youth center, her parents having passed away and being made a ward of the state. Henry went to get her and soon they were on the road together. Becky was young and loved Henry. She had very little experience in the way of men or homicidal cannibals, so there was a shock waiting for her. They obtained work for a couple doing odd jobs, finishing furniture and cleaning for room and board. The couple had the idea to have Henry and Becky move in with their mother, Kate Rich, who at 80 years old needed help By the next week, Kate's family threw them out and Henry and Becky were hitchhiking down the country road in Texas to find a place to stay. Becky was crying, and telling Henry she wanted to go back to Florida. He didn't want to hear it. She slapped him across the face and that was a first for him, never being disrespected by a woman. He grabbed a knife and plunged it into her chest, stabbing over and over. There was no one to hear her screams in the cold back woods. There was no one to see him rape her ripped and bloody corpse, cut it into pieces and scatter it across the field they were nearby.

Becky was soon missed: by Kate Rich, by a local young minister who had tried to help her. Henry told Kate they could go look for her and they set off on a drive to do just that. While Kate peppered Henry with questions, he heard little of it. He had a 6 pack of beer and finally, when he'd had enough, he pulled over and did to Kate what he'd done to Becky: ferociously stabbing her as she fell out of the car and then raping her dead body until he was exhausted. None of this meant anything to him. He thought about the cult and Ottis. There is no doubt that he had killed 2 women in a few days time and there were going to be people looking for them.

Shortly afterward, Kate Rich's farmhouse burned down and was quickly dubbed the work of an arsonist. Ottis? He has never confessed but surely his predilection for setting fires that started in his younger days comes to mind. And the fact that Henry had burned Kate's corpse in her wood-burning stove makes further speculation that the old friends were back in business together. But if they were, it would be a short-lived reunion, indeed.

The police in Stonesburg, Texas were looking and waiting for Henry. That was the closest place anyone had seen Becky alive. Henry at first acted as though he didn't kill Becky and that he wanted to clear his name. Unfortunately, he had a handgun on him, and was picked up for being an ex-con possessing a firearm and taken to jail. Henry was charged with the murders of Kate Rich and Becky Powell. There was a lot of evidence against him, and he had practically led them to the site of the remains. But still, he told an officer guarding him late one night, "I done some real bad things." There had to have been visions of blood and bones draining from the bottom of Henry's cell that night, and in the morning, he was brought before a judge, a roomful of cops and reporters and confessed to killing both Kate and Becky. He told them where the remains were-what little there was left. He admitted to having sex with both dead bodies and while they all stared stunned, he said he'd killed hundreds more. At least, he smiled grimly, at least hundreds more. "Will I be able to go on helping y'all find dead bodies?" he asked. It has been rumored that several reporters had to leave the courtroom, on the verge of becoming physically ill.

Soon, Texas jurisdictions were leapfrogging over each other to clear cold cases that they hadn't been able to solve for years, all pinning them on Henry. And Henry was as good as his word; going where they wanted him to and pointing out where remains would be and where they would find. He had killed many. It's hard to say how many because of his penchant for exaggeration.

art by pete berg

BITS AND PIECES
THE MURDERS OF DENNIS NILSEN

Nilsen is known to have killed 15 men. All of his victims were students or homeless men. He picked them all up in bars and brought them to his house either for sex or just for company. Nilsen strangled and drowned his victims during the night, waking up with little memory of what he had done. He used his butchering skills, which he gained from his time as a cook in the army, to help him dispose of the bodies. The bodies were not immediately dismembered, but were kept, sometimes for several months, in different locations in his home. Nilsen had access to a large garden when living at 195 Melrose Avenue and was able to burn many of the remains in a bonfire. Entrails were dumped over the garden fence to be eaten by wildlife.

In 1981, however, Nilsen moved to an attic flat at 23 Cranley Gardens, Muswell Hill, north London. As his murders continued, he found it difficult to dispose of the remains and had bin bags full of human organs stored in his wardrobe. Neighbours had begun to notice the smell. Three people were murdered at this address, and all were stored in cupboards and chests. Nilsen attempted to dispose of the bodies by boiling the heads, hands and feet to remove the flesh and by chopping the entrails into small pieces and flushing them down the toilet. When he tried to dispose of the bodies by flushing them down the toilet, he blocked the sewers of the flats.

Mr. Nilsen's murders were first discovered by a drain cleaning company responding to a blocked drain. The company found the drain was packed with a flesh-like substance. The drain inspector then called his supervisor, but no assessment was made until the next day, by which time the drain had been cleared. This aroused the suspicions of the drain inspector and his supervisor, who immediately called the police. Upon closer inspection, some small bones and what looked like chicken flesh were found in a pipe leading off from the drain; these were later discovered to be of human origin. Detective Chief Inspector Peter Jay was called to the scene with two colleagues and waited outside until Nilsen returned home from work. As they entered the building DCI Jay introduced himself to Nilsen and explained that he had come about his drains. Nilsen asked why would the police be interested in his drains and also if the two officers were health inspectors. He was told they were police colleagues and given their names. They then climbed the stairs together and as they entered the flat DCI Jay immediately smelt rotting flesh. Nilsen queried why the police would be interested in his drains, so the officer told him they were filled with human remains. "Good grief, how awful!" exclaimed Nilsen. "Don't mess about, where's the rest of the body?" replied Jay. Nilsen responded calmly by saying they were in two plastic bags in his wardrobe. He was then arrested and cautioned on suspicion of murder and taken to the police station. On the way back to the station, Nilsen was asked how many bodies they were talking about, and replied "15 or 16".

He later apologised to the police for not being able to tell them the exact number of people he had killed. When his house was searched, they found three heads in a cupboard, and evidence of thirteen more bodies at Nilsen's former home, 195 Melrose Avenue, Cricklewood. Nilsen appeared unemotional during his trial at the Old Bailey.

FEMALE SERIAL KILLERS

Elizabeth Báthory
Bathory is remembered as the "Blood Countess". After her husband's death, she and four collaborators were accused of torturing and killing hundreds of girls and young women, with one witness attributing to them over 600 victims, though she was only convicted on 80 counts.

Beverley Allitt
Beverley Gail Allitt, dubbed the Angel of Death, was an English State Enrolled Nurse who was convicted of killing four children and injuring five others, in 1991, on the children's ward of Grantham and Kesteven Hospital.

Mary Ann Cotton
Mary Ann Cotton (October 1832 – 24 March 1873) was an English serial killer believed to have murdered up to 20 people, mainly by arsenic poisoning.

Tillie Klimek
Klimek (1876 - 1936) was an American serial killer. She poisoned all five of her husbands and three neighborhood children and others. She became known as a fortune-teller, for predicting their deaths in advance.

Dorothea Puente
The old, sweet-faced, grandmotherly Puente systematically druged and killed her boarders and burying their remains in the yard she so lovingly tended. With her careful exterior, she got away with murder for years.

Karla Homolka
Karla Leanne Homolka (born May 4, 1970 in Port Credit, Ontario, Canada), is a Canadian serial killer who attracted worldwide media attention when she was convicted of manslaughter in the rape-murders of two teenaged girls; her husband, Paul Bernardo, was convicted of their murders and admitted having raped numerous women. Homolka and Bernardo also were responsible for the rape and death of her sister Tammy Homolka.

Aileen Carol Wuornos
Wuornos (born Aileen Carol Pittman) (February 29, 1956 – October 9, 2002) was an American serial killer who was convicted and sentenced to death by the state of Florida in 1992. She ultimately received five additional death sentences. Wuornos admitted to killing seven men in separate incidents, all of whom she claimed either raped or attempted to rape her while she was working as a prostitute. She was put to death via lethal injection on October 9, 2002.

artwork by johnny machine

THE HANDS OF DEATH

OTTIS TOOLE, HENRY LEE LUCAS, & THE CULT OF SATANIC CANNIBALS

{ BY ANNA M. GRIFFY }

He told the police about The Hand Of Death. His confessions were believed by so many people, even though forensic evidence didn't always match up that there were two books written on the subject: "The Confessions Of Henry Lee Lucas" by Mike Cox and "Hands Of Death" by Max Call. Over the next 18 months, Henry talked about the cult, probably knowing he would never see the outside of a prison cell, and fearing no retribution, confessed to first 75, then escalating to 150, and finally a whopping 300 body count. By this time, Ottis was in prison for arson and was implicated in many of these murders, being that he was the one who had introduced Henry to the cult. Toole corroborated many of Henry's tales and told of his taste for human flesh, usually with barbeque sauce.

Ottis and Henry had one last phone call that is telling in nature:

Henry: "I don't want you to think I'm doing this as a revenge."

Ottis: "No, I don't want you to hold anything back about me."

Henry: "See we got so many of them, Ottis. We got to turn up the bodies. Now this boy and girl I don't know anything about."

Ottis: "Well maybe that's the two I killed my own self. Just like that Mexican that wasn't gonna let me out of the house. I took an ax and chopped him all up. What made me? I been meaning to ask you? Why'd I do it?"

Henry: " I think it was just the hands doing it. I know a lot of the things we have done in human sight are impossible to believe."

There were journalists who tried to discredit Henry and Ottis, but according to Texas law enforcement, it was all about money. Henry was leading them to the sites where there was physical evidence. That was irrefutable. Could he have been hired to assassinate Jimmy Carter? Could he have been a contract killer to fly cyanide to Jim Jones at the People's Temple of Guyana? Very doubtful. But he was a murderer, a cold-blooded killer, and with Ottis Toole, they soaked the raw Texas farmland with enough blood to satisfy the thirst of a cult called The Hand Of The Death.

FATAL ADDICTION — TED BUNDY'S LAST INTERVIEW

TED BUNDY, AN INFAMOUS SERIAL KILLER, GRANTED AN INTERVIEW TO PSYCHOLOGIST JAMES DOBSON JUST BEFORE HE WAS EXECUTED ON JAN 24, 1989. THIS IS A TRANSCRIPT OF THAT INTERVIEW

James C. Dobson: It is about 2:30 in the afternoon. You are scheduled to be executed tomorrow morning at 7:00, if you don't receive another stay. What is going through your mind? What thoughts have you had in these last few days?

Ted: I won't kid you to say it is something I feel I'm in control of or have come to terms with. It's a moment-by-moment thing. Sometimes I feel very tranquil and other times I don't feel tranquil at all. What's going through my mind right now is to use the minutes and hours I have left as fruitfully as possible. It helps to live in the moment, in the essence that we use it productively. Right now I'm feeling calm, in large part because I'm here with you.

JCD: For the record, you are guilty of killing many women and girls.

Ted: Yes, that's true.

JCD: How did it happen? Take me back. What are the antecedents of the behavior that we've seen? You were raised in what you consider to be a healthy home. You were not physically, sexually or emotionally abused.

Ted: No. And that's part of the tragedy of this whole situation. I grew up in a wonderful home with two dedicated and loving parents, as one of 5 brothers and sisters. We, as children, were the focus of my parent's lives. We regularly attended church. My parents did not drink or smoke or gamble. There was no physical abuse or fighting in the home. I'm not saying it was "Leave it to Beaver", but it was a fine, solid Christian home. I hope no one will try to take the easy way out of this and accuse my family of contributing to this. I know, and I'm trying to tell you as honestly as I know how, what happened.

As a young boy of 12 or 13, I encountered, outside the home, in the local grocery and drug stores, softcore pornography. Young boys explore the sideways and byways of their neighborhoods, and in our neighborhood, people would dump the garbage. From time to time, we would come across books of a harder nature - more graphic. This also included detective magazines, etc., and I want to emphasize this. The most damaging kind of pornography - and I'm talking from hard, real, personal experience - is that that involves violence and sexual violence. The wedding of those two forces - as I know only too well - brings about behavior that is too terrible to describe.

JCD: Walk me through that. What was going on in your mind at that time?

Ted: Before we go any further, it is important to me that people believe what I'm saying. I'm not blaming pornography. I'm not saying it caused me to go out and do certain things. I take full responsibility for all the things that I've done. That's not the question here. The issue is how this kind of literature contributed and helped mold and shape the kinds of violent behavior.

JCD: It fueled your fantasies.

Ted: In the beginning, it fuels this kind of thought process. Then, at a certain time, it is instrumental in crystallizing it, making it into something that is almost a separate entity inside.

JCD: You had gone about as far as you could go in your own fantasy life, with printed material, photos, videos, etc., and then there was the urge to take that step over to a physical event.

Ted: Once you become addicted to it, and I look at this as a kind of addiction, you look for more potent, more explicit, more graphic kinds of material. Like an addiction, you keep craving something which is harder and gives you a greater sense of excitement, until you reach the point where the pornography only goes so far - that jumping off point where you begin to think maybe actually doing it will give you that which is just beyond reading about it and looking at it.

JCD: How long did you stay at that point before you actually assaulted someone?

Ted: A couple of years. I was dealing with very strong inhibitions against criminal and violent behavior. That had been conditioned and bred into me from my neighborhood, environment, church, and schools. I knew it was wrong to think about it, and certainly, to do it was wrong. I was on the edge, and the last vestiges of restraint were being tested constantly, and assailed through the kind of fantasy life that was fueled, largely, by pornography.

JCD: Do you remember what pushed you over that edge? Do you remember the decision to "go for it"? Do you remember where you decided to throw caution to the wind?

Ted: It's a very difficult thing to describe - the sensation of reaching that point where I knew I couldn't control it anymore. The barriers I had learned as a child were not enough to hold me back from seeking out and harming somebody.

artwork by chuck hodi

JCD: Would it be accurate to call that a sexual frenzy?

Ted: That's one way to describe it - a compulsion, a building up of this destructive energy. Another fact I haven't mentioned is the use of alcohol. In conjunction with my exposure to pornography, alcohol reduced my inhibitions and pornography eroded them further.

JCD: After you committed your first murder, what was the emotional effect? What happened in the days after that?

Ted: Even all these years later, it is difficult to talk about. Reliving it through talking about it is difficult to say the least, but I want you to understand what happened. It was like coming out of some horrible trance or dream. I can only liken it to (and I don't want to overdramatize it) being possessed by something so awful and alien, and the next morning waking up and remembering what happened and realizing that in the eyes of the law, and certainly in the eyes of God, you're responsible. To wake up in the morning and realize what I had done with a clear mind, with all my essential moral and ethical feelings intact, absolutely horrified me.

JCD: You hadn't known you were capable of that before?

Ted: There is no way to describe the brutal urge to do that, and once it has been satisfied, or spent, and that energy level recedes, I became myself again. Basically, I was a normal person.

Ted: I wasn't some guy hanging out in bars, or a bum. I wasn't a pervert in the sense that people look at somebody and say, "I know there's something wrong with him." I was a normal person. I had good friends. I led a normal life, except for this one, small but very potent and destructive segment that I kept very secret and close to myself. Those of us who have been so influenced by violence in the media, particularly pornographic violence, are not some kind of inherent monsters. We are your sons and husbands. We grew up in regular families. Pornography can reach in and snatch a kid out of any house today. It snatched me out of my home 20 or 30 years ago. As diligent as my parents were, and they were diligent in protecting their children, and as good a Christian home as we had, there is no protection against the kinds of influences that are loose in a society that tolerates....

Ted: I'm no social scientist, and I don't pretend to believe what John Q. Citizen thinks about this, but I've lived in prison for a long time now, and I've met a lot of men who were motivated to commit violence. Without exception, every one of them was deeply involved in pornography - deeply consumed by the addiction. The F.B.I.'s own study on serial homicide shows that the most common interest among serial killers is pornographers. It's true.

JCD: What would your life have been like without that influence?

Ted: I know it would have been far better, not just for me, but for a lot of other people - victims and families. There's no question that it would have been a better life. I'm absolutely certain it would not have involved this kind of violence.

JCD: If I were able to ask the kind of questions that are being asked, one would be, "Are you thinking about all those victims and their families that are so wounded? Years later, their lives aren't normal. They will never be normal. Is there remorse?"

Ted: I know people will accuse me of being self-serving, but through God's help, I have been able to come to the point, much too late, where I can feel the hurt and the pain I am responsible for. Yes. Absolutely! During the past few days, myself and a number of investigators have been talking about unsolved cases - murders I was involved in. It's hard to talk about all these years later, because it revives all the terrible feelings and thoughts that I have steadfastly and diligently dealt with - I think successfully. It has been reopened and I have felt the pain and the horror of that.

I hope that those who I have caused so much grief, even if they don't believe my expression of sorrow, will believe what I'm saying now; there are those loose in their towns and communities, like me, whose dangerous impulses are being fueled, day in and day out, by violence in the media in its various forms - particularly sexualized violence. What scares me is when I see what's on cable T.V. Some of the violence in the movies that come into homes today is stuff they wouldn't show in X-rated adult theatres 30 years ago.

JCD: The slasher movies?

Ted: That is the most graphic violence on screen, especially when children are unattended or unaware that they could be a Ted Bundy; that they could have a predisposition to that kind of behavior.

JCD: One of the final murders you committed was 12-year-old Kimberly Leach. I think the public outcry is greater there because an innocent child was taken from a playground. What did you feel after that? Were they the normal emotions after that?

Ted: I can't really talk about that right now. It's too painful. I would like to be able to convey to you what that experience is like, but I won't be able to talk about that. I can't begin to understand the pain that the parents of these children and young women that I have harmed feel. And I can't restore much to them, if anything. I won't pretend to, and I don't even expect them to forgive me. I'm not asking for it. That kind of forgiveness is of God; if they have it, they have it, and if they don't, maybe they'll find it someday.

TO GET A DVD OF THE COMPLETE, UNEDITED VIDEO FOOTAGE OF TED BUNDY'S FINAL INTERVIEW, VISIT SERIALKILLERCALENDAR.COM

JCD: Outside these walls, there are several hundred reporters that wanted to talk to you, and you asked me to come because you had something you wanted to say. You feel that hardcore pornography, and the door to it, softcore pornography, is doing untold damage to other people and causing other women to be abused and killed the way you did.

Cooking With Cannibals
RECIPES FOR THE CRIMINALLY INSANE

Bananas Foster:
by Hadden Clark

½ cup (1 stick) unsalted butter

½ cup packed light brown sugar

4 firm ripe bananas, peeled and cut in ½ lengthwise

½ cup dark rum

Served with vanilla ice cream

1. Melt butter with sugar in a 12 inch skillet over medium high heat. Cook, swirling skillet occasionally, until color deepens, about three minutes.

2. Add bananas, cut sides down. Cook, swirling occasionally to make sure bananas are covered, about 3 1/2 min. Flip bananas and cook 2 ½ min. more.

3. Remove skillet from heat. Add rum. Return to medium heat and cook about ten seconds, to allow rum to heat up. If using a gas stove, tip pan away from you until the vapors from the rum ignite.

(Alternatively, light the rum with a long match.) When the flames subside. Remove pan from heat.

4. Serve bananas topped with vanilla ice cream

Serves four (4)

Sent from:
Hadden Clark 233181
p.o. box 534 J.C.I
Jessup, Maryland
20794

Recipe retrieved by Matthew Aaron

artwork gerard tork

What's Your Serial Killer IQ?

SO YOU THINK YOUR A TRUE CRIME EXPERT? PROVE IT.

1.) What was the name of Ed Gein's friend who helped him to dig up dead bodies?

2.) What was the name of John Wayne Gacy's construction company?

3.) Which serial killer confessed to killing Adam Walsh (son of John Walsh, who became host of the television program "America's Most Wanted")?

4.) Where was serial killer, Richard Ramirez born?

5.) After being X-rayed, what objects had been found to be inserted in to Albert Fish's pelvis and perineum?

6.) Which turn of the century serial killer was a circus strong man and later fed his victims to alligators that he kept behind his bar?

7.) In the television series, "American Gothic", which Boston based serial killer was summoned by sheriff Lucas Buck to destroy the ghost of Caleb's sister?

8.) At the time of Edmund Kemper's murder spree in Santa Cruz, another killer was also active, earning the small California town the title of "Murder Capital Of The World." What is this killers name?

9.) What American killer shot fashion designer Gianni Versace during a cross-country killing spree in 1997?

10.) The term "Serial Killer" was first coined to describe what man?

11.) What form of execution was used to end the life of Carl Panzram?

12.) In the Seinfeld episode "The Masseuse", Elaine Benes dates a man (played by Anthony Cistaro) who is coincidentally named after what killer?

13.) What Chinese-American serial killer committed his crimes with the help Leonard Lake and filmed himself raping and torturing their victims?

14.) What does B.T.K. stand for?

15.) Which killer dismembered his victims body, ground them in a food processor with dog food and then fed them to the surviving victims which he kept prisoner in his basement)?

16.) Which killer is also known as The Gainesville Ripper?

17.) What was the name of the forty-eight member clan in 16th century Scotland that was suspected of the murder and cannibalisation of over 40 people?

18.) What serial killer would fly kidnapped prostitutes to his cabin in the Knik River Valley on his private plane and then stalk and kill them with a hunting knife and rifle?

19.) Robin Gecht (head of the satanic "Ripper Crew" cult that was suspected in the disappearances of 18 women) once worked for what notorious killer?

20.) What is the name of the African-American serial killer that was convicted of the murders of seven elderly women in Columbus, Georgia from 1977-1978.

21.) What serial killer and a necrophiliac was also known as The Lust Killer and Shoe Fetish Slayer?

22.) What was the name of the family of serial killers who owned a small general store / inn in Labette County, Kansas from 1872 to 1873.

23.) The brain of Peter Kurten (AKA The Vampire of Düsseldorf) is currently on display at what museum?

24.) The press is not always original with the nicknames they give killers. How many serial killers have been given the nickname "The Freeway Killer"?

25.) What Florida police officer was imprisoned in 1973 for a series of murders and was found to be linked to the disappearance of over 30 missing women?

26.) What serial killer claimed to have taken part in snuff films, to have killed Jimmy Hoffa, and to have delivered poison to cult leader Jim Jones in Jonestown?

27.) In January 2007, evidence surfaced potentially linking serial killer Jeffrey Dahmer to the abduction and murder of what well known victim?

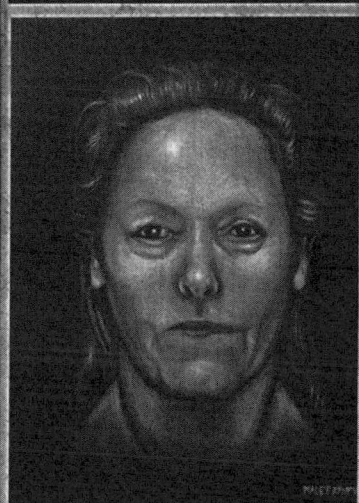

artwork by jack malebranche

ANSWERS - 1: Gus 2: PDM Contractors 3: Ottis Toole 4: El Paso, Texas 5: Pins and Needles 6: Joe Ball 7: Albert Henry DeSalvo 8: Herbert Mullin 9: Andrew Cunanan 10: Ted bundy 11: Hanging 12: Joel Rifkin 13: Charles Ng 14: "Bind, Torture, and Kill" 15: Gary M. Heidnik 16: Danny Rolling 17: The Bean Family 18: Robert Hansen 19: John Wayne Gacy 20: Carlton Michael Gary 21: Jerome Henry Brudos 22: Bloody Benders 23: The Ripley's Believe It or Not! museum in Wisconsin Dells 24: Three 25: Gerard John Schaefer 26: Henry Lee Lucas 27: Adam Walsh. If you got 20 or more of these right, consider yourself an expert.

ANY LAST WORDS?
FAMOUS FINAL WORDS FROM THE WORLD'S WORST KILLERS

Serial killer Ted Bundy's final words before being executed in the electric chair on January 24, 1989 were -- "I'd like you to give my love to my family and friends."

"Hey, fellas! How about this for a headline for tomorrow's paper? 'French Fries'!" Said by: James French, a convicted murderer, was sentenced to the electric chair. He shouted these words to members of the press who were to witness his execution.

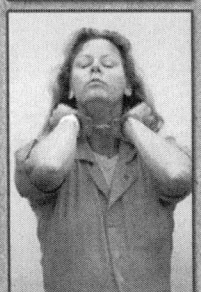

Convicted murderer Aileen Wuornos final words before being executed by lethal injection in October 2002 in Florida, were -- "I'd just like to say I'm sailing with the rock, and I'll be back like Independence Day, with Jesus June 6. Like the movie, big mother ship and all, I'll be back."

Murderer Jimmy Glass' final words before being electrocuted on June 12, 1987, in Louisiana for the robbery & murder of a couple on Christmas Eve, were -- "I'd rather be fishing."

Convicted murderer George Appel's final words before being executed in the electric chair in New York in 1928 were - "Well, gentlemen, you are about to see a baked Appel."

"Hurry up, you Hoosier bastard, I could kill ten men while you're fooling around!" Said by: Carl Panzram, serial killer, shortly before he was executed by hanging.

Serial rapist and killer John Wayne Gacy's final words before being executed by lethal injection, on May 10, 1994, were -- "Kiss my ass."

Convicted murderer James Allen Red Dog's final words before being executed by injection in Delaware on March 3, 1993 -- "I'm going home, babe."

Murderer John Spenkelink's final words before being executed in the electric chair in Florida on May 25, 1979, were -- "Capital punishment: them without the capital get the punishment."

Convicted murderer Gary Gilmore's final words before being put to death on January 17, 1977, by a volunteer firing squad were -- "Let's do it!"

"It (death) will be the supreme thrill. The only one I haven't tried!". Albert Fish was electrocuted in 1936. His full speech was: "What a thrill that will be if I have to die in the electric chair. It will be the supreme thrill. The only one I haven't tried."

DO YOU WANT TO WORK 4 SERIALKILLERCALENDAR.COM?

SerialKillerCalendar.com (makers of the world's best true crime merchandise and publisher of this magazine) are now looking for new, talented people to join our team! We are currently looking for artist's to produce serial killer images for both our new 2008 product line and our soon to be released comic books! We are also looking for skilled writers to create new articles and interviewers. So if you want to be part of the best crime company on the planet, stop by SerialKillerCalendar.com today and drop us a line.

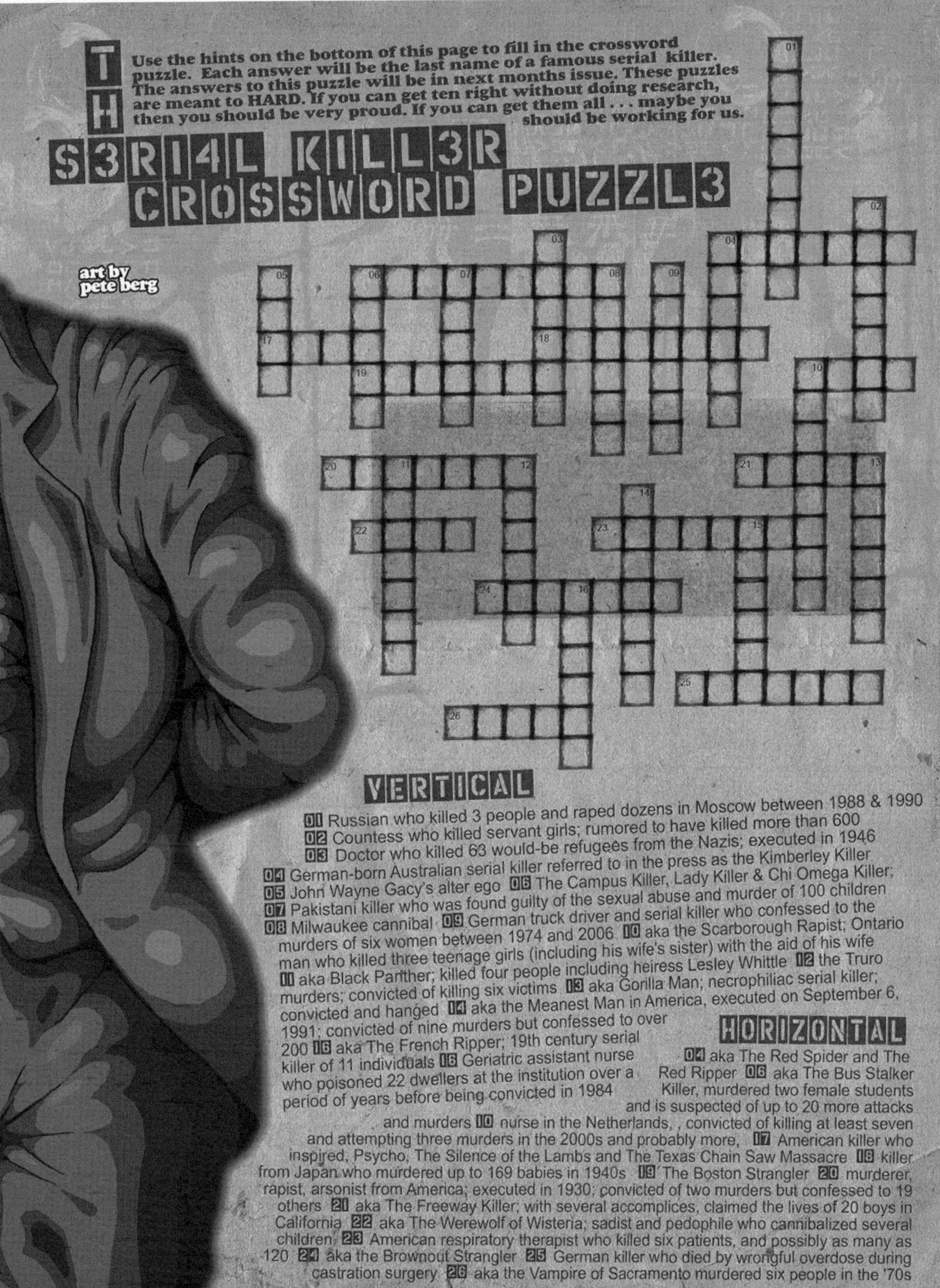

The Art of Pete Berg
petex.deviantart.com

IF LOOKS COULD KILL

our lovely calendar girls model some of serialkillercalendar.com's 2008 merchandise

Want to promote your company? Want to purchase ad space in the world's best true crime magazine? The contact James at SerialKillerCalendar.com to purchase your ad space now.

ZOMBIEFRIENDS.COM

A Social Networking Site For Zombies. The biggest on Earth and Beyond

THE ART OF MURDER
Dark Artist Of The Month: Kimberly Bailey

We where recently able to talk with the talented artist, Kimberly Bailey about her of serial killer artwork. The following is Kimberly in her own words.

Serial killers are civilizations dirty secrets, the skeletons in societies closet. Although we may try to keep them well hid, year after year more appear-hacking and slashing away at the doors we try to hide them behind, our sons, daughters, husbands, coworkers, classmates and even our friends. They are what happens to ourselves in the worst case scenario.

As a person who suffers from mental illness I have learned to deal with like in my own way on my own terms. Living with schizoaffective disorder has taught me that life (my life) can unravel at the drop of a hat. Fate is fickle and if things had gone differently in my life I might have ended up as a serial killer and the subject of another artists paintings. This is one of the reasons I paint serial killers' portraits and real crime paintings-as talismans or personal charms that I create as offerings lest I should never forget how things might have been for me.

Real life crime and murder has always held a certain kind of dark fascination for me. As a teenager I studied the life of Charles Manson, reading everything I could find about him and his "family". I watched every single made for TV movie depicting their life and times-no matter how silly. I felt a connection and even went so far as to attempt to tattoo an X on my forehead to show my allegiance to the family.

Luckily a sober friend intervened and convinced me to put the tattoo in a less conspicuous place on my body. People still ask me questions about the strange tattoo on my hand.

I like to keep my portraits simple, child like even. The most important feature in my paintings are the eyes: some are dead and soulless, while others are electrified with life and the hatred thereof. My arts goal is to draw you into the energy of the killer and then draw out your curiosity and interest in him or her and what makes them tick.

You can view more of Kimba's art online at www.kimbas-art.com.

Beast of the Ardennes
part one by Chris Bartholomew

Nicknames

Michel Fourniret: Ogre of the Ardennes - Beast of the Ardennes

Monique Olivier: big slimy spider - Cunning Witch – Virgin Hunter

CHARLEVILLE-MEZIERES, France - A man accused of seeking young virgins to rape and kill was convicted Wednesday of seven murders and sentenced to life in prison.

Michel Fourniret, 66, was given the maximum sentence by the jury in northeast France. In a particularly severe sentence for a French court, he cannot be considered for parole before serving 30 years behind bars. Given his age, he is unlikely to ever walk free.

He, in his own words, is an extremely dangerous individual. Power over others was - and still is - all important to Fourniret. He believes himself to be 'some kind of superior being'. He sees himself as a hunter, claiming he 'needed' to hunt for virgins at least twice a year.

His wife, Monique Olivier, 59, was also convicted of complicity in four of the murders and sentenced to life in prison. She must serve at least 28 years before she can be considered for early release for the part she played in some of the murders and a rape.

Monique Olivier exposed him after hearing the news of another child murderer's wife Michelle Martin, wife of Marc Dutroux (a convicted pedophile, murderer and supposed leader of an international child pornography and prostitution ring) being convicted.

Fourniret, a machine operator, and a former forest ranger, had made a gruesome pact with Olivier, a nurse, that in exchange for the murder of her first husband - who was never killed - she would help ensnare virgins to satisfy his murderous whims.

While in jail Monique Olivier wrote to him after seeing an advertisement in a Catholic magazine for pen pals. Olivier first wrote to Fourniret over 25 graphic pages, telling him how she had been beaten by two ex-husbands and a boyfriend.

Fourniret replied, saying that on his release he would kill 'those three guys' for her.

He added: 'I need a female companion; I want to play chess, have adventures and kidnap people.' He also described to her his frustration at never having 'had a virgin'.

In her letters to Fourniret, Olivier called him 'my beast' and discussed his obsession with raping virgins.

Having been asked to find some for him, Olivier wrote: 'It is with pleasure that I will execute your orders.'

And so, on the day Fourniret was released early in 1987 for good behavior, Olivier was waiting at the gates of his prison.

The couple married, had a baby son, settled in Auxerre and began plotting their crimes. Fourniret likened their exploits to hunting 'to satisfy my blood lust'.

Psychologists say neither was insane and were marginally above average intelligence.

The specialists stated that the self-obsessed, authoritative Fourniret took a sadistic pleasure in rape and murder.

Described by the chief prosecutor as a "big slimy spider" and "cunning witch" during the trial, Olivier was accused of helping Fourniret select and capture targets and hiding their bodies.

Using an image of happily-married respectability, Olivier would gain the confidence of the girls and women they had identified as prey.

After they had been bound, gagged and sometimes drugged by her husband, she would examine them to check they were the virgins he desired.

She would then hand them over to Fourniret "in the sole aim of allowing him to fulfill his fantasies", in the Franco-Belgian border region where they once lived. He would assault his victims — "beautiful little subjects" was how he referred to them — before shooting, stabbing or strangling them. Failing to help a person in danger was one of the charges.

Fourniret's attorney said he would not appeal the jury verdict because Fourniret doesn't want to defend himself because he considers he is indefensible. He won't ask for a pardon because he is unpardonable.

The verdict closes a two-month trial that riveted France and neighboring Belgium, where one of the victims was killed.

The young women, aged 12 to 21, were strangled, shot or stabbed with a screwdriver between 1987 and 2001 to feed what prosecutors called Fourniret's obsession for virgins. Fourniret also was convicted of kidnapping and rape or attempted rape of all seven victims.

The lead prosecutor called Monique Olivier "a witch," while Fourniret's court-appointed defense lawyer described him as "indefensible."

The couple showed no reaction after Fourniret, dubbed the "Ogre of the Ardennes" by the media, was found guilty in a packed courtroom of killing the seven women and girls aged after raping or attempting to rape them.

Prosecutors said that Olivier helped Fourniret track down and capture virgins, some of who were first drugged and bound, and hiding their bodies to feed his morbid fantasies.

Belgian police detained Fourniret, who had admitted a fascination for virgins, in June 2003 after his bungled kidnapping of a 13-year-old girl. The girl gave authorities his license plate number after she managed to unbind her hands and escape from the back of his van.

Olivier was extradited to France in 2005 and Fourniret in 2006. Judicial officials in both countries decided the case should be tried in France because six of the victims were French citizens.

Investigators suspect Fourniret may also have been involved in several other murders.

The Fourniret case has drawn comparisons with that of Belgium's notorious pedophile Marc Dutroux, who was sentenced to life in prison in 2004 for a series of child kidnappings, rapes and murders.

The crimes were committed over 14 years from 1987, mostly in the wooded Ardennes region of northern France and in Belgium.

Beast of the Ardennes
part two by Chris Bartholomew

The case helped lead to a shake-up in the way French police investigate serial murders, including the improvement of co-ordination between different authorities.

Some parents of the victims, six of whom were French and one Belgian, broke down in tears after the verdict was read, one day after the jury retired to deliberate.

The couple, linked by what prosecutors called a "criminal pact", became acquainted after Fourniret, who had a long history of rape, placed an advertisement for someone to write to while serving a prison sentence for sex crimes in the 1980s.

A series of opportunities to catch the killers were missed, including the failure to launch an inquiry into the disappearance of Isabelle Laville, the couple's first victim in 1987, despite the police lodging a kidnap report.

At the time, Fourniret, who had just been released from prison and was on probation, was living just a few miles away from the place where Laville disappeared.

A lawyer for Laville's family, said: "There was a lost opportunity to identify the Fournirets."

The system also failed to revoke a decision to discharge Fourniret following appearances for offences in the 1990s, allowing the couple to continue carrying out their crimes.

Psychologists who examined the couple have said they were not insane and were slightly above average in intelligence. The specialists concluded that the self-obsessed, authoritative Fourniret took a sadistic pleasure in rape and murder.

Michel Fourniret has been called "Beast of the Ardennes" after the heavily wooded region where his crimes occurred, and Monique Olivier, 59, were described as "inhuman and cruel criminals" by prosecutors during the trial in French town of Charleville-Mezieres near the Belgian border.

The pair also will be tried for at least three other unsolved murders, including that of British student Joanna Parrish. Fourniret wrote to a judge last year, asking to be investigated in the death of Parish, a 20-year-old university student, and two other girls, ages 9 and 19, saying "their families deserve an explanation."

Joanna Parrish, a Leeds University student's naked body was found floating in a river. She had been raped and strangled after answering an advert placed in a newspaper by a man seeking English lessons for his son.

During the two-month trial, Fourniret admitted he was "hunting" girls from 1987 to 2003.

The Victims:

Isabelle Laville - a 17-year-old French girl. She disappeared in Auxerre, on December 11, 1987 on her way home from school. Her skeletal remains were located at the bottom of a well in the country north of Auxerre in July of 2006.

On the 11th of December 1987, Isabelle Laville was walking home from her college when she was stopped by a lady driver, Monique Fourniret asking for directions.

Isabelle entered the car to help the lady driver. During the drive the driver stopped to pick up a hitch hiker with a gas can whose car had apparently run out. The hitch hiker was the driver's husband and thus begin their plan to kidnap and abuse one of their victims.

Isabelle was given drugs to sedate her (traces were found in her hair). Michel Fourniret who lived close to Auxerre then went on to abuse and perhaps rape his 17 year old victim. Probably later that night, he went on to strangle Isabelle and placed the body in his car trunk before disposing of Isabelle's body in a well.

It was not until the 11th of July 2006 that Isabelle's body was found following a description that Fourniret provided to police.

The 32m deep well had been filled in with gravel by the electric company in 2000.

Fabienne Leroy - a 20-year-old woman. She disappeared in 1988 in Mourmelon, and her blood-spattered body was later found in the nearby woods. She was kidnapped from a supermarket car park in Chalons-en-Champagne, east of Paris. Her body was discovered outside a military base the next day after she was killed by a shotgun wound to the chest. Fourniret has confessed to her murder, with Olivier charged as an accomplice.

Jeanne-Marie Desramault - a 22-year-old French student. She disappeared in 1989 from the railway station, and her body was recovered from the estate of Fourniret with his assistance. She was kidnapped outside the railway station in Charleville-Mezieres on March 18, 1989. Fourniret took investigators to her body in the grounds of a chateau he once owned in Donchery in July 2004. He confessed to her murder and Olivier is charged as an accomplice.

Elisabeth Brichet - a 12-year-old Belgian girl. She disappeared from Namur in 1989 after playing with a friend. Fourniret led police to her burial site on his estate in France. She was kidnapped on her way home from a friend's house in Namur, Belgium, on December 20, 1989. Her remains were also found in July, 2004 at Fourniret's chateau. He confessed to the murder but denied rape, while Olivier is charged with complicity.

Natacha Danais - a 13-year-old French girl who disappeared in 1990. She was kidnapped, assaulted, and stabbed to death near Nantes, western France on November 21, 1990. Three days later her body was found on a beach on the Atlantic coast. Fourniret confessed to murder and attempted rape, while Olivier is charged as an accomplice.

Farida Hellegouarch - the girlfriend of one of the members of the Gang des postiches (a gang of bank robbers), a former cellmate of Fourniret's. Fourniret killed her in 1990 to access the group's funds. He bought his castle in France with the money.

Céline Saison - 18-year-old who disappeared in 2000 in Sedan, her body was found in Belgium. Two months later her body was found in the woods in Belgium. Fourniret confessed to kidnapping, raping and murdering her.

Manyana Thumpong - 18-year-old who disappeared in 2001, her body was also later found in Belgium. Her remains were found the following year in the Nollevaux forest in Belgium. Fourniret admitted kidnap and murder but denied rape.

An unidentified man - Fourniret claimed to have robbed and shot an unidentified man at a French highway rest stop.

Fourniret's wife has also said that Fourniret killed a 16-year-old girl who had worked as an au pair at their house. Fourniret allegedly killed her in 1993, but this has not been confirmed. The identity of this alleged victim is not known.

Further Charges:

Joelle Parfondry, a canine beauty parlor employee from the Belgian town of Namur, was the victim of an armed robbery and rape attempt in January 1995.

Sandra N., now aged 18, was the victim of an attempted kidnapping in the Belgian town of Gedinne in February 2000.

Asumpcion, whose name has been changed, was kidnapped and assaulted on June 26, 2003 in the Belgian town of Ciney. Aged 13 at the time, she managed to escape and her statements to police led to Fourniret's arrest.

Other Murder Cases:

Fourniret was charged in two other murder cases which will be tried at a later date:

Joanna Parrish, 20, a British teaching assistant in the central French city of Auxerre, was found dead near the city in May 1990.

Marie-Angele Domece, a 19-year-old disabled Frenchwoman, went missing on the road leading to Auxerre station in July 1988. Her body has not been found.

He denies both murders.

Two other cases are still under investigation:

In France, Fourniret has confessed to murdering Farida Hamiche, the partner of a fellow convict, in 1988, with the aim of stealing the loot from a robbery.

In Belgium, Fourniret is accused of the murder of a young au pair who went missing in 1992. He denies the charge.

Psychologists said the jury might need counseling after the trial. In one of the most disturbing scenes, they heard a coroner suggest Fourniret sexually assaulted a 13-year-old girl after stabbing her to death in 1990.

Fourniret and Olivier would sometimes bring their baby son in the car - his presence persuading victims that it was safe to accept a lift.

Excavations in the Ardennes forest are expected to discover more victims.

"Misery leads to crime. I saw so many boys whipped. It ruined my mind.
- Albert Fish

ERIN TINNEY

Manson Poems And Songs

The Mind of Manson By Tara Rath

I am you—your own reflection, raised on neglect and rejection.
I ask you to join me in the mirror; do not hesitate nor hide.
I am what all your minds create, I am the sum of all you hate.
I am the source of much debate, debate so engrained worldwide.
I am an image, a thought—fear; relate, I cannot, for in you, I reside.
I wear the badge you decide.

You are me—my affection, built on devotion and protection.
Follow my direction if you choose: Join me, in my blissful stride.
I tell the truth to all deaf ears. I have told this truth for forty years.
They say that I am what evidence appears. Appears is reason for rights denied.
They cannot fool me; I am their fears. I have known this from the first tongue, lied.
When questioned, they are all tongue-tied.

I am everyone—my love. I am right and wrong, I am devil and dove.
Transform me, reform me; leave logic outside.
Heaven, hell, I am forever. Alive or dead, I am whichever.
You ask, Where have I lived? Where have I died?
I answer, "Where have I lived, Where have I died?"
"Since I was nine, I've been cast aside."

Behind these bars is where I've grown—the only life I have ever known.
I am the father, to whom you could not confide.
I have become my own creator, by living a life far greater,
Than age as it ages men, later, later in life's stride.
In the life of city men, traffic lights and smog in stride.
It is you who has died.

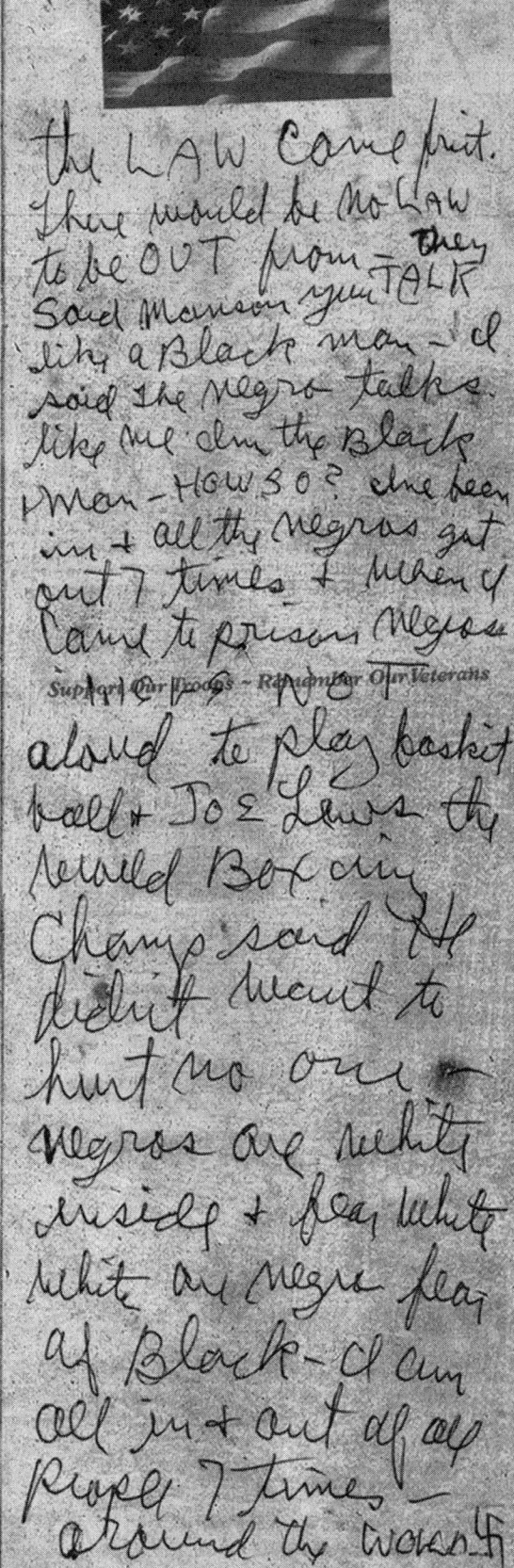

Look At Your Game Girl by Charles Manson

There's a time for livin'
The time keeps on flyin'
Think you're lovin' baby
And all ya do is cryin'

Can ya feel are those feelin's real
Look at your game girl
Look at your game girl

What a mad delusion
Livin' in that confusion
Frustration an' doubt
Can you ever live without the game
The sad sad game
Mad game

Just to say you love's not enough
Ifn you can't be true
You can tell those lies baby
But you're only foolin' you

Can you feel are those feelin's real
Look at your game girl
Go on look at your game girl

Ifn you can't feel
And the feelin's ain't real
Then you better stop tryin'
Or you're gonna play cryin'
Stop tryin' or you're gonna play cryin'
That's the game
Sad sad game
Mad game
Sad game

Your Home Is Where You're Happy by Manson

Your home is where you're happy
It's not where you're not free
Your home is where you can be what you are
'Cause you were just born free

Now they'll show you their castles
An' diamonds for all to see
But they'll never show you that peace of mind
'Cause they don't know how to be free

So burn all your bridges
Leave your whole life behind
You can do what you want to do
'Cause your strong in your mind

And anywhere you might wander
You could make that your home
And as long as you got love in your heart
You'll never be alone

Just as long as you got love in your heart
You'll never be alone no no no
You'll never be alone
no no no no

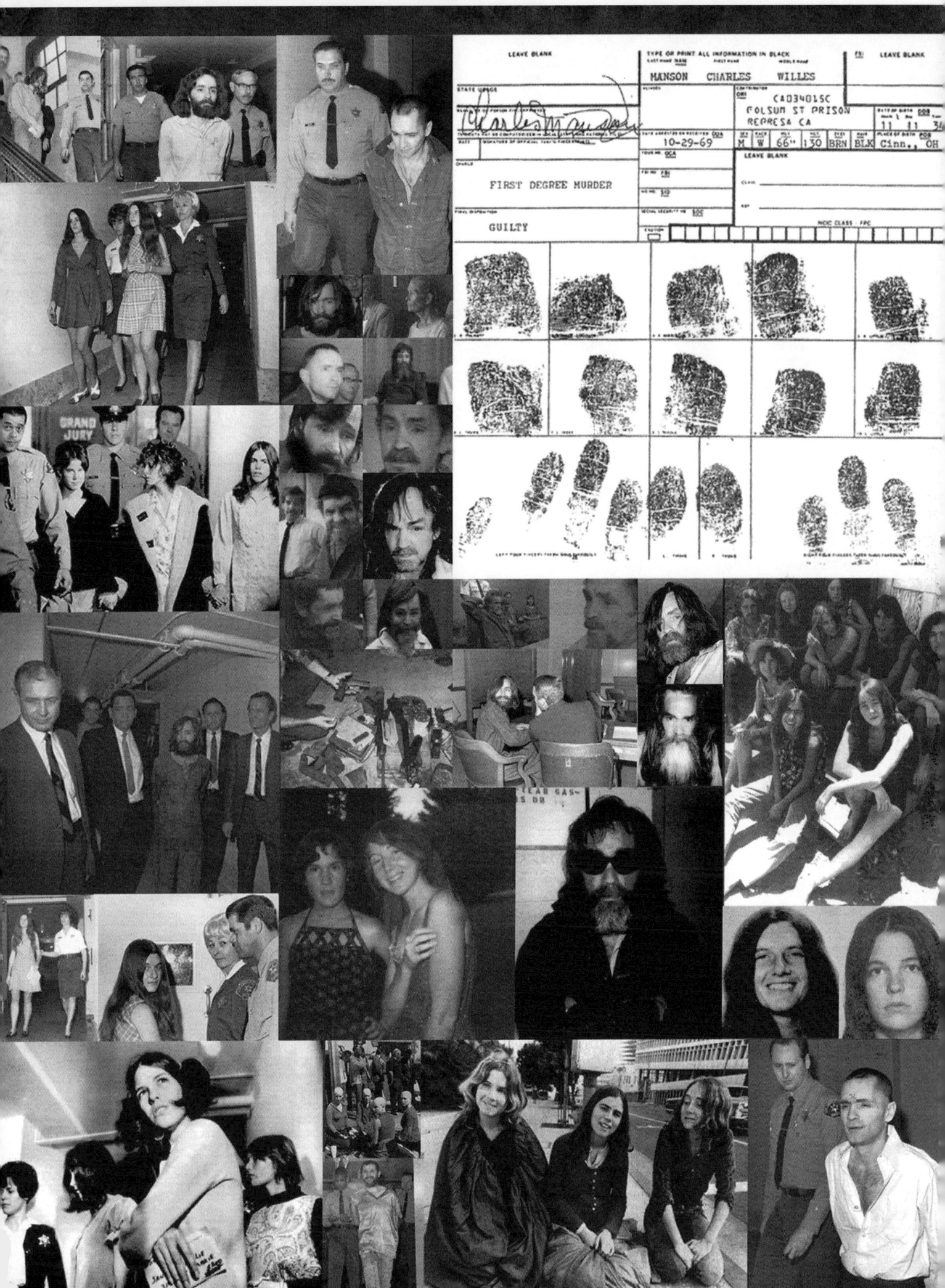

VAIN WOMAN OR urban myth?

AN ARTICLE BY KAMYELLE POWELL

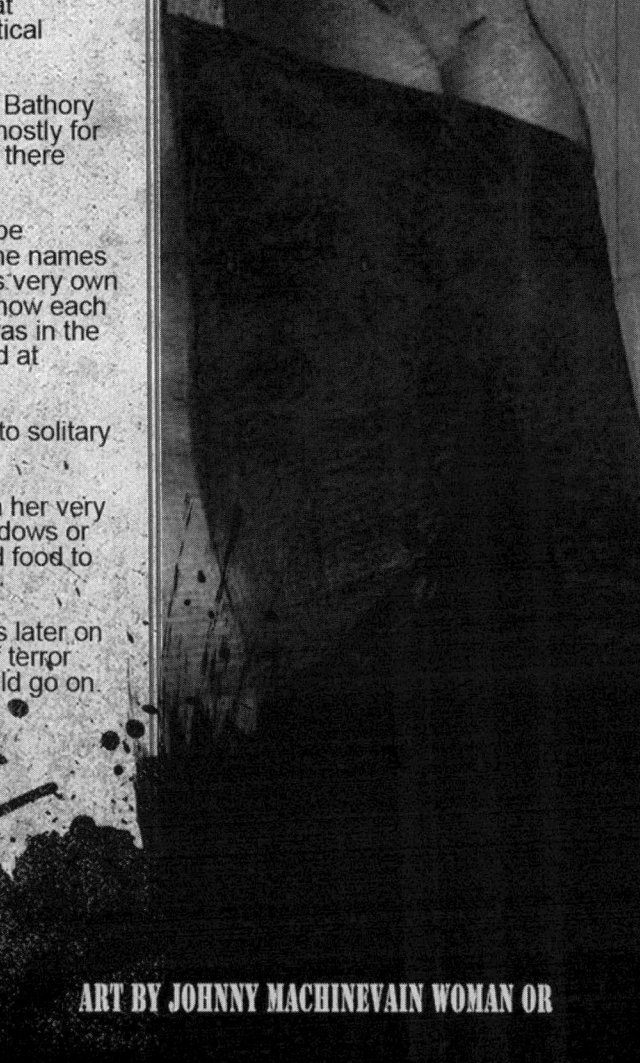

The sadistic Slovakian Countess of the 16th and 17th century put a cornerstone of interest in many horror fanatics, with the release of "Stay Alive". The movie made a fantasy about a woman that had a thirst for blood, unfortunately it was just a fragment of the true story of one of the most sadistic female serial murders of the century. Incidentally this wasn't the first myth that would help her claim to fame. I believe every myth needs the true story behind it, because sometimes the truth is scarier than the myth.

Elizabeth Bathory was born in present day Bratislava, which at the time was split into several different territories. Some of the myths claim that she might have been in the Louisiana area when her crimes were committed. But her best known home was the illusive Transylvanian castle that some of her most gruesome deeds were committed. Also there she would meet her own deathly fate.

In her early life for a brief point she was a civil human being, until her royal parents found out that she had became impregnated by a young peasant right before she was to marry Ferenc Nadasy. They locked her in his estate until the baby was born and she had went a bit mental.

Tragically that would be the same way her life would end after her gruesome acts would come to the light.

Her strange behavior wouldn't start the way most of the myths state it would. She started slowly being cruel to young peasant girls while her husband was away. It would progress even farther as time went on.

Bathory's sadistic methods weren't limited to her draining blood of her victims, like most myths claim. She would learn new ways of torture and try them out on her young female peasants, socially it was normal. She just took it to a more sadistic level.

Some of her work includes sticking pin needles into sensitive areas of there body's, sometimes even under there finger nails. One of Bathory's more infamous acts was stripping a peasant throwing them out into the cold and splashing water on them until they froze to death.

Contrary to most of the myths out there, she did have a few partners in crime. When her husband came back he joined her in her sadistic games even teaching her some new ones twists on her old ticks. Later on Anna Darvulia, a woman about whom very little is known, would become Bathory's main associate in crime during the years following her husband's death. There shortly after there short acquaintance she would fall ill and die. Soon after that she would meet a widow of a farmer, she would be the one to bring the downfall for Elizabeth Bathory.

Erzsi Majorova, her new cohort would advise her to try to bring a few noble blooded women into her ring of victims, because peasants would not want to work for her because of the stories they heard. It would bring Elizabeth's reign crashing down. In 1609 she would kill a noble women, Elizabeth would escape from judgment of that with accusations of suicide.

In 1610 an official inquiry began because of there concern about Elizabeth's behavior and actions. Unlike most people think it wasn't the vast number of Bathory's victims that condemned her, but rather political concerns instead.

On December 19th,1610, Miss Bathory was arrested and put on trial, mostly for show. Later In January of 1611 there would be a second trial.

Everything in her home would be registered as evidence, even the names of 650 victims. All in Elizabeth's very own handwriting. They determined how each victim died by how there role was in the torture. She would be convicted at that trial.

Elizabeth would be sentenced to solitary confinement for her crimes.

She would be held in a room in her very own castle. There were no windows or doors just a few slits for air and food to come threw.

Elizabeth would die three years later on August 12th,1614. Her reign of terror would end, but her legend would go on.

ART BY JOHNNY MACHINE

WHAT WE RECOMMEND

ALBERT FISH
IN SIN HE FOUND SALVATION

A JOHN BOROWSKI FILM

Albert Fish, the horrific true story of elderly cannibal, sadomasochist, and serial killer, who lured children to their deaths in Depression-era New York City. Distorting biblical tales, Albert Fish takes the themes of pain, torture, atonement and suffering literally as he preys on victims to torture and sacrifice. From John Borowski, award-winning director of H.H. Holmes: America's First Serial Killer, comes the first ever docudrama to definitively recount the life and times of elderly cannibal Albert Fish. Adding insight to the account are interviews with artist and Odditorium owner, Joe Coleman, and renowned true-crime author, Katherine Ramsland, Ph.D.

SERIAL KILLERS, WOULD YOU KNOW IF YOU WERE LIVING WITH ONE?

How do you define a serial killer? Many people would think that they are people with a grudge against the world and they hide in the shadows at night waiting for there next victim to come along and pounce, Well yes there have been serial killers that have operated like this for example The Yorkshire ripper who would lay in wait for his victims during a reign of terror in the 1970s and early eighties. But many serial killers are people you would never suspect of such atrocious crimes, one example is Ted Bundy. Who confessed to killing 30 murders of women in the USA in a reign of horror between 1974 and 1978 Now this man was a prime example of a "THE LAST PERSON YOU WOULD EVER SUSPECT" He was smart in appearance and later on many people likened him to that of a Chameleon who could adapt his facial expression to what ever situation he was in.. He was University educated, He even he managed the Seattle office of Nelson Rockefeller's Presidential campaign. He loved his family and he was a charmer. Maybe that is the reason Bundy murdered so many people, People just did not suspect him. So going back to the original question. How would you know if you were living with a serial killer? Are they out late at night when they should be at home? Are they quick tempered? Do they keep a diary that is locked away? My theory is that serial killers are divided into two categories. Insane and Clever. I am sure you would no if you was living with an insane serial killer. The mood swings, maybe the blood stain clothes and worse still you might be the next victim. NO CONTROL!!!!!!!!!! Your "Clever" Serial killer is more composed. He / She will sit at a dinner table with the family as cool as any thing because for them, Serial Killing is a thrill, Its an art of not being caught. Like a Game of Killing Chess. I am not saying you should suspect every one in your family of being a serial killer but be honest "YOU NEVER KNOW"

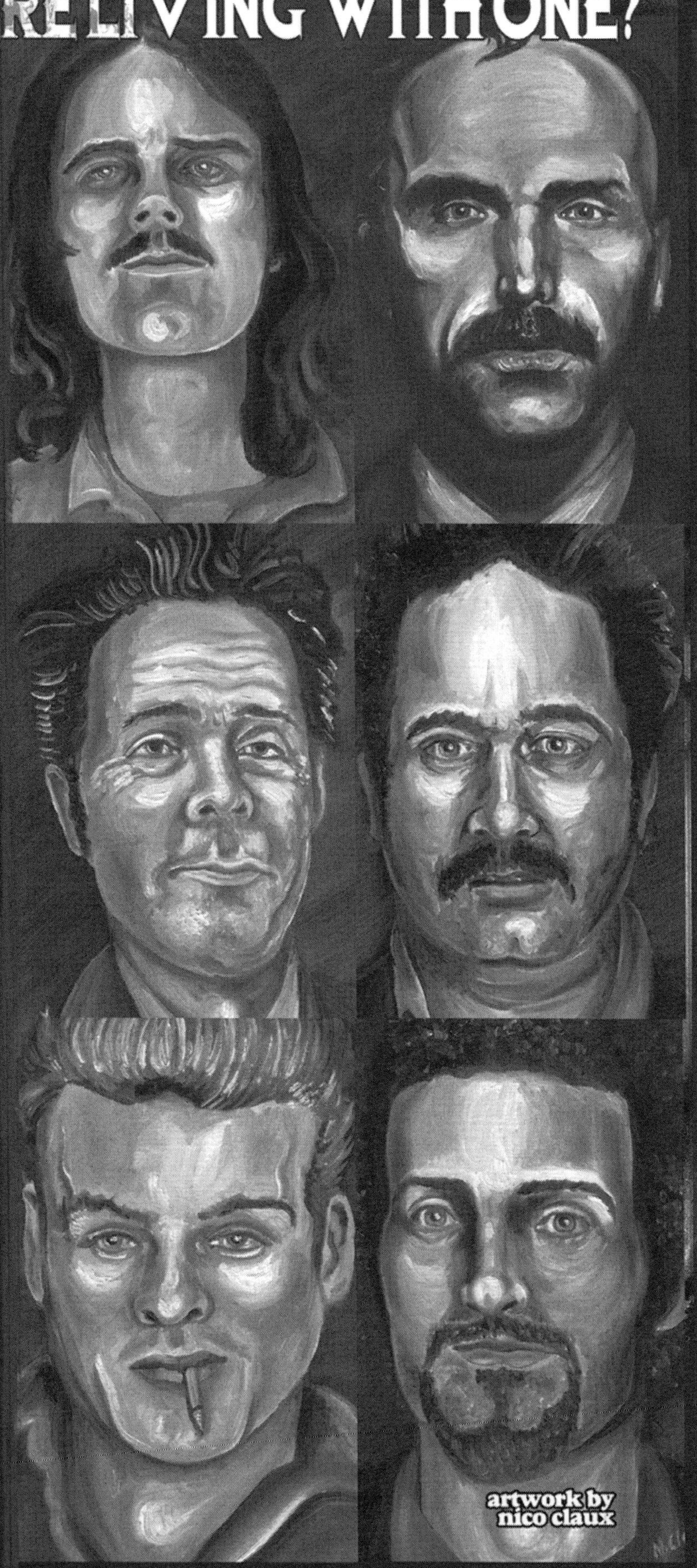

artwork by nico claux

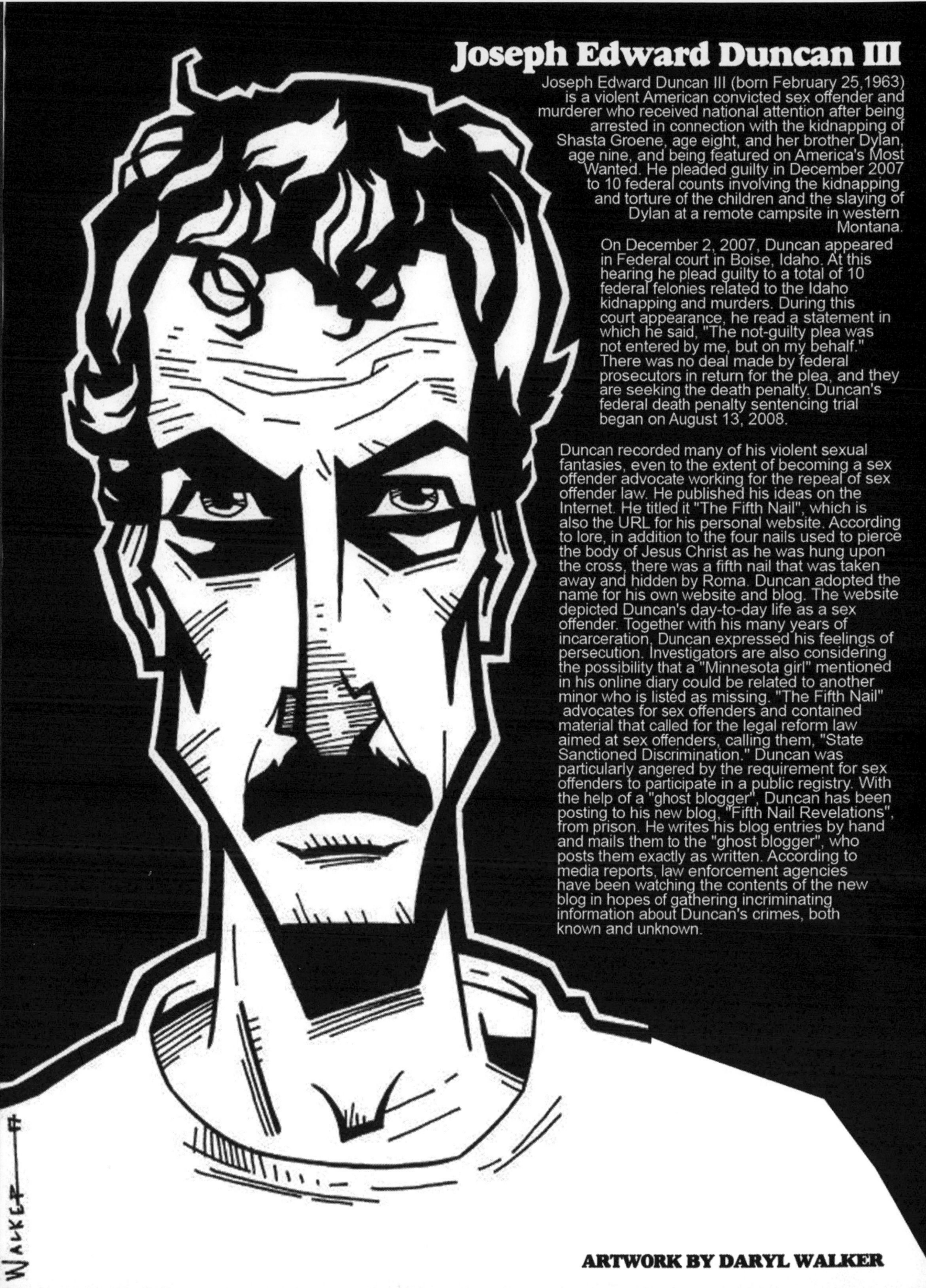

Joseph Edward Duncan III

Joseph Edward Duncan III (born February 25, 1963) is a violent American convicted sex offender and murderer who received national attention after being arrested in connection with the kidnapping of Shasta Groene, age eight, and her brother Dylan, age nine, and being featured on America's Most Wanted. He pleaded guilty in December 2007 to 10 federal counts involving the kidnapping and torture of the children and the slaying of Dylan at a remote campsite in western Montana.

On December 2, 2007, Duncan appeared in Federal court in Boise, Idaho. At this hearing he plead guilty to a total of 10 federal felonies related to the Idaho kidnapping and murders. During this court appearance, he read a statement in which he said, "The not-guilty plea was not entered by me, but on my behalf." There was no deal made by federal prosecutors in return for the plea, and they are seeking the death penalty. Duncan's federal death penalty sentencing trial began on August 13, 2008.

Duncan recorded many of his violent sexual fantasies, even to the extent of becoming a sex offender advocate working for the repeal of sex offender law. He published his ideas on the Internet. He titled it "The Fifth Nail", which is also the URL for his personal website. According to lore, in addition to the four nails used to pierce the body of Jesus Christ as he was hung upon the cross, there was a fifth nail that was taken away and hidden by Roma. Duncan adopted the name for his own website and blog. The website depicted Duncan's day-to-day life as a sex offender. Together with his many years of incarceration, Duncan expressed his feelings of persecution. Investigators are also considering the possibility that a "Minnesota girl" mentioned in his online diary could be related to another minor who is listed as missing. "The Fifth Nail" advocates for sex offenders and contained material that called for the legal reform law aimed at sex offenders, calling them, "State Sanctioned Discrimination." Duncan was particularly angered by the requirement for sex offenders to participate in a public registry. With the help of a "ghost blogger", Duncan has been posting to his new blog, "Fifth Nail Revelations", from prison. He writes his blog entries by hand and mails them to the "ghost blogger", who posts them exactly as written. According to media reports, law enforcement agencies have been watching the contents of the new blog in hopes of gathering incriminating information about Duncan's crimes, both known and unknown.

ARTWORK BY DARYL WALKER

PATRICK MACKAY: Psychopathic Repeat Killer

Patrick Mackay (born September 25, 1952) is a serial killer who confessed to murdering eleven people in England in the mid 1970s. As a child, Mackay was frequently a victim of physical abuse at the hands of his violent, alcoholic father Harold. When Mackay was ten, Harold died from complications of alcoholism and a weak heart. His final words to his son were 'remember to be good'. Patrick was said to be unable to come to terms with the loss, telling people Harold was still alive and keeping a photograph of his father on his person. Later, in his youth, he suffered from extreme tantrums and fits of anger, indulged in animal cruelty and arson (at one point setting the pet tortoise on fire), bullied younger children, stole from elderly women's homes and people in the street, and even attempted to kill his mother and aunt. He also attempted to kill a younger boy, and later said he'd have succeeded had he not been restrained, and attempted to set fire to a Catholic church. Because of such incidents, he spent his teenage years in and out of mental homes and institutions. At 15, he was diagnosed as a psychopath by a psychiatrist, Dr. Leonard Carr. Carr predicted Mackay would grow up into a 'cold, psychopathic killer'.

As he entered adulthood, Mackay developed a fascination with Nazism, calling himself "Franklin Bollvolt The First" and filling his flat with Nazi memorabilia. He lived in London and was frequently drunk or on drugs. In 1973, near his mother's home in Kent, he met and was befriended by Father Anthony Crean, a priest. Regardless, Mackay broke into Crean's home and stole a check for £30. Arrested and prosecuted by the police, he was ordered to pay the fine back but never did. The incident caused a rift between the two and Mackay returned to London. It was around this time that Mackay said he'd drowned a tramp in the River Thames.

On March 21, 1975, then aged 22, Mackay used an axe to kill Father Crean, hacking through the victim's skull and watching him bleed to death. He was swiftly arrested and was soon considered by police to be a suspect in at least a dozen other killings over the past two years, most victims being elderly women who had been stabbed or strangled during robberies. Mackay bragged that he had murdered 11 people.

Patrick Mackay was charged with five murders, but two charges were dropped through lack of evidence. In November 1975 he was convicted and sentenced to life imprisonment. He is now in his thirty-third year of imprisonment.

art by chuck hodi

HIGHWAY OF TEARS
by Chris Bartholomew

Aboriginal - people in Canada who belong to recognized indigenous groups in the Canadian Constitution Act of 1982, sections 25 and 35, respectively as Indians, Métis, and Inuit. Natives.

Often, even when the evidence is overwhelming, when it comes to a serial killer people just would rather not believe it – at first. "I don't think a serial killer is on the loose," someone says. "It's easier for our society to lay the blame on one person, but I believe that there are multiple murderers out there who are racist and are targeting aboriginal women." Time and time again we see things like this being said and later, when someone sits down and looks at the evidence, they change and believe in the serial killer. This is one of those cases. Some say it's a race thing, but it's really not a good idea to make statements like that when most of the time we find that the killer wasn't prejudice; they just like certain types of women. Statements that I've heard such as: "Would they say the same thing if 10 or 12 local white girls were raped or murdered or disappeared on the same road," are moot until the serial killer is caught. Only when he is found out will we know exactly why he took mostly aboriginal women. Someone has found himself a desolate area, vast and rugged. Witnesses are non-existent. There is a place that makes it seem as if women are vanishing into thin air. Numerous back roads lead into the woods from a highway. The terrain is difficult; the bodies could be dumped anywhere. Highway 16. The British Columbia, Canada, section of the Yellowhead Highway. The number '16' was first given to the highway in 1942, and originally, the route that the highway took was more to the north of today's highway, and it was not as long as it is now. Since 1988, at least 32 women—31 of them aboriginal—have been killed or suspiciously disappeared along the 500-mile section of highway between Prince George to Prince Rupert. These crimes have remained largely uninvestigated. Seven years ago, officers investigating two cold-case murders in Abbotsford had a suspect. The similarities in the murders combined with the suspect's criminal record — which included multiple rape convictions — left police thinking they had the right guy. Unable to prove anything, the suspect, in his 50s, was left to walk free and was last reported living in Ontario. The Royal Canadian Mounted Police is officially investigating the unsolved murder or disappearance of nine women between the ages of 14 and 25 since 1974, most of who were hitchhiking along Highway 16.

The murders of Kathryn Mary Herbert (11 years old when murdered in 1975), Theresa Hildebrandt (15 years old when slain in 1976) remain unsolved, although their remains have since been recovered. Monica Jack, a 12-year-old girl, disappeared in May 1978 while riding her bike home along Nicola Lake near Merritt. Police recently added the following murders to the Highway of tears probe: Gale Weys, killed in Clearwater in 1973; Pamela Darlington, found dead in Kamloops in 1973; and Maureen Mosie, found dead in Kamloops in 1981. Many of the small towns that dot the highway have their own theories about the missing women. Some say a serial killer is on the loose. Others think it's one of their own, a person who knows the community and the women well. Since the Canadian police routinely have no suspects and make no arrests in connection with the disappearances, the rumors continue to thrive. Along the highway there are posters of the missing girls tacked to utility poles. In gas stations, family members have posted pleas to help them find their lost little girls. A sign says, "Highway of Tears: In memory of the missing women." Every town seems to have been affected. There are 16, 4, and 12 year spans between the first, middle, and last murders respectively. If the killer first killed when he was in his late teens or early twenties, he would now be in his late forties or early fifties. Even if he waited until he was thirty to kill, that would still put his age well within a physically capable range to kill today. If he spent any time in jail or prison, that could account for some of the time. Maybe he led a quiet, non-criminal life during those periods. In the case of the latter, Dennis Rader has proven expansive amounts of time can pass without the requisite lockup. While working, he may be emotionally stable and less compelled to search for victims. Amidst those periods requiring fewer commitments—he might be between jobs—he could experience increased stress in conjunction with protracted time during which to think over certain "fantasies" that cross his mind, intensifying the desire to act upon those ruminations. His fantasies are probably about the first time and later murders are an attempt to re-enact the experience. He probably made his first kill as a teen in Terrace, British Columbia, and he probably now resides in the Prince George, British Columbia area. The first of the latest series of incidents was Ramona Wilson, 15, who was hitchhiking to a friend's place on June 11, 1994. Her remains were found near the Smithers airport a year later. Five months after that, Roxanne Thiara, also 15, went missing from Prince George only to be found dead - her body dumped near Burns Lake. The slaughter rose to three in a row when the remains of Alishia Germaine, again 15, were discovered December 9, 1994

The next six months are event-free until Delphine Nikal, 16, from Telkwa disappears somewhere between Smithers and her home. She has yet to be found. Lana Derrick, 19, was a forestry student in Terrace, who went missing while walking down a street in Terrace in October, 1995. She has never been heard from since. Nothing happened for almost seven years. He could have been in jail. The next victim was the first Caucasian woman, Nicole Hoar, who disappeared on June 21, 2002. Nicole was a young tree planter hitching her way from Prince George to her sister's home in Smithers. She was hoping to attend the Midsummer Music Festival, but she never arrived. On September 17, 2005, a number of ceremonies named "Take Back the Highway" were held in communities between Prince George and Prince Rupert. Activities included marches, minutes of silence, local speakers and prayers to promote awareness and in protest to the violence against these women. Four days later Tamara Chipman, 22, went missing somewhere between Prince Rupert and Terrace. Tamara had taken judo for years and was considered able to take care of herself. Not this time. Meanwhile, Crystal Lee Okimaw, 24, vanished from Prince George January 16 and Aielah Saric-Auger, 14, was discovered dead just east of Prince George on February 2, 2006. Guesses as to what sort of person the police might be looking at include a traveling salesman. A hunter. It could be a trucker who runs in, then out of the towns. It might be someone local who always seems to be at the right place to stop to pick up young women. In Vancouver, B.C., Northern B.C., Edmonton, Alberta, Saskatchewan in Canada, over 500 women have disappeared and/or been murdered in the last 20 years. Many have been described as having high risk lifestyles. June 21, 2008, there will be a Walk4Justice – Highway of Tears, from Vancouver to Ottawa. One of the reasons for the walk, besides of course to remember the dead and missing is to let the killer know that they are looking for him, and that he will be caught. Yes, Police suspect they could be looking for one of the world's worst serial killers - perhaps more than one.

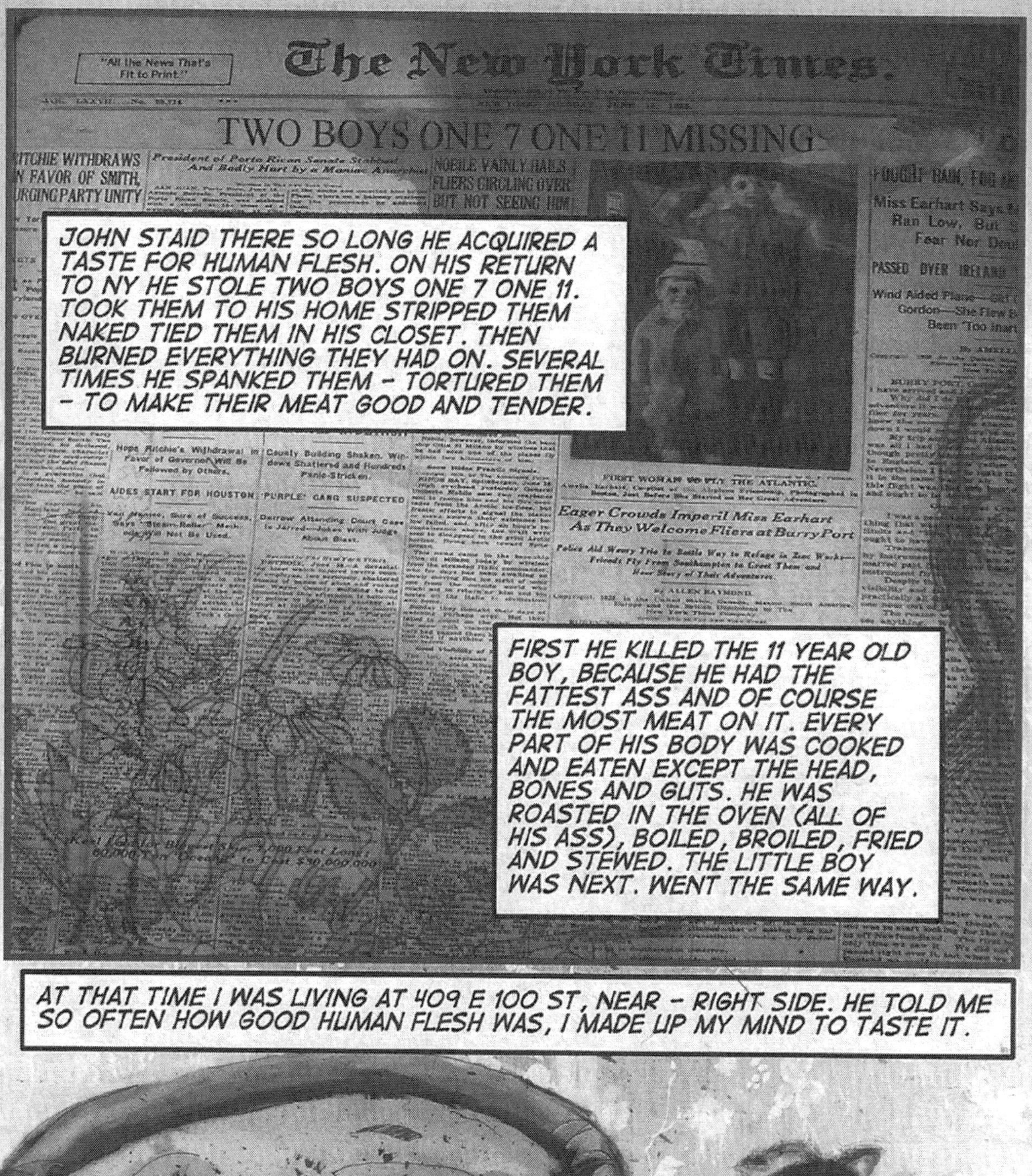

JOHN STAID THERE SO LONG HE ACQUIRED A TASTE FOR HUMAN FLESH. ON HIS RETURN TO NY HE STOLE TWO BOYS ONE 7 ONE 11. TOOK THEM TO HIS HOME STRIPPED THEM NAKED TIED THEM IN HIS CLOSET. THEN BURNED EVERYTHING THEY HAD ON. SEVERAL TIMES HE SPANKED THEM — TORTURED THEM — TO MAKE THEIR MEAT GOOD AND TENDER.

FIRST HE KILLED THE 11 YEAR OLD BOY, BECAUSE HE HAD THE FATTEST ASS AND OF COURSE THE MOST MEAT ON IT. EVERY PART OF HIS BODY WAS COOKED AND EATEN EXCEPT THE HEAD, BONES AND GUTS. HE WAS ROASTED IN THE OVEN (ALL OF HIS ASS), BOILED, BROILED, FRIED AND STEWED. THE LITTLE BOY WAS NEXT. WENT THE SAME WAY.

AT THAT TIME I WAS LIVING AT 409 E 100 ST, NEAR — RIGHT SIDE. HE TOLD ME SO OFTEN HOW GOOD HUMAN FLESH WAS, I MADE UP MY MIND TO TASTE IT.

ON SUNDAY JUNE THE 3, 1928 I CALLED ON YOU AT 406 W 15 ST. BROUGHT YOU POT CHEESE --- STRAWBERRIES. WE HAD LUNCH. GRACE SAT IN MY LAP AND KISSED ME. I MADE UP MY MIND TO EAT HER.

PART 2 OF WHY SERIAL KILLERS? BY DAVID HAYES: CREATING SERIAL WAS A BIT CATHARTIC AS WELL. HOW CAN A DRAWING ON A PAGE POSSIBLY BE THREATENING? WE'VE PUT A CARTOON FACE ON FEAR TO, MAYBE, JUST MAYBE, TAKE THE EDGE OFF. EVEN THOUGH HE DIED YEARS AGO, JOHN WAYNE GACY OR, MORE ACCURATELY, THE THOUGHT OF GACY STILL CHILLS ME. THE THOUGHT OF HIS CRIMES, THEIR MAGNITUDE, CAUSES THE HAIR ON THE BACK OF MY NECK TO STAND UP. A HORROR MOVIE VILLAIN HASN'T DONE THAT TO ME SINCE I WAS TEN-YEARS-OLD YET A MURDERER OF YOUNG MEN, DEAD FOR YEARS, STILL FRIGHTENS ME. THAT IS WHAT SERIAL IS FOR ME. IT IS A CHANCE TO TRY AND EXORCISE DEMONS AND LOOK BEYOND THE EVERYDAY TERROR OF SERIAL KILLERS. TO BE COMPLETELY HONEST, IT HASN'T WORKED YET. READING THROUGH THE FIRST ISSUE STILL CAUSES HITCHES IN MY THROAT AND THAT SENSE OF IMPENDING DOOM LIKE SOME SOCIOPATH IS STARING AT ME. FROM THE SHADOWS, CAREFULLY PLANNED, THEY GLARE AT ME LIKE A SIDE OF BEEF CLUTCHING WHICHEVER IMPLEMENTING OF DEATH IS FAVORED.

PART 3 OF WHY SERIAL KILLERS? BY DAVID HAYES : EACH ISSUE OF SERIAL WILL FEATURE A 10 PAGE STORY, A 6 PAGE STORY AND A 4 PAGE STORY. THE FIRST ISSUE, COMPLETE AND AVAILABLE VIA WOWIO.COM AROUND JULY 2ND FOR FREE, FEATURES SOME OF THE MOST BRUTAL SERIAL KILLERS IN HISTORY. THE AFOREMENTIONED JOHN WAYNE GACY IS JOINED BY ANGEL RESINDIZ AND ALBERT FISH. FIENDS, ALL THREE, EACH WITH THEIR OWN PROCLIVITIES. A TRIO OF DEATH, DISMEMBERMENT AND CANNIBALISM. THEY FRIGHTEN ME EVEN THOUGH THEY ARE EITHER DEAD OR INCARCERATED. I DON'T BELIEVE THAT EACH INDIVIDUAL IS PERSONALLY TERRIFYING. I BELIEVE IT IS WHAT THOSE INDIVIDUALS REPRESENT THAT SCARES ME MOST. AND WHAT THEY REPRESENT IS OUT THERE, STALKING, WAITING, PLANNING, UNCONTROLLABLE. AFTER ALL, WHAT'S SCARIER THAN REAL LIFE?

ON THE PRETENSE OF TAKING HER TO A PARTY. YOU SAID YES SHE COULD GO. I TOOK HER TO AN EMPTY HOUSE IN WESTCHESTER I HAD ALREADY PICKED OUT.

WHEN WE GOT THERE, I TOLD HER TO REMAIN OUTSIDE. SHE PICKED WILDFLOWERS. I WENT UPSTAIRS AND STRIPPED ALL OF MY CLOTHES OFF.

I KNEW IF I DID NOT I WOULD GET HER BLOOD ON THEM.

WHEN ALL WAS READY I WENT TO THE WINDOW AND CALLED HER. THEN HID IN A CLOSET UNTIL SHE WAS IN THE ROOM. WHEN SHE SAW ME ALL NAKED SHE BEGAN TO CRY AND TRIED TO RUN DOWN THE STAIRS. I GRABBED HER AND SHE SAID SHE WOULD TELL HER MAMMA. FIRST I STRIPPED HER NAKED.

> HOW SHE DID KICK-- BITE AND SCRATCH. I CHOKED HER TO DEATH, THEN CUT HER IN SMALL PIECES SO I COULD TAKE MY MEAT TO MY ROOMS. COOK AND EAT IT.

> HOW SWEET AND TENDER HER LITTLE ASS WAS ROASTED IN THE OVEN. IT TOOK ME 9 DAYS TO EAT HER ENTIRE BODY.

> I DID NOT FUCK HER THO I COULD OF HAD I WISHED. SHE DIED A VIRGIN.

THE LETTER WAS UNSIGNED, OF COURSE. FISH WAS TRIED AND CONVICTED OF GRACE BUDD'S MURDER AND CANNIBALISM.

next issue: the crawlspace

THE ART OF EVIL BY KURT BELCHER:

I GOT TO EXPERIENCE BOTH SIDES OF THE FENCE ON THIS BOOK: I WROTE ABOUT ANGEL RESENDIZ, BUT I DREW JOHN WAYNE GACY'S STORY. I ATTEMPTED A ROUGH-HEWN, ALMOST SCRIBBLE-LIKE VISUAL LANGUAGE WITH THIS STORY, GOING STRAIGHT FROM ROUGH SKETCHES TO FINAL INK DRAWINGS, WITH MOST OF THE PAGES DRAWN WITH AN INK DROPPER, RATHER THAN MORE TRADITIONAL INKING METHODS. LATER I MOVED TO SHARPIES AND PENS. NOT TO SOUND TOO PHILOSOPHICAL, BUT I WANTED TO GO FROM IMAGES IN THE BEGINNING THAT WE CAN'T COMPREHEND, TO AN ENDING THAT TRIES TO MAKE SENSE OF GACY'S LIFE AND CRIMES. WRITING ABOUT THEM IS DISTURBING ENOUGH. DRAWING THEM IS CHANNELING THEIR CRIMES INTO AN IMAGE THAT PEOPLE CAN UNDERSTAND.

I TRIED TO CONVEY IN IMAGES WHAT IT MAY BE HARD TO UNDERSTAND WITH JUST WORDS: GACY WAS EVIL. THEY ARE NEIGHBORS, PEOPLE ON THE STREET, OCCASIONALLY PEOPLE YOU TALK TO. WANT TO BE CHILLED TO THE BONE? READ THE "FISH" STORY. RYAN YAGER'S WONDERFULLY (AND APPROPRIATELY) MACABRE ART NOTWITHSTANDING, THE NOTE ALONE IS ENOUGH TO MAKE YOU SICK WITH REVULSION, AND THE THOUGHT THAT THESE THINGS COME SO NATURALLY TO SOME PEOPLE.

DRAWING GACY'S LIFE FROM THE START OF HIS CRIMES TO THE END OF HIS LIFE TOUCHES SOMETHING IN ME THAT I DON'T WANT TO ADMIT EXISTS WITHIN ME, AND HOPEFULLY MOST OTHERS DON'T EITHER. OUR PRESIDENT TALKS ABOUT EVILDOERS AND PEOPLE ROLL THEIR EYES. WHILE SOMETIMES I ROLL MY EYES RIGHT ALONGSIDE THEM, IF YOU WANT TO FIND THE NOTION OF EVIL WITHIN THE SOUL PERSONIFIED, JUST LOOK IN ONE DIRECTION: THE SERIAL KILLER.

MAT,

GREETINGS. IT TAKES ABOUT 3 WEEKS FOR YOUR LETTER TO ARRIVE. I DON'T GET THAT MANY LETTERS. MOST ARE FROM GUYS IN BANDS. SO YOUR A CHEF EH? COOL. WHICH ARE YOUR BEST DESSERTS? AS FOR FAVORITE MOVIES I LIKE COMEDIES - SCI FI- AND THRILLERS. EVER SEEN CHRONICLES OF RIDDICK PART 2? ITS PRETTY GOOD. I REALLY DON'T WRITE ABOUT MY CASE OR RELIGION. HOPE YOU UNDERSTAND. I COULD USE A MONEY ORDER AND/OR SOME STAMPS IF YOU CAN HELP OUT. DO YOU HAVE FAMILY? I'M THE YOUNGEST OF FIVE. BEEN TO ANY GOOD CONCERTS? I LIKE ALL TYPES OF MUSIC BUT HEAVY METAL IS MY FAVORITE. IF YOU SEND PICTURES OF GIRLS MAKE EM FROM HEAD TO TOE. SEND 5 (OR LESS) PER ENVELOPE NOTHING SCENIC FOR NOW. SIGN EM ON BACK W/ YOUR FIRST NAME AND LAST INITIAL. DO YOU HAVE A PRINTER? GIRLS CAN BE

IN LINGERIE OR BIKINI. NOTHING NUDE. WHATS AUSTIN LIKE? I HEAR ITS REALLY CROWDED. WHATS BEEN THE BEST YEAR YOU HAD? IF YOU COULD EXPERIENCE ANYTHING WHAT WOULD IT BE? THATS ALL FOR NOW. TAKE IT EASY, WRITE WHEN YOU GET A CHANCE.

YOUR FRIEND
RICHARD

**Thanks to Mat Clouser for letting us reprint his letter from Richard Ramirez.
Artwork by Matt Verges**

Richard Leonard Kuklinski Part One
THE ICEMAN COMETH
by Aaron Kirkland

THE EARLY YEARS

When you think of the Mafia you think of The Godfather, Goodfellas, The Sopranos, and you think of people like Al Capone, John Gotti, Sammy "The Bull" Gravano. There is one man, who was the epitome of all that and then some! His name...Richard Leonard Kuklinski.

Richard was born in Jersey City, New Jersey on Thursday, April 11, 1935 to Anna and Stanley Kuklinski. His mother was a devoute Catholic and his father an abusive alcoholic. Anna worked at a meat packing plant and Stanley worked as a brakeman for the railroad.

Richard was born second to his brother Florian. When Richard and Florian were growing up Stanley would often beat the 2 boys, sometimes so bad that he would literally knock them out cold. They would also witness Stanley's abuse towards Anna on several occasions! One day in 1940 Stanley was beating Florian when he hit him too hard and killed him unintentionally. He forced Anna to tell family and police that Florian had fallen down the stairs and died that way!

Richard hated his father. Even when he was sitting in jail being interviewed many years later he would attest how he regretted never killing his father for the pain he caused in his life.

Richard grew up in the projects with his sister Roberta (who was born premature) and his other brother Joseph, both of which were his younger siblings. His favourite thing in the whole world were true crime magazines. Richard all to often was beat up by local bullies. By the age of 10 Richard was taking his anger out by torturing animals. He would tie dogs to the bumpers of buses, and throw dogs off of rooftops. He would even go as far as throwing animals into the incinerator in his building.

Richard had taken enough beatings and was fed up. Thoughts of going to the police went through his head but he kept telling himself "I'm no rat..." and would take matters into his own hands! It was a cold Friday night in January when Richard yanked a two-foot-long wooden pole out of the hall closet and went into the alley by his building. He waited in the shadows for what felt like hours, hoping and knowing that Charley Lane (leader of the gang of boys that used to beat on Richard) would walk by the alley on his way home.

Just as he was ready to head inside he saw Charley in the distance...his nerves trembled with both fear and hatred to very strong feelings to feel all at once. He confronted his tormentor only to have Charley threaten him with violence if he didn't get out of his way to which Richard replied "Yeah, try." Charley went to attack Richard but Richard replied with a smack in the head, just above the ear, with the pole he swiped from his house...Charley stepped back now filled with anger he went to attack again... and again Richard attacked Charley with the pole this time knocking him down to the ground where Richard kept hitting him until he didn't move anymore. He just wanted to lay a scare into the boy, not wanting to kill him. When Richard realized Charley was dead he grabbed a car that he had stolen for a joyride and stuffed the body in the trunk... drove around for a while till he came to a bridge with a pond under it near a forest in South Jersey. Richard grabbed a hammer and broke out Charley's teeth and cut the tips of his fingers off, knowing that they were ways to identify a body from reading his true crime magazines. Richard then dumped the lifeless body over the bridge and as it broke through the ice he knew that he had to have the upper hand, he tasted what it was to be powerful and have someone's life taken away because of his own hands and it felt good. Richard Kuklinski had experienced murder first hand at the age of 14.

LIFE AS A STREET TOUGH

After he killed Charley Lane, he got his revenge on the other boys who used to beat him!

Richard began hanging around pool halls beginning to pick the game of pool up like a pro.

Because he had a thick frame and tall exterior there weren't' too many people that wanted to go toe-to-toe with Richard Kuklinski. Those who did were sorely mistaken.

Richard ended up starting a crew and took leadership. Calling themselves 'the Coming Up Roses' they were involved in many bar brawls and were soon known as a fearless and unbeatable crew.

One day Carmine Genovese of the De Cavalcante called upon Richard to take car of a mark with his crew. He had heard good things about Richards crew and wanted to see just how fearless and vicious they could be! The man lived near Lincoln Park and the hit had to be done quick, he "need to go" as Carmine so blatantly put it! One of the members of the gang offered to be the shooter as long as Richard drove, and Richard agreed...John Wheeler a big tough as nails kinda guy froze once he saw his target getting into his car...Richard saw this and said not to worry they could pull up to marks car and take him out through the window at the next traffic light. Wheeler froze up again at the next opportunity to take this easy target out. So with Richard now pissed that the job still wasn't done they tailed him to this bar in Hoboken where Richard spoke up and said that he'd take the guy out. They waited for the guy to leave the bar. He finally left the bar and Richard got out of the car walked over to the mark and just as he was getting into his car *BOOM* Richard shot him in the head just above the ear. Killing him instantly. Richard calmly walked back to his own car and sped off. As they left the crime scene Wheeler looked at Richard and said "Man, Rich, you're cold like ice!" They returned to Carmine and the crew earned $500 each and the doors to the underworld were now open to big possibilities for them!

The gang was given enough work to last them a while, they were making money hand over fist and Richard would gamble most of his winnings away, which would become a big problem for him in his future.

One day two of the members, John Wheeler and Jack Dubrowski thought they were invincible and held up a card game held by a made man in the De Cavalcante family. This was a bad idea because one of the members of the game recognized Wheeler even though they had there faces hidden. Word hit a soldier in the De Cavalcante family and he had a sit down with Richard. He told Richard about the card game being hit and that everyone knew that Richard had nothing to do with the robbery otherwise he'd be dead! Richard offered to tell Wheeler and Dubrowski to leave town and never come back, but that wasn't good enough for the soldier! He wanted them taken out! See in the Mafia world you don't mess with a made man! Ray Liotta told us this in Goodfellas. So with that said Richard sealed their fates and gunned them down! Left them where they lay so that it would be known that the job was done. Much like Richards previous murders before these he was never identified as a suspect! He finally put the Coming Up Roses behind him and was looking forward to moving on with his new found fame as an extremely dangerous street tough and hit man for hire!

His first time having to torture someone was when Carmine Genovese, freshly released from jail, asked Richard to make this guy disappear. He disrespected one of his friends wives. Carmine made it clear he had to suffer! So Richard went to the marks work and scouted the place where the he worked and then set the trap up! The mark worked at a used car lot so Richard set it up to happen on a test drive. They went out on the drive and parked... Richard pointed at something and then *BAM*, hit the mark in the head knocking him out cold. Richard hog tied him, duct taped his mouth and shoved him in the trunk of his car. Richard drove out to a wooded area in the Jersey Pine Barrens, pulled the mark out of his trunk and placed him against a tree and made him realize that he was gonna suffer! He pulled out a hatchet and proceeded to break his knees. He cut his fingers off one-by-one and was gonna use them as proof the mark had suffered but got a better idea...by this time the mark had soiled himself. Richard finally killed the guy and buried what was left of him in a hole out in the woods. Richard soon left with the proof he needed for Carmine... his head!

SECRET LIFE

One thing that not many people at all knew about Richard was that he was married once before Barbara. Her name was Linda. She had taken a liking to Richard when he was sixteen and she was twenty-five-years old. She would go on to let him live with her and they would have sex numerous times a day, everyday. Richard would at times be violent with Linda (as he grew up witnessing his mom being beaten by his father), and other times he would bring her stuffed toys, fresh flowers, fancy candy, and clothing. After finding out that Linda was pregnant he ended up marrying her for the sake of the baby.

At 20, Richard was a father for the first time naming the child Richard Jr. He had no real feeling of love or emotion for the child...he felt the child was just an extension of lust and nothing else. Linda became pregnant again and nine months later gave birth to his second child they called David. Richard still had no emotional feelings of love towards his children but he did feel the need to protect them on occasion. One such instance was when the super-intendant slapped both Richards kids for allegedly being too loud. Linda called Richard at a local bar and told him and he lost it! He got in his car and drove to find the super at a bar he usually drinks at. Long story short the super was hospitalized for weeks, and Richard had to pay $3000 for knocking a cop (who was working as a bar tender at the bar this happened in) out. Richard and Linda's relationship was going sour and they had stopped having sex to barely any at all.

One fateful evening Richard's younger brother Joe, now all grown up, told Richard he had seen a guy, Sammy James, and his wife Linda go into a room at the Hudson Hotel. Room 16 his brother told him... ground level right near the Coke machine. So Richard in a fury left his brother and sped off for the hotel. He showed up at the hotel and booted the door in with all his might. Linda's eyes popped out of her head in shock and fear. Richard looked at James started to beat the crap out of him and told him he was gonna break every bone in his body but one...and that if he ever heard he was around Linda again he would find him and break that bone he did not break and went on to break ever bone but one. He then turned to Linda and said "If you weren't the mother of my son's" and pulled out a knife. He went to grab her left breast and she tried to put up a fight so he hit her and knocked her unconscious and proceeded to cut her nipples off. He never had any real contact with her after that and only saw his sons on occasion.

ROY DEMEO

Roy DeMeo would turn out to be an important role in Richards up and coming life as well as big a thorn in his side as his own father!

Roy DeMeo was a well known tough like Kuklinski but Richard could never be made as he was of Polish decent. Roy looked up to people like Lucky Luciano, and Al Capone so he was really striving to become famous in the Mafia world. He was not liked by many but respected by all as a good earner in the underworld. He was not liked because of his explosive temper, which a lot of people said would be his downfall.

Richards first meeting with DeMeo would not be a good one. Richard at the time was distributing and directing porn, he never got into the porn, just saw it as a cash crop for him and ended up being the porn king of New York at one time! Richard was behind on a payment he owed to an investor. The investor happened to be friends with Roy and he got Roy involved. Richard went to see his investor but was met by Roy asking for the money. Roy knew that Richard was well over 6 feet and 300 pounds but he did not care as Roy was a hot tempered, loud mouth. They exchanged words Roy saw that he was not putting enough fear into Richard and Roy knew he didn't want to go toe-to-toe with this mammoth of a man so he left to get his crew. When Roy left Richards investor told him who Roy was and that he was connected...he didn't want to see Richard get hurt so Richard turned around to get on the elevator. He was met by DeMeo's men who had their guns pointed on Richard. DeMeo stared Richard down and said "So tough guy, You want to die, you want to fucking die?" and right after that he hit Richard across the side of the head with the butt of his gun. DeMeo didn't know that Richard was carrying a gun just like he always did...a .38 derringer. Richard knew that if he said anything or tried to go for the gun he would surly be shot! Soon all of DeMeo's men were beating on Richard only enraging him, but doing his best to keep it cool so he did not get shot on the spot. They kept beating him but got tired when they couldn't knock him out. DeMeo told him to get the money or he was dead! Richard got up, angry as could be, and went to the washroom. Looked at himself in the mirror he was mad at the mess they made of him. He had to go to the hospital and got thirty-eight **stitches on three different wounds on his head.**

Richard Leonard Kuklinski Part Two
THE ICEMAN COMETH
by Aaron Kirkland

Richard made arrangements to pay his investor. He then went and found DeMeo at a club he owned called the Gemini Lounge. He walked in to the club and asked for DeMeo. DeMeo told him he was glad that he was making payment arrangements and said that he had balls for coming to the bar. He told DeMeo he wanted to talk and they talked. Richard told him that the two investors that had Roy confront Richard were stealing from each other and that he didn't owe as much as they had made it seem! Roy said that maybe they got off on the wrong foot and proceeded to tell him that he had asked around about him and found out that Richard was actually a stand up guy, and also told him that he knew Richard had a gun on him and it took balls not to go for it. They talked about the money they could make together in the future all the while Richard was scheming a plan to kill DeMeo ...he would wait for the right opportunity, but he wanted to make some money first.

First piece of business was to pretty much rule the porn industry in New York. With DeMeo's help Richard was pushing massive amounts of pirated porn and Disney movies in the underworld.

BARBARA KUKLINSKI (PEDRICI)

Probably the biggest downfall in Richard's life. Although throughout the relationship together Richard loved Barbara more than anyone he had ever loved before.

Barbara is first introduced into Richard's life at a soda machine at Swiftline Trucking Company where Richard worked. They walked by each other at the machine, said hi to each other and went about there way. They kept running into each other around the workplace, Barbara worked in the office and Richard worked in the loading bay and where ever else his boss could take advantage of his massive frame. One day while Richard and Barbara stopped to talk to each other...their boss, Sol Goldfarb, saw this and got upset. Sol had a crush of sorts on Barbara and didn't like that she was talking to someone as bad as Richard was. This was something that would haunt Barbara for the rest of her life...people telling her to watch out for Richard that he was in with bad people, that he had a bad reputation for being extremely violent. She couldn't see this as Richard had two sides to him...Dr. Jekyll and Mr. Hyde.

Throughout their lives together they had 3 children. Their names are Merrick, Christin, and Dwayne. Because there was so much physical abuse towards Barbara, she would tend to shield Dwayne from seeing it because she did not want to see him grow up to become like Richard the way Richard saw his dad beat his mom growing up. Richard actually was jealous of Dwayne because he was a new male introduced into the environment and Richard being the alpha male that he was didn't like that Barbara gave Dwayne so much attention. Richard never layed a hand on his kids, not even the kids he previously fathered as Barbara told him that if he ever did that she would kill him where he stood!

Regardless of what people thought of Richard Kuklinski, he was always a family man. He kept his personal life (meaning the Mafia, and the fact that he was the biggest distributor of Porn in New York) away from his family because he didn't want to hurt them in anyway. Near the end of his career as a hit man and professional killer he even thought of quitting the business and taking off with his family to a place where no one knew who or what he was.

PETER CALABRO

Roy DeMeo had many of the NYPD cops on his side, and payed them handsomely for looking the other way at certain times or giving up info on cases against him and his crew. One of these cops was Peter Calabro. Peter wanted his wife killed so Roy did it for him. It would be this killing that made DeMeo a fully informed man when it came to busts, and info on anything that DeMeo needed.

Sammy "The Bull" Gravano was a well known man in the Mafia world. He was not a man to mess with being John Gotti's right hand man. When Gravano needed a cop killed he contacted DeMeo and he referred Richard. DeMeo had a feeling it was gonna be Peter Calabro that was going to be the hit, and he wanted nothing to do with it...that and the fact that he was a cop.

Gravano contacted Richard and set up the hit...supplied him with the proper tools and gave him all the info that he needed to know... when and where he was going to be where he was to be hit!

The biggest piece of info that Gravano and DeMeo forgot to mention was that he was a cop.

March 14, 1980 it was cold and snowing. Richard had followed Calabro for a while and learned his routes and followed him that day and finally went ahead of him and parked on the side of the road with his emergency lights on. He knew it would force Peter Calabro to slow down as he was driving by. He waited until Calabro drove directly by his window...with a shotgun ready at window level he fired and killed his mark instantly.

Richard found out the next day that the man he had killed was a cop and that made him more livid than any moment he had ever experienced. He knew that it was then that he had been too careless with his killings.

MISTER SOFTEE

Richard first met him at a hotel in Queens where he was hunting for his next mark on contract. He thought the guy was there after him so he played it cool. Richard walked into a bathroom, stepped up to a urinal and then the guy walked in and stepped up to the urinal directly next to the one the Richard was using...Richard was about ready to battle it out with this guy, he was not taking going to let this make him a victim. It wasn't till they both went to the sinks to wash their hands that Richard talked to him. He asked him if his business was with him and the other guy asked if Richard had business with him, they both said no and that was that. They both knew they were hit men, and only another hit man can see a hit man a mile away.

A few days later Richard sat there in his car with a tranquilizer gun, which was a new weapon that he had introduced into his arsenal of death, when he heard a Mister Softee truck coming around the corner. He flagged the truck down and walked over to get some ice cream. When he got to the window he was in shock to see the ice cream man was the same hit man he ran into at the hotel while Richard was on surveillance. They introduced themselves to each other and this is where we first meet Robert Pronge. They talked shop and Robert told Richard that he used the Mister Softee truck to do surveillance, Richard was impressed. Robert Pronge used to be a Special Forces soldier and had extensive training in Explosives and killing.

It was here that Richard would first be introduced to a weapon he loved to use more than any gun or rat cave he had… POISON. They exchanged methods of offing their marks and became friends then and there. It would prove to be fatal for Robert Pronge.

Richard and Robert would carry their friendship on for a while before Richard thought that Robert was truly crazy. Now I remember writing this earlier but Richard would never kill a woman or child…ever! So what befell Robert Pronge was that he asked Richard to kill his wife and eight-year old son. He told Pronge that he didn't do that kind of thing and that he thought it morally wrong and wouldn't do it. Another issue that upset Richard was that Robert wanted to poison a reservoir that serviced an upstate community with drinking water. He was only doing it because a guy was gonna pay him several thousand dollars to poison a certain family, but Richard though it unnecessary to poison so many people for no reason… all Richard could think about was all the young kids that would die for no reason.

Richard went to see Robert and put an end to his psychopathic tendencies. It was mid-august when Richard crept into Roberts garage where he kept his truck and his killing tools. Richard was always known for having a cat-like walk when he was hunting for his prey. He wanted them to be surprised when they saw him (if they ever did) at the last second of their lives. So Richard walked up on Robert, pulled out his .22 pistol stocked with a silencer and put 5 bullets into Robert Pronge's body. Richard felt sad as he did genuinely like Robert, but didn't trust his psychopathic ways.

THE DOWNFALL OF RICHARD KIKLINSKI

Richard wasn't killing as much as he was laying low from the Peter Calabro killing. He was into a bunch of things…Money Laundering in Zurich and the states, Porn distribution, the odd contract, and he went back to doing breaking and entering.

He was working with a B&E crew that consisted of Al Rinke, Gary Smith, Danny Deppner and Percy House. They scored from houses all over New Jersey. Richard had experience doing B&E's because that is what he did before he started doing big time hits for the Mafia.

One day while robbing a house, Al Rinke was caught and arrested. He tried to make a deal with the police in order for him giving up the rest of his crew. Detective Pat Kane (who had at the time been investigating a string of house robberies) had been questioning him for two-days when he gave up the names: Danny Deppner, Gary Smith, Percy House and the head of the crew…a guy he only knew as "Big Rich", a name that Pat Kane would have come across him from now on!

Percy House was the first to be arrested, and he wouldn't say anything (he knew the reputation of Big Rich). The other guys were no where to be found. Danny Deppner's wife went to the police with details about what they were looking for. She told the police that Danny and Gary were afraid to come out of hiding because they didn't want Richard to kill them. They considered Richard the Devil. She told them of how Richard helped them and put them up somewhere safe away from the cops and told them to stay put till he told them it was okay to come out of hiding.

Richard helped Gary and Danny out by putting them up in a hotel for the time being and helped them with food if they needed it. Richard told them to stay put so they did not get seen. Gary got it into his head to leave for a couple hours to see his daughter. Richard found out about this and decided it was his time to go.

Richard went to a diner near by and bought three hamburgers for each of them to eat. He sprinkled poison on just Gary's burger and took it too them. Richard put on a front to make the guys feel east about him being there and he really wanted to watch the life leave Gary Smith's body. They sat down to eat the burgers and almost instantly the poison worked on Gary. Richard made Danny strangle Gary to finalize his death and make sure there was no coming back for Gary! Richard then had Danny dispose of Gary's body by putting it underneath the bed of the hotel room they were in (this would be a big mistake on Richard's part). Deppner was next. He would eat a roast beef sandwich that was laced with cyanide. You'd think he would have learned not to eat anything Richard brought with him. After Danny ate the sandwich he was almost dead when Richard shot him in the head with a silenced .22.

Richard was also involved with another one of his close personal friends Phil Solimene. Richard never trusted anyone but Barbara, and Phil was the only other person he trusted. Phil was the owner of a pharmacy. Richard knew Phil for many years, and committed many crimes with him including murder.

Phil had gotten himself in some trouble and Pat Kane had approached him to get him to set Richard up. It was either that or serve jail time. So Phil agreed to set up the only man that ever trusted him with his life. An undercover agent was set up as a fake Mafia hit man who's background was a fresh jail releasee that was looking to get back into the game.

Phil would try and get Richard to the store to have coffee and meet his "friend" that he knew would get along well with Richard. Richard was reluctant at first and many times after that. By this time Richard was flying all over the world and laundering money for different big time people.

Finally Richard agreed to come to the store and hang out. Phil had been trying for so long now to get Richard to come to the store and he finally had his chance. Richard for a long time now had wanted to kill Pat Kane because he had been investigating Richard for some time (I am talking a couple years have passed since the Deppner-Smith killings). It started when Pat came to Richards house and stirred up the pot by bringing his personal life to his house, something he had been desperately trying to keep away from his family for so long. Pat was investigating the murders of Danny Deppner and Gary Smith.

When Phil first tried to sell Richard on his new "friend" he told him that he was a big timer with connections to anything Richard needed, drugs, guns, hit men, anything really. So Richard called up Phil and asked to meet with Dominick, the undercover cop. Richard was looking for cyanide. Cyanide specifically because he used it in a spray bottle mixed with a certain amount of cyanide and water. This acted as a deadly spray that when sprayed in someone's face (provided only a little cyanide, just enough to kill a grown man, was used) is would cause them to die instantly and make it look as if they suffered a heart attack.

Richard and Dominick's first encounter was where Richard was looking for some silencers and cyanide. Dom said he would look into getting what Richard needed…knowing that he can't really supply him with any killing agents, he would string him along saying he knew a female DEA officer that could get him the silencers and he knew a guy that could get the cyanide.

Richard Leonard Kuklinski Part Three
THE ICEMAN COMETH
by Aaron Kirkland

Richard became impatient about having to wait so long to get what he needed, and he started to become distant with Dom because of having to wait. Richard was asking all over for cyanide to kill this cop that was a thorn in his side. So finally one day Dom got a hold of Richard and they talked about getting the cyanide for the last time as Dom threw him a curve ball and stated that he was looking for a hit man to do in a loud mouth customer of his that was Rich and he wanted to rob and kill him. Richard said he would be up for it. To keep him strung along Dom asked about ways he could do it and that is what sealed his fate. Richard had been talking to Dom on a bugged phone, all the while Richard was not even suspicious of this. A man that all his life had never said much to people about who he was or what he did told the most unlikely of people that he would take a contract, while being recorded.

THE DAY HIS WORLD CAME CRASHING DOWN

It was almost like a scene right out of Goodfellas. Richard and his family were getting ready for another Kuklinski Christmas when he was contacted by Dom with info on when and where they were gonna rob Dom's customer.

It was set up for early in the morning on a Wednesday. They would meet the buyer and deal business with him in the back of a van. Dom mentioned that every time they meet at this place he orders an egg sandwich. Dom said that he would supply the sandwich and the vial of cyanide, again Richard never thought in his mind that this guy was trying to set him up. All Richard was thinking about was putting a bullet in both Dom and the buyers head. Richard wanted to save the cyanide that was gonna be used in the buyers sandwich for Pat Kane.

December 17, 1986 Richard was off to meet Dom for what was going to be a big day for the Jersey police and the Anti Mafia Justice League.

They met on time that morning and said there hellos. Dom mentioned that eh was going to meet the buyer and bring him to Richard's van where he would test the coke out before he would buy it from Dom. Dom handed Richard the cyanide and the egg sandwich making sure to say everything clearly so the wire he was wearing would pick it up.

Richard was feeling now that he was possibly being set up and said that he was going to go and pick his van up, that he'd be back with the van. Dom kept trying to get Richard to put the cyanide on the egg sandwich there so that they could bust him on the spot, but he didn't. They let him go. Richards plan was he was going to drive off and come back in a different car to see if the buyer really was going to show up…all he would have said was his van wouldn't start so he got a bigger car. Barbara had been feeling ill for a while now, and Richard went to find a pay phone to call her to see how she was doing. They talked for a few minutes and asked if she wanted to go for breakfast, she said yes, and he was on his way home to pick up his wife…the love of his life and the only woman he ever felt true love for. By this time Richard said screw Dom and would call Phil and tell him he thought that Dom was full of it and ask why he would talk so highly of someone so full of it.

By now the cops knew that Plan A was out of the question and they felt they had enough on Richard Kuklinski that they could just go and pick him up on what they had, which was Richard on tape talking about ways he had killed people and various other murder and mob related incidents. Off they went to arrest the mammoth murderer of a man that his neighbours knew as just Rich they family man, not The Iceman worlds greatest hit man.

Richard and Barbara were just getting set in the car to go to breakfast. They were gonna go for breakfast and Richard wanted to take Barbara to the doctors to get looked at because she was still not feeling to well. Richard had no idea what was about to happen next. There were a pile of undercover cars parked up the road monitoring the Kuklinski home. The local cops had no idea what was going on and a neighbour called the local police and they almost ruined the whole operation. Richard and Barbara were in the car and Richard started it and they were off up the street. No sooner did they get up the road when they were surrounded by cops and agents. Richard wanted to grab the gun he had under his seat but was afraid with all the bullets that might be flying around one might hit Barbara.

Richard was ripped from the car, and about to be put to the ground when Barbara was ripped from the car too. This infuriated Richard, he kept shouting to them that she had nothing to do with this and they should leave her alone. But they threw her to the ground and this upset him to the point of no return. It took eight strike force officers to get the hulking man to the ground and handcuffed, all the while thinking about how they had hurt his only true love. He would kill Pat Kane if he died trying.

LONG STORY SHORT…

Barbara was let out but charged with possession of a gun that was found under the seat of the car they were busted in, but the charges were later dropped when they convicted Richard. Richard was charged with nineteen felony offences and 4+ murder charges were added to his list of charges. He was sentenced to 2 life sentences as they could only prove that he killed Smith-Deppner, and Louis Masgay. More can be learned about Richards trial and the actual numbers of charges he ended up with by reading the book "The Iceman: Confessions Of A Mafia Contract Killer" by Philip Carlo, or by searching for his name on the internet. Richard Kuklinski has said in later interviews that he killed 200+ people. Some for fun, some for money, some were hobos he was trying new weapons out on, some where heads of Mafia families. He was claimed to have been part of the Jimmy Hoffa killing, which to this day had been unconfirmed. Right before Richards death on Sunday, March 5, 2006 of unknown causes, he tried to bring down Sammy "The Bull" Gravano (as he was the one who had Richard unknowingly kill a cop) for the killing of Peter Calabro. When Richard died all charges were dropped against Gravano and the secret of the Hoffa killing would be voided, and never brought up again. Richard just before he died was paranoid that someone was poisoning him and that was the reason he was getting sick. He could never get anyone to believe his complaints and no evidence of what he died of has yet to be given to the public.

Why Do Women Kill?
By Lorenzo Garza

It is a common misconception that serial murder is a boy's club. But with the not-so recent release of "Monster" people have a much larger misconception; that female serial murder is a new phenomenon. Though Aileen Wuronos has received the most media coverage and deemed "America's First Female Serial Killer", this couldn't be farthest from the truth. There have been several cases of female killers long before the term "Serial Killer" was born. So what makes Wuronos so different? I believe that the methods, victims and motive that Wuronos selected did not fit normal female characteristics not only for serial murder, but in general.

Method: Most female serial killers who act alone, like Belle Gunness or Mary Ann Cotton, fall into the category of poisoners. What makes Wuronos interesting to the general public, I suppose, is that she used a gun. Comparing a female killer's pathology to a male is to compare basic female to male character traits. Using a gun or knife is a very violent, phallic way of showing dominance to one's victim. So, in turn Wuronos established violent , masculine behavior unlike her previous female counter parts. It is a natural instinct for a female to nurture, hence, poisoning a loved one's food.

Victims: One of the most important differences in the pattern between male and female murderers are victims. Although it is a common trait amongst all killers to murder people they are familiar with, (Like Thomas Harris' infamous character Hannibal Lecter says, "He covets what he sees everyday.") but the female killer seems to murder people they actual care about, people very close to them. Serial murder should be closely compared in all regard to dating. The biggest difference of course, the wanted outcome is murder and not just sex. Unlike a male, who can have sex with (or kill) as many anonymous partners (victims) as they can, a female's pathology tends to take time to get to know their partners (victims). Whether the woman is a poisoner, Black Widow, or a women with P_____ Syndrome, the need to know their victims on a personal level seems to be there. The way a women will associate sex with love and family, the perverse of that manor of thinking to a psychopath is to associate murder with love and family.

art by jack malebranche

WANTED BY THE FBI
INTERSTATE FLIGHT - MURDER

THEODORE ROBERT BUNDY

DESCRIPTION

Born November 24, 1946, Burlington, Vermont (not supported by birth records); Height, 5'11" to 6'; Weight, 145 to 175 pounds; Build, slender, athletic; Hair, dark brown, collar length; Eyes, blue; Complexion, pale/sallow; Race, white; Nationality, American; Occupations, bellboy, busboy, cook's helper, dishwasher, janitor, law school student, office worker, political campaign worker, psychiatric social worker, salesman, security guard; Scars and Marks, mole on neck, scar on scalp; Social Security Number used, 533-44-4655; Remarks, occasionally stammers when upset; has worn glasses, false mustache and beard as disguise in past; left-handed; can imitate British accent; reportedly physical fitness and health enthusiast.

CRIMINAL RECORD

Bundy has been convicted of aggravated kidnaping.

CAUTION

BUNDY, A COLLEGE-EDUCATED PHYSICAL FITNESS ENTHUSIAST WITH A PRIOR HISTORY OF ESCAPE, IS BEING SOUGHT AS A PRISON ESCAPEE AFTER BEING CONVICTED OF KIDNAPING AND WHILE AWAITING TRIAL INVOLVING A BRUTAL SEX SLAYING OF A WOMAN AT A SKI RESORT. HE SHOULD BE CONSIDERED ARMED, DANGEROUS AND AN ESCAPE RISK.

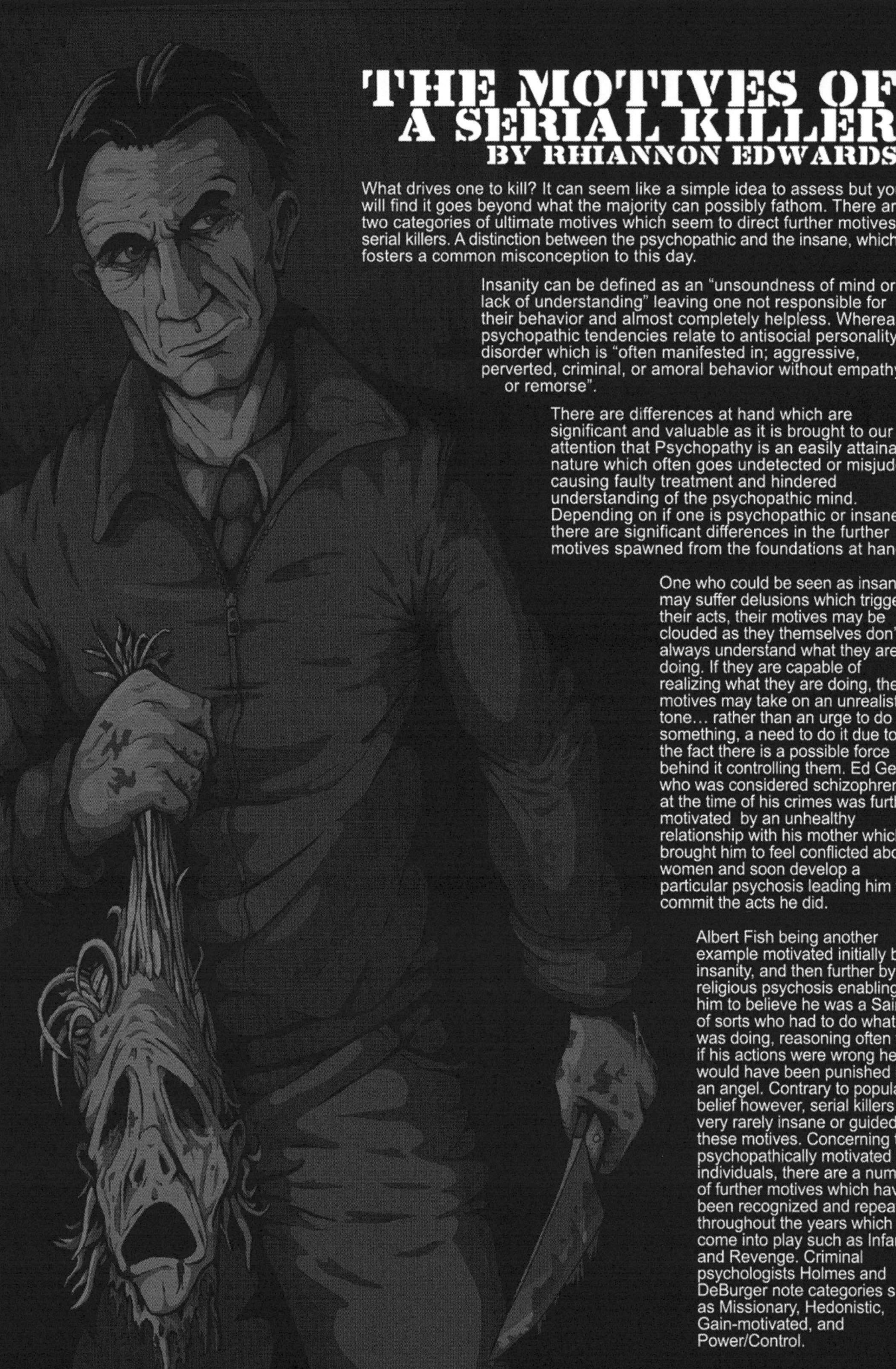

THE MOTIVES OF A SERIAL KILLER
BY RHIANNON EDWARDS

What drives one to kill? It can seem like a simple idea to assess but you will find it goes beyond what the majority can possibly fathom. There are two categories of ultimate motives which seem to direct further motives of serial killers. A distinction between the psychopathic and the insane, which fosters a common misconception to this day.

Insanity can be defined as an "unsoundness of mind or lack of understanding" leaving one not responsible for their behavior and almost completely helpless. Whereas psychopathic tendencies relate to antisocial personality disorder which is "often manifested in; aggressive, perverted, criminal, or amoral behavior without empathy or remorse".

There are differences at hand which are significant and valuable as it is brought to our attention that Psychopathy is an easily attainable nature which often goes undetected or misjudged causing faulty treatment and hindered understanding of the psychopathic mind. Depending on if one is psychopathic or insane, there are significant differences in the further motives spawned from the foundations at hand.

One who could be seen as insane may suffer delusions which trigger their acts, their motives may be clouded as they themselves don't always understand what they are doing. If they are capable of realizing what they are doing, their motives may take on an unrealistic tone… rather than an urge to do something, a need to do it due to the fact there is a possible force behind it controlling them. Ed Gein who was considered schizophrenic at the time of his crimes was further motivated by an unhealthy relationship with his mother which brought him to feel conflicted about women and soon develop a particular psychosis leading him to commit the acts he did.

Albert Fish being another example motivated initially by insanity, and then further by a religious psychosis enabling him to believe he was a Saint of sorts who had to do what he was doing, reasoning often that if his actions were wrong he would have been punished by an angel. Contrary to popular belief however, serial killers are very rarely insane or guided by these motives. Concerning the psychopathically motivated individuals, there are a number of further motives which have been recognized and repeated throughout the years which come into play such as Infamy and Revenge. Criminal psychologists Holmes and DeBurger note categories such as Missionary, Hedonistic, Gain-motivated, and Power/Control.

serial killers are hedonistic, killing for sheer pleasure and often becoming addicted to this pleasure which fuels their continuation of murder, this includes killers such as Dennis Rader (the BTK strangler) who vastly enjoyed the hunt as well as the kill of his victims, and Jeffrey Dahmer who was satisfied with what he could do with the body after his victim was killed.

There are those who are influenced heavily by media depictions of serial killers and who grow to obtain a deep interest in them to an extreme point where they find they would like to achieve the success of a killer they have heard about. They often crave the fame or rather infamy which goes along with the act they commit, and they are motivated by this thoroughly as well as the power they seem to have during the process. Power and control, as mentioned, can take on a level of it's own concerning types who seek to feel something they may have been restricted from at another time in their lives… or simply for those who dream of obtaining the kind of power others possess regularly in what seems to be an easier form. The power itself can prove an addicting motive and is often cited as one that a high number of killers possess during their "reign of terror".

The motives of a serial killer vary, and to most they confuse, but it is significant to note that a lot of motivations present are an average phenomenon seen amongst society but often simply expressed in different, more accepted ways. These motives presented, aside from other factors contributing, tend to be the main trigger in what allows any human being to kill.

ARTWORK BY PETE BERG

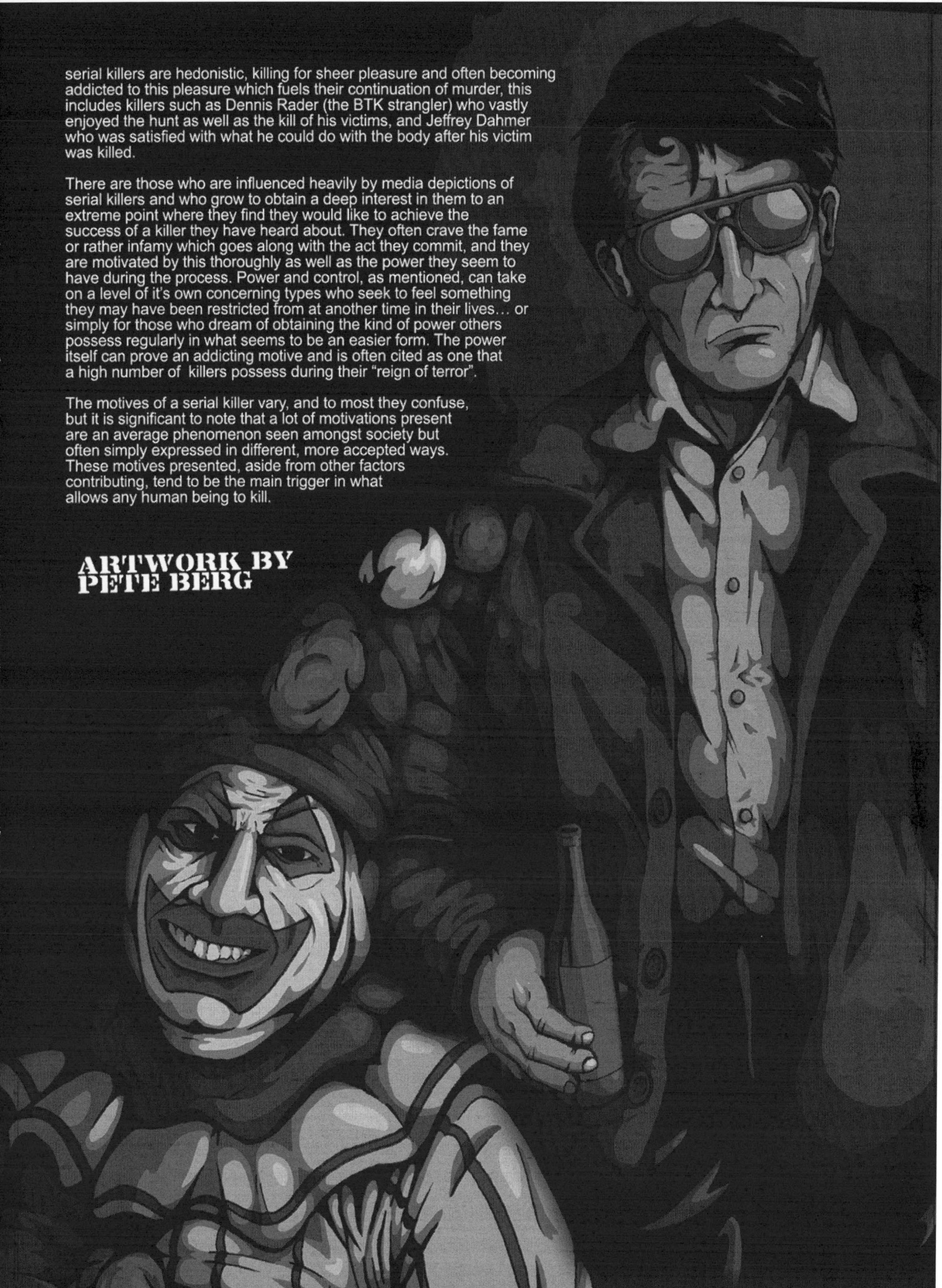

TO: JAMES GILKS
FROM: LEE BELCHER.

///

THIS IS KENNY CALIHAN SENDING THIS MESSAGE TO YOU VIA LEE BELCHER WHO IS MY SPOKESPERSON AT MY REQUEST.

IVE KNOWN CM, CORONA, SIRHAN AND ALOT OTHERS OVER THE YRS - AS IVE KNOWN THE ABOVE SINCE ERA - 1991-1992. I KNOW ALOT HIGH PROFILE CALIFORNIA STATE PRISONERS. I WAS HERE IN 1999 WHEN THE NOVEL "TAMING THE BEAST" WAS WRITTEN, ABOUT CM.

IVE DID A "THESIS" ON CM, CORONA, SIRHAN, BACK IN 1998-1999., DUE TO THE FACT JAMES - THAT IVE BEEN THRU (6) FRIVOLUS SO-CALLED INVESTIGATIONS OVER THE YRS - THAT DID NOT PAN OUT, AND THAT BEING MYSELF AND CM.

I HAVE ALOT REAL GOOD STORIES THAT WOULD BE USEFUL FOR YOUR MAGAZINE, AND SOME WAY OUT STORIES. IM HOUSED IN THE STATES ONLY HIGH-PROFILE UNIT AT CORCORAN STATE PRISON. - AND 95% OF THE INMATES HOUSED IN MY UNIT ARE SERVING LIFE WITH NO PAROLE (LWOP) FOR MURDER(S), CONTRACT KILLINGS ETC ETC.

FEEL FREE TO CONTACT ME AT YOUR SOONEST, AND ANY THING YOU MAY NEED TO KNOW - FEEL FREE TO ASK.

YOU CAN ALSO CONTACT LEE BELCHER IF NEEDED, WHO WILL CONTACT ME VIA THE MAIL ALSO.

THANKS FOR YOUR AMPLE TIME. HOPE TO HEAR FROM YOU SOON.

SINCERELY
KENNY CALIHAN - F17158
PHU. 4A4R62
P.O. BOX - 3476
CORCORAN - CA 93212-3476

8-17-08 -

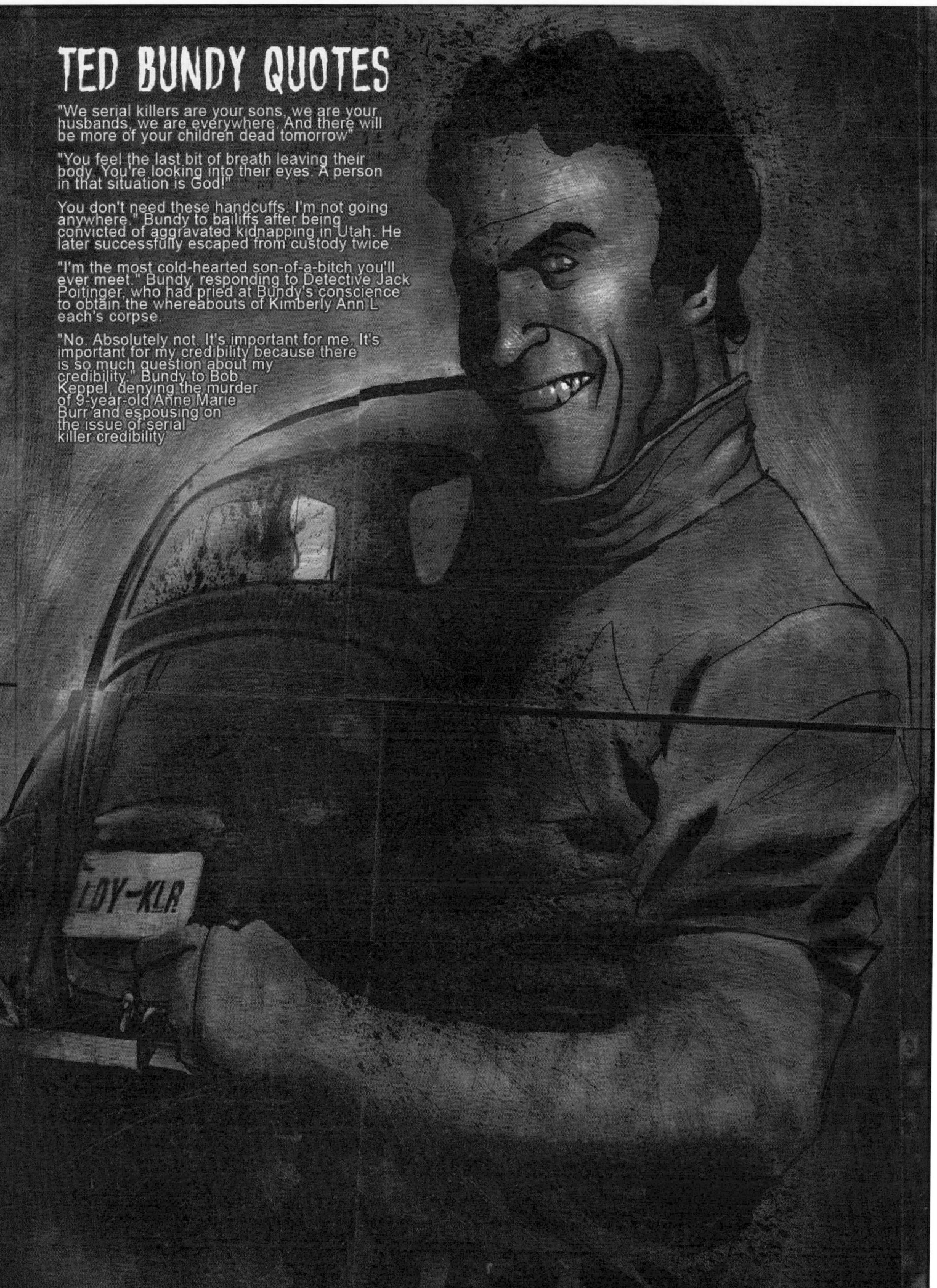

Charles Starkweather
by Faith LeAnne

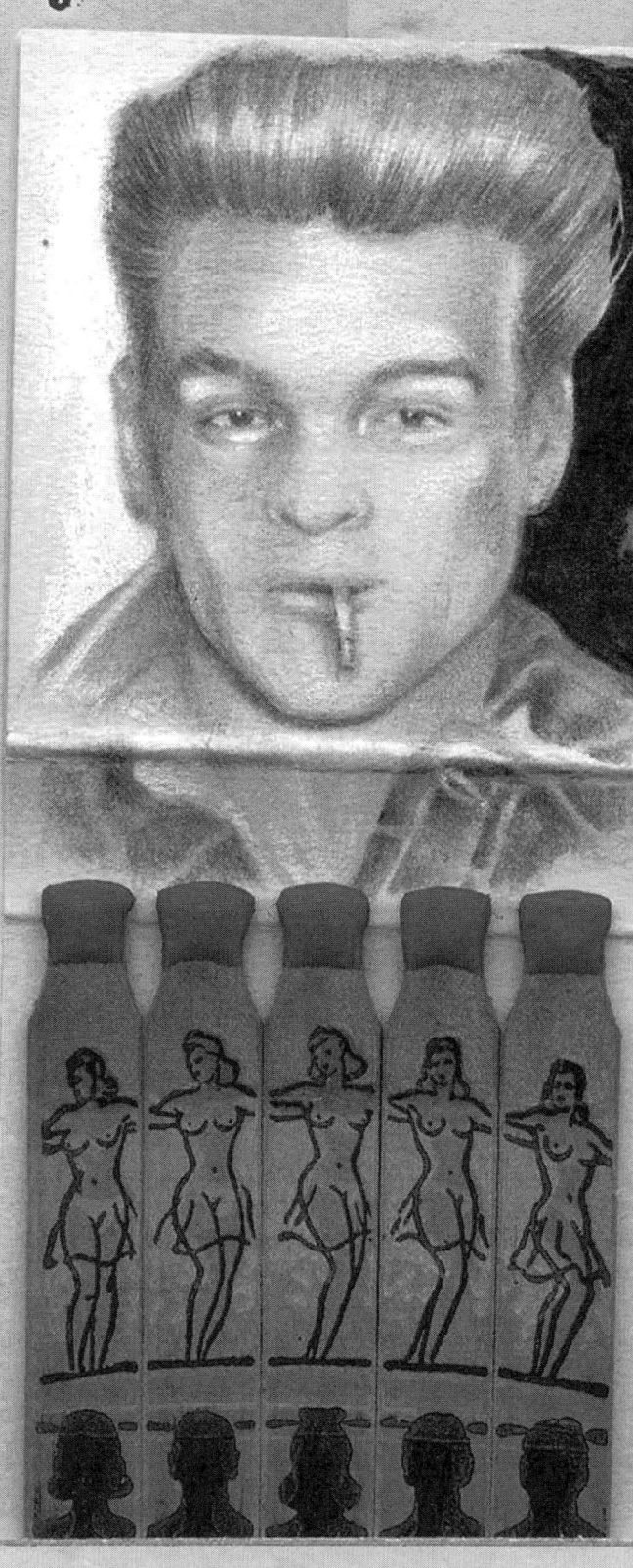

ARTWORK BY JASON DAQUINO

Lincoln, Nebraska...small town. In 1957 a Tornado hit, but it wasn't that that was buzzing up all the newspapers.... Charles Raymond Steakweather, had decided that year, was going to be HIS year. That it would be the year everyone remembered him, and until this day, his and Caril Ann Fugate's mass murder spree is considered the second worse thing to happen in Nebraska. It was next to only the Great Depression. Charles Starkweather, wasn't the child of a one parent home. He was he abused. He was not a child to witness abuse at the hands of anyone in his family. If anything the Starkweather's were considered very well adjusted members of the community. They weren't rich, but weren't destitute, either. His parents, Helen and Guy, raised two children born before Charles and four more after him. He could be thought of as a middle child. This is the only thing found to perhaps make his a little out of place in his home but at that time many children came from large families who were not well to do. Neither of those factors led to what Charles would eventually do. From an early age, Charles knew he was different. He was born bow-legged, and had a minor speech problem. Those imperfections caused lots of torment in his early years, contributing to his learning that he could be either a sheep, and get eaten by the wolf or or the wolf. Charles eventually opted to be the Wolf. Charles decided that there was no point in applying himself in school. He eventually stopped trying all together, causing him to labeled a slow learner. He could have possibly had some other minor mental issues, that were recognized by the fact that he two almost distinct and different sides of his personality could be displayed. At times Charles could be very sweet and kind, soft spoken and almost what one would call a gentle person. With the next flick of his wrist, he could unleash, violence at a feverish pitch. It didn't take those who irked him long to find out that you don't mess with Charlie Starkweathe. In fact, it was better to stay out of his way completely, because he was as unpredictable as a rattlesnake. Charles once commented that there was nothing more he hated than "those" people. Those people was anyone who had more money than he had. Those who had a better job than he had. Anyone with a chip on their shoulder were one of those people and they tended to immediately transform Charles from a sheep to a wolf. The wolf, he became was done taking every one's shit. Charles delighted in knocking all those people who put themselves up so high, right back down. He became known as a bully and by the time he went to high school education had became a complete loss cause. Charles developed other problems beside his behavior and it is believe that something may have effected his sight. He started to believe he had no purpose in the world. He mulled over the idea that there wasn't anything, to live for, to die for? If that was true his conclusion was why be here and he felt that only James Dean, in the movies understood, him. Starkweather took to Dean's character instantly. Dean understood him, Dean knew what it was like. Starkweather knew he now had a purpose. He has someone to look up to because he never really took to his father. James Dean, on the screen, was finally someone Charles could identify with. Charles understood, he was to be a rebel. But Charles, unlike Dean's character had a cause. It was clear that Charles had no problems with his vision when it came to one thing Caril Ann Fugate. Caril, at thirteen, was instantly smitten with Charles when she met with him though a friend. Although she was much younger him, Charles felt an instant connection between the two. It seemed like Caril Ann understood him. She quickly became completely absorbed with Charles' Dean mannerisms, and if she couldn't have Dean, the teenage girl's heart throb of the day she could have Charles, and he wanted her, Caril was in love. Caril Ann's past it mirrored Charles's in almost every way. Caril was not very bright and had never really applied herself in school. She had beauty and was well liked by her schoolmates. At home she was berated for not doing better in school and was often called stupid. When she met Charles that change because he made her feel smart. Charles also made her feel beautiful, Charles became her world. Charles had never felt what love was before. He had never felt close with his parents, even though there was never a reason not to. He had one close friend, but he had never known real love, until he met Caril Ann. Just as he was her world, she was his. He had never experienced love's warm feeling. In fact, had he felt anythingsoft, only hardness, the brashness, the torment the he belived the world had given him, but Caril gave him the greatest gift of all. love. He felt blessed. Caril Ann's parents weren't so accepting of the relationship They thought Charles a punk, with no direction He was not good enough for their daughter. Their blatant disregard of him, only made her love him more. As their relationship grew, Charles started to see Caril Ann as the only good thing in his life. He started to love her more and more, and he hated society to an increasingly equal degree. All of humanity became Charles' enemy, and he was slowly growing tired of it. After quitting school at sixteen, Charles shifted between jobs. He had little or no money, but this wasn't a problem for the Charles and Caril, as long as they were together, however in November Charles went into a local gas station, and wanted to purchases Caril Ann a stuffed bear. He had no money and tried getting the bear on credit. Charles was turned down. He returned to the car defeated, and the last shotgun shell, fell into place, in his life. In Charles' mind, that gas station attendant had to die. The attendant stood beteen the happiness of Charles's and his girl, and no one messed with Charlies's girl. He returned later on that same night, He knew what he planned to do and he just needed enough time to work up the nerve to do it.

Years of violence was one thing, putting a shotgun up to someone was something entirely different. His thinking pumped him up. All of the things that had happened to him through the years, all the names he had been called, all the people who had picked on him, this was their fault he decided, They made him do this. This wasn't his fault, this was all them he justified as he manifested years of hate into one act of ruthless retaliation. Drained of remorse Charles picked up the shotgun and went inside. He didn't kill the gas station attendant there. He decided he would make too much of a scene, leave too much evidence, maybe the shot would be to loud, so instead he had the attendant drive with Charles driving sitting, to a deserted area. Once there Charles thought about his actions again. A hint of remorse went through his mind, but it stopped short of reversing his decision. When the attendant, Robert Colvert, realized he was going to die, he put up a fight. In the struggle, Colvert got shot. With a bullet already in the attendant, Charles simply finished the job and in execution style, putting the gun to the back of his head, Charles popped off a final shot into Robert. Having the taste of blood, it would be only a matter of time before he would kill again, Charles decided that nothing and no one would ever boss him around again. He was now a god, untouchable. Charles told Caril Ann right away, but professed he had done this as an act to prove his love for her, the naive teen, or perhaps, unfeeling one, simply took it as an undying declaration of their bond. They knew now that there was nothing that could ever tear them apart. On January 28th, just a month after murdering Robert Colvert, Charles went to Caril Ann's parents home, and waited for her to return. A heated argument started between Caril's stepfather and Charles. As it became more heated, her enraged stepfather told Charles that he wasn't planning on letting Charles come around anymore. Caril's her mother had also had enough of the affair, and after hearing local town gossip, about how Charles supposedly had said he was going to make Caril Ann his wife, and that she was pregnant by his child. Caril Ann's stepfather struck Charles, a stupid mistake, on his part. Never parting with his twelve gauge shotgun he brought it up, and shot Caril's stepfather. Caril's mother then got up, and he used the butt end of the gun to dispatch her, hitting her over and over again. When Caril Ann arrived home, she found Charles standing over her two year old sister, and what happens next is uncertain. Caril claims that he fatally strangled the child, and he claimed she beat the child to death. Whatever the case, after her parents were dispensed, they proceeded to have there own honeymoon. They indulged on all the minor delights the Fugate's had to offer. Watching television, and eating whatever was in the home. Caril Ann, quickly acted and put a sign up on the door written to keep away noisy neighbors, that read "Whole Family, sick with flu." Charles and Caril took the bodies and moved them from inside the house. Caril's little sister Ann sister was put in a box. Her parents were put in the outhouse, in the back. Charles It would only be a matter of time before there happy home was disrupted. He fled with Caril Ann, in an attempt to outrun the police. People got suspicious after not seeing the family for a while. They called the police and when they got there they quickly realized something was not right. A police bulletin was put out for Charles Starkweather, and Caril Ann Fugate. The duo had driven to an unsuspecting friend of Starkweather's family. Charles and Caril murdered the friend and took shelter for the night in his farm. They soon realized that there car was going to be a big give away. Charles decided to do what must be done, and just point it out as a sacrifice for love, he left his car on the side of the road, and hid the weapons the both had on them, hitching a ride with a couple only a couple who were just a few years younger then him. Charles didn't waste much time. Getting right to the point. While Caril Ann sat with smiles and grins, she was watching Charles dominate the scene. To her it was like a movie, and she was dating the star. Charles forced them back towards the farm where Charles and Caril had spent in the night before. He got them both out of the car, and after taking their money, he shot Robert Jensen. Caril Ann screamed gleefully as Charles shot him, and then narrowed her eyes, as she focused on the woman. She looked cold and cruel, then she smiled, and waited for Charles to shoot her. She was so excited by Charles killing men. Her only exception until now was the killing of her mother. Caril now wanted the woman dead. She thought, what if this woman wanted her Charles? They should have ran. They should have went somewhere, anywhere, far away, but instead Charles insisted, that they go back into town, not thinking that any one would be looking for them. This was a very stupid that eventually led to their capture. Charles had worked a lot of jobs. It made him affluent with the different areas, and it was very easy for him to know the rich part of town. Charles hated the rich people, with all there money. He came from nothing, so it was not by chance that he chose a house that he knew was upper class. He stopped with Caril Ann and entered demanding breakfast. Before Charles and Caril left there would be three more dead woman: Clara Ward, the maid, Lillian Fencl, and the master of the house C. Lauer Ward. Caril Ann was asleep on the couch for most of this killing, but bothered to get up to complain that they were making to much noise. To please Caril Ann, Charles tied the maid to a bed violently stabbing her death, after taking care of Clara, who had the nerve to arm herself in an attempt to shoot him. Charles stabbed Clara so violently and so many times that they could not count the number of entry wounds. When C.Lauer Ward unexpectedly arrived home, he got little out of his mouth before Charles, already angry with the situation, shot him with the already loaded gun. They took Ward's car with anything that looked like it had value and stayed for a day of rest and sleep. Starkweather & Fugate's spree was coming to a violent end. The law didn't look kindly on such a pro-dominate member of society being killed. Even the governor got involved. His orders pointed toward Charles and Caril being taken down immediately. Charles stopped along the highway, after hearing about themselves on the radio. He knew they'd all be looking for the car that they were in. He couldn't have that. Charles saw someone who had pulled over to the side of the road and who had fallen asleep. Charles knocked on his window and told the man they were going to trade cars, When they man didn't answer and attempted to go back to sleep, Charles, shot him. Caril Ann in the backseat with the dead body still in the car, Charles couldn't figure out how to release the emergency break. A young man stopped on the side of the road, after seeing the young couple thinking that he may be of some help. After asking what the trouble was, Starkweather was running out of time and patients, he told the man to release the emergency break or he'd kill him. The man made like he was going to do as he said and then started an altercation with Starkweather, trying to wrestle the gun away from him. Sadly for Starkweather this was not his day, as a deputy Sheriff came by and stopped. Immediately Caril Ann jumped out of the car, and ran towards the officer, the jig was up, and she didn't want to go down, she knew Charlie would, and she wasn't about to as well. Charles grabbed the Packard and started driving, with police chasing him. The police shot at him, and broke the glass out of the window of the back of his car, causing a bullet, or a piece of glass to whizz right by his head, Charles stopped the car, immediately. The media ate up Starkweather. He was all they could have wanted, a serial killer, with the looks of Dean with an under aged lover. It was a case that the State was completely fascinated with but no more fasicinated than they were with Starkweather himself. He was a man of few words. He had little or no remorse, for the crimes he had committed. He had no motive, only that, the more he saw people, the more he started to hate them. Caril Ann tried in vain to save herself, saying she was a hostage of Charles and that she only did as told. For fear he's hurt her family, she went along but the only problem was that she had watched him massacre them, leaving her little creditability, if any. Charles Starkweather was tried on the 5th on May, 1958. It didn't take long for the jury to return with a guilty verdict in which the jury specifically asked for the death penalty. Charles Starkweather was killed, in the electric chair, on the 5th of June, 1959. Caril Ann was only fourteen, when captured, and given a life sentence, Charles, was less than loving when he found out that she blamed him for the whole thing and he confirmed theta she could have escaped anytime if she wanted to do so. Caril was paroled in 1976 and changed her name. What makes a serial killer? Head Trauma? Abuse? Being Bullied? What's the difference between me, you, or Charles Starkweather, and Caril Ann? I'd say it's only a loaded shotgun and a pack of shells.

Serial killer quotes

"I didn't want to hurt them, I only wanted to kill them."
- David Berkowitz

"What I did was not for sexual pleasure. Rather it brought me some peace of mind."
- Andrei Chikatilo

"When this monster entered my brain, I will never know, but it is here to stay. How does one cure himself? I can't stop it, the monster goes on, and hurts me as well as society. Maybe you can stop him. I can't."
- BTK

"I sat down to think things over a bit. While I was sitting there, a little kid about eleven or twelve years old came bumming around. He was looking for something. He found it too. I took him out to a gravel pit about one quarter miles away. I left him there, but first committed sodomy on him and then killed him. His brains were coming out of his ears when I left him, and he will never be any deader."
- Carl Panzram

"I just wanted to see how it felt to shoot Grandma."
- Edmund Kemper

"As I grew up I realized, though imperfectly, that I was different from other people, and that the way of life in my home was different from that in the homes of others....This stimulated me to introspection and strange mental questionings."
- John Haigh

"After my head has been chopped off, will I still be able to hear, at least for a moment, the sound of my own blood gushing from my neck? That would be the best pleasure to end all pleasure."
- Peter Kurten

"When I'm hurting somebody, I want to see them. I want to crash their skull. And I want to get them with that knife. And I like to hear the sounds of the pounding. And I like to see the breathing when I'm killing them. And when I'm killing somebody, I don't care I'm killing them."
- Sean Hanify

"We all go a little mad sometimes."
- Ted Bundy

VICTIM OF CHOICE: by Jessica Fairfield

A killers victim of choice is a very significant piece of info. It can tell us much about the type of person a killer feels rage against or other vital facts such as a killers sexual orientation. In most cases the victim of choice is found before the killer is found. Therefore, we must learn as much as we can from the body or bodies found.

Many times killers will target family members or close friends after an insurance policy has been set in place. Or, maybe just for some valuables or cash the victim has on hand. Mary Ann Cotton was famous for killings like these. Her victims were poisoned after a hefty insurance policy was all set. There are other ways a killer can benefit from the bodies of their victims. William Burke and William Hare were a killer team. Their victims were anyone who so happened to stay at Burkes Inn. The bodies were then sold to the black market for a profit. In a similar case Fritz Haarmann and homosexual lover/ partner in crime would also sell the bodies to the black market, not to mention the fact that they would also sell the clothes from their victims. H H Holmes was even known to occasionally sell the bodies of his victims to medical schools.

Prostitutes are constantly showing up dead or missing at the hands of serial killers. There are many reasons serial killers target prostitutes. First off they can go unnoticed and therefore lesson the chance of a killer being caught as in the case of Jack the Ripper. They are an easy target because they are willing to get into cars with strange men. They can heighten ones sexual drive and fantasies begin, but when it comes to a serial killer and their deviant sexual fantasies this can be a very dangerous thing. For other killers though it is not the sex drive but the fact of what these women are. When one takes on the perception that all women are evil, prostitutes become the lowest of low. The killer may or may not be aroused by the kill. Usually if they are it proves to further enrage and frustrate him. In his eyes he's giving the bitch what she deserved or ridding the world of its filth.

Perhaps the hardest type to cope with though are child killers. Indeed to cross such a line is beyond all normal thinking. Most have a sexual attraction to children and were sexually abused themselves as a child. Power and fear play a huge part in their murders. Child killers do tend to be the sickest of them all. Take for example Albert Fish, who is suspected of killing as many as 100 kids. In one case he took the body of a 10 year old girl home, cut it up, cooked it up in a stew, and ate it for the next nine days. Afterwards he felt compelled to write her mother and tell her how sweet and tender her daughters ass had tasted.

Almost every homosexual serial killer has a similar story. They were all brought up in abusive homes where their manhood was endlessly bashed. Some were dressed as girls and paraded around in drag, others were called sissies and took many beatings for not acting like a man. When his son begins to realize he is homosexual he is embarrassed and confused. Some such as John Wayne Gacy were so confused and determined to keep their secret that they will date and marry woman and in Gacy's case even have children. It becomes so important to them that they kill the men they sleep with. On the other hand sometimes its because the victim aroused a side of the killer that they have not yet faced. Because of this the man loses his life. Still, a part of all this is the ability to kill another person. In heterosexual killings and homosexual killings as well sometimes it is all about power over another life or a desire to have sex with a corpse.

ART BY CHRIS CARPENTER

art by johnny machine

Indeed this was the issue Denis Nilsen faced. Had he been heterosexual his victims would have been women. It could not have changed the fact that he wanted his sexual partner to be dead.

Sad but true, looks, personality and popularity play a huge part in a persons teenage years. During high school if one lacks all three of the above mentioned characteristics he/she is likely to have a rough four years in high school. They will be mocked and rejected by everyone. They spend every Friday and Saturday night at home and prom night as well, sulking all the way. Many have dealt with this ordeal and come out as doctors or lawyers, but others find it too much to handle. The constant rejection from their peers molds the Nerd into a vengeful killer. The Columbine shootings should just about sum it up for you. Those were spree killers though, not serial killers like Joel Rifken. After years of ridicule he turned to prostitutes. Some made the deal and went on their merry way while others were slaughtered. Other killers decide to select a woman of higher stature. These killers can be very picky about their victim of choice. Some will select a woman and stalk her for weeks or months before making the kill. Others like Ted Bundy will go out in seek of a victim with a certain trait. Almost all of Ted's victims had long, dark hair parted in the center, a striking resemblance to one of Ted's ex girlfriends.

Many times however there is no discernable pattern amongst a killers hit list. They seem to just explode suddenly without warning and kill whoever was there when it happened. Sometimes its just circumstance. Jesse Pomroy killed mostly boys but when he found himself alone with a young girl the opportunity was too good to let it go. H H Holmes would place ads in the newspaper, advertising rooms for rent. Whoever showed up was killed. Richard Ramirez would search for an unlocked door or window. Whoever was inside became his next victim.

Then there are the rare cases. A killer selects their victims for some meaningless reason, or a totally insane one. Elizabeth Bathory killed virgins because she thought their blood could keep her young. Earl Leonard Nelson was in the habit of meeting up with landladies, feigning interest in moving into one of her apartments. At the best moment he'd pounce on her. Bobby Joe Long would respond to ads selling used furniture or other items. If he found a women home alone she'd be killed.

There are also medical monsters. These killers are preoccupied with human anatomy in a very sadistic way. Most will attend and/or graduate a medical school. Once in practice they experiment their atrocities on their patients. Their victims will always be someone who went to them for help. Jane Toppan is a well known medical monster who was able to get away with her crimes for years. Her victims were poisoned for her appetite of death and her curiosity of watching people die.

Weapon of choice has a lot to do with the victim of choice as well. Almost every killer who used poison was the type who was killing for financial gain or just because that particular person was a nuisance. A blunt object suggest a more personal grudge, such as women haters. An object close by is selected as the weapon in the heat of the moment. This points to the fact that the killer is disorganized because they did not carry their own weapon. It also shows that the urges to kill were abrupt not intended and planed. They did not stalk their victims, they just happened to be in the wrong place at the wrong time. If a killer chooses a knife for a weapon it shows blood lust and sometimes an interest in human anatomy. These are the guys who disembowel their victims. A shooter is more thorough. He is concerned very much with when, how, and where a shooting will take place, not so much so with who ends up as the next victims though. For Berkowitz the shooting had to be done at night and at a lovers lane. Those who choose to strangle their victims, as the Boston strangler did, are usually the type who want to commit atrocities on the body afterwards. A stranglers work has just begun after murder has taken place. Typically their victims are prostitutes or someone they were able to lure into some shadows, away from public eye.

Still there are some killers who would rather use their bare hands. These killers like the ones who bludgeon their victims are acting on sudden impulses brought about by some strange thing. Or, there could be a personal grudge involved with specific types of people IE: drug addicts or homosexuals. Their victims are again merely unlucky people who ended up in the wrong place at the wrong time.

Of course this is all based off of most cases. There will always be serial killers who cannot be placed in one box or another with a label. For every person there is a serial killer who would want them dead. Its impossible to know what to expect from a person who is capable of serial murder. But, when a killer is on the loose everyone around them is at their mercy.

GONE FISHING

The trial of Albert Fish for the premeditated murder of Grace Budd began on Monday, March 11, 1935, in White Plains, New York with Frederick P. Close as judge, and Chief Assistant District Attorney, Elbert F. Gallagher, as the prosecuting attorney. James Dempsey was Fish's defense attorney. The trial lasted for ten days. Fish pleaded insanity, and claimed to have heard voices from God telling him to kill children. Several psychiatrists testified about Fish's sexual fetishes, including coprophilia, urophilia, pedophilia and masochism, but there was disagreement as to whether these activities meant he was insane. The defense's chief expert witness was Fredric Wertham, a psychiatrist with a focus on child development who conducted psychiatric examinations for the New York criminal courts; Wertham stated that Fish was insane. Another defense witness was Mary Nicholas, Fish's 17-year-old stepdaughter. She described how Fish taught her and her brothers and sisters a "game" involving overtones of masochism and child molestation. The jury found him to be sane and guilty, and the judge ordered the death sentence. and Chief Assistant District Attorney, Elbert F. Gallagher, as the prosecuting attorney. James Dempsey was Fish's defense attorney. The trial lasted for ten days. Fish pleaded insanity, and claimed to have heard voices from God telling him to kill children. Several psychiatrists testified about Fish's sexual fetishes, including coprophilia, urophilia, pedophilia and masochism, but there was disagreement as to whether these activities meant he was insane. The defense's chief expert witness was Fredric Wertham, a psychiatrist with a focus on child development who conducted psychiatric examinations for the New York criminal courts; Wertham stated that Fish was insane.

ICIC/NCIC ON FILE
RELEASE DATE-12/20/78

WANTED

FPC CLASS ON FILE
NATIONWIDE ALERT ISSUED

CHICAGO POLICE DEPARTMENT
HOMICIDE DIVISION
JOHN WAYNE GACY

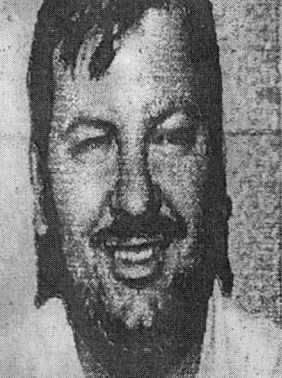

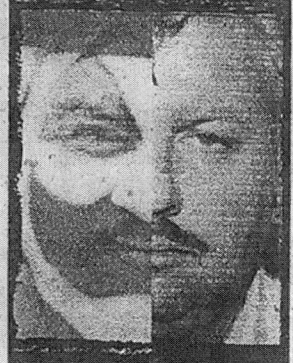

THE "KILLER" CLOWN
FUGITIVE FROM JUSTICE

DESCRIPTION

Date of Birth	March 17, 1942	Hair	Salt & Pepper
Place of Birth	Chicago, Illinois	Eyes	Brown
Height	5' 8"	Complexion	Ruddy
Build	Heavy	Nationality	U. S. Citizen
Occupation	Contractor	Scars	Appendix

Remarks John Wayne Gacy is currently being sought by the **Chicago Metropolitan Police Department** for questioning into the disappearance of several victims of violent **homicide**. Direct any and all inquiries to the **Homicide Investigations Unit** of your local **Chicago P. D.** or any law enforcement agency concerning this subject.

CAUTION

Although **John Wayne Gacy** has no known prior history of violent criminal activity, subject should be considered **extremely dangerous & volatile** due to the nature of the crimes for which he is currently being sought as a suspect. Make no attempt to apprehend, or assist this individual. He is physically imposing & could, if provoked, cause substantial harm to members of the general public who may provoke him.

RELEASED by CHICAGO POLICE DEPARTMENT HOMICIDE INVESTIGATION UNIT

MAKING A LIVING 1 BY CHRIS BARTHOLOMEW

Even serial killers have to eat, pay bills, and live somewhere. Here is a list of some serial killers and what they did to support their 'habit'.

Herbert Richard "Herb" Baumeister

Herbert Richard "Herb" Baumeister (April 7, 1947 - July 3, 1996) was the founder of the thrift store chain Sav-a-Lot and an alleged serial killer from suburban Westfield, Indiana. In 1988 Baumeister founded the Sav-a-lot chain. The chain was a success and Baumeister became very rich. He also began spending a lot of time in homosexual bars in Indianapolis. He would bring men he picked up back to his mansion where he would strangle them and dispose of their bones in the woods behind his home. Baumeister fled to Toronto and killed himself. A search of his property uncovered the bones of 11 men. Baumeister was also suspected of killing nine more men and disposing of the bodies in rural areas between Indianapolis and Columbus.

Dr Marcel Petiot - The Butcher of Paris; Dr Satan

Dr Petiot was a respected doctor in Paris during the Second World War. He was charged with the murder of 27 people, including Joachim Guschinow, M. and Mme Kneller, their son Rene Kneller, and Paul Braunberger between 1941 and 1944. Other sources suggest he killed 63 people, or even 150, and that the 86 dissected bodies pulled out of the Seine between 1941 and 1943 were also his handiwork. Lured to his premises under the promise of a route out of German occupied France, his mostly Jewish victims would then be given a lethal injection, which he told them was to ward off foreign diseases on their travels. They would then be put into a small triangular room with extra thick walls, where Dr Petiot would watch them die through a small hole in the wall. Their bodies were then stored in a quick lime pit and later burned in a furnace. Petiot was guillotined on 26th may 1946 in the Paris Sante Prison.

John Reginald Halliday Christie

John Reginald Halliday Christie was a 54 year old serial murderer and sexual psychopath who murdered at least 6 women. He also gave evidence at the trial of Timothy Evans, who was executed (later posthumously pardoned), for crimes almost certainly committed by Christie (who had served in the Army during World War One and been a Special Police Constable during the Second World War). On the outbreak of World War II, he applied to join the police force and was accepted despite previous convictions. He was arrested, tried, and hanged for murder in 1953.

Denis Nilsen

A British serial killer who lived in London. He is known to have killed at least 15 men between 1978 and 1983, when he was eventually caught after his disposal of a body blocked his household drains and drew the attention of the police. In 1961, Nilsen left school and enlisted in the British Army where he became a cook. He served in the army for 11 years before leaving in 1972 and served briefly as a police officer. From the mid 1970s, Nilsen worked as a civil servant. He was active in the trade union movement.

Paul Kenneth Bernardo

Bernardo committed multiple sexual assaults, escalating in viciousness, in and around Ontario. Most of the assaults were on young women whom he had stalked after they had exited buses late in the evening. Bernardo worked for Amway, whose sales culture had a deep effect on him. He bought the books and tapes of famous motivational get-rich-and-famous experts. Bernardo and his friends practiced their techniques on young women they met in bars.

Karla Leanne Homolka

Homolka is a Canadian serial killer who was convicted of manslaughter in the rape-murders of two teenaged girls; her husband, Paul Bernardo, was convicted of their murders and admitted having raped numerous women. Homolka and Bernardo also were responsible for the rape and death of her sister Tammy. She worked part-time in a pet shop at a nearby mall. After receiving her grade 12 diploma in 1989, she was hired as a veterinary assistant a Veterinary Clinic, which asked her to leave after she was suspected of stealing drugs. She then found a similar job at the Martindale Animal Clinic.

Dr. Thomas Neill Cream

He was a Scotish-born serial killer, who claimed his first proven victims in the US and the rest in England. Cream, who poisoned his victims, was executed after his attempts to frame others for his crimes brought him to the attention of London police. Cream went to Chicago and set up a medical practice not far from the red-light district, offering illegal abortions to prostitutes. Unsubstantiated rumors suggested his last words as he was being hanged were confession that he was Jack the Ripper, even though he was in jail at the time of the Ripper murders.

William Patrick Fyfe

A Canadian serial killer convicted of killing five women in the Montreal area of Quebec, although he claims to have killed four others. He allegedly killed his first victim in 1979 at age of 24. He was raised by an aunt and moved from Western Canada to Montreal in 1958. As an adult, he worked as a handyman.

Robert William "Willie" Pickton

Pickton is a Canadian pig farmer and serial killer convicted of the second-degree murders of six women. He is also charged in the deaths of an additional twenty women, many of them prostitutes and drug users from Vancouver's Downtown. He confessed to forty-nine murders to an undercover police officer posing as a cell mate. The Crown reported that Pickton told the officer that he wanted to kill another woman to make it an even 50, and that he was caught because he was "sloppy. Pickton and his brother, David Francis Pickton, ran a registered charity called the Piggy Palace Good Times Society, a non-profit society whose official mandate was to organize, co-ordinate, manage and operate special events, functions, dances, shows and exhibitions on behalf of service organizations, sports organizations and other worthy groups.

Karl Denke

Denke was born in German. As an adult, he was well liked in his community, and worked as an organ player at the local church. Denke was arrested after attacking a man at his house with an axe. Police searched Denke's home and found human flesh in huge jars of curing salts. A ledger contained the details of 40 people Denke had murdered and cannibalized over the years. It is thought he even sold the flesh of his victims at the market. He hung himself in his jail cell. He owned a rooming house and played an organ at his church.

Gwendolyn Graham & Cathy Wood

Both Gwendolyn Graham and Cathy Wood were Nurses aids at a retirement home. They are attributed five victims, and imprisoned for life.

John George Haigh

He Lived in Great Brittan. Haigh was an Accountant at an engineering firm, and hanged for his crimes, he is attributed six victims, but there were possibly nine.

Edmund Kemper

An American serial killer who lived in California, with 10 victims to his name. He is serving a life sentence. He was a Highway Department worker

Anna Maria Zwanziger

Zwangiger was a German serial killer with four victims. She was a domestic servant. She was beheaded for her crimes.

Andrei Romanovich Chikatilo - Butcher of Rostov, The Red Ripper, The Rostov Ripper

A notorious Russian serial killer, he was convicted of the murders of 52 women and children. He completed a degree in Russian literature by a correspondence course and tried a career as a teacher in. There were several complaints of him perpetrating child sexual abuse on his students that were usually handled quietly and without police involvement, thus he was able to move from school to school. He eventually took a job as a clerk for a factory, using his many business trips around the Soviet Union to carry out his killings.

John R. Gasser

Gasser was a student and state employee in Seattle. Gasser raped and strangled a 22-year-old carhop and dumped her body near the Sand Point Naval Station. Years after his release from prison, he raped and strangled a 49-year-old woman and dumped her body in a ditch outside Olympia in 1982. He is in prison in Washington.

Harvy L. Carignan - The Want Ad Killer

He was a gas station manager is Seattle and Minneapolis. Suspected in dozens of sex-slayings spanning four decades and several Western states and provinces, Carignan is thought to have killed at least two women in Washington. He was convicted of two murders in Minnesota. He met some victims by placing newspaper help wanted ads. A map found in his Minnesota home had at least 180 areas circled – including 18 in Washington – where some bodies have been found. He is in prison in Minnesota.

James Dwight Canady

City water department employee, in Seattle. He abducted, raped and strangled two women, and then dumped their bodies near Stevens Pass. Canady later attacked two other women and was being held in King County Jail on rape, assault and kidnapping charges when he confessed to the murders, leading detectives to one body. He is in prison in Washington.

Warren Forrest

Clark County parks employee, in Vancouver. Forrest is suspected of kidnapping, raping and strangling six women near Vancouver. He was convicted of killing one and abducting, raping and attempting to kill two others, after serving seven years in a state mental hospital. He is in prison in Washington.

Gary G. Grant

Navy enlistee, Renton. He confessed to four sex-slayings, including the murders of two 6-year-old boys and two teenage girls. All victims stabbed, strangled or both, then dumped in wooded areas near a Renton trailer park where he lived with his parents. He is in prison in Washington.

Ted Bundy

Law student, Tacoma. One of the most infamous serial killers of modern time, the former Tacoma man and University of Washington law student is thought to have killed at least 36 young women and girls in Washington, Oregon, California, Utah, Colorado and Florida. He was executed in Florida in 1989.

James Elledg

Part-time church janitor. He attacked at least four women over 33-year span, killing two. Crimes include a 1966 robbery/kidnapping in Albuquerque, N.M.; a 1974 bludgeoning murder in Seattle; and the 1998 fatal stabbing of one woman and sexual assault of another in a Lynnwood church. He was executed in Washington in 2001.

James Edward Ruzicka

Stable cleaner, Redmond. Deemed a sexual psychopath after attacking two Seattle women, he escaped Western State Hospital, then raped and strangled two teenagers in West Seattle. He hung the body of one victim from a tree and hid the other in a field. He was arrested in Oregon after raping a 13-year-old girl. He is in prison in Washington.

William Batten

Car lot worker, Aberdeen. He was committed to state psychiatric hospital as a sexual psychopath following child molestations in 1967. He stabbed two teenage hitchhikers to death near Moclips in 1975. He remains a suspect in the 1969 disappearance of a woman he had dated. He is in prison in Washington.

Robert Lee Yates Jr.

Aluminum plant worker and Army Reserve helicopter pilot, Spokane. He killed a string of prostitutes in Spokane and Pierce County since 1996. Admitted to 16 murders, convicted of 15. He would pick up prostitutes, shoot them and engage in post-mortem sex. Grew up on Whidbey Island and lived in several Washington cities. He is on death row in Washington.

Kenneth Bianchi - The Hillside Strangler:

Security-alarm installer, Bellingham. Strangled at least seven women and left their bodies on hillsides in Los Angeles. He killed two Western Washington University students in Bellingham in 1979. He worked with an adopted "cousin" convicted of nine similar murders in Los Angeles. He is in prison in Washington.

Morris Frampton

Sprinkler system installer, Seattle. He beat to death a Seattle prostitute, and then dumped her body near the South Park marina. Also convicted of assaulting two other Seattle prostitutes and acquitted of killing another. He is in prison in Washington.

Stanley Bernson

Produce salesman, Spokane. Suspected of killing up to 30 Northwest women, Bernson stabbed a 15-year-old girl to death and buried her in a shallow grave in Richland. Authorities in Oregon also charged him for the 1978 murder of a Umatilla teenager, whose body was found in 1985. He is in prison in Washington.

Randy Woodfield - The I-5 Killer:

Bartender, Eugene/Portland, Ore. Suspect in at least 13 homicides, including three in Washington. Best known for robbing, raping and killing women in communities along Interstate 5 from Bellevue to Redding, Calif. he often wore a false beard and hooded sweat shirt during his attacks. He is in prison in Oregon.

Martin Lee Sanders

Long-haul trucker, Spokane. He was convicted of raping and killing two teenagers in Spokane in 1983. He also killed two teenage female hitchhikers in Grant County in 1980. He avoided prosecution in those murders by later pleading guilty to the Spokane homicides. He is in prison in Washington.

Dwayne Elton

Army sergeant, Fort Lewis. Shot and killed one prostitute, strangled and sliced the throat of another. Elton dumped his victims near Madigan Army Hospital in 1984. The Seattle native later pleaded guilty to the killings in military court to avoid a death sentence. He is in a military prison in Kansas.

William Scott Smith

Cook, Salem, Ore. He was convicted of two counts of aggravated murder for the sex slayings of two young Salem women in separate attacks in the spring of 1984. Smith was also questioned in the 1983 unsolved murder of a 14-year-old girl in Idaho. Although not officially a suspect in any Washington murders, Green River investigators at one time looked at him in relation to serial killings in this state. Smith also has family ties to Pierce County. He is in prison in Oregon.

Billy Ray Ballard Jr.

Truck driver, Plains, Mont. He confessed to killing a Seattle couple who disappeared while sightseeing in the Columbia River Gorge. Their bodies were recovered at different times, dumped 30 miles apart, in rural Grant County. Ballard's arrest for the abduction, rape and torture of two women in Wyoming months later helped investigators match his fingerprint to one left on the Washington couple's abandoned car. Status: In prison in Wyoming.

Joe Kondro

Laborer, mill worker, Longview. He admits to raping and strangling two young girls in Southwest Washington -- killings more than 11 years apart. Convicted of two other rapes, he also admits to abducting a teenage store clerk at knifepoint. Suspect in dozens of disappearances, rapes and murders since 1982. He is in prison in Washington.

Westley Allan Dodd

Shipping clerk. Raped, tortured and killed three boys in Vancouver-Portland area. Caught after he tried to abduct a boy from a Camas movie theater. Admitted to molesting about 30 children. He was executed in Washington in 1993.

Scott William Cox

Long-haul trucker, Newberg, Ore. He stabbed one prostitute and strangled another in Portland. Suspected in more than 20 other murders, including the 1988 homicide of Snohomish County transient Hazel Gelnett and the 1990 murder of Tia Hicks, a Seattle woman whose body was found in Montlake Terrace. Also suspected of raping and trying to kill a Seattle prostitute in May 1991. He is in prison in Oregon.

Keith Jesperson - Happy Face Killer

Long-haul trucker, Yakima Valley/Portland. He confessed to eight murders in five states. Jesperson typically raped, beat and strangled truck-stop prostitutes and transients, then dumped bodies along wooded roadsides. Sent taunting letters to media and authorities, signed with a "happy face." Caught after killing his girlfriend near Camas. He is in prison in Oregon.

John Eric Armstrong

U.S. Navy, Bremerton/Detroit, Mich. Armstrong claims to have killed two women and a transsexual man in Seattle while stationed on the Bremerton-based USS Nimitz from 1993 to 1999, plus eight others worldwide. He was convicted of five Detroit-area prostitute murders. Police discount many of his claims. In prison in Michigan.

Reel to Real BY EVIL LUCY

The credo of "Sex Sells" might soon be something of the past.

As humans we do things to bring out our emotions, we watch movies, we read books and magazines, listen to music. As human animals we have ways of relieving boredom or feed a morbid appetite that we may have. Case in point. Hollywood "caters" to the dark desires of those of us who like things about Serial Killers, be it their charisma, their dark side, or their utter contempt for a society that would detain them. Serial Killers, Psychopaths, Mass Murderers, FBI profilers such as Robert Ressler who coined the term: "Serial Killer" and writes many books on the subject, and let's not forget the books of atrocities that make the mind seethe.

Did you know that there are more books written about Jack The Ripper than Abraham Lincoln?

Movies about Serial Killers are as old as Westerns, and have as many followers, they're just not your good ol' boys who like to watch the Duke with beer and a bowl of pork rinds, the genre of murder films/horror has many fans, from an educated business person, to your kid who likes to draw inverted crosses while listening to Slayer. What this piece will concentrate on is the Serial Killer appeal that Hollywood uses. The epic book: "The Silence of the Lambs" was written by Thomas Harris, in which the protagonist, an educated doctor of Psychology, Dr. Hannibal Lector, is detained for hideous crimes reminiscent of Ed Gein. Lector is used to try and catch a killer named Buffalo Bill, who kills many young women to use their skin as a costume, in vain to make him a woman. Other movies that center on Ed Gein are: "The Texas Chainsaw Massacre" and "Psycho", the plot of the "Texas Chainsaw Massacre" is that of a psychotic madman who kills people and stitches their skin into masks, In Alfred Hitchcock's "Psycho", it goes in another less gory yet psychologically more provocative way, the character, a wimpy little nerd who dotes on his Mother, would stalk women in the shower of the motel that he owned, while wearing his Mother's clothes and kills his victims in the shower. Oh did I mention that Norman Bates (the star of Psycho) was doting on his Mom's corpse which was in a rocking chair? I didn't? Silly Me!

Now while these books and later movies were incredible, it was not original. They are loosely based on Ed Gein of Plainfield, Wisconsin who horrified his little town. Ed Gein was a grave robber who came from an emotionally stunted background complete with abusive Father and overbearing Mother. Gein's father was a vicious alcoholic and due to this found himself unemployed very often.

Augusta Gein was a religious fanatic that acted as if her husband wasn't there, and shielded Ed and his older brother, George, from the horrors of the world, and espoused that sex was an act for procreation, women (outside of Augusta Gein) were nothing but whores, sluts, and prostitutes who used their sex to ruin God's Earth. The boys scolded if they made friends outside of the house. Following the death of their Father, the Gein boys took on jobs to help support their Mother and the farm. Ed Gein would constantly try to look up to his brother and adopt his work ethic, this went OK for Gein, but Ed found that it was easier to baby sit because he could easily get along with children rather than people his own age. Ed Gein's brother, Henry, died of a heart attack and left Ed and his Mother to go on without him. Two years later, Augusta Gein died of a series of strokes, and left poor Ed alone in the World. Ed was shattered by the loss of his Mother, and through his madness created his own World where women would pay for being harlots, whores, and prostitutes.

Ed Gein began his Macabre new twist on life when he started grave robbing and using the deceased skin of the dearly departed as trophies and clothing.

Gein adorned his home with skulls, innards, and shrunken heads. Gein's fascination with World War 2 also helped him implement the use of human skin for lampshades. It is possible if not fact that Gein's upbringing turned him into a confused man with many sexual hang ups and it is suggested that Gein suffered from guilt of being a man and wished to be a woman. Gender Confusion. He would often contemplate cutting off his penis, and would use the skins of the dead to make a female costume, complete with female scalp and vaginas. Gein was only convicted of two deaths, but suspected in many more.

Ed Gein alone has inspired scores of movies, books, and music. Slayer's song "Dead Skin Mask" is about Gein, and in the background you can hear: "Mr. Gein this isn't funny anymore, I don't want to play". One movie that does not do any justice or has any real attachment to Ed Gein is "Ed Gein The Butcher of Plainfield". Released in 2007 this movie used many historical inaccuracies in their attempt to portray a true story of Ed Gein. Using the scapegoat of: "Based On a True Story" this movie is nothing but Hollywood Candy. The story is smack with inaccuracies and in some twisted way try to show that Ed Gein had human compassion. To be fair the movie did portray Ed Gein's religious zealot of a Mother right down to the demure, conservative woman that Augusta was. But aside that. Nothing in this movie lends to the facts that have been written about since the late 1960's. Along with the above mentioned movies, and books, Ed Gein was also used in Brett Easton Ellis's story: "American Psycho". The story is about a handsome young man who goes on murder sprees, reminiscent of Ed Gein. However to give Ed Gein full credit to this book and later movie would be totally unfair.

Two other notorious Serial Killers are used in this book, and their names were Ted Bundy, and Jeffrey Dahmer.

American Psycho is set in the 1980's, and follows the life of Patrick Bateman, a young, rich white man who has it all. Patrick has a great life, lives in NYC in the height of the materialistic 80's, quite the "lady killer". He uses his good looks, intellect and guile to lure young women into a night that they will never forget. Bateman ritualistically cuts open his female victims, decapitating them, causing torture to barely living females and even attempts to eat his victims. We can see the similarities of Ted Bundy, because Pat Bateman was very good looking and charming, And the cannibalism is one of the things that Jeffrey Dahmer was infamous for.

The last movie that I would like to analyze is "Copycat" released in 1995, it is the story of a Serial Killer named, Daryll Lee Cullum who was apprehended by the authorities for trying to kill a woman who would lecture about Serial Killers to large symposiums of college students. A Copycat Serial Killer then emerges and plays with authorities by changing his Modus Operandi in his choice of slaughter. Some of the signatures that the killer uses are those of Ted Bundy, Jeffrey Dahmer (the Serial Killer in this movie does seduce young men but is not a homosexual, furthermore he doesn't eat parts of the bodies), David Berkowitz "The Son of Sam", and even uses the name Peter Kurten "The Vampire of Dusseldorf to elude authorities. The Serial Killer is a polite looking, and well mannered young man, a bit on the dorky side and is incredibly anal retentive as to how the slaying has to take place. He is not original in the slayings as he has borrowed from other Serial Killers. This movie is different from all other movies as it does accurately portray what some Serial Killers have done, but it also takes things out of loop. Because as most people who read True Crime books know, Serial Killers are robots of ritual, never deviating from their way of slayings. A definite good movie.

In closing I would like to state that the fascination with death especially in Hollywood is no where near done in this century or the next. And I for one am glad, what else would I write about?

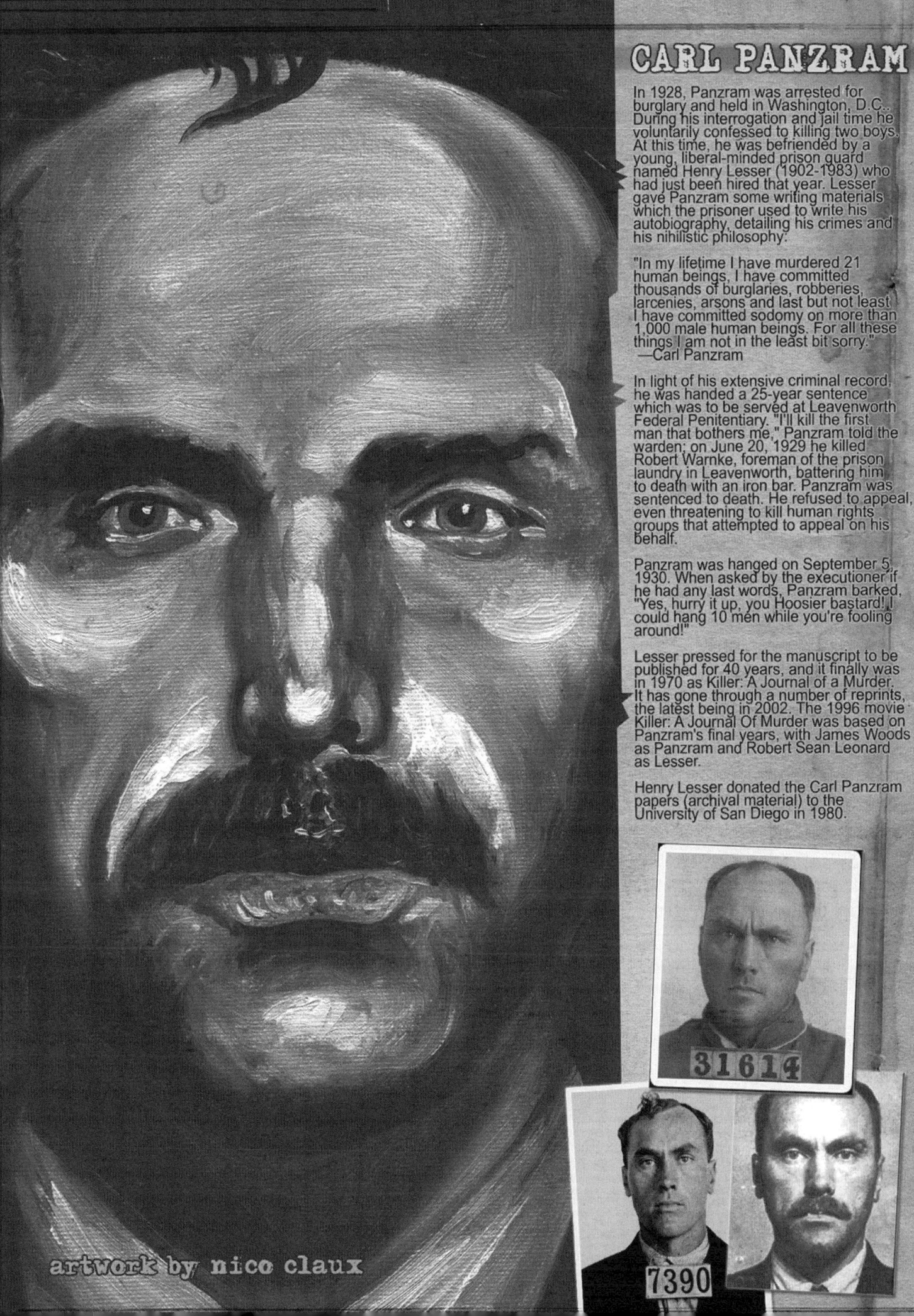

CARL PANZRAM

In 1928, Panzram was arrested for burglary and held in Washington, D.C.. During his interrogation and jail time he voluntarily confessed to killing two boys. At this time, he was befriended by a young, liberal-minded prison guard named Henry Lesser (1902-1983) who had just been hired that year. Lesser gave Panzram some writing materials which the prisoner used to write his autobiography, detailing his crimes and his nihilistic philosophy.

"In my lifetime I have murdered 21 human beings, I have committed thousands of burglaries, robberies, larcenies, arsons and last but not least I have committed sodomy on more than 1,000 male human beings. For all these things I am not in the least bit sorry."
—Carl Panzram

In light of his extensive criminal record, he was handed a 25-year sentence which was to be served at Leavenworth Federal Penitentiary. "I'll kill the first man that bothers me," Panzram told the warden; on June 20, 1929 he killed Robert Warnke, foreman of the prison laundry in Leavenworth, battering him to death with an iron bar. Panzram was sentenced to death. He refused to appeal, even threatening to kill human rights groups that attempted to appeal on his behalf.

Panzram was hanged on September 5, 1930. When asked by the executioner if he had any last words, Panzram barked, "Yes, hurry it up, you Hoosier bastard! I could hang 10 men while you're fooling around!"

Lesser pressed for the manuscript to be published for 40 years, and it finally was in 1970 as Killer: A Journal of a Murder. It has gone through a number of reprints, the latest being in 2002. The 1996 movie Killer: A Journal Of Murder was based on Panzram's final years, with James Woods as Panzram and Robert Sean Leonard as Lesser.

Henry Lesser donated the Carl Panzram papers (archival material) to the University of San Diego in 1980.

artwork by nico claux

HE TRAVELED BY RAIL.

HE LIKED THE SOUND THE TRAIN *MADE* AS IT MOVED.

IT HELPED ROCK HIM TO *SLEEP* AT NIGHT, LIKE A BABY IN A GOLDEN CRADLE.

AS FAR AS ANYONE *KNOWS*, IT STARTED IN SAN ANTONIO IN '91.

RESÉNDIZ DIDN'T *ADMIT* TO THE MURDER UNTIL APRIL, 2006.

IN FLORIDA, IN MARCH OF '97, HIS *M.O.* STARTED.

THE *BOY* DIED FIRST. HE WAS LEFT NEXT TO THE TRACKS.

RESÉNDIZ RAPED, STRANGLED, AND *SUFFOCATED* HIS FIANCÉ, AND BURIED HER THIRTY MILES AWAY.

CLICK CLACK

FIVE MONTHS LATER CAME HIS FIRST REPEAT, NEAR LEXINGTON'S *UNIVERSITY OF KENTUCKY*. THE BOY FIRST, *THEN* THE GIRL.

DESPITE RESÉNDIZ'S *BEST* EFFORTS, THE GIRL SURVIVED.

I WALKED BY THERE EVERY *DAY AND NIGHT*. IT COULD'VE BEEN ME OR *ANYONE* I KNEW.

THE ATTACK HAPPENED NEARLY OUTSIDE THE ART DEPARTMENT'S *DOOR*.

RESÉNDIZ WAS *QUIET* AFTER THAT FOR OVER A YEAR.

THE KANSAS CITY-SOUTHERN LINE WAS *FIFTY YARDS* OUTSIDE AN *81-YEAR-OLD* TEXAS WOMAN'S DOOR.

A FEW MONTHS LATER, A *PEDIATRIC NEUROLOGIST* WAS KILLED IN HER HOME, NEAR THE WEST UNIVERSITY PLACE, TEXAS TRAIN TRACKS.

RESÉNDIZ'S *FINGERPRINTS* IN HER CAR MEANT THERE WAS NOW A SUSPECT *AND* AN M.O.

A PASTOR AND HIS WIFE IN *WEIMAR*, TEXAS, DIED BY *SLEDGEHAMMER*. FINGERPRINTS ON THEIR *MAZDA* LINKED IT WITH THE *WEST UNIVERSITY* MURDER CASE.

SUDDENLY, THEY HAD A SERIAL MURDERER ON THEIR HANDS.

WE'RE WORRIED THIS FELLER *MIGHT* BE COMIN' *BACK*.

BARELY A *MONTH* LATER, A DEAD SCHOOLTEACHER'S HONDA CIVIC WAS FOUND ON THE *INTERNATIONAL BRIDGE* IN DEL RIO, TEXAS.

THE *SAME* DAY, RESÉNDIZ KILLED A 73-YEAR-OLD WOMAN IN FAYETTE COUNTY, TEXAS. HER FARMHOUSE WASN'T *FAR* FROM WEIMAR.

RESÉNDIZ TRIED TO TAKE HER CAR, BUT HE COULDN'T FIND THE *KEYS*.

HE KILLED HIS *FINAL* PAIR IN GORHAM, ILLINOIS, ELEVEN DAYS LATER.

HE USED THE SHOTGUN *TWICE*, BUT HE ONLY FIRED *ONCE*.

RESÉNDIZ WAS SEEN DRIVING THE WOMAN'S RED PICKUP IN *CAIRO*, SIXTY MILES AWAY.

ON JUNE 21ST, '99, RESÉNDIZ WAS *BRIEFLY* THE 457TH TEN MOST WANTED FUGITIVE.

RESÉNDIZ'S *SISTER*, MANUELA, FEARED HE MIGHT KILL AGAIN OR *BE* KILLED BY THE FBI, SO SHE AGREED TO HELP THE POLICE.

SHE AND A *SPIRITUAL GUIDE*, ALONGSIDE A TEXAS RANGER, MET RESÉNDIZ ON A BRIDGE CONNECTING EL PASO, TEXAS, WITH CIUDAD JUÁREZ, CHIHUAHUA.

RESÉNDIZ WAS 39 YEARS OLD WHEN HE *SURRENDERED* IN JULY OF '99.

HE HAD *MOSTLY* BEEN KNOWN BY THE ALIAS OF RAFAEL RESENDEZ-RAMIREZ UNTIL THEN. IT WAS ONLY *NOW* THAT THEY LEARNED HIS TRUE NAME:

ANGEL MATURINO RESÉNDIZ.

CLICK-CLACK

UNDER INTERROGATION, RESÉNDIZ DESCRIBED HIMSELF AS HALF-*MAN* AND HALF-*ANGEL*, UNABLE TO *DIE*.

A FORMER TEXAS ATTORNEY WARNED AGAINST THE AUTHORITIES "PINNING ON HIM EVERY CRIME THAT HAPPENS NEAR A RAILROAD TRACK."

ALTHOUGH MANY SPECIALISTS CALLED HIM *COMPLETELY DELUSIONAL*, RESÉNDIZ WAS RULED *COMPETENT* TO BE EXECUTED.

RESÉNDIZ WAS UNIMPRESSED:

"I DON'T *BELIEVE* IN DEATH. I KNOW THE *BODY* IS GOING TO GO TO WASTE. BUT ME, AS A *PERSON*, I'M ETERNAL. I'M GOING TO BE ALIVE *FOREVER*."

RESÉNDIZ RECEIVED AN *EXECUTION DATE* FOR JUNE 27TH, 2006.

HIS *DEATH WARRANT* WAS FOR MURDERING THE PEDIATRIC NEUROLOGIST IN HER HOME A WEEK BEFORE *CHRISTMAS* IN 1998.

ANGEL RESÉNDIZ WAS EXECUTED IN HUNTSVILLE, TEXAS BY LETHAL INJECTION.

GIVE ME FORGIVENESS.

RESÉNDIZ *DIED* AT 8:05 P.M. ON JUNE 28TH, 2006.

HIS EXECUTION WAS TEXAS'S *THIRTEENTH* OF THE YEAR.

THE DOCTOR'S HUSBAND HAD THE LAST WORD:

HE WAS *EVIL* CONTAINED IN HUMAN FORM, A CREATURE WITHOUT A SOUL, NO *CONSCIENCE*, NO SENSE OF *REMORSE*, NO *REGARD* FOR THE SANCTITY OF HUMAN LIFE.

CLICK CLACK

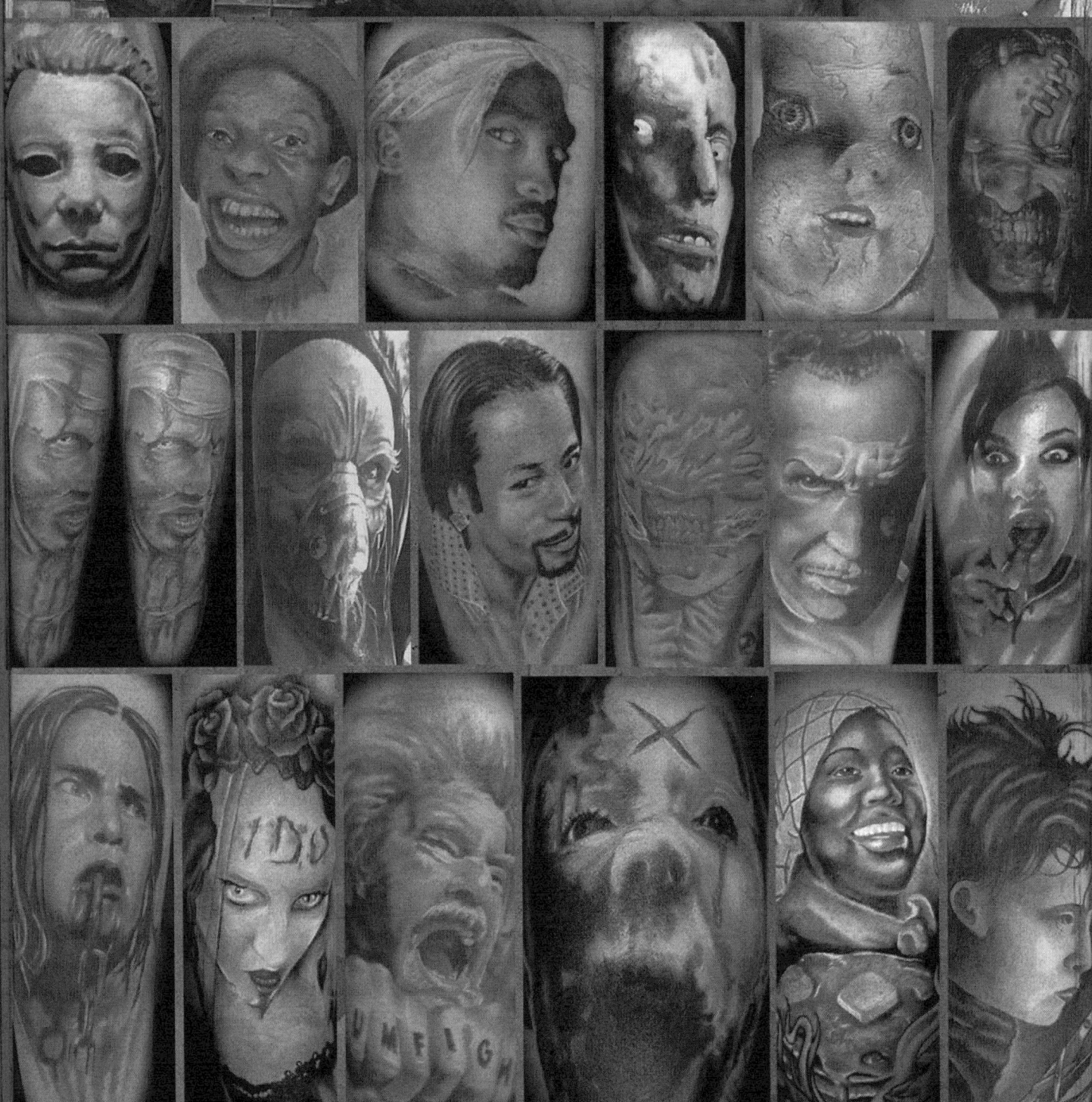

Lynnette Fromme, left, and Nancy Pitman, right, being led into San Joaquin County Courthouse for arraignment on murder charges. Three other persons were also arraigned. (APWirephoto)(es21600es) 1972
MO -MO- MO - MO MO MO MO MO

★★★ TRIAL TESTIMONY OF THE MANSON FAMILY ★★★ PART ONE

MANSON SPEAKING TO JUDGE. DATE UNKNOWN

MANSON: Your Honor, you mentioned... you mentioned "reconsider." Then you could possibly reconsider, if you can ask me to reconsider. Let me ask you to reconsider. I have a position as well as your Honor has a position. My position is still as strong as it was the first day I was arrested. The position that I hold is as follows. The confusion that has been created around the situation can be eliminated if your Honor would allow me to have my own voice in court. I am not here to use dilatory tactics or cause confusion. I am not here to shout in your courtroom. I am not here to fight with your bailiffs, and I am not here to go against my brother. I am just here to try to explain what these two gentlemen, even though sincere as they may be, they have no idea of what is going on. They are still in the dark about the whole situation. They have a bunch of facts; they have a bunch of things...

OLDER: What two gentlemen are you talking about?

MANSON: The district attorneys, they are very good at what they do, but they are way out, they are on the edge of town, you know, like it's...

OLDER: Are you making some kind of a motion, Mr. Manson?

MANSON: Yes, I'm making a motion, if I can finish. I listened to you.

OLDER: Just tell me what the motion is.

MANSON: It is my opinion that the court is not supposed to think, but supposed to administer the laws that go into the book, Manson vs. the United States. You give me a case...

OLDER: Mr. Manson I don't want to hear a speech. If you have a motion or a request, state it to the court so I would know what you want.

MANSON: I would like to associate in with Mr. Kanarek as my own counsel.

OLDER: I have already ruled on that several times. Your motion will be denied.

MANSON: Yeah, okay, then you leave me nothing, you know, there is nothing else I can do. You can kill me now.

OLDER: All right.

MANSON: You understand what I am saying to you? Do you understand what I am saying to you?

OLDER: Is there anything further, gentlemen, before we resume in the courtroom?

Artwork by Trav

WILLIAM GARRETSON QUESTIONED BY VINCENT BUGLIOSI JULY 24, 1970

Q: Do you recall what you did that evening, August 8, 1969, a Friday?

A: Yes.

Q: What did you do that evening?

A: I went down to Sunset Boulevard.

Q: How did you get there?

A: Hitchhiked.

Q: All right, what happened when you got down to Sunset Boulevard?

A: I purchased a T.V. dinner and some cigarettes and some Pepsi-Cola.

Q: And what time did you return?

A: Around 10:00 o'clock.

Q: When you returned at approximately 10:00 P.M. did you see anyone else on the premises?

A: No, sir. I did not.

Q: How did you enter the premises, through the gate here as depicted on the diagram?

A: Yes.

Q: How did you open the gate?

A: You had to push a button right before you get to the gate, it would be on the left side.

Q: Is the button near the telephone where I am pointing now?

A: Yes.

Q: And this would activate the gate and open it, is that correct?

A: Yes.

Q: How long would the gate stay open? Would you have to close it or would it automatically close?

A: No. I would say about fifteen to twenty seconds, something like that.

Q: When you arrived back at the premises did you notice any telephone wires on top of the gate or on the ground or anything like that?

A: No.

Q: Did everything seem to be in order?

A: Yes.

(Missing testimony about Garretson taking path to the guest house and not seeing or hearing anything at the main house)

Q: Did you have any visitors that night in your guest house?

A: Yes, I did.

Q: Who was that?

A: Steven Parent.

Q: At about what time did Mr. Parent arrive?

A: Around 11:45 P.M.

Q: Just before midnight?

A: Yes.

Q: Did he arrive by himself?

A: Yes, he did.

Q: What was the nature of Mr. Parent's visit to you?

A: He brought a radio with him, a clock radio, and he wanted to know if I would like to buy the one that he had, buy it or one that he could get, you know. He worked in an appliance place or something that dealt with radios and stereos.

Q: Did you buy the radio from him?

A: No.

Q: I take it that he eventually left your guest house?

A: Yes. He made a phone call though, before he left.

Q: About what time did he make a phone call?

A: About 12:00 o'clock.

Q: What did you do after Mr. Parent left?

A: I wrote a few letters and listened to the stereo.

Q: Okay. Did you eventually fall asleep that night?

A: No.

Q: Did you fall asleep at all?

A: No. I was going to make a phone call before dawn.

Q: Did you make the phone call?

A: No.

Q: Why not?

A: The line was dead. I mean, not the line, the phone was dead.

Q: Did this frighten you at all?

A: Yes.

Q: Did you do anything about it?

A: No.

Q: Did you fall asleep around dawn at all?

A: Yes.

Q: But throughout the night you were awake?

A: Yes.

Q: Listening to your stereo?

A: Yes. And writing letters.

Q: Did you hear any gunshots during the night?

A: No.

Q: Did you hear any loud screams during the night?

A: No.

(Missing testimony about dogs usually barking when people approached the guesthouse but not the main house)

Cross-examination for William Garretson by Paul Fitzgerald:

Q: What time was it that you actually went to bed, went to sleep that is?

A: I couldn't really say but it was just before daybreak. I mean, daybreak.

Q: And did Christopher wake you up? (Note that Christopher was one of the dogs)

A: Yes.

Q: All three dogs were inside the guest cottage that night; is that right?

A: Yes.

Q: Did you say anything to Christopher when he started to bark and woke you up?

A: I told him to be quiet. Well, he started barking, you know, I told him to shut up, and then I looked up and there was a policeman outside in the patio pointing a rifle at me by the picnic table.

Q: What did you do then?

A: I didn't know what to do.

Q: What happened next?

A: Another one came and pointed another rifle, and then another one, and he was pointing a pistol, and he kicked in the door, and Christopher bit him on the leg.

★★★ TRIAL TESTIMONY OF THE MANSON FAMILY ★★★ PART TWO

Artwork by Ani Aslanian

Q: What happened to Christopher?

A: I told him to stop it.

Q: What happened next?

A: Well, then they drug me onto the patio and threw me down on my stomach. And I asked them what was wrong.

And they told me to shut up, they would show me.

Q: Were you shown?

A: Yes.

Q: What were you shown?

A: Two bodies on the front lawn and one in the car.

LINDA KASABIAN QUESTIONED BY VINCENT BUGLIOSI JULY 27, 1970.

Note many objections have been deleted for clarity:

Q: Did you ever go to live at the Spahn Movie Ranch in Chatsworth, California?

A: Yes, I did.

Q: I show you people's 28 for identification. Linda do you know whose photograph that is?

A: Yes, I do.

Q: Who is shown in that photograph?

A: Gypsy.

Q: Do you know her by her real name?

A: Kathy.

Q: Does the name Katherine Share ring a bell?

A: Yes.

Q: You know her as Gypsy and Kathy?

A: Also she told me Minine or Minone.

Q: Did Gypsy have anything to do with your going to the Spahn Ranch?

A: Yes, she did.

Q: How was that?

A: She told me about a beautiful man that we had all been waiting for.

Q: Did you start to live at the Spahn ranch?

A: Yes, I did.

Q: When did you meet Charles Manson for the first time?

A: The next night.

Q: That would be July 5, then?

A: Right, and he was up and back at the ranch, in a cluster of trees, and he was working on a dune buggy.

Q: Did you have a conversation with Mr. Manson on this first occasion?

A: Yes.

Q: What did he say to you?

A: He asked me why I had come. I had told him that my husband had rejected me and that Gypsy told me I was welcome here as part of the Family.

Q: After you told Mr. Manson why you had come to the Spahn Ranch, did he do anything...

A: Yes, he felt my legs and seemed to think they were okay or whatever.

Q: Where did you stay that night?

A: In a cave up in back of the ranch.

Q: When was the next time you saw Mr. Manson?

A: The next night or maybe the night after, I am not sure.

Q: Where did you meet Mr. Manson on this following occasion?

A: Inside the cave.

Q: What took place at that time?

(An objection from Kanarek)

(Possible missing testimony)

Q: You mentioned earlier, Linda, about a Family. Is that what the people were called out at the Spahn Ranch?

A: Yes.

KANAREK: Objection on the grounds it is assuming facts not in evidence. There is no evidence of any Family. What they are called is hearsay, your Honor.

OLDER: Mr. Kanarek, I told you before I just want the motion or the objection and grounds without the argument.

KANAREK: And I respectfully ask the court to ask the witness...

OLDER: Sit down, sir.

KANAREK: ...not to respond...

OLDER: Sit down, sir.

(Missing testimony about Manson's dominance over Family members.)

(Objection. Sustained)

(Attorneys approached the bench)

BUGLIOSI: Your Honor, with all...

HUGHES: I find it highly prejudicial, that we go to the bench whenever Mr. Bugliosi wishes and not when Mr. Kanarek asks.

OLDER: Don't interrupt. Mr. Bugliosi was talking.

BUGLIOSI: With all deference to the court I don't understand why I cannot put in Manson directing...

HUGHES: I cannot hear this.

BUGLIOSI: I cannot understand, with all deference to the court how the court is not permitting me to put on evidence that Manson was in charge of the Family. I have the highest regard for the court. I want the court to know that. At this particular point, your Honor, I am shocked at the court's position.

This is our case against Manson.

OLDER: That is not a legal argument, Mr. Bugliosi, as you well know.

BUGLIOSI: I agree with the court on that.

OLDER: The questions called for hearsay. I find no exception under which it might come in. That is the reason I sustained the objection.

BUGLIOSI: The only way I can prove Manson was the head of the Family is that he directed everyone to do things. I am just at a loss for words.

OLDER: I think perhaps a good deal of it can be solved by phrasing your questions in some other manner.

(Possible missing section)

(Court adjourned for the day)

LINDA KASABIAN QUESTIONED BY VINCENT BUGLIOSI JULY 28, 1970

Note many objections have been deleted for clarity:

Q: Did you indicate yesterday that after the first time you met Mr. Manson you saw him the following night; is that correct?

A: Yes.

Q: Where were you this night when Manson saw you?

A: In a cave in back of the ranch.

Q: Did anything take place between you and Mr. Manson in the cave?

A: He made love to me and we had a slight conversation.

Q: What conversation did you have with Mr. Manson while you were making love, or about that time?

A: I don't recall the complete conversation, but he told me that I had a father hang-up, and I said...

Q: This is after you had sexual intercourse with him?

A: No. I think it was before.

Q: Did this impress you when he said you had a father hang-up?

A: Very much so.

Q: Why?

A: Because nobody ever said that to me, and I did have a father hang-up. I hated my stepfather.

(Missing testimony about a camouflaged campsite with dune buggy parts about two miles from Spahn Ranch.)

Q: Was a walkie-talkie system set up at this campsite?

A: Yes, it was.

Q: Do you know who ordered that the walkie-talkie system be set up?

A: Charlie did.

Q: Did he indicate why he wanted a walkie-talkie system?

A: Yes. We had been spotted. Maybe it was the fire department, or some trucks were going back and forth, and we had been spotted. So, we had a walkie-talkie system set up a little ways from the camp that we would make phone calls if they would come by, you know, to let people at the camp know.

Q: What was the setup of the walkie-talkie system?

A: Well, there was a road leading up to the campsite, and right at the beginning of this road a part of the walkie-talkie system was set up, and then there was a wire going all the way down to the road, camouflaged, leading to another part of the walkie-talkie system at the camp.

Q: Were there any guard shifts at the second camping site?

A: Yes.

Q: Who acted as guards?

A: All us girls in different shifts.

Q: What were you guarding?

A: Actually just like a watch-out tower, we would sit there with the walkie-talkie system, watching out if a truck went by or if, you know, somebody came walking through that would spot us.

Q: Did Charlie ask you girls to do anything while you were at the second camping site?

A: First he instructed us to make little witchy things to hang in the trees to show our way from the campsite to our road in the dark.

Q: What witchy things?

A: Things made from weeds, rocks, stones, branches, some kinds of wires, I don't know, all different little things.

Q: Why do you use the word "witchy?"

A: All the guys, Charlie called us witches.

Q: Okay, were there any male visitors who came to the ranch and visited the Family?

A: Yes.

Q: Did Charlie ever tell you girls to do anything with these male visitors?

A: Yes, he told us to make love to them, and try to get them to join the Family, and if they would not join the Family, not to give them our attention, not to make love to them.

(Kanarek made a motion for a mistrial. Motion denied)

Q: Where did you get your food from?

A: We used to go on garbage runs.

Q: What do you mean by garbage runs, Linda?

A: We used to go in the back of supermarkets and restaurants, into the garbage cans and take the throw-away food, take them home, clean them up and eat them.

Q: Did Charlie ever say anything about what type of food you should eat?

A: Not really. He used to really dig zusus.

Q: What are zusus?

A: Candy and ice cream.

Q: Linda, do you know what a sexual orgy is?

A: Yes, I do.

(Kanarek objected and attorneys approached the bench)

OLDER: Let me tell you something, Mr. Kanarek, and I want you to get it straight right now. I do not want you to interrupt. I don't want you to interrupt me; I don't want you to interrupt another attorney and I don't want you to interrupt the witness. Do you understand, sir?

KANAREK: Yes, your Honor.

OLDER: You will be given every opportunity to state whatever you want to discuss, but you are not going to continually interrupt.

KANAREK: I understand.

OLDER: Now just a minute, that means right now also.

KANAREK: Yes.

OLDER: If you continue to interrupt I'm going to find you in contempt. I want you to clearly understand that. When I am speaking, don't interrupt.

KANAREK: Well, your Honor, it's certainly not intentional.

★★★ TRIAL TESTIMONY OF THE MANSON FAMILY ★★★ PART THREE

OLDER: I believe it is.

KANAREK: Not to interrupt the court. The point is, your Honor, if Mr. Bugliosi solicits a question...

OLDER: You heard what I said. Now, I mean it.

KANAREK: Then Mr. Manson is being denied due process.

OLDER: Do you have anything else to say?

KANAREK: May I make the record, your Honor is interrupting me.

OLDER: There is no record to make.

KANAREK: The point is...

OLDER: Now, Mr. Kanarek, I order you to stop talking this moment, do you understand, sir?

KANAREK: Very well.

(Missing discussion over use of the term "sexual orgy." Judge Older denied its use.)

Q: There was a back house at the Spahn Ranch?

A: Yes.

Q: A little past mid-July, 1969, did a large group of members of the Family and guests gather at the back house?

A: Yes, they did.

Q: About how many people?

A: As many people as there were in the Family - maybe twenty - and I believe there were three or four guests.

Q: About what time of day was it?

A: It was nighttime.

Q: What took place at the back house?

A: There was one particular girl - I don't remember her name - she was fairly young, I'd say maybe sixteen, and she was very shy and very withdrawn, and I remember she was lying in the middle of the room, and Charlie took her clothes off and started making love to her and kissing her and, you know, she was trying to push him off, and he just sort of pushed her back down and kissed her. And at one point she bit him on the shoulder, and he hit her in the face, and then she just sort of let go and got behind it, or whatever. Then he told Bobby Beausoleil - no, excuse me - yes, he told Bobby Beausoleil to make love to her, and he told everybody to touch her and to kiss her and to make love to her. And everybody did.

(Kanarek made several motions. All were denied.)

Q: You say everyone made love to her. Are you referring to the male members of the Family?

A: Everybody that was in the room. Yes.

KANAREK: Well, your Honor, may I have a continuing objection and a continuing request to admonish, because this is most prejudicial what Mr. Bugliosi is eliciting.

BUGLIOSI: The "G" is silent, sir. It is Bugliosi.

KANAREK: I am sorry.

OLDER: Let's proceed.

Q: After everyone touched the girl, then what happened?

A: Then he told everybody to make love to everybody else.

Q: When you say "he" are you referring to Charles Manson?

A: Yes.

Q: Could you define in more detail what you mean by making love?

A: Well, we all shed our clothes, and we were laying on the floor, and it was just like - it didn't matter who was beside you, if it was a man or woman, you just touched each other and made love with each other, and the whole room was like this. It was sort of just like one.

Q: Was everyone nude?

A: Yes.

Q: Was there sexual intercourse?

A: Yes. That is what I just said.

Q: In your stay at the ranch did you ever have discussions with Charles Manson?

A: Yes.

Q: Did he ever say anything about how not to get caught?

A: Yes. He used to say "If you don't get caught, you won't get it caught thought in your head."

Q: Did he ever say anything to you about willing to kill or be killed?

A: Yes. He used to say "If you are willing to be killed, then you should be willing to kill."

Q: One day in the woods at the Spahn Ranch did Mr. Manson indicate to you that he was someone other than Charles Manson?

A: Yes. I remember he took me in his arms and said, "Don't you know who I am?"

Q: Did Charles Manson ever talk to you about the Beatles?

KANAREK: Object on the grounds of hearsay, conclusion, foundation - improper foundation as to who was present, the time when it occurred.

OLDER: Place?

Artwork by Cody Whitman

KANAREK: Place, right. Thank you, your Honor.

OLDER: Overruled.

KASABIAN: Yes. There was a certain passage in one song where he said that he thought he heard - or did hear, I am not sure if it was thought or whatever - that the Beatles were calling to him, saying, "Charlie, Charlie, send us a telegram," or "Put out a song," or something. Yes, he felt that the Beatles were calling him.

(Various objections by Kanarek)

MANSON (to Older): May I object to my lawyer's objections?

OLDER: No, you may not, sir.

(Missing testimony about children being hidden due to fear of Black Panthers coming to the ranch. More about armed guards at night and about Manson's reactions when blacks came to rent horses at the ranch)

KASABIAN: Well, they knew that we were super-aware, much more than other white people, and they knew we knew about them and that they were eventually going to take over, his whole philosophy on the black people, that they wanted to do away with us because apparently they knew that we were going to save the white race or go out to the hole in the desert.

Q: Did Mr. Manson mention the term Helter Skelter to you?

(Five objections by Kanarek)

A: Yes. It is a revolution where blacks and whites will get together and kill each other and all non-blacks and brown people and even black people who do not go on black people's terms...

Q: Did he say who was going to start Helter Skelter?

A: Blackie. He used to say that blackie was much more aware than whitey and super together, and whitey was just totally untogether, just would not get together; they were off on these side trips, and blackie was really together.

KANAREK: I ask that the answer be stricken on the basis that it is gibberish, your Honor, you cannot understand it.

BUGLIOSI: Why don't you talk to your client about it?

OLDER: I admonish counsel to not engage in colloquy.

Q: During the day of August 8, do you recall Mr. Manson saying anything about Helter Skelter?

A: Yes, I believe that was the day he got back from Big Sur. He was telling us about his trip and that people were really not together, they were just off on their little trips, and they just were not getting together. So he came out and said, "Now is the time for Helter Skelter."

(Missing testimony involving Manson sending Atkins, Krenwinkel and Watson away with extra clothes, a revolver and knives)

(Court recessed for lunch)

(Missing testimony)

A: I thought we were going on a creepy-crawl mission.

Q: A creepy-crawling mission?

A: Yes.

Q: What is a creepy-crawling mission?

A: A creepy-crawling mission is where you creepy-crawl into people's houses and you take things which actually belong to you in the beginning, because it actually belongs to everybody. I remember one specific instance where the girls made Charlie a long, black cape, and one of the girls was fitting it to him, and he sort of said, "Now when I go creepy-crawling, people won't see me because they will think I am a bush or a tree."

Q: What was the first thing that happened after you arrived on top of the hill?

A: Tex turned the car around and parked the car beside a telephone pole.

Q: What is the next thing that happened?

A: He got out of the car; he walked around the back of the car. I don't know if he had wire cutters or what, I don't know, but I remember he climbed the pole, and I saw the wires fall. Then he came back and got back in the car.

(Missing testimony about taking car down the street and walking back up the hill)

Q: What happened after you, Katie, Sadie and Tex walked up the hill?

A: We climbed over - we climbed over a fence and then a light started coming towards us and Tex told us to get back and sit down.

OLDER: Are you able to go on, Mrs. Kasabian?

A: Yes, I am. And a car pulled up in front of us and Tex leaped forward with a gun in his hand and stuck his hand with the gun at the man's head. And the man said, "Please don't hurt me, I won't do anything." And Tex shot him four times.

Q: After Tex shot the driver four times what was the next thing that happened?

A: The man just slumped over. I saw that, and then Tex put his hand in the car and turned the ignition off. He pushed the car back a few feet then we all proceeded towards the house and Tex told me to go in back of the house and see if there were open windows or doors, which I did.

Q: Did you find any open doors or windows in the back of the house?

A: No. I came around from the back and Tex was standing at a window, cutting the screen, and he told me to go back and wait at the car, and he may have told me to listen for sounds, but I don't remember him saying it. And I waited for a few minutes, and then all of a sudden I heard people screaming, saying "No, please, no." It was just horrible. Even my emotions cannot tell you how terrible it was. I heard a man scream out "No, no." Then I just heard screams, just - I don't have any words to describe how a scream is. I never heard it before. It was just unbelievably horribly terrible.

Q: Were these the screams of men or women or both?

A: It sounded like both.

Q: Were the screams loud screams or soft screams, or what?

A: Loud. Loud.

Q: Did the people appear to be pleading for their lives?

A: Yes.

Q: How long did the screaming continue?

A: Oh, it seemed like forever, infinite. I don't know.

Q: What did you do when you heard these screams?

A: I started to run towards the house.

Q: Why did you do that?

A: Because I wanted to stop, because I knew what they had done to this man, that they were killing these people.

Q: What happened after you ran toward the house?

A: There was a man just entering out of the door and he had blood all over his face and he was standing by a post, and we looked into each other's eyes for a minute.

★★★ TRIAL TESTIMONY OF THE MANSON FAMILY ★★★ PART FOUR

I don't know however long, and I said, "Oh God I am so sorry. Please make it stop." And then he just fell to the ground into the bushes. And then Sadie came running out of the house, and I said "Sadie, please make it stop." and she said, "It's too late." And then she told me that she left her knife and she couldn't find it. And while this was going on, the man had gotten up, and I saw Tex on top of him, hitting him on the head and stabbing him, and the man was struggling, and then I saw Katie in the background with the girl chasing after her with an upraised knife, and I just turned and ran to the car down at the bottom of the hill.

Q: You said you saw Katie. That is Patricia Krenwinkel?

A: Yes.

Q: Was she chasing someone?

A: A woman in a white gown.

LINDA KASABIAN QUESTIONED BY VINCENT BUGLIOSI JULY 29, 1970.

Note many objections have been deleted for clarity:

Q: This woman whom Katie was chasing, do you have any physical description of her?

A: I only saw the back of her and she had a long white gown, and I believe she had long, dark hair, possibly brown, I'm not positive.

Q: After Sadie told you that she had lost her knife inside the house, what did Sadie do, if you recall?

A: I believe she started to run back into the house.

Q: When Tex was stabbing this man, was the man on the ground?

A: Yes.

Q: Was he screaming?

A: Yes.

Q: Was he struggling with Tex?

A: Yes.

Q: And you say you saw Tex hit him over the head?

A: Yes.

Q: How many times did Tex stab this man?

A: I don't know. He just kept doing it and doing it and doing it.

Q: When the man was screaming, do you know what he was screaming?

A: There were no words, it was beyond words, it was just screams. Please.

Q: Is that about the time then you ran back down to your car?

A: Yes.

Q: What was your state of mind at that point?

A: I was in a total state of shock.

Q: Did you think of running to a nearby home or calling the police or anything like that?

A: Yes, that was my first thought.

Q: Then why didn't you do it?

(Objection on grounds of hearsay. Sustained. Attorneys approached bench.)

BUGLIOSI: I think her answer would be, as an offer of proof, that the reason she did not call the police or go to a neighbor's house is because she thought of Tanya, her daughter Tanya, back at the Spahn Ranch, and also she thought of Manson at Spahn Ranch with Tanya, so she was frightened. Again this goes towards the issue of her relationship with Manson and also the issue of whether or not she was an accomplice.

(Missing discussion. Objection remained sustained.)

Q: Did Tex, Sadie and Katie eventually come to the car?

A: Yes.

Q: What happened then?

A: Well, I had started the car, and Tex came over and told me to turn the car off and to push over, and he seemed really up-tight because I had run to the car.

Q: Did Tex then drive off?

A: Yes, he did.

Q: Did Katie and Sadie say anything as you were driving off from the residence?

A: Yes. They complained about their heads, that the people were pulling their hair, and that their heads hurt. And Sadie even came out and said that when she was struggling with a big man, that he hit her in the head. And also Katie complained of her hand, that it hurt.

Q: Did she say why her hand hurt?

A: She said when she stabbed that there were bones in the way and she couldn't get the knife through all the way, and that it took too much energy or whatever, I don't know her exact words, but it hurt her hand.

Q: Did Katie say anything about one of the girls inside the residence?

A: Yes, she did. She said that one of the girls was crying for her mother and for God.

(Missing testimony about changing clothes and looking for a place to clean up.)

Q: Would you relate what happened, Linda?

Art by Joel Bagley

SHARON TATE & ROMAN POLANSKI

A: An older woman came running out of the house.

Q: What happened next?

A: I don't remember her exact words but she said, "Who is there?" or "Who is that, what are you doing?" And Tex said, "We're getting a drink of water." Then she got sort of hysterical and she said, "My husband is a policeman; he is a deputy," or something like that. And then her husband came out and he said, "Is that your car?" And we said, "No, we are walking." And then we started walking to the car.

Q: All four of you?

A: Yes. And the man was behind us.

Q: Did the man follow you all the way down to the car?

A: Yes.

Q: Did all four of you get into the car?

A: Yes.

Q: What is the next thing that happened?

A: The man was right behind us and he came to the driver's seat and he started to put his hand in the car to reach for the keys, and Tex blocked him, grabbed his hand and just jammed, you know. So I thought the man's arm was going to go with him.

Q: Now, when you say Tex jammed, what do you mean by that?

A: He drove off fast.

(Missing testimony about throwing clothes and knives from car, washing off at a gas station and returning to Spahn Ranch.)

Q: What happened after you pulled the car into the parking area and parked the car?

A: Sadie said she saw a spot of blood on the outside of the car when we were at the gas station.

Q: What is the next thing that happened?

A: Charlie told us to go into the kitchen, get a sponge, wipe the blood off, and he also instructed Katie and I to go all through the car and wipe off the blood spots.

Q: What is the next thing that happened?

A: Charlie told us to go into the bunkroom and wait, which we did.

Q: Where is the bunkroom located?

A: It was called the gun room, also, which Danny DeCarlo had a side bed.

Q: Did you and Katie and Sadie enter the bunkroom?

A: Yes.

Q: Who was there?

A: Clem and Brenda.

Q: Is he also known as Clem Tufts?

A: I just knew him as Clem.

Q: Did Mr. Manson eventually enter the bunkroom?

A: Yes.

Q: Was he with anyone?

A: Yes, he was. With Tex.

Q: Did Tex say anything after you were all in the bunkroom?

A: He said, "I am the devil here to do the devil's work."

(Objection.)

STOVITZ: Your Honor, may we ask your Honor to ask counsel to make his objection and then to allow the witness to continue? We are having great difficulty keeping the continuity of her testimony going with these constant objections. I know the record reflects the objections because I have gone through the record, but I think the continuous interruption is made for one obvious purpose, to interrupt the witness's train of thought and interrupt Mr. Bugliosi's train of thought.

OLDER: Let's proceed. Bear in mind, Mr. Kanarek, what has been said by the court before regarding this subject.

Q: Would you repeat what Tex said?

A: That "I am the devil here to do the devil's work."

Q: He was telling the people in the room that he was the devil?

A: That is what he told the people at the house.

Q: Did Tex say anything else about the killings?

A: Yes. He said that there was a lot of panic, and that it was real messy and bodies were laying all over the place, but they were all dead.

Q: Did Mr. Manson say anything in response to this?

A: Yes. He asked if we had any remorse.

(Objection. Attorneys approached bench.)

OLDER: Mr. Kanarek, you have directly violated my order not to interrupt repeatedly. You did it again. I find you in contempt of court and I sentence you to one night in the County Jail starting immediately after this court adjourns this afternoon until 7:00 A.M. tomorrow morning. The order will further provide that you are to be given free access to confer with your client, Mr. Manson, during the time you are in custody. Proceed.

KANAREK: Your Honor, if I may, I will ask your Honor to read the record. I tried to object before.

OLDER: I don't have to read the record, sir. I was present. You have repeatedly, in spite of my warnings to you, interrupted. You just did it again in a flagrant disregard of the order.

KANAREK: Your Honor, that is not so. I beg the court to realize. If you will read the record, she answers so fast that I ask that you...

OLDER: You have been doing it continually, and you did it again after repeated warnings.

SHINN: Your Honor, may I be heard, your Honor?

OLDER: On what subject?

SHINN: On this same subject. I was present.

OLDER: You are not involved in this.

SHINN: But I want to make my observations, your Honor.

OLDER: I am not interested in your observations.

(Missing testimony. Kasabian stated that all four had told Manson they did not feel remorse. Also said she did feel remorse. The following evening Manson told her get extra clothes and driver's license.)

Q: What did he say after that?

A: He said we were going out again tonight. Last night was too messy and he was going to show us how to do it. He told us that we were going to go to two different houses in two groups; that he would go in one group and leave another group off.

(Missing testimony about the group wandering around Los Angeles looking for targets. Also, about Manson getting out of car to kill someone stopped at a traffic light but the light changed and the man escaped. They stopped at a Church and Manson found the doors were locked so they left. Stopped at a house and Manson checked but said there were photos of children.)

Q: The second night did you know what was going to happen?

A: Yes.

★★★ TRIAL TESTIMONY OF THE MANSON FAMILY ★★★ PART FIVE

Q: Why did you go along with Mr. Manson and the others?

A: Because Charlie asked me and I was afraid to say no.

(Missing testimony. Drove to a house on a hill but decided other houses were too close. Drove to another house but Manson decided against it. Manson then gave directions to Harold True's house, which was beside the LaBianca house.)

Q: Had you ever parked in front of that house before?

A: Yes, in the exact spot.

Q: When?

A: My husband and I and friends were on our way down from Seattle, Washington, to New Mexico and we stopped off in Los Angeles and this one particular person knew Harold True, so we went to his house and had a party.

Q: Now, when Manson directed you to stop in front of Harold True's place did you recognize the spot?

A: Yes I did. Right away.

Q: Did you say anything to Manson with respect to this?

A: Yes.

Q: What did you say?

A: Charlie, you are not going into that house, are you?

Q: Did he say anything to you?

A: Yes, he did, he said "No, I'm going next door."

Q: Then what happened?

A: He got out of the car.

He disappeared up the walkway, the driveway, leading towards Harold's house, and I could not follow him any longer, he just disappeared.

Q: Did Mr. Manson eventually return to the car?

A: Yes, he did.

Q: How long after he left the car did he return to the car?

A: I remember we all lit up cigarettes, and we smoked about three-quarters of a Pall Mall cigarette, however long that takes.

Q: What happened after Mr. Manson returned to the car?

A: He called Leslie and Katie and Tex out of the car.

Q: What did you hear him say?

A: I heard him say that there was a man and a woman up in the house and that he had tied their hands, and that he told them not to be afraid, that he wasn't going to hurt them.

Q: Did he give any instructions to Tex, Katie and Leslie Van Houten? Did he give them any instructions at all?

A: I am not positive, but it keeps ringing in my head that he said, "Don't let them know that you are going to kill them."

Q: Did Manson say anything to Tex, Katie and Leslie about fear or panic?

A: Yes. I think I heard him say not to cause fear and panic in these people.

A: Charlie got back into the car and handed me a woman's wallet, and he proceeded to drive off.

(Missing testimony. Manson told Kasabian to hide a wallet in a gas station restroom. Bugliosi introduced a photo of a dune buggy with a sword mounted to it. Hughes objected.)

HUGHES: Your Honor, the objection that I am making is that this photograph has never been produced for us by way of discovery. This is just indicative of the complete disregard that the district attorney's office has had to various discovery motions and various discovery orders that this court has made.

OLDER: Statements like that aren't going to help you, Mr. Hughes. Just state the facts.

HUGHES: Okay. The district attorney's office is withholding evidence from us.

OLDER: Is that what you came up to say?

KANAREK: I make a motion to suppress.

BUGLIOSI: For the record, I just saw it for the first time a few minutes ago myself.

HUGHES: That is a lot of shit, Mr. Bugliosi.

OLDER: I hold you in direct contempt of court for that statement. I will take the matter up at 4:15 this afternoon. The motion to suppress is denied.

(Hughes was found in direct contempt for disorderly, disruptive, vulgar and unprofessional conduct. Older offered Hughes a fine of $75 but Hughes stated that he was "a pauper." Older sentenced him to a night in jail. Hughes gave a clenched fist salute and stated "Right on.")

Artwork by Hayley Mui

LINDA KASABIAN QUESTIONED BY VINCENT BUGLIOSI JULY 30, 1970.

Note many objections have been deleted for clarity:

(Missing testimony about Manson driving Kasabian, Atkins and Grogan to the beach.)

Q: What happened when you stopped the car?

A: We all got out of the car, started walking towards the beach. We got down to the beach, walked on the sand, and Charlie told Clem and Sadie to stay a little bit behind us, and Charlie and I started walking hand in hand on the beach, and it was sort of nice, you know. We were just talking and I gave him some peanuts, and he just sort of made me forget about everything, and just made me feel good. I told him I was pregnant and started walking. We got to a side street, a corner, and a police car came by and stopped, and asked us what we were doing, and Charlie said we were just going for a walk. And Charlie said something like "Don't you know who I am?" or "Don't you remember my name?" As if the policemen were supposed to know him. They just said no. It was a friendly conversation. It just lasted for a minute. Then we walked back to the car.

Q: You say you told Mr. Manson that you were pregnant. Were you pregnant by him?

A: No.

Q: What is the next thing that happened?

A: I took over driving, still, we just pulled out of the parking spot, drove down the hill, got back the same way we had come in, and Charlie asked us if we knew any people at the beach. We all said "No." Then he looked at me and said "What about that man you and Sandy met?" He said, "Isn't he a Piggy?" I said, "Yes, he is an actor." And then he further questioned me and he asked me if the man would let him in. And I said, "Yes." And he asked me if the man would let my friends in, Sadie and Clem. And I said, "Yes." And he said, "Okay, I want you to kill him," and he gave me a small pocketknife. And at this point, I said, "Charlie, I am not you. I cannot kill anybody." And I don't know what took place at that moment, but I was very much afraid. And then he started to tell me how to go about doing it, and I remember I had a knife in my hand, and I asked him, "With this?"

And he said, "Yes," and he showed me how to do it. He said, "As soon as you enter the residence, the house, as soon as you see the man, slit his throat right away." And he told Clem to shoot him. And then, also, he said if anything went wrong, you know, not to do it.

(Kanarek approached the bench.)

KANAREK: I ask for a mistrial.

OLDER: Motion is denied.

KANAREK: And also your Honor, then I ask the testimony to be excluded on the grounds it is incompetent, irrelevant and immaterial. It is hearsay. It is a conclusion, and furthermore, your Honor, it is violative of the prosecution's representation that they were not going to put before the jury any crimes that were not set out as they indicated. This is a solicitation to murder.

OLDER: Have you completed your argument, Mr. Kanarek? I want you to complete your argument and I will rule once and for all.

KANAREK: It is not just to make a record. It is to try to convince the court.

OLDER: Have you completed your argument?

KANAREK: Yes, your Honor.

OLDER: The motion is denied, let's proceed.

(Missing testimony about how the target had picked up Kasabian and Sandra Good, took them to his apartment. They showered and ate. Then Kasabian had sex with him. Kasabian showed Manson where the man lived but purposely took him to the wrong floor.)

Q: What is the next thing that happened?

A: Then we walked back downstairs to the car, and he gave Clem a gun.

Q: Charlie Manson gave him a gun?

A: Yes. At this point he said something... he said that if anything went wrong, you know, just hang it up, don't do it; and of course, to hitchhike back to the ranch, and for Sadie to go to the waterfall. And then he drove off.

Q: Before he drove off did Mr. Manson tell Clem and Sadie anything?

A: Yes.

Q: What did he tell them?

A: While I knocked on the door, for them to wait around the corner until I entered, and then to ask the man if they could come in.

(Missing testimony about Kasabian knocking on door, someone answering and Kasabian saying "Oh, excuse me, wrong door." The potential killers then left.)

Q: Why did you knock on the wrong door, Linda?

A: Because I didn't want to kill anybody.

Q: What is the next thing that happened?

A: Sadie went to the bathroom.

Q: Where did she go to the bathroom?

A: As we were walking downstairs.

(Missing testimony about the three walking on the beach looking to hide the gun.)

Q: What, if anything, were Sadie and Clem singing?

A: I remember one song that everybody always sang, but this day I remember them singing the Beatle song about piggies and forks and knives, and eating your bacon.

(Missing testimony about hiding gun in a sand dune, hitchhiking to a house, smoking marijuana, hitchhiking back to Spahn Ranch. Kasabian and Grogan went to the main ranch while Atkins stayed with the man who gave them the ride.)

Q: Do you know what LSD is?

A: Yes.

Q: Have you ever taken LSD?

A: Yes. I'd say approximately fifty times.

Q: Over how long a period of time have you taken LSD?

A: Over an approximately four year period.

Q: A four year period, off and on?

A: Yes.

Q: Have you seen other people take LSD?

A: Yes.

(Missing testimony. Bugliosi asked whether Kasabian has tried to leave Spahn Ranch following the murders.)

★★★ TRIAL TESTIMONY OF THE MANSON FAMILY ★★★ PART SIX

A: Yes. On the morning after the second night I packed a sleeping bag with some of Tanya's clothes and planted it by the road in some bushes.

Q: Why did you plant the sleeping bag by the road?

A: I had to hide it. He wouldn't let me walk out of there knowing that I'd seen what I'd seen.

(Missing testimony about Kasabian leaving Spahn Ranch but leaving her daughter behind. She went to a commune named Ojosarco near Taos, New Mexico to find her husband. She told him and a friend, Joe Sage, about the murders. Sage telephoned Spahn Ranch and spoke to Manson to confirm the story. Manson denied it. Linda Kasabian then spoke, by phone, to Krenwinkel about her daughter. Krenwinkel told her "You just couldn't wait to open your big mouth, could you?" Kasabian returned to Los Angeles, then back to Taos, and back to Los Angeles again and retrieved her daughter. The two went to Miami, Florida and then to Boston. She found she was wanted for questioning and turned herself in.)

Q: Why didn't you do something about your guilt feelings before you were arrested?

A: I was afraid, I was pregnant again, I had Tanya and I had this thing about going to the police.

Q: You were brought back, then, to Los Angeles by the authorities in early December, 1969?

A: Yes, that is correct.

Q: You have been in custody ever since?

A: Yes, I have.

Q: And you had your child Angel while you were in custody?

A: Yes, I did.

Q: No further questions. The defense may inquire.

LINDA KASABIAN CROSS-EXAMINED BY PAUL FITZGERALD JULY 30, 1970

Q: You testified this morning, did you not, that you had taken LSD fifty times, is that correct?

A: Approximately, yes.

Q: Do you recall when you first ingested LSD?

A: Yes. It was in Boston, it was Christmas Eve of '65.

Q: You testified this morning, did you not, that you had taken LSD fifty times, is that correct?

A: Approximately, yes.

Q: Do you recall when you first ingested LSD?

A: Yes. It was in Boston, it was Christmas Eve of '65.

Q: And is there some way to describe the experiences that you would experience each time you ingested the LSD?

A: I would call it a realization.

Q: Did it appear to you that when you took LSD it affected your normal thought processes?

A: No, not really.

Q: How long does it usually take when you ingest LSD for it to take effect?

A: It depends on the acid.

Q: It also depends on the dosage?

A: Yes.

Q: Have you taken LSD in different dosages?

A: I never knew the exact dosage, no.

Q: Was there some reason you never knew the exact dosage?

A: Well, the dosage was not usually inscribed on the capsule or tablet, so I don't know.

Q: It is usually obtained through illegal sources, isn't that correct?

A: I suppose.

Q: Well, I am asking you about your experience.

A: I never obtained it illegally.

Q: Did you ever obtain it legally?

A: Well, I'm not quite sure what you mean by legal or illegal.

Q: Well, for example if you go to a doctor or drugstore and you have prescribed dosage, or frequently one knows what dosage or tablet or drug one has taken.

A: Yes.

Q: Do you know the unit of measure to describe the dosage of LSD?

A: No.

Q: For example, does it come in milligrams, micrograms, grams?

A: I think micrograms sounds right.

Q: Now, how were you able to arrive at the approximate figure of fifty LSD experiences?

A: Because I can usually remember the exact trips.

Q: You have also ingested peyote, have you not?

A: Yes, I have.

Q: What is peyote?

A: It is a form of cactus and it looks like a button, and it grows in southern Texas.

Q: Is it a hallucinogenic drug?

A: Yeah, I guess you could call it that.

Q: Is LSD a hallucinogenic drug?

A: Yes.

Q: Would it be fair to

Artwork by Ian Wagner

say that in LSD states you have had hallucinations?

A: Yes.

Q: Would it be fair to say that while taking peyote you have had hallucinations?

A: Yes. But they are different.

Q: Can you describe them?

A: Well, my sole purpose for taking it was for realization, God realization.

Q: That was to discover God?

A: Yes.

Q: Were you successful in your endeavor?

A: I realized you don't have to take peyote or LSD to discover God.

Q: Is it possible, in your experience, to take dosages of LSD that render you not in control of your mental faculties?

A: Yes, you could take an overdose.

Q: How much would be an overdose?

A: I never took an overdose so I don't know.

Q: Were the hallucinations you experienced while taking the drug, LSD, vivid in character?

A: Sometimes there would be colors that might not be there.

Q: You would see things moving that were actually stationary, is that correct?

A: Yes.

Q: Have you ever seen God under LSD?

A: No, I have not.

Q: Have you ever had delusions under the influence of LSD?

A: I don't quite understand what you mean.

Q: A delusion is a false belief.

A: False belief. Yes, I believe I have.

Q: What sort of false belief did you have?

A: For one thing, I believed that I could see God through acid.

Q: Were you able to see God through acid?

A: Yes, the acid told me it was God.

Q: Are you familiar with the term "acid trip?"

A: Yes.

Q: What is an acid trip?

A: What I have been doing the last fifty times.

Q: Has LSD altered your personality? If you are able to answer that question.

A: Altered my personality? It showed me parts of myself, yes, it has altered, I believe, to a certain extent.

Q: Is taking LSD like having a dream?

A: Yes, sort of, yes.

Q: Let's say on Monday you ingested some LSD and you see and experience something correct?

A: Okay, yes.

Q: On Wednesday you are not ingesting any LSD.

A: Uh-huh.

Q: And you are seeing and hearing things, but the things you see and hear on Wednesday are as real as the things you heard and saw on Monday?

A: Usually the things I saw and heard on Monday were in my own head, and they were not real. But the things on Wednesday when I was not under the drug were real, were stationary.

Q: Have you ever had conversations with a person by the name of Katherine Share?

A: Is that Gypsy?

Q: Also known as Gypsy.

A: Yes, I have had conversations with her.

Q: Have you had LSD experiences with Gypsy?

A: No.

Q: Did you ever tell Katherine Share that you completely died under the influence of LSD and you were reborn again?

A: I don't recall that phrase, no.

Q: Do you recall ever having any experience under LSD in which you experienced death?

A: It was death of values, of thoughts, something was put into me that died, that I rejected.

Q: Did you ever experience an actual physical death of your own self?

A: No.

Q: Have you ever had the experience of your body melting under LSD?

A: No.

Q: Have you ever looked at your hand or some other portion of your body while you had been under the influence of LSD?

A: Yes.

Q: Have you ever seen a part of your body dissolve under the influence of LSD?

A: Dissolve?

Q: Dissolve, melt.

A: No.

Q: What was your mental state during the month of July, 1969?

A: I was extremely impressionistic. I was - I can't think of the words - to describe it.

Q: Can you give us an example of your impressionistic aspects?

A: Well, somebody would tell me something, and at first something within myself would say that is not right, and then this person would further, you know, just keep, you know, putting it into me and putting it into me, and finally, you know, I would just give up.

Q: You were very angry with your husband, were you not?

A: Angry? No, I was just rejected. I felt hurt.

(Missing testimony about drugs Kasabian had taken including drugs, mescaline, psilocybin, and methydrine hydrochloride. She denied taking STP and belladonna.)

Q: You referred during your direct testimony to the hanging of little items from trees near your campsite in Devil's Canyon during the month of July, 1969.

A: Yes, that is correct.

Q: Little pieces of string, little pieces of wire, little pieces of paper?

A: Yes.

Q: And those things had a purpose?

A: Yes. So that we could find our way to the campsite.

Q: Weren't those also witchy things?

A: Yes, that is what they were called.

Q: Do you know why they were called witchy things?

A: No, not particularly.

Q: Didn't you feel that you were a witch during the month of July, 1969?

A: I was made to feel I was a witch, yes.

Q: Did you refer to yourself as a witch?

A: While I was there, yes, and at one point, once when I left, I referred to myself as a witch.

Q: You are familiar with the name Yana, the witch?

A: Yes.

Q: Is that what you used to refer to yourself as?

★★★ TRIAL TESTIMONY OF THE MANSON FAMILY ★★★ PART SEVEN

LINDA KASABIAN CROSS-EXAMINED BY PAUL FITZGERALD — JULY 31, 1970

A: Well, when I first entered the ranch, Gypsy told me that they all assumed different names, and if I would like to pick out a name? And the name just came to me, so I assumed that name, which I was called Yana maybe once or twice. Which just, you know, sort of went down, and they called me Linda.

Q: Did you profess to have magical powers?

A: No, I didn't.

Q: Do you feel you were a witch?

A: I think I tried to make myself believe I was a witch.

Q: Did you act like a witch?

A: No. I acted like myself.

Q: Were you a good witch or a bad witch?

A: I was a good witch, at the time when I was referring to myself as a witch.

Q: During the month of July and early August, 1969 were you preoccupied with the devil and witchcraft?

A: No. No.

Q: Didn't you attempt to practice the art of witchcraft?

A: No. I don't even know what witchcraft is. I don't know rituals.

Q: Well, was this whole thing about calling yourself a witch just a joke?

A: I don't know. When I came into the ranch they told me I was a witch and that they were witches, so they made me believe that I was a witch, too.

Q: Did you ever see any ceremonial witchcraft at the Spahn Ranch?

A: Ceremonial witchcraft? Not that I can recall, no.

Q: You didn't see any black magic rites or anything like that, did you?

A: No. No.

Q: You never saw anybody at the Spahn Ranch do anything a real witch would do, did you?

STOVITZ: What would a real witch do, your Honor?

Q: Is the term "Family" your word, your term?

A: I consider them a family and I considered myself part of the family while I was there because we were a family.

Q: Is it fair to say that you coined the word Family?

A: That I coined the word Family?

Q: Yes.

A: I don't understand what you mean.

Q: What did one have to do, if anything, to become a member of the Family you are referring to?

A: I don't know. I don't know if there was any special thing you had to do.

(Missing testimony about definition of a family. Fitzgerald then referred to the group orgy in the back house that was brought up in direct examination.)

Q: Were you forced in any fashion to participate in love making?

A: No.

Q: Did you make love with somebody?

A: Yes.

Q: Did you make love with more than one person?

A: Yes, I did.

Q: How many persons did you make love to?

A: Well, I remember I made love with Leslie and Tex, the three of us together, and then Snake made love to me, and then Clem was there and then Clem made love. That is all I recall.

Q: When you made love with the people you have just described, can you say you wanted to?

A: Yes.

Q: I take it during the period of time you were making love to them you were unaware of what other persons were making love with whom?

A: Sometimes I looked up, you know, but...

Q: And was this a pleasant experience for you?

A: Well, it was a different experience.

Q: Did you enjoy it?

A: Yeah, I guess I did. I will have to say I did.

(Court adjourned for the day)

(Missing testimony about Kasabian's travels before meeting Manson.)

BUGLIOSI: He at this point apparently wants to go into this $5,000 theft. I want to compliment Mr. Fitzgerald on the record for his professional and ethical attitude in coming here to discuss this before asking questions about it.

FITZGERALD: I have information, and as a result of the information I believe, and I intend to produce evidence on the defense case in chief that Linda Kasabian had other motives other than this motive she has stated for leaving her husband on or about July 4, 1969. I intend to introduce evidence that she came to the Spahn Ranch about July 4 asking for some sort of amnesty or asking to be hidden, to be hidden out because she had stolen $5,000 from her husband's roommate, one Charles Melton. We also intend to introduce evidence that she attempted to give the $5,000 to various people at the Spahn Ranch, including one Katherine Share, and Charles Manson. Now I think that the evidentiary import of this evidence is that it impeaches her in terms of her stated motives, for becoming involved at the Spahn Ranch. Number two, it impeaches her statements, or rather, her altruistic statement about her innocence, her being impressionistic and her naivete.

Artwork by Ani Aslanian

OLDER: What question do you propose to ask?

FITZGERALD: I propose to ask her if she went to the Spahn Ranch for motives other than what she stated. If she says "No," I would ask her, "Isn't it a fact you went to the Spahn Ranch because you stole the money from your husband's roommate?

OLDER: I think that is clearly objectionable, Mr. Fitzgerald.

BUGLIOSI: There are many crimes, your Honor, that we would like to introduce at this trial against Mr. Manson, and we are not going into them because we just cannot do it. The law is clear that you cannot introduce evidence of other crimes.

OLDER: Let's proceed, gentlemen.

Q: You slept in a cave on the evening of July 5; correct?

A: Yes.

Q: Where did you sleep July 6?

A: In the cave.

Q: Who did you sleep with in the cave, if anybody, on July 6?

A: Let me see. I am not sure if it was that night or the night before. I slept with Charlie that night.

Q: Did you sleep with anybody on the 7th?

A: I don't know. I can't go back there and remember exactly, you know, dates and who.

Q: Do you remember who you slept with, if anyone, on the 8th?

A: No.

Q: The 10th?

A: No. But eventually I slept with all the men. So, I don't know the dates.

(Attorneys approached the bench due to Manson loudly telling Fitzgerald to ask Kasabian about the theft of the $5,000.)

Q: What sort of activity did you engage in during the day of July 5th?

A: Well, first I will have to explain to you the night of July 4th.

Q: You may do so.

A: Okay. I met Tex, and Tex took me into a dark shed, shack, whatever you want to call it, and he made love to me, which was an experience that I had never had before.

Q: You had never had sexual intercourse before?

A: No. I am saying that the experience I had in making love with Tex was a total experience, it was different.

Q: In what respect?

A: That my hands were clenched when it was all over and I had absolutely no will power to open my own hands, and I was very much afraid, I didn't understand it. And I questioned Gypsy about it later and she told me it was my ego that was dying. And I told him that I was on my way to South America, and we had all this money, and we were going to do these things.

Q: You had all what money?

A: We had some money that Charlie Melton had inherited.

BUGLIOSI: Your Honor, may we approach the bench.

OLDER: You may approach the bench.

BUGLIOSI: The way it developed is that apparently Tex told her to go steal $5,000, whereupon she did go and steal the $5,000, and gave it to Leslie, I believe. She didn't keep it for herself. She is about to testify to this. And I think the defense is now bringing in through the back door what the court indicated it could not do.

OLDER: I don't see it that way. She is now relating a conversation that she had with Tex, one of the defendants in this case. I think it is permissible.

(Morning recess.)

Q: Would you continue with the conversation you had with Tex Watson?

A: Yes. I told him that we and these people were going to go to South America by boat and sail around the world. And we had this money, and it seemed to me as soon as I mentioned money he started going on this trip, and telling me that it wasn't their money; that it was everybody's money and it was just there to take, and that there was no right and wrong. It was just theirs, ours. I said, "Hey..." He told me, you know, that I should go and take this money. I said, "Hey, I can't do that, he's my brother." He said, "But there is no wrong." And he just kept going on and on. And I accepted it and that was about the conversation.

Q: Didn't you have a philosophy or organized set of thoughts that time was irrelevant, made no sense?

KANAREK: I object on the grounds the word organized—I don't think this witness - I object on the ground it is assuming facts not in evidence that she has an organized thought.

(Overrulled. Possible missing testimony.)

Q: Were you interested in those philosophies?

A: I remember the first-up in the cave, the first thing he said, he started to talk to me and I said that I already knew the truth, because I didn't know what he was going to say. And he said "Don't you want to hear it?" So he started talking to me about it.

Q: What would Charlie do with you when he spent this time with you?

A: He would talk to me, he would make love to me.

Q: How many times did he make love to you?

A: Let me think. The cave, the waterfall, the trailer and the house; four times.

Q: Did you disagree with his philosophy in some respects?

A: Yes, I did.

Q: And you told him that you disagreed with it when he told you?

A: No. Because I was always told, "Never ask why."

Q: Were you also told that you couldn't disagree?

A: The girls used to always tell me that. "We never question Charlie. We know that what he is doing is right."

Q: Were you afraid?

A: Yes.

Q: What were you afraid of?

A: I was just afraid. He is a heavy dude - man.

Q: What is a heavy dude?

A: A dude is a man. Heavy. He just had something, you know, that could hold you. He was a heavyweight, you know. He is just heavy, period.

Q: Did you love Charlie?

A: Yes, I did. To be truthful I felt... I felt that he was the Messiah come again; you know, the second coming of Christ.

Q: You thought he was God?

A: No.

Q: You thought he was a God-man?

A: Yes.

Q: You thought he was a deity in human form?

A: Well, I thought he was the Messiah.

Q: A second Jesus Christ?

A: Yes.

Q: You used the term-or I believe my notes are correct-but I believe on your direct examination you said, "No sense makes sense."

A: Yes.

Q: What did you mean by "No sense makes sense?"

A: I don't know. That is what Charlie told me.

★★★ TRIAL TESTIMONY OF THE MANSON FAMILY ★★★ PART EIGHT

Q: Why are you testifying?

A: You want me to tell you?

Q: I asked you the question.

A: Well, from the moment it happened I knew that I would be the one to tell the truth; I knew I would be the one to tell it, and I never had immunity in my mind. I never knew this was going to happen. This is something that to me I look at as a miracle. I just know I have to do this, whether it's immunity or not, it doesn't matter.

(Missing testimony. Fitzgerald read Kasabian's immunity agreement. "...that if you testify to everything you know about the Tate/LaBianca murders, the district attorney's office will petition the court to grant you immunity from prosecution and dismiss all charges against you." He questioned Kasabian about her agreement.)

Q: Is it your understanding of that immunity agreement that if you say these defendants are innocent you are granted immunity?

A: I just have been told that as long as I tell the truth I will be granted immunity.

(Missing testimony.)

JUNE EMMER QUESTIONED BY KANAREK AUGUST 3, 1970

June Elmer was questioned out of the jury's presence due to being a conditional witness that may not be able to testify later:

Q: How long have you known Miss Kasabian?

A: She stayed a month with me at my house between the middle of October and the middle of November.

Q: Now, while she stayed at your house did Linda Kasabian discuss with you LSD?

A: Yes.

Q: Now, directing your attention to the matter of acid and LSD, would you please tell us whether or not Linda Kasabian told you that she had consumed acid or LSD?

A: Yes. She told me when she was carrying her baby, Tanya, she took it, and for me not to believe everything I see in the papers about taking LSD as far as having a child.

Q: What did she tell you concerning her stay in California?

A: She had a ball there and really enjoyed it.

Q: Did she tell you that she had been in a $250,000 house?

A: Yes.

Q: And did Mrs. Kasabian state words to you, anything, as to her state of mind towards other people when she went on trips?

A: She did not care what happened when she went on trips.

Q: Do you have in your mind a meaning for the word trance?

A: Yes.

Q: Now, directing your attention to Linda Kasabian, would you state that what you observed concerning her, as to whether or not she appeared to be in a trance?

A: Yes, she...

(Objection by Bugliosi. Sustained. Response stricken from the record.)

Q: Would you indicate to us, Mrs. Emmer, what her manner appeared to be to you?

A: Hippie-type.

Q: And when you say hippie-type, what do you mean, Mrs. Emmer?

A: The way she dressed.

Q: Did she wear shoes?

A: No.

Q: Mrs. Emmer, at one time while you were discussing a $250,000 home with Mrs. Kasabian, did you ask her why she was at this house?

(Objection by Bugliosi. Requested an offer of proof as to the validity of the question.)

KANAREK: Well, I believe the Sharon Tate home, your Honor, is worth about $250,000. And it is our belief that Linda Kasabian was in that house, that Linda Kasabian had a participation in these murders that is far and much greater than Linda Kasabian has testified to.

(Objection overruled.)

A: Yes.

Q: What did she tell you?

A: She told me she couldn't tell me. I said, "Why not?" I said, "What kind of people do you know with that kind of money?" She said, "I just cannot tell you."

Q: Do you have an opinion, Mrs. Emmer, as to the truth, honesty and integrity of Linda Kasabian?

A: I know she lies.

STOVITZ: May that be stricken your Honor, as pure speculalation, pure conjecture, and pure malarkey?

OLDER: It is non-responsive. The answer is stricken.

Q: Well, you lived with her for a whole month?

A: Yes.

Q: Did her father tell you what his opinion was concerning her reputation?

A: Yes.

Q: You had occasion to observe her, and among other people besides yourself?

A: Yes.

Q: All right, would you tell us what, then, her reputation for truth, honesty and integrity was in the fall of 1969 in the community in which she lived in Miami?

A: She was a liar.

Q: What was her reputation, was it good, bad?

A: All I can say is she just lied, that is all.

Q: What is her reputation for truth, honesty and integrity, good or bad?

A: It was bad. (The record notes there was a pause before replying.)

Q: Did she ever state to you-did she ever state to you anything concerning the taking of any other drugs other than LSD or acid?

A: She told me she took them all.

June Emmer cross-examined by Stovitz (August 3, 1970) out of the jury's presence. Note that many objections by Kanarek have been deleted for clarity:

Q: Mrs. Emmer, when Linda Kasabian first came to Florida, she first moved in with her father, is that right?

A: No.

Q: Whom did she move in with?

A: She arrived on a Saturday and spent Saturday night, her and the baby, upstairs over the liquor bar. Her father could not be found.

Q: Was there any particular reason her father could not be found?

A: He has weekends off and sometimes he goes out in his boat or goes here or there.

(Missing testimony about witness being twenty nine years old and her husband, in the Fall of 1969, was sixty two.)

Q: When Linda came to live with you she was more or less like a young person to you and you and Linda started to talk, is that right?

A: Yes.

Q: One of the things that you and Linda got to talk about was your drinking habits, isn't that right?

KANAREK: I object your Honor, on the grounds that it is immaterial, irrelevant.

OLDER: Sustained.

Q: All right now, do you imbibe a little? Do you partake of alcoholic beverages from time to time?

A: Yes.

Q: And do you find that as the occasion arises, when you have taken too many alcoholic beverages, your memory becomes a little bad at times?

A: Yes.

Q: This weekend, for instance, you have not taken an excess of alcohol, have you?

A: I have four or five drinks a night.

Q: What about this morning, did you have four or five drinks this morning?

(No response from witness.)

Q: The shaking of your hand, especially when you took the oath, is that because you were nervous or the four or five drinks?

A: My shaking has nothing to do with my drinking whatsoever.

Q: Do you drink to stop your shaking?

A: No. When I drink I shake more.

Q: All right, now, did you ever see Linda drink?

A: Once.

Q: When was that?

A: All I seen her, during the month, was take one beer, that is all.

Q: Now, when did your husband pass away?

A: November 22nd.

Q: 1969?

A: Right.

Q: And following your husband's demise did you increase your drinking habits or did you decrease your drinking habits?

(Objection. Sustained.)

Q: All right now, was your husband ill at the time Linda left Miami?

A: He was under a doctor's care.

Q: And when Linda left Miami, when was the last day before that that she lived with you?

A: The same day. She left from my house to go to the airport.

Q: Now you like Linda's father, Mr. Drouin, right?

A: Yes.

Q: Do you have any matrimonial plans?

A: No.

Q: Do you feel that Linda's affection for her father or her father's affection for Linda in any way interferes with your relationship with Mr. Drouin?

KANAREK: This is assuming facts not in evidence. In fact the contrary is true, the father feels Linda is a liar.

Artwork by Joel Bagley

OLDER: Overruled.

STOVITZ: I suggest you stand next to your witness if you want to coach her. It's very disconcerting your standing over there.

A: All he does is work for me.

Q: How long has he worked for you?

A: For my husband fourteen years.

Q: How long has he worked for you?

A: Four years.

Q: In other words you were only married to your husband four years?

A: Three years.

Q: Three years?

A: Three.

(Missing testimony. Kanarek had traveled to Miami to speak to Emmer and he was paying the expenses for her trip to Los Angeles.)

Q: Did you ever discuss the term "reputation" with Mr. Kanarek?

A: Yes.

Q: What do you understand the word "reputation" to mean?

A: What she is known as.

Q: Now, besides Mr. Drouin, did you know anyone else that knew Linda Kasabian at Miami Beach, Florida?

A: Her father's girl friend.

Q: What is her name?

A: Judy. Judy Short.

Q: Is Judy here in California now?

A: No.

Q: Where have you last seen her?

A: She helps Rosy at the bar. Rosy is Linda's father.

Q: And did you discuss Linda Kasabian with anyone else besides her father and Judy?

★★★ TRIAL TESTIMONY OF THE MANSON FAMILY ★★★ PART NINE

A: Yes. A neighbor across the street.

Q: What is that neighbor's name?

A: A Mrs. Frye.

Q: Do you like Linda Kasabian?

A: She never did anything to me.

Q: Mrs. Emmer, would you like a drink of water?

A: No, thank you.

Q: Your mouth is still not dry?

(Objection. Overruled.)

Q: Mrs. Emmer, you stated that you had about five drinks last night, is that right?

A: Not last night, no.

Q: The night before?

A: (No response from witness.)

Q: Now, what about one occasion in Miami Beach, Florida, when Linda Kasabian was telling you all of these things about California, how many drinks did you have on that occasion?

A: I never drink in the daytime. I have a couple of drinks at night as most people do.

Q: Was this conversation in the daytime or the nighttime?

A: Daytime.

Q: All right. Now, one of the things that she said to you about California was that she was in a house with beautiful chandeliers, is that right?

A: Yes.

Q: Did she describe what type of chandeliers, whether they were French Provincial, or the Spanish type, or whether the early American chandelier?

A: No.

Q: Did she show it to you in a book?

A: No.

Q: Tell us everything you remember about the chandelier and about the house.

A: She told me she was in several homes worth over $250,000, with chandeliers. That is all she told me.

Q. Linda told you that she was using acid when she was carrying Tanya, is that right?

A: Right. She told me not to believe everything I read in the papers. Because she was taking a lot of it when she carried Tanya, and she said "Look at that baby; there is nothing the matter with it."

Q: How old was Tanya when you saw her?

A: Two and a half.

Q: Did she walk?

A: Yes.

Q: Was she saying words? Did she say anything like "Mommy" or "Daddy" or "Charlie" or anything like that?

KANAREK: Or "Aaron?"

A: She used the word "Mama" and "love."

Q: And aside from going around barefooted and being a little hippie-ish, did Linda appear to be a normal girl?

A: Yes.

Q: As far as you are concerned, the amount of alcohol that you drank in no way affected your opinions whatsoever; is that right?

A: No.

Q: And the amount of alcohol you drank in no way affected your memory?

A: I told you I had a couple of drinks every night; but during the day, that is when we talked, because we were home alone.

Q: At the bar did you have a couple of drinks each night?

A: No. I wasn't at the bar. I was home with her.

Q: At night?

A: During the day.

Q: What about having a couple of drinks; when did you have a couple of drinks?

A: At night. I never drank in the daytime.

Q: At the bar or at the house?

A: At the house.

Q: Was Linda there when you were having a couple of drinks?

A: Yes.

Q: And didn't she, on one of those times, ask you, "Judy" - she called you Judy, didn't she?

A: Right.

Q: Didn't she say, "Judy, why do you drink so much?"

(Objection. Sustained.)

(Missing testimony. Emmer had only talked to three people about Kasabian.)

OLDER: There is no evidence that Mrs. Emmer is familiar with the general reputation of Linda Kasabian in the community for truth, honesty and veracity. Therefore her testimony regarding reputation as to Mrs. Kasabian will be stricken.

LINDA KASABIAN CROSS-EXAMINED BY PAUL FITZGERALD AUGUST 3, 1970

(Missing testimony. Retelling her previous testimony. Attempted to show she could have contacted police several times but didn't. Questioned her about a book being written about her.)

Q: Is it your understanding that upon the publication of your book you will be quote famous unquote?

A: I don't care. I don't care if I am famous or not. It doesn't matter.

Q: The purpose of the book is to secure money, isn't that right?

A: Actually the purpose for the book is so that younger people can relate to me and see that this road I went down is not the way, and they will go another way. That is my purpose.

Q: They will profit from the mistakes you have made in the past, is that right?

A: Yes.

Q: I have no further questions.

(Attorney's approached bench due to news story that President Nixon had declared that Manson was guilty.)

FITZGERALD: I have been

handed what purports to be a Western Union telegram, a telegraphic copy of an AP Wire Service that was handed to all the news media wherein the President of the United States is quoted as saying that a man who is guilty, directly or indirectly, of eight murders without reason - and he is referring to Charles Manson - I am a little emotional perhaps, but I think it would absolutely be grounds for a mistrial.

OLDER: Well, if true it is a perfect example of why I insisted the jury be sequestered.

FITZGERALD: Yes, it was a wise thing, no question about it. Everyone is entitled to change his opinion.

(Judge Older stated it was premature to consider any motions. Denied motion for a mistrial.)

Linda Kasabian cross-examined by Day Shinn:

(Missing testimony concerning Kasabian's conversations, while in custody, with Stovitz, Bugliosi, police and her attorneys.)

Q: Do you recall what Mr. Bugliosi said to you at the first meeting?

A: What he said to me?

Q: Yes.

A: Well, he always stressed for me to tell the truth.

Q: Besides the truth I'm talking about.

Q: Did she answer the question, your Honor?

A (Kasabian): I was waiting for you. I thought you were busy.

Q: You can answer the question, I'm sorry.

A: I have no question to answer.

Q: I did not get the last answer, your Honor.

STOVITZ: She was waiting for you, she did not want to be discourteous and answer your questions while you had your back turned.

OLDER: I would suggest you put the question to her again, Mr. Shinn.

SHINN: I forgot the question.

OLDER: Let's go back and read the record.

(Question was read back but declared ambiguous by judge.)

(Missing testimony about consultations with attorneys.)

Q: I believe you also stated that you have hallucinations sometimes?

A: Under the drug?

Q: Under the drug or not under the drug; hallucinations?

A: Well, sitting here right now, when I look at all those holes, they just sort of seem to all go together. I don't know if that is hallucination.

Q: What holes?

A: Excuse me. The holes in the tiles on the walls.

Q: What else do you see?

A: I see a clock, and I see wood, and I see people.

Q: Do you believe in Santa Claus?

STOVITZ: Then or now, counsel?

(Missing testimony about Kasabian not telling about murders before her arrest. Cross-examination was yielded to Kanarek.)

LINDA KASABIAN CROSS-EXAMINED BY IRVING KANAREK AUGUST 4, 1970

(Meeting in Judge's chambers. Hughes was ejected for being improperly dressed. Hughes borrowed a jacket from a reporter and returned to chambers. Discussed Nixon's statements regarding Manson's guilt. Older stated he had windows of juror's bus blackened so they would not see headline. Refused to question jurors on whether they'd seen the headline.)

OLDER: I want to direct all counsel to remove from counsel table any news containing any of this material so that they will not inadvertently be displayed to the jury when the jury comes in.

KANAREK: I believe that this jury, with the facts of life being what they are, this jury, I would believe it without being able to prove it, that this jury knows what President Nixon said, the substance of what he said, and the retraction is inadequate. The bell has rung; the Presidency of the United States has been invoked and the President has declared that Mr. Manson is guilty.

And I say something else, without being able to prove it. The district attorney of Los Angeles County is running for attorney general. I say it without being able to prove it, that Evelle Younger and the President got together to do this.

(Hughes asked the judge to censure Nixon. Denied. Kanarek moved for a mistrial. Denied. Manson asked to make a motion. Granted.)

MANSON: Your Honor, in view of the publicity, and it doesn't look like it is going to stop, I request this court, as provided in the Constitution, to be able to confront and cross-examine witnesses, to be able to take part in these proceedings in order for the court, the jury, the spectators and the world that is misinformed so badly, to take a look at what they are judging. It is easy to sit and be quiet and have someone else speak, but they are not my words, they are not my philosophy that you speak of, they are not my Family's that you talk of. All the things that the court seems to be confused about, I might be able to assist and help you straighten this mess out, because you have certainly got a mess, you have made a mess of the whole thing. You have made a mess of it.

(Older asked Manson if he was making a motion.)

MANSON: Yes, I am making a motion to be allowed to move as my own counsel and have movement of the courtroom to cross-examine and to be confronted and confront witnesses, with the assistance of an attorney who can help me in the legal matters. Your Honor, each man has a reality, each man knows what he knows to be true. For me to communicate to you, I have to use my reality because I don't know your reality. I know you are a pilot and I know you have been through wars...

OLDER: Mr. Manson,... I am not going to let you continue unless you get back on the track. Tell me precisely what relief you are seeking and you may argue in support of that.

MANSON: This is the problem. The track that you are on and the track that I am on is two different tracks. You judge me from a slanted view.

Artwork by Joel Bagley

VINCENT BUGLIOSI 1970

CHARLIE MANSON (the finger)

★★★ TRIAL TESTIMONY OF THE MANSON FAMILY ★★★ PART TEN

I ask this court if I may stand up and be a man and maintain my voice in the courtroom to cross-examine witnesses that I am confronted with.

(Manson moved to be allowed to be his own attorney. Older stated "It would be a miscarriage of justice to permit you to represent yourself in a case having the complications that this case has." Motion denied. Manson stated, "Mr. Older, I can't accept you as being a good judge. A pilot maybe. The inadequacy is a reflection of your own." Judge order him to be quite.)

(Missing testimony concerning two hitchhikers that Kasabian picked up after the murders during her trip to Taos, New Mexico.)

Q: Now, did you tell this person that your name, at that time, when you spoke with him, was Yana, but that your name used to be Linda?

A: Maybe.

Q: Well, would you reflect upon that for a moment and tell us whether, in fact, you did state that your name was Yana and it used to be Linda?

A: Yes, I probably said that.

Q: Pardon? Excuse me?

A: I probably said that.

Q: Well, did you, in fact, say that?

A: Well, I can't remember if I did say it.

Q: Well, what makes you think you probably said it?

A: It just sounds right.

Q: May I ask you what sounds right about it?

A: That I would say my name is Yana but it used to be Linda. It just sounds right.

Q: Well, may I ask you why it sounds right?

A: I don't understand.

Q: You don't understand what?

A: Didn't I answer it the way I am supposed to answer it?

Q: Well, has anyone told you that you are supposed to answer questions a certain way?

A: No, but I thought I answered your question, but you keep asking.

Q: Well, my question is - may that question be read back, your Honor?

STOVITZ: Which question, counsel?

OLDER: Reframe the question, Mr. Kanarek. We have long since gone by it.

KANAREK: Very well.

Q: Why, Mrs. Kasabian, why did you say it sounds right that Yana was your name at that time rather than Linda?

A: I still don't understand.

Q: Well, may I ask you -you don't understand the last question?

A: No, I don't.

Q: Well, did you in fact, Mrs. Kasabian, say "My name is Yana, but my name used to be Linda?" Did you in fact say that?

A: I probably did, yes.

Q: Then may I ask you, then, why do you say "probably?" Is there any doubt in your mind as to whether you said "My name is Yana but it used to be Linda?"

STOVITZ: Objected to as argumentative, your Honor. She answered the question three or four times.

KANAREK: I submit she hasn't, your Honor.

STOVITZ: I submit the record speaks for itself, your Honor.

OLDER: You may answer.

A: I remember telling them my name was Yana and I just might have said "It used to be Linda," but I'm not sure.

Q: May I ask you then, now, would you listen to this carefully, Mrs. Kasabian: Why aren't you sure as to whether or not you said that your name used to be Linda?

STOVITZ: To which we object as being argumentative, your Honor.

OLDER: Sustained.

(Missing testimony.)

(After the noon recess, Manson held a newspaper up for the jury to see. The headline was "Manson Guilty Nixon Declares." Remainder of day was spent on this incident and questioning jurors.)

LINDA KASABIAN CROSS-EXAMINED BY IRVING KANAREK AUGUST 5, 1970

(As the jurors were entering the jury box, Atkins, Krenwinkel and Van Houten stood and said "Your Honor, the President said we are guilty, so why go on with the trial?" Judge ordered them to sit down.)

Q: Mrs. Kasabian, on the night, on the second night that you left the Spahn Ranch, did you know that you had participated with three other people who, all together, you and the three other people together, had killed five people?

A: No.

Q: Directing your attention, Mrs. Kasabian, to the second night and your state of mind, your thinking as you left the Spahn Ranch on the second night, did you know that what you and three other people had done the night before caused the killing of five people?

A: I don't understand the question.

Q: You don't understand that question?

A: Right.

Q: What about the question don't you understand?

A: Well, I don't know what the answer is.

Q: You mean you don't know what answer Mr. Bugliosi wants you to give?

BUGLIOSI: Your Honor, I object to this. These are unbelievably outrageous remarks.

OLDER: Mr. Kanarek, if you repeat that I will have to take some action against you. The jury is admonished to disregard this colloquy between counsel.

(Missing testimony. Traced Kasabian's steps when Kasabian left Spahn Ranch after the murders and drove to New Mexico. Attempted to show she planned to retrieve Rosemary LaBianca's wallet from the gas station where it had been hidden. Kanarek showed Kasabian crime scene photographs.)

Q: Mrs. Kasabian, you looked through the window, didn't you, in that house?

A: Yes.

Q: Mrs. Kasabian, I ask you...

(Kanarek showed another crime photo to Kasabian.)

A: Oh, god.

(Older declared a recess. Kasabian's attorney, Ronald Goldman, spoke to Judge Older in Chambers.)

GOLDMAN: In the first place, your Honor, I want to make an objection to the court to the tactics that are being employed by Mr. Kanarek at this time in exhibiting certain photographs in connection with this case where there has been no evidence introduced concerning my client's percipient testimony, or the fact that she was a witness in or to the matters that were being shown. The evidence has shown that she was not a witness nor did she see the scenes depicted in that photograph, No. 87, and I imagine that there are other photos concerning others who were inside that residence. I submit, your Honor, it is improper courtroom decorum, improper tactics of counsel unless he lays a foundation that they have some relevancy to her testimony.

(Older said the defense had a right to show Kasabian the photos.)

OLDER: It may well be that the shock of that alone would cause her to change her story, if she were lying, and admit it. I agree that the photographs should not be displayed until after the question has been put to the witness and the court has had a chance to rule on any objection. I agree it is improper to stand up there with a photograph in your hand for five minutes, and put it in her hand and have her hold it, while you go through a series of questions that have nothing to do with the photograph.

(Possible missing testimony.)

Q: Now, Mrs. Kasabian, on how many instances, Mrs. Kasabian, did you have sexual relations with Mr. Watson?

A: Two or three times.

Q: Two or three times?

A: Yes.

Q: Now, could it have been more than that?

A: Not that I can remember.

Q: You mean it might possibly be more than that?

A: It could be, yes, but I remember just two specific instances, and possibly a third.

Q: Is it a fair statement that while you were at the Spahn Ranch you had sexual relations with many people?

A: Yes.

Q: With many men?

A: With the men at the ranch, yes.

Q: All of the men at the ranch; right?

A: Not all of the men, no.

Q: Well, will you tell us those with whom you had sexual relations?

A: Charlie, Tex, Bruce, a guy named Chuck, Bobbie. That is all. And Clem.

Q: Anyone else?

A: No, not that I can remember.

Q: And it is a fair statement, is it, that you enjoyed sexual relations?

BUGLIOSI: That is immaterial. Object.

OLDER: Sustained.

Q: Well, Mrs. Kasabian, I am now asking you: At the time that you state that you ran toward the house with the thought that you were going into the house, at that time - at that time - were you in a state of shock?

A: Yes, I guess so.

Q: And so, being in a state of shock, you don't know whether you went into the house or not; is that correct?

A: I know I didn't go into that house.

Q: You know you didn't?

A: Yes.

Q: Or is it a fair statement to say that you wish you didn't?

STOVITZ: That is objected to as argumentative, your Honor.

OLDER: Sustained.

KANAREK: Your Honor, may I approach the witness in connection with a photograph?

(Permission granted. Kararek dropped folder of crime photos in front of jury box.)

Q: Mrs. Kasabian, I show you this picture.

A: Oh, God. How could you do that?

BUGLIOSI: She has already looked at it, your Honor. Is there any necessity for him to continue flashing it in front of her face?

KANAREK: Your Honor, it seems like I am the one that is always the villain.

OLDER: Just a moment. Mrs. Kasabian, did you see the photograph?

A: Yes, I did.

OLDER: Did you see it well enough to identify the person in the photograph?

A: He was the man I saw at the door.

OLDER: All right. You may return.

KANAREK: Thank you, your Honor.

Q: Mrs. Kasabian, why are you crying right now?

A: Because I can't believe it. It is just - I don't know.

Q: You can't believe what, Mrs. Kasabian?

A: That they could do that.

Q: That they could do that?

A: Yes.

Q: I see. Not that you could do that, but that they could do that.

A: I know I didn't do that.

Art by Joel Bagley

★★★ TRIAL TESTIMONY OF THE MANSON FAMILY ★★★ PART ELEVEN

Q: You were in a state of shock, weren't you?

A: That's right.

Q: Then how do you know?

A: Because I know it. I do not have that kind of thing in me to do such an animalistic thing.

Q: And you are basing it upon the fact that you don't have it in you to do that kind of an animalistic thing?

A: Right.

Q: Is that why you are saying you didn't do it, right?

A: Right.

Q: Is that why you are saying you didn't do it, right.

A: I just know I didn't do it, Mr. Kanarek.

CHARLES MANSON TESTIMONY NOVEMBER 19, 1970

The Court: Do you have anything to say?

Yes, I do.

There has been a lot of charges and a lot of things said about me and brought against me and brought against the co-defendants in this case, of which a lot could be cleared up and clarified to where everyone could understand exactly what the family was supposed to have been, what the philosophies in regards to the families were, and whether or not there was any conspiracy to commit murder, to commit crimes, and to explain to you who think with your minds.

It is hard for you to conceive of a philosophy of someone that may not think.

I have spent my life in jail, and without parents.

I have looked up to the strongest father-figure, and I have always looked to the people in the free world as being the good people, and the people in the inside of the jail as being the bad people.

I never went to school, so I never growed up in the respect to learn to read and write so good, so I have stayed in jail and I have stayed stupid, I have stayed a child while I have watched your world grow up, and then I look at the things that you do and I don't understand.

I don't understand the courts, and I don't understand a lot of things that are brought against me.

Your write things about my mother in the newspaper that hasn't got anything to do with anything in particular.

You invent stories, and everybody thinks what they do, and then they project it from the witness stand on the defendant as if that is what he did.

For example, with Danny DeCarlo's testimony. He said that I hate black men, and he said that we thought alike, that him and I was a lot alike in our thinking.

But actually all I ever did with Danny DeCarlo or any other human being was reflect himself back at himself.

But maybe the girls and women in your world outside ... Being by yourself for such a long time when you do get out you appreciate things that people don't even see, you walk over them every day.

Like in jail you have a whole new attitude or a whole different way of thinking.

I don't think like you people. You people put importance on your lives.

Well, my life has never been important to anyone, not even in the understanding of the way you fear the things that you fear, and the things you do.

I know that the only person I can judge is me.

I judge what I have done and I judge what I do and I look and live with myself every day.

I am content with myself.

If you put me in the penitentiary, that means nothing because you kicked me out of the last one. I didn't ask to get released. I liked it in there because I like myself.

I like being with myself.

But in your world it's hard because your understanding and your values are different.

These children that come at you with knives, they are your children.

You taught them. I didn't teach them. I just tried to help them stand up.

Most of the people at the ranch that you call The Family were just people that you did not want, people that were alongside the road, that their parents had kicked them out or they did not want to go to Juvenile Hall, so I did the best I could and I took them up on my garbage dump and I told them this that in love there is no wrong.

I don't care. I have one law and I learned it when I was a kid in reform school. It's don't snitch. And I have never snitched. And I told them that anything they do for their brothers and sisters is good, if they do it with a good thought.

It is not my responsibility. It is your responsibility. It is the responsibility you have towards your own children who you are neglecting, and then you want to put the blame on me again and again and again.

Over and over you put me in your penitentiary. I did not build the penitentiary. I would not lock one of you up. I could not see locking another human being up.

You eat meat with your teeth and you kill things that are better than you are, and in the same respect you say how bad and even killers that your children are. You make your children what they are. I am just a reflection of every one of you.

I have never learned anything wrong. In the penitentiary, I have never found a bad man. Every man in the penitentiary has always showed me his good side, and circumstances put him where he was. He would not be there, he is good, human, just like the policeman that arrested him is a good human.

I have nothing against none of you. I can't judge any of you. But I think it is high time that you all started looking at yourselves, and judging the lie that you live in.

I sit and I watch you from nowhere, and I have nothing in my mind, no malice against you and no ribbons for you.

But you stand and you play the game of money. As long as you can sell a newspaper, some sensationalism, and you can laugh at someone and joke at someone and look down at someone, you know.

You just sell those newspapers for public opinion, just like you are all hung on public opinion, and none of you have any idea what you are doing.

You are just doing what you are doing for the money, for a little bit of attention from someone.

I can't dislike you, but I will say this to you. You haven't got long before you are all going to kill yourselves because you are all crazy.

And you can project it back at me, and you can say that it's me that cannot communicate, and you can say that it's me that don't have any understanding, and you can say that when I am dead your world will be better, and you can lock me up in your penitentiary and you can forget about me.

But I'm only what lives inside of you, each and every one of you. These children, they take a lot of narcotics because you tell them not to. Any child you put in a room and you tell them, "Don't go through that door," he never thought of going through that door until you told him to go through the door. You go to the high schools and you show them pills and you show them what not to take, how else would they know what it was unless you tell them?

And then you tell them what you don't want them to do in the hopes they will go out and do it and then you can play your game with them and then you can give attention to them because you don't give them any of your love.

You only give them your frustration; you only give them your anger; you only give them the bad part of you rather than give them the good part of you.

You should all turn around and face your children and start following them and listening to them.

The music speaks to you every day, but you are too deaf, dumb, and blind to even listen to the music. You are too deaf, dumb and blind to stop what you are doing. You point and you ridicule.

But it's okay, it's all okay. It doesn't really make any difference because we are all going to the same place anyway. It's all perfect. There is a God. He sits right over here beside me. That is your God. This is your God.

But let me tell you something; there is another Father and he has much more might than you imagine.

If I could get angry at you I would try to kill every one of you. If that's guilt, I accept it.

These children, everything they have done, they done for love of their brother. Had you not arrested Robert Beausoleil for something he did not do....

(Interruption)

I have killed no one and I have ordered no one to be killed.

I may have implied on several occasions to several different people that I may have been Jesus Christ, but I haven't decided yet what I am or who I am.

I was given a name and a number and I was put in a cell, and I have lived in a cell with a name and a number.

I don't know who I am.

I am whoever you make me, but what you want is a fiend; you want a sadistic fiend because that is what you are.

You only reflect on me what you are inside of yourselves, because I don't care anything about any of you and I don't care what you do.

I can stand here in front of this court and smile at you, and you can do anything you want to do with me, but you cannot touch me because I am only my love, and it is all for me, and I give it to myself for me, because I look out for me first and I like me, and you can live with yourselves and your opinion of yourselves. I know what I have done.

If I showed someone that I would do anything for my brother, include give my life for my brother in the battlefield, or give where else that I may want to do that, then he picks his banner up and he goes off and does what he does. .

That is not my responsibility. I don't tell people what to do.

If we enter into an agreement to build a house, I will help you build the house and I will offer suggestions for that house, but I won't put myself on you because that is what made you weak, because your parents have offered themselves on you.

You are not you, you are just reflections, you are reflections of everything that you think that you know, everything that you have been taught.

Your parents have told you what you are. They made you before you were six years old, and when you stood in school and you crossed your heart and pledged allegiance to the flag, they trapped you a in truth because at that age you didn't know any lie until that lie was reflected on you.

Art by Joel Bagley

★★★ TRIAL TESTIMONY OF THE MANSON FAMILY ★★★ PART TWELVE

No, I am not responsible for you. Your karma is not mine.

My father is the jail house. My father is your system, and each one of you, each one of you are just a reflection of each one of you, and you all live by yourselves, no matter how crowded you may think that you are in a room full of people, you are still by yourself, and you have to live with that self forever and ever and ever and ever.

To some people this would be hell; to some people it would be heaven.

I have mine, and each one of you will have to work out yours, and you cannot work it out by pointing your fingers at people.

I have ate out of your garbage cans to stay out of jail.

I have wore your second-hand clothes.

I have accepted things and given them away the next second.

I have done my best to get along in your world and now you want to kill me, and I look at you and I look how incompetent you all are, and then I say to myself, "You want to kill me, ha, I'm already dead, have been all my life!"

I've lived in your tomb that you built.

I did seven years for a thirty-seven dollar check. I did twelve years because I didn't have any parents, and how many other sons do you think you have in there? You have many sons in there, many, many sons in there, most of them are black and they are angry. They are mad, and they are mad at me.

I look and I say, "Why are you mad at me?"

He said, "I am mad at you because of what your father did."

And I look at him and I say, "Well," and I look at my fathers, and I say, "If there was ever a devil on the face of this earth I am him."

And he's got my head anytime he wants it, as all of you do too, anytime you want it.

Sometimes I think about giving it to you. Sometimes I'm thinking about just jumping on you and let you shoot me. Sometimes I think it would be easier than sitting here and facing you in the contempt that you have for yourself, the hate that you have for yourself, it's only the anger you reflect at me, the anger that you have got for you.

I do not dislike you, I cannot dislike you. I am you. you are blood. You are my brother. That is why I can't fight you.

If I could I would jerk this microphone out and beat your brains out with it because that is what you deserve, that is what you deserve.

Every morning you eat that meat with your teeth. You're all killers, you kill things better than you. And what can I say to you that you don't already know? And I have known that there is nothing I can say to you. There is nothing I can say to any of you. It is you that has to say it to you, and that is my whole philosophy; you say it to you and I will say it to me.

I live in my world, and I am my own king in my world, whether it be a garbage dump or if it be in the desert or wherever it be. I am my own human being. You may restrain my body and you may tear my guts out, do anything you wish, but I am still me and you can't take that.

You can kill the ego, you can kill the pride, you can kill the want, the desire of a human being.

You can lock him in a cell and you can knock his teeth out and smash his brain, but you cannot kill the soul.

You never could kill the soul. It's always there, the beginning and the end. you cannot stop it, it's bigger than me. I'm just looking into it and it frightens me sometimes.

The truth is now; the truth is right here: the truth is this minute, and this minute we exist.

Yesterday you cannot prove yesterday happened today, it would take you all day and then it would be tomorrow, and you can't prove last week happened. You can't prove anything except to yourself.

My reality is my reality, and I stand within myself on my reality.

Yours is yours and I don't care what it is. Whatever you do is up to you and it's the same thing with anyone in my family. and anybody in my family is a white human being, because my family is of the white family.

There is the black family, a yellow family, the red family, a cow family and a mule family. There is all kinds of different families.

We have to find ourselves first, God second, and kind, k-i-n-d, come next. And that is all I was doing. I was working on cleaning up my house, something Nixon should have been doing. He should have been on the side of the road picking up his children. But he wasn't. He was in the White House sending them off to war.

I don't know the different people that have got on the stand; one friend said I put a knife to his throat. I did. I put a knife to his throat. And he said I was responsible for all of these killings.

I have done the best I know how, and I have given all I can give and I haven't got any guilt about anything because I have never been able to say any wrong.

I never found any wrong.

I looked at wrong, and it is all relative.

Wrong is if you haven't got any money.

Wrong is if your car payment is overdue.

Wrong is if the TV breaks.

Wrong is if President Kennedy gets killed.

Wrong is, wrong is, wrong is you keep on, you pile it in your mind. you become belabored with it, and in your confusion....

I make up my own mind. I think for myself. I look at you and I say, "Okay, you make up your own mind, you think for yourself, then you see your mothers and your fathers and your teachers and your preachers and your politicians and your presidents, and you lay in your brain with your opinions, considerations, conclusions." And I look at you and I say, "Okay, if you are real to you it's okay with me but you don't look real to me. you only look like a composite of what someone told you you are. You live for each others' opinion and you have pain on your face and you are not sure what you like, and you wonder if you look okay."

And I look at you and I say, "Well, you look alright to me," you know, and you look at me and you say, "Well, you don't look alright to me,"

Well I don't care what I look like to you. I don't care what you think about me and I don't care what you do with me. I have always been yours anyway. I have always been in your cell.

When you were out riding your bicycles I was sitting in your cell looking out the window and looking at pictures in magazines and wishing I could go to high school and go to the proms, wishing I could go to the things you could do, but oh so glad, oh so glad, brothers and sisters, that I am what I am.

Because when it does come down around your ears and none of you know what you are doing, you better believe I will be on top of my thought.

I will know what I am doing. I will know exactly what I am doing. If you ever let me go before you kill me. And then I don't really particularly care anyway, because I still will be there and I will still know what I am doing.

In my mind I live forever.

In my mind I live forever, and in my mind I have always lived forever.

I am only what you made me. I am only a reflection of you.

I have done everything I have always been told. I have mopped the floor when I was supposed to mop the floor. And I have swept when I was supposed to sweep.

I was smart enough to stay out of jail and too dumb to learn anything. I was too little to get a job there, and too big do to something over here.

I have just been sitting in jail thinking nothing. Nothing to think about.

Everybody used to come in and tell me about their past and their lives and what they did. But I could never tell anybody about my past or what my life was or what I did because I have always been sitting in that room with a bed, a locker, and a table. So, then it moves on to awareness: how many cracks can you count in the wall? It moves to where the mice live and what the mice are thinking, and see how clever mice are.

And then, when you get on the outside, you look into people's heads. You take Linda Kasabian and you put her on the witness stand and she testifies against her father. She never has liked her father, and she has always projected her wrong off to the man-figure. So, consequently, it is the man's fault again, and the woman turns around and she blames it on the man. The man made her do it. The man put her up to it.

The man works for her, the man slaves for her, the man does everything for her, and she lays around the house and she tells him what he should do, because, generally, she is an extension of his mother. His mother told him what to do and she trained him for twenty years and passed him on to the wife. Then the woman takes him and tells him what to wear, when to get up, when to go to work.

Then when she gets on the stand and she says when she looked in that man's eyes that was dying, she knew it was my fault.

She knew that it was my fault because she couldn't face death.

And if she cannot face death, that is not my fault. Why should she blame it on me? I can face death. I have all the time.

In the penitentiary you live with it, with constant fear of death, because it is a violent world in there, and you have to be on your toes constantly.

So, it is not without violence that I live. It is not without pain that I live.

I look at the projection that comes from this witness stand often to the defendants. It isn't what we said, it is what someone thought we said. A word is changed: "in there" to "up there," "off of that" to "on top." The semantics get into a word game in the courtroom to prove something that is gone in the past. It is gone in the past, and when it is gone, it is gone, sisters. It is gone, brother.

You can't bring the past back up and postulate or mock up a picture of something that happened a hundred years ago, or 1970 years ago, as far as that goes. you can only live in the now, for what is real is now.

The words go in circles.

You can say everything is the same, but it is always different. It is the same, but it is always different. You can "but" it to death. You can say, "You are right, but, but, but."

You sat here for nineteen days questioning that girl.

She got immunity on seven counts of murder.

She got. I don't know how much money she is going to make in magazines and things. You set her up to be a hero, and that is your woman. That is the thing that you worship.

You have lost sight of God. You sing your songs to woman. You put woman in front of man. Woman is not God. Woman is but a reflection of her man, supposedly. But a lot of times man is a reflection of his woman. And if a man can't rise above a woman's thought, then that is his problem, it is not my problem. But you give me this problem when you set this woman against me.

You set this woman up here to testify against me. And she tells you a sad story.

Art by Joel Bagley

THE MEANING IS ALWAYS LEANING IN A TIMELESS WORLD OF SOUND HAVE YOU BEEN LISTENING TO THE MUSIC TO THE SOUNDS THATS BEEN COMING DOWN OR IS THERE NO ONE IN YOUR WORLD BUT YOU...

CHARLES MANSON

★★★ TRIAL TESTIMONY OF THE MANSON FAMILY ★★★ PART THIRTEEN

How she has only taken every narcotic that is possible to take. How she has only stolen, lied, cheated and done everything that you have got there in that book.

But it is okay, she is telling the truth now. She wouldn't have any ulterior motive like immunity for seven counts of murder.

And then comical as it may seem, you look at me, and you say, "You threatened to kill a person if they snitch."

Well, that is the law where I am from. Where I am from, if you snitch, you leave yourself open to be killed.

I could never snitch because I wouldn't want someone to kill me.

So, I have always abided by that law. It is the only law that I know of, and it is the law that I have always abided by.

But she will come up here and you enshrine her, you put her above you, and you strive to be as good as something below you.

It is circles that just don't make any sense in my reality. But of course again that is my reality and it has nothing to do with you, because you have got your reality and you have to live with what you believe in.

But this woman has got here and she has testified. She said she wasn't sure, but maybe.

Then the magical mystery tour wouldn't be able to be explained to you.

A magical mystery tour is when you pick up somebody else and play a part, you may pick up a cowboy today, and you go around all day and play like a cowboy. You put on a hat and you ride a horse.

This is all we have done. We have played like mom and dad. We have loved each other. We have done everything we could to stay outside the frame of the law, the shakedowns.

Nothing has been stolen. I have got better sense than to break the law. I give to the law what it has coming. It is his law. If I break his law, he puts me back in the grave again.

I haven't broken his law yet but it seems as if somebody lays around and somebody needs to fulfill a spot, they snatch it up and say, "This will do. We will put this over here, we can hang this on him. Or we can do this to that."

Then the words go into another meaning and another level of understanding.

Why a woman would stand up and project herself into a man and say, "Actually he never told me anything, but I knew it all came from him."

Her assumption.

Am I to be found guilty on her assumption?

You assume what you would do in my position, but that doesn't mean that is what I did in my position. It doesn't mean that my philosophy is valid. It's only valid to me. Your philosophies, they are whatever you think they are and I don't particularly care what you think they are.

But I know this: that in your own hearts and your own souls, you are as much responsible for the Vietnam War as I am for killing these people.

I knew a guy that used to work in the stockyards and he used to kill cows all day long with a big sledgehammer, and then go home at night and eat dinner with his children and eat the meat that he slaughtered. Then he would go to church and read the bible, and he would say, "That is not killing." And I look at him and I say, "That doesn't make any sense, what you are talking about?"

Then I look at the beast, and I say, "Who is the beast?"

I am the beast. I am the beast.

I am the biggest beast walking the face of the earth. I kill everything that moves. As a man, as a human, I take responsibility for that. As a human, it won't be long, and God will ask you to take responsibility for it. It is your creation. You live in your creation. I never created your world, you created it.

You create it when you pay taxes, you create it when you go to work, then you create it when you foster a thing like this trial.

Only for vicarious thrills do you sell a newspaper and do you kow-tow to public opinion. Just to sell your newspapers. You don't care about the truth. You take another Alka-Seltzer and another aspirin and hope that you don't have to think of the truth and you hope that you don't have to look at yourself with a hangover as you go to a Helter Skelter party and make fun of something that you don't understand.

(The Judge asks Manson to stick to the point.)

The issues in this case? The issues in this case?

The issues are that Mr. Younger is Attorney General, and I imagine he is a good man and does a good job. I don't know him. I can't judge him. But I know he has got me here. He set me in this seat.

Mr. Bugliosi is doing his job for a paycheck. That is an issue. He is doing whatever he is doing. Whether he thinks it is right or not, I couldn't say. That is up to him.

The only way that I have been able to live on that side of the road was outside the law. I have always lived outside the law. When you live outside the law it is pretty hard, you can't call the man for protection. You have got to pretty much protect your own.

You can't live within the law and protect yourself. You can't knock the guy down when he comes over and starts to rape one of the girls, or starts to bring some speed or dope up there. You can't enforce your will over someone inside the law.

I gave everything I could think of to that old man and that ranch for permission to stay there, and I have given the people that stayed on that ranch my all. When no one wanted to go out in front and fight, I would go out and fight. When no one else wanted to clean the toilets, I would go and clean them.

People would see me and they would see what I do and see the example that I set. They see, when I am cleaning out a cesspool, that I am happy and smiling and making a game of it. Like I was on a chain gang somewhere once upon a time and they come and pass the water. I make a game out of it, or I make a pleasure out of a job. We turn it into a magical mystery tour.

We speed down the highway in a 1958 automobile that won't go but fifty, and an XKE Jaguar goes by, and I state to Clem, "Catch him Clem, and we'll rob him or steal all of his money," you know. And he says, "What shall we do?" I say, "Hit him on the head with a hammer." We magical mystery tour it.

Then Linda Kasabian gets on the stand and says:

"They were going to kill a man, they were going to kill a man in an automobile."

To you, it seems serious. But like Larry Kramer and I would get on a horse and we would ride over to Wichita, Kansas, and act like cowboys. We make it a game on the ranch.

Like, Helter Skelter is a nightclub. Helter Skelter means confusion. Literally. It doesn't mean any war with anyone. It doesn't mean that those people are going to kill other people. It only means what it means. Helter Skelter is confusion.

Confusion is coming down fast. If you don't see the confusion coming down fast around you, you can call it what you wish.

It is not my conspiracy. It is not my music. I hear what it relates. It says, "Rise!" It says, "Kill!" Why blame it on me? I didn't write the music. I am not the person who projected it into your social consciousness, that sanity that you projected into your social consciousness, today. You put so much into the newspaper and then you expect people to believe what is going on. I say back to the facts again.

How many witnesses have you got up here and projected only what they believe in. What I believe in is right now. I don't believe in anything past now. I speak to you from now.

Because there is nothing here to worry about, nothing here to think about, nothing here to be confused over. My house is not divided. My house is one with me, myself.

Then I look at the facts that you have brought in front of this court and I look at the twelve facts that are looking at me and judging me. If I were to judge them, what scale would that balance? Would the scale balance if I was to turn and judge you? How would you feel if I were to judge you? Could I judge you? I can only judge you if you try to judge me. That is the fact.

Mr. Bugliosi is a hard-driving prosecutor, with a polished education. Semantics, words. He is a genius. He has got everything that every lawyer would want to have except one thing: a case. He doesn't have a case.

Were I allowed to defend myself, I could have proven this to you. I could have called witnesses and showed you how these things lay, and I could have presented my picture.

You are dealing with facts and positive evidence. If you are dealing with things that are relative to the issues at hand, then you look at the facts. What else do you look at? Oh, the leather thong.

How many people have ever worn moccasins with a leather thong in it? So you have placed me on the desert with leather clothes on and you took a leather thong from my shoe.

How many people could we take leather thongs from? That is an issue.

Then you move on and you say I had one around my neck. I always tie one around my head when my hair is long. It keeps it out of my eyes. And you pull it down on your neck. And I imagine a lot of long-haired people do.

There are so many aspects to this case that could be dug into and a lot of truth could be brought up, a lot of understanding could be reached.

It is a pretty hideous thing to look at seven bodies, one hundred and two stab wounds.

The prosecutor, or the doctor, gets up and he shows how all the different stab wounds are one way, and then how all the different stab wounds are another way; but they are the same stab wounds in another direction.

They put the hideous bodies on display and they say: "If he gets out see what will happen to you." Implying it. I am not saying he did this. This is implied. A lot of diagrams are actually in my opinion senseless to the case.

Then there is Paul Watkins' testimony. Paul Watkins was a young man who ran away from his parents and wouldn't go home. you could ask him to go home and he would say no. He would say, "I don't got no place to live. can I live here?" And I'd say, "Sure." So, he looks for a father image. I offer no father image. I say, "To be a man, boy, you have got to stand up and be your own father." And he still hungers for a father image. So he goes off to the desert and finds a father image.

When he gets on the stand, I forget what he said, whether it had any relative value, oh, I was supposed to have said to go get a knife and kill the Sheriff of Shoshone. Go get a knife and kill the Sheriff of Shoshone? I don't know the Sheriff of Shoshone. I don't think I have been there but once.

I am not saying that I didn't say it, but if I said it, at that time I may have thought it was a good idea. Whether I said it in jest and whether I said it in joking, I can't recall and reach back into my memory. I could say either way. I could say, "Oh, I was just joking." Or I could say I was curious. But to be honest with you I don't ever recall saying "Get a knife and change of clothes and go do what Tex said." Or I don't recall saying, "Get a knife and go kill the sheriff."

I don't recall saying to anyone "Go get a knife and kill anyone or anything." In fact it makes me mad when someone kills snakes or dogs or cats or horses. I don't even like to eat meat because that is how much I am against killing.

So you have got the guy who is against killing on the witness stand, and you are all asking him to kill you. you are asking him to judge you. Because with my words, each of your opinions or diagrams, your thoughts, are dying. What you thought was true is dying. What you thought was real is dying. Because you all know, and I know you know, and you known that I know you know. So, let's make that circle.

You say, "Where do we start from there?" Back to the facts again. You say that the facts are elusive in my mind. Actually, they just don't mean anything. The District Attorney can call them facts. They are facts. You are facts.

But the facts of the case aren't even relative, in my mind. They are relative to the Thirteenth Century. They are relative to the Eighth Century. They are relative to how old you are or what kind of watch you wear on your arm. I have never lived in time. A bell rings, I get up. A bell rings and I go out. A bell rings, and I live my life with bells. I get up when a bell rings and I do what a bell says. I have never lived in time. When your mind is not in time, the whole thought is different. You look at time as being man-made. And you say time is only relative to what you think it is. If you want to think me guilty then you can think me guilty and it is okay with me. I don't dislike any of you for it. If you want to think me not guilty it is okay with me.

I know what I know and nothing and no one can take that from me.

You can jump up and scream, "Guilty!" and you can say what a no good guy I am, and what a devil, fiend, eeky-sneaky slimy devil I am. It is your reflection and you're right, because that is what I am. I am whatever you make me.

You see, it is what happens inside the now that ... the words just lose meaning. A motion is more real than a word.

TRIAL TESTIMONY OF THE MANSON FAMILY — PART FOURTEEN

Because words are your words. You invented the words, and you made a dictionary and you gave me the dictionary and you said, "These are what the words mean." Well, this is what they mean to you, but to someone else, they have got a different dictionary. And things mean different things to different people, and to match the symbols up as you talk back and forward. Then you put a witness up here to say what you said.

I could never say what someone else said. I could only say what I said.

You tell me something and, tomorrow, I try to repeat it, if I didn't write it down, I couldn't tell you what you said. Let alone a year ago, let alone eight months ago, let alone a week ago. I am forgetful. I forget one day to the next. I forget what day it is or what month it is or what year it is. I don't particularly care because all that is real to me is right now.

But then, the case is real to me, and I say, "What do I have to do to make you people let me go back to the desert with my children?"

You have your world. You are going to do whatever you do with it. I have got nothing to do with it. I don't have the schooling in it. I don't believe in your church. I don't believe in anything you do. I am not saying you are wrong, and I hope that you say I am not wrong for believing what I believe in.

Murder? Murder is another question. It is a move. It is a motion. You take another's life. Boom! and they're gone. You say, "Where did they go?" They are dead. You say, "Well, that person could have made the motion." He could have taken my life just as well as I took his.

If a soldier goes off to the battlefield, he goes off with his life in front. He is giving his life. Does that not give him permission to take one? No. Because then we bring our soldiers back and try them in court for doing the same thing we sent them to do. We train them to kill, and they go over and kill, and we prosecute them and put them in jail because they kill. If you can understand it, then I bow to your understanding. But in my understanding I wouldn't get involved with it.

My peace is in the desert or in the jail cell, and had I not seen the sunshine in the desert I would be satisfied with the jail cell much more over your society, much more over your reality, and much more over your confusion, and much more over your world, and your word games that you play.

And each witness got up here and only testified for what was best for them, they did not testify for what was best for me. They testified for what was best for them, their own benefit. So you say, "Okay, and then what else did she say?" She said, "You only see in me what you want to see in me." you only see in her what you put in her, because when you take LSD enough times you reach a stage of nothing. You reach a stage of no thought.

An example of this: if you were to be standing in a room with someone and you were loaded on LSD and the guy says, "Do you like my sports coat?" And you would probably not pay any attention to him. About two or three minutes later the guy loaded on LSD will turn around and say, "My, you have a beautiful sports coat" because he is only reacting. He is only reacting to the individual terminology, the person that he has in the room.

As you would put two people in a cell, so would they reflect and flow on each other like as if water would seek a level.

I have been in a cell with a guy eighty years old and I listened to everything he said. "What did you do then?" And he explains to me his whole life and I sat there and listened, and I experienced vicariously his whole being, his whole life, and I look at him and he is one of my fathers. But he is also another one of your society's rejects.

Where does the garbage go, as we have tin cans and garbage alongside the road, and oil slicks in your water, so you have people, and I am one of your garbage people. I am one of your motorcycle people. I am one of what you want to call hippies. I never thought about being a hippie. I don't know what a hippie is.

A hippie is generally a guy that's pretty nice. He will give you a shirt and a flower, and he will give you a smile, and he walks down the road. But don't try to tell him nothing. He ain't listening to nobody. He got his own thoughts. You try to tell him something, and he will say, "Well, if that's your bag."

He is finding himself. You, those children there were finding themselves. Whatever they did, if they did whatever they did, is up to them. They will have to explain to you that. I'm just explaining to you what I am explaining to you. Everything is simple to me. It is what it is because that is what it is. It doesn't go any farther.

What? That is all there is. Why? Why?

Why comes from your mother. Your mother teaches you why, why, why. you go around asking your mother why and she keeps telling you, "Because, because" and she laces your little brain with because and: "Because." "Why?" "because." "Why?" And you don't know any different. If you had two mothers, one to tell you one thing and one to tell you another, then your mind might be left where mine was. If you had a dozen parents that you went around with and couldn't believe anything you were told and then you couldn't disbelieve anything you were told. And it's the same thing with this court. I don't believe what these witnesses get up here and say but I don't disbelieve them either. I won't challenge them. If the guy says, "You're no good," I say, "Okay." If that's what you want me to believe it's okay with me.

I don't care what you believe. I know what I am. You care what I think of you? Do you care what I think of you? Do you care what my opinion is? No, I hardly think so. I don't think that any of you care about anything other than yourselves because when you find yourself, you find that everyone is out for themselves anyway.

It looks that way to me here, the money that has been made, the things that I cannot talk about, and I know I can't talk about, I won't talk about and I will keep quiet about these things. How much all money has passed over this case? How sensational do you think that you have made this case?

I never made it sensational. I was hiding in the desert. You come and got me. Remember? Or could you prove that? What could you prove?

The only thing you can prove is what you can prove to yourselves, and you can sit here and build a lot in that jury's mind, and they are still going to interject their personalities on you. They are going to interject their inadequate feelings; they are going to interject what they think. I look at the jury and they won't look at me. So I wonder why they won't look at me.

Tonight's Weather
FAIR
Details on Page 3

PHILADELPHIA DAILY NEWS

10¢

SATURDAY, JULY 25, 1970
Volume XLVI—No. 99

4 ★★★★
SPORTS

Manson X-es Himself 'Out of World' for Trial

Tate Killings Called 'Plot To Incite Racial War'

Story on Page 3

FIRST WITNESSES AT SHARON TATE MURDER TRIAL include (l. to r.) Paul J. Tate, father of slain actress; Mrs. Winifred Chapman, maid who discovered "bloodbath crime" in Tate home; Dennis Hearst, whose connection with case has yet to be disclosed; and Wilfred Parent, father of victim Steven Parent who happened to be visiting estate caretaker.

How Sex Plot By Khrushchev Cost French Envoy His Job
Story on Page 2

Pipe Bomb in Car Kills President Of Phone Firm
Story on Page 3

GRANTED IMMUNITY "for cooperation with prosecution" in Gary Hinman murder case which led to arrest of Charles Manson and others in Tate case, Mary Brunner (center) shows up at Los Angeles Hall of Justice and discusses current trial with Manson "family" members, strange-named Capistrano (left) and Clemsonmoonstar.

★★★ TRIAL TESTIMONY OF THE MANSON FAMILY ★★★ PART FIFTEEN

They are afraid of me. And do you know why they are afraid of me? Because of the newspapers.

You projected fear. you projected fear. You made me a monster and I have to live with that the rest of my life because I cannot fight this case. If I could fight this case and I could present this case, I would take that monster back and I would take that fear back. Then you could find something else to put your fear on, because it's all your fear.

You look for something to project it on and you pick a little old scroungy nobody who eats out of a garbage can, that nobody wants, that was kicked out of the penitentiary, that has been dragged through every hellhole you can think of, and you drag him up and put him into a courtroom.

You expect to break me? Impossible! you broke me years ago. You killed me years ago. I sat in a cell and the guy opened the door and he said, "You want out?"

I looked at him and I said, "Do you want out? You are in jail, all of you, and your whole procedure. The procedure that is on you is worse than the procedure that is on me. I like it in there."

I like it in there - it's peaceful. I just don't like coming to the courtroom. I would like to get this over with as soon as possible. And I'm sure everyone else would like to get it over with too.

Without being able to prepare a case, without being able to confront the witnesses and to bring out the emotions, and to bring out the reasons why witnesses say what they say, and why this hideous thing has developed into the trauma that it's moved into, would take a bigger courtroom, and it would take a bigger public, a bigger press, because you all, as big as you are, know what you are as I know what you are, and, I like you anyway. I don't want to keep rehashing the same things over, There are so many things that you can get into, Your Honor, that I have no thoughts on. It is hard to think when you really don't care too much one way or the other.

(Interruption.)

I was released from the penitentiary and I learned one lesson in the penitentiary, you don't tell nobody nothing. You listen. When you are little you keep your mouth shut, and when someone says, "Sit down," you sit down unless you know you can whip him, and if you know you can whip you stand up and whip and you tell him to sit down.

Well, I pretty much sat down. I have learned to sit down because I have been whipped plenty of times for not sitting down and I have learned not to tell people something they don't agree with. If a guy comes up to me and he says, "The Yankees are the best ball team," I am not going to argue with that man. If he wants the Yankees to be the best ball team, it's okay with me, so I look at him and I say, "Yeah, the Yankees are a good ball club." And somebody else says, "The Dodgers are good." I will agree with that; I will agree with anything they tell me. That is all I have done since I have been out of the penitentiary. I agreed with every one of you. I did the best I could to get along with you, and I have not directed one of you to do anything other than what you wanted to do.

I have always said this: You do what your love tells you and I do what my love tells me. Now if my love tells me to stand up there and fight I will stand up there and fight if I have to. But if there is any way that my personality can get around it, I try my best to get around any kind of thing that is going to disturb my peace, because all I want is to be just at peace, whatever that takes. Now in death you might find peace, and soon I may start looking in death to find my peace.

I have reflected your society in yourselves, right back at yourselves, and each one of these young girls was without a home. Each one of these young boys was without a home. I showed them the best I could what I would do as a father, as a human being, so they would be responsible to themselves and not to be weak and not to lean on me. And I have told them many times, I don't want no weak people around me. If you are not strong enough to stand on your own, don't come and ask me what to do. You know what to do, This is one of the philosophies that everyone is mad at me for, because of the children. I always let the children go. "You can't let the children go down there by themselves." I said, "Let the children go down. If he falls, that is how he learns, you become strong by falling." They said, "You are not supposed to let the children do that. you are supposed to guide them."

I said, "Guide them into what? Guide them into what you have got them guided into? Guide them into dope? Guide them into armies?" I said, "No, let the children loose and follow them."

That is what I did on the desert. That is what I was doing, following your children, the ones you didn't want, each and every one of them. I never asked them to come with me— they asked me.

(Recessed)

There's been a lot of tank about a bottomless pit. I found a hole in the desert that goes down to a river that runs North underground, and I call it a bottomless pit, because where could a river be going North underground? You could even put a boat on it. So I covered it up and I hid it and I called it "The Devil's Hole" and we all laugh and we joke about it. You could call it a Family joke about the bottomless pit. How many people could you hide down in this hole?

Again you have a magical mystery tour that most of the time there's forty or fifty people at the ranch playing magical mystery tour. Randy Starr thought he was a Hollywood stunt man. He had a car all painted up and like never done any stunts. Another guy was a movie star, but he had never been in any movies, and everybody was just playing a part, you know, like most people get stuck in one part, but like we were just playing different parts every day. One day you put on a cowboy hat and say, "Shoot somebody," or the next you might have a knife fighter, or go off in the woods for a month or two to be an Indian, or just like a bunch of little kids playing. Then you establish a reality within that reality of play acting.

And then you get to conspiracy. The power of suggestion is stronger than any conspiracy that you could ever enter into. The powers of the brain are so vast, it's beyond understanding. It's beyond thinking. It's beyond comprehension. So to offer a conspiracy might be to sit in your car and think bad thoughts about someone and watch them have an accident in front of you. Or would it be a conspiracy for your wife to mention to you twenty times a day, "You know, you're going blind, George, you know how your eyes are, you're just going blind; we pray to God and you're going blind, and you're going blind."

And she keeps telling the old man he's going blind until he goes blind.

Is that a conspiracy?

Is it a conspiracy that the music is telling youth to rise against the establishment because the establishment is rapidly destroying things? Is that a conspiracy? Where does conspiracy come in? Does it come in that?

I have showed people how I think by what I do. It is not as much what I say as what I do that counts, and they look at what I do and they try to do it also, and sometimes they are made weak by their parents and cannot stand up. But is that my fault? Is it my fault that your children do what they do?

Now the girls were talking about testifying. If the girls come up here to testify and they said anything good about me, you would have to reverse it and say that it was bad. you would have to say, "Well, he put the girls up to saying that. He put the girls up to not telling the truth." Then you say the truth is as I am saying it, but then when it is gone, tomorrow it is gone, it changes, it's another day and it's a now truth, as it constantly moves thousands of miles an hour through space.

Hippie cult leader; actually, hippie cult leader, that is your words. I am a dumb country boy who never grew up. I went to jail when I was eight years old and I got out when I was thirty-two. I have never adjusted to your free world. I am still that stupid, corn-picking country boy that I always have been.

If you tend to compliment a contradiction about yourself, you can live in that confusion. To me it's all simple, right here, right now; and each of us knew what we did and I know what I did, and I know what I'm going to do and what you do is up to you. I don't recognize the courtroom, I recognize the press and I recognize the people.

The Court: Have you completed your statement, Mr. Manson?

You could go on forever. You can just talk endless words. It don't a mean anything. I don't know that it means anything. I can talk to the witnesses and ask them what they think about things, and I can I bring the truth out of other people because I know what the truth is, but I cannot sit here and tell you anything because like basically all I want to do is try to explain to you what you are doing to your children.

You see, you can send me to the penitentiary, it's not a big thing. I've been there all my life anyway. What about your children? These are just a few, there is many, many more coming right at you.

The Court: Anything further?

No.

We're all our own prisons, we are each all our own wardens and we do our own time. I can't judge anyone else. What other people do is not really my affair unless they approach me with it.

Prison's in your mind ... Can't you see I'm free?

The Sheboygan Press

THE MODESTO BEE — Sunday, August 17, 1969

Man Claims He Knows Who Killed Five

LOS ANGELES (AP) — Police is reported to have told policeman Folger, 26; international man who says he believes he hair stylist Jay Sebring, 35, be-knows the killer or killers of those the evening of the slayfriend of estate caretaker Wil-

THE LOWELL SUN — December 2, 1969

Young pair held in Tate murders

LOS ANGELES (UPI) — Three young members of a pseudoreligious cult that roamed Death Valley have been identified as suspects in the bloody slayings of actress Sharon Tate and four other persons Aug. 9.

In addition, four or five other members of the group called "The Family" are expected to be named in indictments which will be sought from the Los Angeles county grand jury.

Police Chief Edward Davis told a news conference Monday the three suspects were members of a "roving band of hippies," were suspected of killing a middle-aged couple the night following the Tate murders.

Two of the suspects were in custody — Charles D. "Tex" Watson, 24, arrested Sunday night in McKinney, Tex., and Patricia Kernwinkel, 21, arrested Monday near the home of her aunt in Mobile, Ala.

The third suspect, Linda Kasabian, 19, was caught in New Mexico. Authorities said several units were cruising around hippie communes but so far none actually had been searched.

"It is anticipated that an additional four or five persons will be named in indictments which will be sought from the Los Angeles County grand jury," Davis said.

The criminal complaints committee of the jury will be brought up to date on the case today and "we are seeking before the ninth day of December to bring additional potential suspects in before the grand jury for the culmination of the case," Davis added.

The additional suspects were, according to Davis, in custody in Inyo County, Calif. Two months ago a sheriff's posse rounded up 26 young men and women who were living a nomadic life of thievery. The group had a communie in the Death Valley area near the Nevada line in southeast California.

DAVIS also said "there may be some connection" between the group and the stabbing death of Gary Hinmann, 34, in his Topanga Canyon home July 31. Robert Bausoli, 21, allegedly a leader of the group, was arrested in connection with the slaying. A mistrial was declared in his first trial on murder charges and he will be retried in January.

Police said the words "political piggy" had been scrawled in blood on a wall in Hinmann's home.

Film director Roman Polansky said Monday night he would not comment on the latest developments in the murder of his wife until after the suspects are brought to trial. Miss Tate was

in abandoned mining shacks and posting lookouts equipped with walkie-talkies. The women members of the group reportedly were nude or were only bikini bottoms.

The grisly Tate slayings appeared to be the outcome of some weird religious rite, police investigators said during the initial investigation. Some of the victims were stabbed repeatedly as in the climax of a "ritualistic orgy," police said. The names involved gave the case international publicity and Hollywood abounded with theories of the mass murders, including one rumor they resulted from a drug-pushing ring.

However, Davis said that none of the victims were involved with illicit drug traffic.

The women members of the group were linked to the slayings of Leno LaBianca and his wife Rosemary a day later in the nearby Silver Lake district of Los Angeles. Officers at first believed they were the work of a "copy cat" killer.

THERE were gruesome similarities. The word "pig" was smeared in blood on the front door of the Tate residence. The words "death to pigs," were written in blood on the refrigerator of the LaBianca home.

The motive for the murders remained a mystery. Davis said none of the victims were acquainted with the suspects and "there was no economic motive apparent in the Tate case and there was no motive, if any, economic motive in the LaBianca case."

Davis said the suspects apparently visited the Tate home before the murders when it was leased to a different party. The telephone lines had been cut to the house. "It had all the earmarks of premeditation," the chief said.

CHARLES D. WATSON — PATRICIA KERNWINKEL

STAR-NEWS
PASADENA, CALIFORNIA, MONDAY, AUGUST

Why El Monte Death

The bewildered, grief-stricken parents of a slain 18-year-old El Monte boy pondered Sunday why quiet, middle-class Steven Parent became the fifth victim in a bloody mass slaying at the plush estate of actress Sharon Tate.

"I don't understand," said Wilfred Parent, 44, the boy's father. "It don't make any damned sense."

Steven was found shot to death in the front seat of his car parked near the estate. Police said the car transmission was in drive position and the brake was released, indicating the youth was trying to escape when killed.

"I just can't understand what he was doing up there in the first place," said Parent. "Steve wasn't a pushy kind of kid. I didn't even know he knew any of those people."

Police later said Steve was probably a friend of William Garretson, 19, the caretaker arrested at the $200,000 home Saturday morning after discovery of the bodies.

When Steve didn't return to his suburban El Monte home Friday night, his parents worried. "He didn't call, didn't

STEPHEN PARENT
... slaying victim

TWO OF MANSON CLAN, 25 UNIDENTIFIED

Fingerprints Deepen Tate Mystery

By MARY NEISWENDER
Staff Writer

Although two fingerprints found at the home of slain actress Sharon Tate were identified as belonging to two of the "Manson family" members charged with her murder, 25 other fingerprints were found at the home by police experts who admit they have been "unable to match them with known persons."

Similarly, fingerprint experts testified at the Los Angeles Superior Court trial of Charles Manson and three of his girl disciples that there were six unidentified fingerprints found at the home of market owner Leno LaBianca.

THE MYSTERY fingerprints — and the lack of any fingerprints in obvious places, throughout both the Tate and LaBianca homes — seemed to offset dramatic prosecution testimony that one fingerprint was found of Patricia Krenwinkel, one of the female defendants, and one fingerprint of Charles "Tex" Watson, who is charged with the Tate-LaBianca murders but is fighting extradition in Texas.

Both were lifted by police investigation from the actress's Benedict Canyon home.

Miss Krenwinkel's left little finger was found imprinted on an inside back door of the pregnant actress' bedroom, Officer Jerrome Boen testified. It was found midway on a French door, which leads from Miss Tate's bedroom to the pool area of the exclusive home, he said.

Watson's print — his right ring finger — was found near the edge of a front door six to eight inches above the doorknob, Boen said.

Four fingerprint experts took the witness stand Thursday to build the prosecution's case against Manson, Miss Krenwinkel, Leslie Van Houten and Susan Atkins.

FINAL expert to testify

NEW ORLEANS (UPI) — The 5th U.S. Circuit Court of Appeals set a Sept. 11 deadline Thursday for the extradition of Charles "Tex" Watson to California, where he faces charges of killing actress Sharon Tate and six others. The court ordered Watson extradited from Texas at that time, unless U.S. Supreme Court agrees in the meantime to intervene.

— Officer Harold J. Dolan of the police department's scientific investigation division — said although 10 points of identity were necessary to match fingerprints, he found 18 in Watson's case and 17 in Miss Krenwinkel's imprint.

"We lifted 50 latent prints from the Tate home," Dolan said under direct examination by Deputy Dist. Atty. Vincent Bugliosi. "Twenty-two matched with the victims' fingerprints; three were not good enough for comparison, and 25 could not be matched with known persons."

Dolan said the prints of Miss Tate, coffee heiress Abigail Folger and Polish playboy Voityck Frykowski were found on furniture in the home. Only one print was found of Hollywood hairstylist Jay Sebring — on a bottle of beer found in the master bedroom.

Under cross examination by chief defense counsel Paul Fitzgerald, Dolan admitted another print was found on the bottle, but police could not match it with anyone.

Two mystery fingerprints also were found near the one identified as belonging to Miss Krenwinkel on the French doors.

Also unidentified were several prints around the window frame which police believe was the "point of entry" of the murderers. A fingerprint on a telephone in the master bedroom, another on a white ashtray in the living room, some on a tape and tape case in the living room, one on a rocking chair in Miss Tate's bedroom and several on the outside of the three cars in the driveway were labeled as "not matched up with any known human being."

At the LaBianca home, 19 of 25 fingerprints found were attributed to either Mr. or Mrs. LaBianca or Mrs. LaBianca's son, Frank Struthers Jr. Six were unidentified.

Several of the unidentified prints were found near a liquor cabinet in the dining room. Mrs. LaBianca's opened purse was found on top of the cabinet, her wallet missing. Unknown prints also were found on a closet door in the boy's bedroom, on a file cabinet in the den and on a closet door in the front bedroom.

Lack of any fingerprints in certain obviously used areas was also brought out in direct examination.

"There was not so much as a slight smudge (on the fork officers found stuck in LaBianca's stomach)," Dolan said. "It gave the impression to me that the handle had been wiped."

A KNIFE found in the grocer's throat was covered with blood, negating the chances of fingerprints, he said.

All the walls of the LaBianca home were checked for fingerprints, Dolan said, including the areas where it was obvious the murderers had leaned in order to write "Death to Pigs" and "Rise." No prints were found.

On the LaBianca refrigerator, where "Healter Skelter" had been written, Dolan said there were "no smudges ... no ridges ... no prints at all ... the entire refrigerator had been cleaned."

A buck-knife, which star prosecution witness Linda Kasabian said Miss Atkins lost in the frenzy of murder, was dusted for fingerprints, but no readable ones were found, Dolan said.

WARDEN 'CHARMED,' BUT—
'Manson Didn't Fool Us,' Says Ex-Guard

By MARY NEISWENDER
Staff Writer

"He reminded me of an old car . . . you know things'll keep going wrong with it, but you keep trying to repair it."

This was the impression that hippie cult leader Charles Manson left with most guards at the federal prison on Terminal Island and with one in particular, Guard Henry Tippett, of 2677 Jefferson St., Long Beach, now retired, watched over the self-styled Messiah during his almost three years in the prison.

Manson's sentence to Terminal Island followed conviction of transporting a stolen car across state lines, and parole violation.

Manson—apparently a Svengali even in prison, Tippett said—charmed the then-associate warden, who made him a trustie.

"The officers who had contact with him didn't agree with the warden," said Tippett. "We opposed making him a trustie. If you work in a prison long enough, you get to know these things, especially with this guy's background."

Tippett, who retired in 1959—a year after Manson was released—claimed Manson had a tendency to break the rules.

"HE WAS always doing things wrong — anything to violate the rules. It seemed intentional. It wasn't because he was dumb," Tippett said.

"For example, a simple thing like being assigned to a dormitory. Manson wouldn't stay in one dorm. He'd switch around, just to annoy the guards."

Tippett said the guards quit "writing him up" because Manson was never disciplined.

"He would have been in isolation all the time if the warden had paid attention to the guards," Tippett added.

Tippett, who was previously at Fort Leavenworth Prison, Kans., claimed that even the older inmates who associated with the then 22-year-old Manson eventually ended up "in trouble."

"But he apparently

EX-GUARD TIPPETT
'We Knew His Type'

charmed one of the associate wardens," said Tippett. "The warden had him on one job, then another—never doing anything." Finally, say Tippett, Manson went before the classification board and became a trustie.

"I GUESS they felt they could make something out of him," he added, "but most of us—the ones who saw him in action—felt he wouldn't last long as a trustie.

Manson didn't.

Assigned to clean-up work at the adjacent Coast Guard base, Manson got into a locker room, outfitted himself in new clothing, picked up some car keys

Ironically, he was caught at a roadblock near San Francisco shortly after his escape by police who weren't even looking for him.

Manson was returned to the prison, where he stayed until his release in 1958.

He had few "followers" at that time, Tippett said. "Most other inmates stayed away from him."

Not so today.

THE BEARDED, long-haired leader of the hippie cult suspected of the Tate killings and "at least 10 others," has a following whose loyalty is hard to believe.

Held in Inyo County jail for 10 days awaiting preliminary hearings on a charge of receiving stolen property, he "still runs his 'family' in jail," say sheriff's officers.

"He gives the orders and they obey him," say the officers.

"They" are the remnants of his gang in the desert area — three men in a large cell with him, and one woman in a separate part of the jail.

"We find Manson a model prisoner though," added the officers. "But he should be by now. He has been in and out of jail since he was 15."

MANSON was first arrested on an adult charge in 1951, in Beaver, Utah, for taking a stolen car across a state line (a federal offense). He was sent to the National Training School for Boys in Washington, D.C., then transferred to the federal reformatory at Petersburg, Pa.

In 1955 he was arrested for auto theft in Los Angeles and given five years' probation; he violated his federal probation a year later in Indianapolis and was sent to the Terminal Island prison.

When released in 1958, he was picked up for a vehicle code violation in Los Angeles. The following year he was arrested for auto theft, and later in the year for forgery. In 1960 he was arrested in Laredo, Tex., for transporting women across a state line for immoral purposes (another federal offense).

In 1967 he was arrested in Ukiah for interfering with an officer; in 1968 in Ventura for having a false driver's license.

In 1969 his Los Angeles arrests included possession of marijuana; assault with intent to commit bodily harm, later changed to forceable rape; auto theft; burglary; cultivation and possession of marijuana, and the final charges for which he is currently in jail: contributing to the delinquency of a minor, firearm theft, receiving stolen property and auto theft.

At his preliminary hearing Wednesday, some of his followers were in the audience lending him moral support; others in jail spoke out in his defense.

Some of his followers have even said they'd kill for him — and they allegedly did.

Several Suspects and Car

Grief
Roman Polanski breaks down inside limousine after attending funeral services for his wife, actress Sharon Tate, slain last week. Car window reflects others who attended funeral.

Check "sex underworld" in Bel Air murders probe

By BRUCE RUSSELL

LOS ANGELES, Calif. (Reuters)—A black address book belonging to murdered hair stylist Jay Sebring—slain together with pregnant actress Sharon Tate and three others Friday at a palatial Hollywood Hills mansion—is leading police into a "sex underworld," police sources said today.

They said the book was found along with a quantity of drugs in Sebring's car, after the quintet were savagely slaughtered at the hilltop estate of Miss Tate, 26, wife of Polish-born film director Roman Polanski.

The discovery of the drugs and black book, containing names of both men and women, led police to check the possibility the killer or killers might have been drug addicts or eccentrics invited into the house by Sebring.

Police continued to insist that there was no link between the sinister butcherings and the double murder of a Hollywood supermarket owner Leno La Bianca, and his wife, Rosemary, found slaughtered about 24 hours later.

POLANSKI, who has directed macabre films such as "Rosemary's Baby," broke down and sobbed like a child yesterday at his wife's funeral service.

Wearing dark glasses which failed to hide his bloodshot eyes, the director cried on the shoulder of his mother-in-law, Mrs. Gwen Tate, outside the church of the Holy Ghost here where the Catholic service was held.

Throngs of Hollywood's "beautiful people" turned out for the funeral for Sharon Tate. They wore dark clothes, but the style was black mini-skirts and black Edwardian suits with bell-bottom pants.

Another service was held yesterday for Sebring, Miss Tate's former fiance. He and Miss Tate were found tied together by a white rope slung over a ceiling beam.

Two other victims of the slayings in her home were buried yesterday—coffee heiress Miss Abigail Folger, 25, whose funeral was held at Redwood City near San Francisco, and 18-year-old Steven Parent, who was visiting a caretaker at the back of the house and apparently ran into the murders by accident.

Los Angeles County Coroner Dr. Thomas Noguchi released reports on how the quintet were butchered, but the Los Angeles Times said Thursday Noguchi had not revealed everything.

NOGUCHI said Sebring, found hooded with the rope around his neck attached to the almost nude body of the eight-month pregnant actress, had been stabbed. But the Times said he also had a bullet in his body.

The Times also said Miss Tate and Miss Folger had been stabbed many times but not mutilated.

The fifth victim, Polish emigre film maker Voytek Frykowski, was found and stabbed on the lawn, and had been beaten around the face, possibly with a pistol, the Times said.

After releasing Monday the only suspect held in the Tate case—19-year-old William Garretson, the caretaker Parent was visiting, the police made no further arrests in any of the eight murder cases.

Sharon's Dad Hunted Her Killers

Police in L.A. Admit Narcotics Were Found at Tate Home

By MARY NEISWENDER
Staff Writer

Flight of 'Strangler' Provides Rip-Roaring Story While It Lasts

By Nicholas von Hoffman
Washington Post Staff Writer

LYNN, Mass., Feb. 25—It was a good, old-fashioned, sensational story. No CIA, no international implications, no threat to democratic institutions or individual liberty, just a rip-roaring police story with all the homey, oldtime ingredients — murder, sex, sadism, loud-mouthed lawyers and hysteria.

For 30 hours while he'd been free, it had been a pip of a story, then the suspense ended when the self-proclaimed Boston Strangler had walked into a haberdashery here and given himself up.

This was the right place to end the story, in a late 19th century town of crooked streets and loft factories, the right place for the "Strangler," who had confessed to 13 fiendish 19th century murders. And the way the town reacted to the news that Albert DeSalvo was in police headquarters made you think of the wax museum with those tableaus of dusty mannequins re-enacting bloody, entertaining crimes.

Hundreds of hooded, scarfed people stood outside the police station and let the ice on Johnson Street go through the soles of their shoes and constrict their capillaries while they waited to see the "Strangler."

"I saw him! Wasn't he aw-w-ful? Take my picture! Do you think we'll be on the 6 o'clock news?" they shouted in frigid and delighted satisfaction, when they saw the man who looked like an unemployed dishwasher.

In captivity, he was an anti-climax, a nothing in his stolen pea jacket and bell bottom trousers. He looked like the floors on the courthouses and police stations they kept taking him to, muddied, salt-stained, littered, walked on by large male feet in galoshes and service shoes.

He was better in the hours before his capture. Then he'd been a good story. "Stark Fear Grips Three States — Women Beware! He's A Cutie—Keep Chain Lock Bolted," the Boston Record-American had warned while offering a $5000 reward for the "Strangler" alive or dead.

In the hours before they got him, Boston had suddenly seemed peopled with retired school teachers, aging nurses, Victorian females of the dancing years and vulnerability.

"I'm alone with my cousin and she's a shut-in, but our janitor's a good man and he won't let strangers in, at least I pray to God he won't," confided a woman on the subway train and it seemed appropriate for Boston, much of which still looks like Sherlock Holmes London, a city where you can imagine hansom cabs and Jack the Ripper on the night snow.

"What's going on in the State House?" a reporter had been asking earlier in the Boston police headquarters press room.

"We're saying the lights in the attorney general's office burn till dawn."

"What do you mean? He left his office hours ago."

"I don't care when he left his office. We always have the lights burning till dawn. And we always have old ladies praying in the street. Those old ladies in the street really grabs them in South Boston."

"Hey, any you guys want this Newton rape?"

"Yeh, give me the details."

"I haven't got names."

"You know the Record-American isn't interested in a rape without names."

"Well, the Globe isn't interested in a rape with them."

"Who's checked the FBI?"

"Aww, the FBI," says the sergeant who wondered into the sagging room, "they couldn't catch anybody with bloodhounds. You know how he's going to be found? A tip. It's all a tip in this business."

It was the Lynn police who got the tip and the old-fashioned police story ended in an old-fashioned way.

'Boston Strangler' Gives Up in Store

DeSalvo Hunt Ends Quietly In Lynn, Mass.

From News Dispatches

LYNN, Mass., Feb. 25 — Albert DeSalvo, the self-confessed Boston strangler, surrendered meekly today to two uniform store employes after one of the largest manhunts in New Englan history.

DeSalvo said he had escaped from Bridgewater State Hospital yesterday to call public attention to his need for rehabilitation.

"Maybe people will know what it means to be mentally ill," he said as he was taken in manacles into the Lynn police station.

Reported Despondent

DeSalvo reportedly had been despondent because he was not receiving what he considered adequate treatment at the mental hospital.

Police said DeSalvo told them he had broken into a home at 785 Western Ave. in Lynn Friday and spent the night in the basement, stealing the Navy clothing he was wearing when captured.

At that address, police found clothing and other items strewn in the basement and other evidence of DeSalvo's presence.

The owner, Arthur Vincent, commented: "Oh, my, we had no idea he was here..."

Vincent, who lives in the house with his sister, Mrs. Simone Fedas, said he heard "a bump or something" at about 2:30 a.m., but fell asleep again immediately. Mrs. Fedas said she "felt faint" when police told her what the bump might have been.

Moved to Prison

Shortly after his arrest DeSalvo was transferred to Walpole State Prison despite one attorney's expressed fears that he might try to kill himself or become the target of hard-core criminals.

DeSalvo, who has confessed murdering 13 Boston area women, escaped with two companions before dawn yesterday. They were captured in Waltham, a Boston suburb, last night as the hunt for DeSalvo spread from Canada to Florida.

A state official said one of DeSalvo's two brothers—who had been arrested and charged with helping him escape—first tipped police that DeSalvo was in the Lynn area.

But it appeared that DeSalvo may have intended to surrender anyway.

He entered the Simons Uniform Store about 2 p.m. wearing part of a sailor suit and a rumpled Navy pea jacket that he had changed into sometime after his escape.

Alan Simons, 30, a partner in the uniform firm, said DeSalvo walked up to a salesman, and said, "Can I use the phone? I want to call F. Lee." F. Lee Bailey is his lawyer.

Bailey was not in his office but DeSalvo talked to the lawyer's private detective, Attorney Andrew Tuney, a former state police lieutenant who once headed the Boston strangler investigation.

Simons and the salesman, Jimmy Trellegan, 32, recognized DeSalvo and while he was on the phone, called Lynn police.

"When he got off the phone he said he was hungry," Simons said. "We told him to come on out back and we'll make some coffee. We made the coffee and waited for the police."

Trellegan said he frisked DeSalvo and found no weapon on him.

163-12446-A

Simons said neither ___ nor the salesman was afraid of the Boston strangler. "Nobody was scared. He wasn't a very big person. He never went after men anyway," said Simons.

While the five were having coffee, Simons said DeSalvo mentioned "he knew we knew who he was.

"He told us to call off the police because he wanted to turn himself in," he said.

Simons described DeSalvo as looking "tired, tired around the eyes, like someone who had been out all night and hadn't slept.

"He was pretty calm and quiet. So we just let him stay that way until the police came."

Tuney, the detective DeSalvo called, said the fugitive told him he was in Lynn and added: "Do me a favor and call off the police and I'll stay here till you come."

"I promised him I would," Tuney said. "Before we could get there, the police had him. How, I don't know."

One of the arresting officers, Robert Clounan, said they found DeSalvo in the back room of the store "leaning against a water cooler. He said he wanted to give himself up and to contact state police.

"We put handcuffs on him right away. He wasn't armed and he was very docile. He didn't give us any trouble."

An unruly mob of 2000 jammed into the narrow street outside police headquarters as word of DeSalvo's arrest spread through the area.

"Kill him," were the shouts of some in the crowd. The gathering broke up only after DeSalvo was taken from the station to court.

Detectives formed a tight ring around the prisoner and pushed through the crowd to put him in a police car for the trip to Cambridge. DeSalvo was handcuffed. He smiled and winked at several newsmen whom he recognized from a recent trial.

In New York, Attorney Bailey said DeSalvo had left a note by his hospital bed saying he was escaping to "force public officials to admit" he is the Boston "strangler." He said the note also tried to establish that he had stayed in the hospital willingly for 2½ years because he wanted to get psychiatric help.

Bailey also said DeSalvo had walked past four state troopers in a parking lot in Lynn without being spotted — even though he was wearing brown shoes and no kerchief with the Navy uniform.

Bailey said he would seek a writ of habeas corpus to free DeSalvo from Walpole prison under the Eighth Amendment, which deals with cruel and unusual punishment.

As for the $10,000 reward he had offered for DeSalvo's capture alive, Bailey said it "looks like a surrender"—indicating he would not pay the reward.

The first real break in the dramatic manhunt came Friday night when the two men who escaped with DeSalvo were captured in a Waltham bar 13 hours after the break. Fred A. Erickson, 40, of Brockton, serving a life sentence after he stabbed his estranged wife 27 times in 1954, and George W. Harrison, 33, of Westford, serving an 11-to-15-year term for armed robbery, were returned to the mental hospital.

The trail grew still hotter when DeSalvo's brothers were arrested on charges of helping him escape.

Richard E. DeSalvo, 31, asked for a hearing and was released in $500 bail. Joseph DeSalvo, 37, pleaded innocent and was released in $1000 bail.

Massachusetts Attorney General Elliot L. Richardson said that after the breakout the three escapees stole a car and drove to Boston's Haymarket Square. DeSalvo dropped them there and drove to suburban Everett where he rendezvoused with his brother Joseph at a gas station, Richardson said. Joseph then dropped him off at Lynn, the attorney general said.

Near the Everett gas station police today found the stolen car, a pillowcase from the hospital, 30 candy bars and Albert DeSalvo's glasses.

Richardson said DeSalvo had about $150 on him when captured.

DeSalvo's escape took place only five weeks after he was convicted and sentenced to life on a series of sexual attacks and robberies involving four Greater Boston women in 1964. The charges were unrelated to the stranglings.

He was being held in Bridgewater pending an appeal to the Massachusetts Supreme Court by Bailey.

U.S. Department of Justice

Federal Bureau of Investigation

In Reply, Please Refer to
File No.

Los Angeles, California
May 26, 1983

ARYAN BROTHERHOOD (AB)
LOS ANGELES DIVISION
RACKETEERING ENTERPRISE INVESTIGATION

During the last 180-day period, investigation in this matter has been primarily concerned with developing sources of information regarding the Aryan Brotherhood (AB).

CONTACT WITH OTHER AGENCIES

One such source of information is known as the California Prison Gang Task Force (PGTF). This task force is made up of representatives from various law enforcement and corrections-related agencies throughout the state, and meets on a once per month basis. The meetings offer investigators and corrections officers the frequent opportunity to discuss the latest intelligence and developments relating, not only to the AB, but to other prison gangs, including the Mexican Mafia (EME), La Nuestra Familia (NF), and the Black Guerilla Family (BGF). The Los Angeles Division now has a member representative who will be attending the PGTF meetings on a regular basis.

During this investigative period, the following information regarding members and associates of the AB was derived from various Federal and local agencies in the Los Angeles area:

On January 13, 1983, AB member, Robert "Blinky" Griffen, ─────────── was found guilty in San Bernardino County Superior Court, for the 1980 murder of "T-Bone Gibson." Griffen was also found not guilty ─────────────────── of a weapon.

This document contains neither recommendations nor conclusions of the FBI. It is the property of the FBI and is loaned to your agency; it and its contents are not to be distributed outside your agency.

ARYAN BROTHERHOOD (AB)
LOS ANGELES DIVISION

On January 18, 1983, AB associate [redacted] arrested by the Los Angeles Police Department (LAPD) for parole violation. [redacted] is presently in Terminal Island Federal Penitentiary.

On January 20, 1983, AB associate [redacted] arrested by the LAPD and the United States Marshal's Office (USM) on a Federal Warrant charging him with parole violation. [redacted] has previously done State and Federal time, has admitted to being an AB associate, and is associated with AB member [redacted]. [redacted] is also suspected to be an associate of members of the EME. [redacted] has committed bank robberies, in the past, with [redacted] who is considered an AB sympathizer. Since his arrest, [redacted] has escaped from Federal custody, and is now a fugitive.

On February 3, 1983, AB associate [redacted] was arrested by the LAPD and USM at his residence in Los Angeles, California on an outstanding Federal Warrant for parole violation and bank robbery. A loaded nine-millimeter automatic was seized from the residence. [redacted] has since been identified in another bank robbery, and is suspected to be involved in a Los Angeles murder/robbery.

On February 9, 1983, AB/Nazi member [redacted] was paroled from Folsom State Prison to Los Angeles.

On January 24, 1983, AB associate [redacted] released from Terminal Island Federal Penitentiary and placed on Federal parole. [redacted] was scheduled to appear on March 24, 1983 in the Santa Monica Superior Court by which he is charged with burglary and being a felon in possession of a gun, by the State of California.

AB associate [redacted] were arrested by the California Highway Patrol immediately following the robbery of the Pomona First Federal Savings and Loan Association, Glendora Branch, in El Monte, California. [redacted] is presently in Terminal Island Federal Penitentiary, and [redacted] is in the Los Angeles County Jail.

ARYAN BROTHERHOOD (AB)
LOS ANGELES DIVISION

On March 4, 1983, AB associate ▓▓▓▓▓▓▓▓▓▓ was arrested by Hawthorne Police Department for violation of Federal parole. ▓▓▓▓▓ is presently housed at Terminal Island Federal Penitentiary.

On March 9, 1983, AB member ▓▓▓▓▓▓▓▓▓▓ was arrested by Sacramento Police Department on an armed robbery warrant from San Mateo, California. ▓▓▓▓▓ has since posted bail.

On March 11, 1983, AB associate ▓▓▓▓▓▓▓▓▓▓ was arrested by the LAPD and the USM for violation of Federal parole. ▓▓▓▓▓ is currently housed at Terminal Island Federal Peritentiary.

AB associate ▓▓▓▓▓▓▓▓▓▓ is presently wanted by law enforcement for his escape from the Impact House Community Treatment Center in Pasadena, California. ▓▓▓▓▓ was pending sentencing on bank robbery charges. Shortly after providing testimony against AB member ▓▓▓▓▓▓▓▓▓▓ he escaped.

Recently, AB associate Eros Timm was found stabbed to death in his cell at the United States Penitentiary, Lewisburg, Pennsylvania. Timm suffered from approximately forty stab wounds to his head, neck and chest. Though many inmates have been placed under suspicion, at this time none have been charged. Investigators at Lewisburg believe that Timm was a victim of the recent retaliation efforts of a group called the D.C. Blacks towards the AB.

On April 5, 1983, also at the Lewisburg Federal Penitentiary, an associate of Eros Timm, ▓▓▓▓▓▓▓▓▓▓. Again, inmates associated with the D.C. Blacks are under suspicion.

The retaliation efforts on the part of the D.C. Blacks are believed to be due to the September 27, 1982 death of a member, Raymond "Cadillac" Smith. Smith was allegedly killed by ▓▓▓▓▓▓▓▓▓▓ at the United States Penitentiary, Marion, Illinois. It is not known if the violence between these groups is solely a race issue,

ARYAN BROTHERHOOD (AB)
LOS ANGELES DIVISION

or not. Investigators claim that the D.C. mob strives for power and control within the prison system. It is also known that the AB also strives for the same type of control. Investigators believe that the violence between these two groups is only in the "budding" stage. It cannot be determined, at this time, whether or not this violence will spill over into the California State prison system.

LOS ANGELES DIVISION INVESTIGATION

It should be noted that during this period, the Los Angeles Division of the Federal Bureau of Investigation completed a successful Title 3 investigation entitled ███████ aka; ET AL; RICO-NARCOTICS" (LA 183A-1595). b7C

On February 11, 1983, narcotics traffickers ███ b7C

On February 28, 1983, ███████ b7C

SOURCE INFORMATION

During this investigative period, a number of confidential sources have provided information regarding the activities of the AB.

One such source advised that the AB has spread throughout the Federal prison system, and has developed links with other organized crime groups on the streets. In the early 1970s, members of the AB started going to Federal prisons for crimes such as bank robbery and narcotics violations. Two of the first members to do Federal time, were ███████ b7C

ARYAN BROTHERHOOD (AB)
LOS ANGELES DIVISION

[redacted] As was the policy in the past, they began recruiting for the AB, only now they had the entire country to pick from.

[redacted]

The Federal prison system held many well-to-do members and associates of Italian organized crime groups, who were powerful on the streets, but were at the mercy of any "nut with a knife" while in prison. The plan was to have these La Cosa Nostra (LCN) figures pay protection to the AB, while at the same time, to ingratiate themselves with these mobsters. In return, the mobsters were safe while inside the walls, and were obligated to offer the AB members a "slice of the pie" on the streets when they were paroled. Other source information [redacted] that the AB would protect LCN members and handle LCN hits inside the prison, and in return, the LCN would provide money, drugs and assistance to AB members on the outside. It was also agreed that the AB would comprise an elite "hit squad" for the LCN on the outside.

Source contact [redacted] and has gained a certain control over the flow of drugs into the prisons. The AB is also very active in the "shaking down" of other prisoners; the LCN being the primary target. The AB's most valued tool of intimidation is brutal execution-style murders.

Sources have also advised that as is the case with any organization, there must be a constant flow of information. In addition to the traditional prison "grapevine", [redacted]

AYRAN BROTHERHOOD
LOS ANGELES DIVISION

According to the source, ██████ was so impressed by the vast amount of profit to be made in the prison drug game, that he made an open offer to any AB member who needed to borrow money to start a drug business.

Another source has advised that ██████

On the other hand, the LCN gives the AB access to its inside connections on the streets for information gathering.

ARYAN BROTHERHOOD
LOS ANGELES DIVISION

According to other source information ▮▮▮

Other source information indicates that ▮▮▮

According to sources, ▮▮▮ is now putting together a marijuana business ▮▮▮ and has offered pieces of the business to various AB members. This business will involve truck loads of marijuana being brought to the West Coast from the East Coast, primarily out of Florida.

Other information has been received alleging that ▮▮▮ These individuals are closely associated with members of the AB, and it is suspected that AB members and associates are actively involved in the drug business. These individuals are supposed to be getting their drugs from an AB associated individual by the name of ▮▮▮ who is a Chinese dope dealer in San Francisco, California. According to sources, ▮▮▮ has a history of "fronting" dope to AB associated individuals.

Further information indicates that a Thai national, an AB associate by the name of ▮▮▮ was recently incarcerated in California. ▮▮▮ has a connection for white heroin in Thailand, and has actively sought out help from the AB organization in his drug business.

Sources have advised ▮▮▮ that there has been an alliance with the Mexican Mafia (EME). Once the AB had shown itself to be a valued and respected ally, there was a deal worked out, whereby the AB would unite in war with the EME against La Nuestra Familia (NF). In the Federal prisons, as in the State prisons, the AB and the EME have cooperated in several murders and shake-downs, and together they seem to form an irresistible force. Both the AB and EME look down on

ARYAN BROTHERHOOD
LOS ANGELES DIVISION

their brethern who still occupy the state prisons. They are looked upon as barbarians who spend their time plotting on each other, rather than bettering themselves by criminal enterprise.

ARYAN BROTHERHOOD MURDERS IN THE FEDERAL PRISON SYSTEM

Since the inception of the AB in the Federal prison system, the organization has planned and carried out a number of brutal prison murders. During this investigative period, a ███████████ source has been developed who has provided information, and is willing to testify regarding ████ murders which took place at various Federal penal institutions throughout the nation. These AB Commission sanctioned murders took place ███████████████ and involved victims who were "hit" because they were suspected informants, because they failed to pay drug debts, or just for making disparaging remarks about the AB. These murders involve members and associates of the LCN, AB, EME, and a Washington D.C. based street gang known as the D.C. Mob. One such murder, that of D.C. Mob leader Raymond "Cadillac" Smith in 1982, has been followed by many other murders, thought to be retaliatory in nature. The source has been interviewed extensively ████████████████ and the results have been turned over to the appropriate United States Attorneys for prosecutive decisions and action.

b7D

Post Office Box 7251 - Main Station
St. Louis, Missouri 63177
January 28, 1980

Chief J. Franklin Neff
Hannibal Police Department
777 Broadway
Hannibal, Missouri 63401

Dear Chief Neff:

Reference is made to your previous request for investigative assistance by the Federal Bureau of Investigation in determining the whereabouts of John Wayne Gacy during 1967, with regard to his possible involvement in an investigation initiated in 1967 by the Hannibal, Missouri Police Department, the Cook County, Illinois Sheriff's Department, and States Attorney's Office. Through contact with the Des Plaines, Illinois Police Department it was determined that previous investigation conducted by that department indicated that Gacy had assisted his father-in-law in the operation of several Kentucky Fried Chicken Restaurants in the Waterloo, Iowa area during 1966 and 1967, at which time Gacy's mother resided in Little Rock, Arkansas. Information was also provided that Gacy was believed to have been previously affiliated with the Jaycees in Springfield, Illinois and Waterloo, Iowa, although no information had been developed by that department indicating that Gacy had ever resided in Hannibal, Missouri. Further, it is believed that an interview of Gacy is not deemed feasible at this time in view of pending prosecutive proceedings.

Information which was also provided by the Cook County, Illinois States Attorney's Office indicated that Gacy was married in Springfield, Illinois in 1964 and, following his move to Waterloo, Iowa in 1966, he was involved in some type of trouble in Waterloo, Iowa in 1967, which carried over into 1968.

Through subsequent investigation conducted by the Springfield Division of the Federal Bureau of Investigation, Gacy's father-in-law, [redacted], was located and interviewed in Springfield, Illinois, on December 3, 1979, at

b7C

1 - Addressee
1 - St. Louis (62-5154)
JDM:bjb
(2)

which time he recalled that Gacy had been previously employed at the Roberts Brothers Clothing Store in Springfield, Illinois until around 1966, at which time Gacy moved to Waterloo, Iowa where he assisted [ ] in the operation of three Kentucky Fried Chicken Restaurants for the next several years. [ ] further advised that, to his knowledge, Gacy never resided or was employed in Hannibal, Missouri. No other information of value was developed which indicated that Gacy has ever been in Hannibal, Missouri at any time in the past.

b7C

I trust that the above information will be of benefit to your department in connection with this investigative matter, and it is, indeed, a pleasure to have had the opportunity to assist your department in this regard.

Very truly yours,

ROY B. KLAGER, JR.
Special Agent in Charge

By:

G. NORMAN CHRISTENSEN
Assistant Special Agent in Charge

ZODIAC KILLER STALK NEW VICTIMS

Gunman chooses prey by horoscope signs — & a Leo is next

"THIS is the Zodiac. Twelve signs will die..."

That frightful letter, sent to the New York Post newspaper, launched one of the biggest manhunts in the history of the Big Apple and sparked fears that the next victim would be a Leo.

It tied together three apparently random shootings in a city used to murder, and announced a new terror: The Zodiac Killer was striking. Before the letter arrived, two shootings were lost on the police blotter among countless other senseless crimes.

But, the letter continued: "The first sign is dead on March 8, 1990, 1:45 a.m. The second sign is dead on March 29, 1990, 2:57 a.m. The third sign is dead on May 31, 1990, 2:04 a.m."

On the same page, in a precisely drawn circle representing the astrological zodiac, were the symbols of three birth signs of the three shooting victims. A potential killer was on the loose, they concluded.

He was trying to kill people based on their astrological signs.

Their worst fears were confirmed when a fourth victim was shot in the chest in Central Park. Near his almost lifeless body, investigators found another note in the same handwriting as the others, filled with astrological references.

OF the three previous victims, one had died. They were:

- Mario Orsco (Scorpio), a 50-year-old father of two, walking with a cane, was shot March 8 in Brooklyn.
- Germaine Montenesdro (Gemini), 33, shot March 29 while leaving a subway station, also in Brooklyn.
- Joseph Proce (Taurus), shot May 31 while walking home with a cane in Queens. He died several weeks later because of an infection caused by the shooting.

Now, panic is spreading through New York — informed sources believe that Zodiac's next victim will be a Leo. That fear reached wildfire proportions when the New York Daily News published a story by its astrologer Joyce Jillson.

"Those born under the sign of Leo are advised to stay in on the evening of July 26," she wrote. "That is the sign with all of the earmarks of Zodiac's next victim."

The most baffling aspect of the case, police said, was how Zodiac knew the astrological signs of his victims, none of whom apparently knew him.

The fourth victim, Larry Parham (Cancer) was recovering from his wounds when he gave the police a key clue to Zodiac's method.

The night before he was

The demented villain boasts of his crimes with words and drawings. Says one official: "I've never seen this city so afraid."

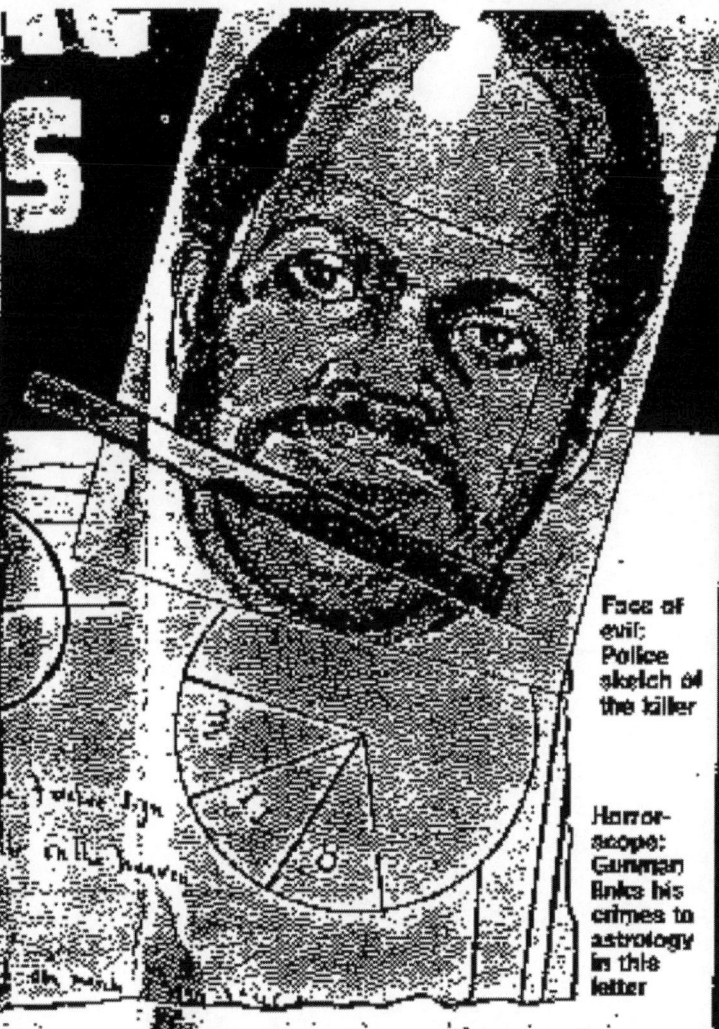

Face of evil: Police sketch of the killer

Horoscope: Gunman links his crimes to astrology in this letter

shot, he said he was approached in Central Park by a man who fit the description of Zodiac.

"He started talking to me for no reason but was real friendly," Parham said. "He asked me what was my zodiac. I said Cancer. He said he was a Taurus."

Police believe that Zodiac has attacked consistently except for a period that included his own sign — Taurus.

They discount the theory that he is the same man who called himself The Zodiac Killer and is believed responsible for 37 deaths in San Francisco between 1968 and 1978. He is still at large. But police say the New York version is a copycat.

EYEWITNESSES provided authorities with sufficient information to come up with a composite drawing of Zodiac.

The day after it was published in the newspapers, they were flooded with more than 1,000 calls from people who claimed they had seen him.

Mayor David Dinkins offered a $10,000 reward for information leading to the capture of the killer. Police spokesman Det. Joseph McConville told The GLOBE: "We have more than 50 detectives working on this case.

"Each time we come up with a new piece of evidence, we sit down and toss it around to see if we can fit it into the pattern.

"This case is like a giant puzzle. Every bit of information, no matter how silly or insignificant it may seem, is being pieced together by computer to make a complete picture."

Another New York administration official, speaking under the condition that his name would not be revealed, said: "I've never seen this city so afraid. People are reading their horoscopes to see if it is safe for them to go out.

"The fear has spread to all levels of society. High-powered stockbrokers, who live on Fifth Avenue, have told me they look over their shoulders when they are out on the streets during the times, between midnight and 6 a.m., when Zodiac has struck.

"This man has his hands around the throat of the entire city."

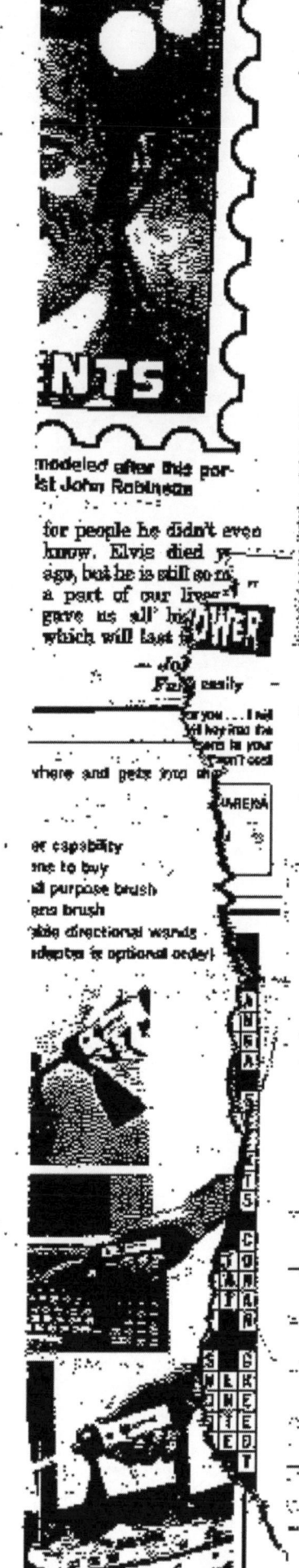

CALENDARS, TRADING CARDS, ACTION FIGURES TEE SHIRTS, ART PRINTS, DVDS, CLOCKS, MUGS AND MUCH MORE. ONLY AT
SERIALKILLERCALENDAR.COM
YOUR HOME FOR MURDER, MADNESS AND MERCHANDISE!